CATASTROPHE!

Survivors

of the

Super Volcano

MAY 2021

H V Loren

Acknowledgements

To my wife for indulging me during the slow process of learning to write in a different style and while seeking information and knowledge.

To my editors and those who were prepared to read drafts and suggest improvements in documents that were unpolished and often boring:

My wife Ria and my son Johan; Erica vd Watt, Ingrid Maas, Jennifer Els, and Gert Claassen.

I must give special thanks to Frank Redman of Texas, my mentor and editor for the revised edition of the book. He helped to improve the book and taught me a lot.

To Johan Kotze who adapted images to create the front page.

ISBN: 978-1-5210-3490-3

Authors Note:

For many years I read and wondered about the very ancient world: the discoveries and the many tales not fully explained. Within the limits of the possible, I speculated and developed theories. I could not publish my speculations without proof, therefore I started writing a novel covering these ideas. I used characters, living in south facing valleys and organized in Clans, whose life, experiences, and crisis answered these questions.

I justify my assumptions in the endnotes. I found support of some of the ideas in the writings and presentations of today's many futurists, thinkers, and sages, for example, Lisa Randall, Robin Dunbar, Yuval Harari, Brian Green, Michio Kaku, Jared Diamond, Raymond Kurzweil, amongst many others. The list grows continuously.

This novel came to depict pre-historic Clans living meaningful lives, which remained stable for many generations without the requirement of growth. The Catastrophic eruption of the Toba Super Volcano, 74 000 years ago, changed everything.

More thoughts to share and comment on at:
www.supervolcano.inf & www.illoreaens.com

The setting

During the ice age, the climate was mild in the south-facing valleys where the Clans lived. They had access to an abundance of fruit, nuts, roots, and starchy tubers as well as small game for meat.

The reflective ice sheets caused a cold, dry but healthy climate with low rainfall. Large deserts spread over all the continents while huge quantities of water remained captured in the ice, lowering sea levels. The Great Mountain Range caught enough moisture to maintain a perpetual snow cover over the high peaks, allowing snow melt and fountains to water the Clan Valleys and to create soggy bogs on the plains lower down, where another hominin species roamed in small groups, killing competing bands for the limited resources available there.

The advancing and retreating ice sheets ground up the earth surface to powdery dust, which at a later stage would be carried into the Black Sea depression to form the deep silt layer at the bottom of today's sea.

We know many Homo species existed before the Toba eruption: sapiens (that's us), neanderthals, heidelbergensis, floriensis, luzinensis, denisovans, erectus, and many more. All had pursued a hunter-gatherer type lifestyle that slowly became more sophisticated as their brains, and that of their forebears, grew larger over millions of years. Then, over a few hundred thousand years the larger brains of one species developed intelligence on par or exceeding that of the humans of today, while others remained more primitive.

It was a difficult environment in which to survive. The volcanic winter following the Toba eruption, made it infinitely worse for the different *Homo* species who roamed the earth. According to scientists, a genetic bottleneck developed and only a few breeding pair survived the resultant Catastrophes. Details remain controversial.

How did any survive?

<><><>

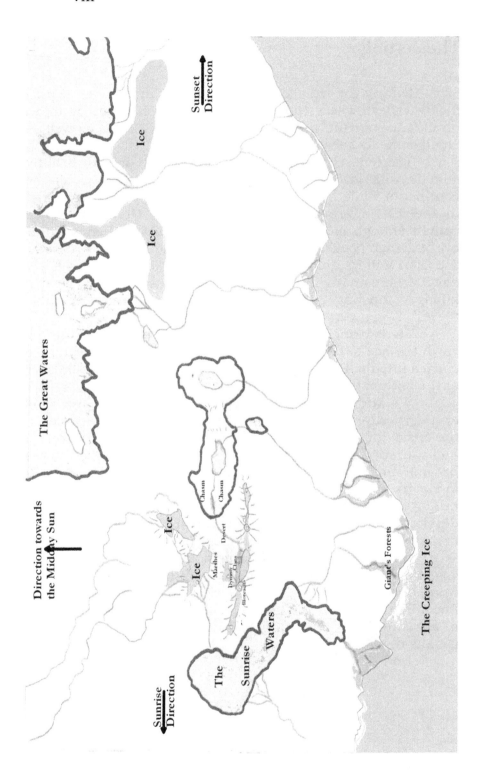

Contents

Prologue

The magma chamber has been building for millions of years, growing slowly but steadily. Mighty explosions released some of the pressure in extremely long intervals. The eruptions only helped to allow more and hotter lava to accumulate. 500,000 years passed while the pressure increased. From deep within the earth gas bubbles formed, rising through the molten rock, causing the ground to swell and subside in long, continuous waves. The waves traveled around the earth but no hominid noticed, even though animals and birds became restlessness.

A growing bulge formed in the middle of an ancient archipelago. With increased frequency, earth tremors warned of an impending disaster. With each tremble, nearby birds took to the air while animals uneasily sniffed the air before searching for safety. Great herds thundered west over the plains. Insects crawled into cracks and then appeared again, instinctively knowing they could be crashed. Reptiles, able to survive in water, sought refuge there.

The hominins living within a few thousand miles from the Super Volcano site, now noticed the strange behavior of the birds and animals. They were anxious but did not know what to expect or what to do.

The humans living far away to the west had developed a stable social structure and ideal living conditions. Mental challenges made their hunter-gatherer lifestyle interesting. Their intelligence and technological innovation allowed a long, healthy and comfortable life. The Clan sizes were limited to approximately what we now call the Dunbar number. It prevented faction forming and ensured long term stability over uncountable generations. They continued with their daily activities, oblivious of danger. Even those with the ability to know, did not recognize the threat from the east, which promised extinction.

Finally, the earth's mantle could not contain the stress. Disaster struck. Toba, the greatest Super Volcano in at least twenty-five million years, erupted. This Catastrophe occurred recently, only seventy-four thousand years ago. It and its aftermath destroyed life all over the world. But some Hominids survived.

Chapter 1 – Abduction

Something was wrong! Questa heard a rustle and saw a repulsive face peering through the bushes. Terrified, she swung round, burst through the undergrowth and forced her way towards the clearing. Before she could reach the relative safety of open ground, strong arms grabbed her from behind and pulled her back into the dense thicket. She could not see her assailant and just managed to cry out before a huge hand smothered any further sound.

Suppressing her panic, she used her considerable strength in an effort to wrench loose. None of the self-defense tricks she learned during her training could break the grip. She struggled, struck out and scratched wildly. A smell of sweat, smoke and rancid fat nearly overwhelmed her. Ignoring the stench, she managed to grab the heavy spear that her attacker carried and stabbed backward. The spear connected something firm, barely yielding, but whatever was holding her did not even respond. It only changed its grip and wrenched the spear from her hand.

The three Clansmen from the Dynasty still kept themselves busy on the far side of the orchard. They did not see the attack. They had seen Questa disappear into the vegetation surrounding the stream and were waiting for her to reappear. Then they heard her scream. Keeping their spears ready, they looked at one another, then stormed towards the bushes.

Questa's captor held her immobilized while a few of the huge creatures charged past them to confront the Clansmen.

The foremost grabbed the long throwing spear of the first Clansman, ignoring the sharp point. The jagged edges cut the creature's hand, heightening its excitement. It hit the Clansman with an open hand, spattering blood over his face.

The Clansman's head twisted to the side. The force of the impact threw him sideways. He crumpled to the ground. His body jerked twice and then he lay still, killed by a single blow.

Horror overwhelmed Questa's senses. She could not move; could not even cry out.

Her assailant still held her, its huge hand covering her mouth and much of her face. She nearly choked. She tried to bite, but without success. She desperately wanted to turn her face away and close her eyes from the horrid scene, but was powerless to do so. Transfixed by the sight, she kept watching.

A number of the excited creatures pushed past the body of the Clansman and his killer.

The second Clansman halted his rush forward and stepped back, his spear still pointing at the creatures. One of the creatures swiped the Clansman's spear to the side, causing him to twist to the right and then, as he recoiled, hit him full in the face. Blood spurted from the Clansman's nose while his head snapped back violently. The blow lifted him bodily from the ground, throwing him backward to where he landed stretched out — dead too.

The third Clansman dropped his spear and ran.

The creatures watched as he fled and did not pursue him. They gestured, uttering guttural noises while looking at the two bodies. They appeared surprised, as if they did not understand that they had just killed two Clansmen.

The attack and the slaying of the Clansmen were so sudden, so unexpected, that Questa had trouble comprehending what was happening. In shock she froze, involuntarily closing her mind against the horror. As if in a daze, she heard the creature still holding her, call the others. It waved its spear past her head. She started struggling, twisting and turning, trying to loosen her captor's grip, but it tucked her under its arm without any trouble, not noticing her efforts or her weight.

With a final roar, it turned and made its way through the undergrowth, heading up the slope.

Suspended from a crooked arm, Questa abandoned her useless struggles. She tried to slow her thumping heart by taking a few deep breaths, but the putrid smell of her assailant made it difficult.

The attack had driven away all thoughts previously occupying her mind. She had let her natural vigilance lapse, concerned with the secrets of the Dynasty, the secrets Usux had revealed so recently. Her mind filled with the horror she had just witnessed and a growing panic threatened to engulf her.

With an effort, she forced herself to calm down. *How could everything have gone so horribly wrong? The day had been so* beautiful. *The fragrance of the new season proclaimed vigor and growth.*

When she had exited the Dynasty's cave Habitat, the sun-drenched slopes invited her to explore. All seemed safe.

She forced her body to go limp, hoping that the creature would release her, would allow her to wriggle loose, but her assailant did not show any sign of yielding.

Questa managed to take a few more deep breaths and took control of her racing brain, *With my training, I should be able to find a means of escape. I have to think rationally, analyze my situation... What are these creatures? What are they doing here? What are they going to do to me?*

Her first thought was that the Primitives had attacked, but that did not make sense, *The Primitives always attack from the plains. They never venture onto the mountain slopes. Even the Clan valleys scare them. These attackers don't look like Primitives. They are much bigger.*

Only the bottom half of her captor's body was visible. All she could determine was that it was male. The others were also males, taller than she was. Their torsos were huge and bulky with legs like tree trunks. Their arms were not sinewy but heavy, maybe as thick as the thighs of the strongest Clansmen of her valley. They were all similar—massive, strong and hairy. She wondered why they looked familiar, even though they were so very different from the Clans. Although huge, they were not much taller than some Clansmen she knew.

Then she realized, *Oh, yes! Their proportions are similar to ours, except for their size. They are brawny, not obese. They walk with a heavy, swinging gait, probably because of their thick legs, but their arms are not excessively long. Even their large hands are in proportion, like ours. They are definitely not apes.*

Questa scrutinized the others. Though similar in body type except for size, their faces were ugly. Their eyes were deep-set with brows sloping backward, and they lacked the delicate chin that the Clan-members found a mark of beauty. They lacked the elongated temples of the Clans.

Long, reddish hair was tied back. Reddish-blond fuzz, not quite beards, partially hid their features. Thick down of a similar color covered their arms and legs.

Her captor's legs were heavily muscled and even sturdier than those of the others. The part of his body that she could observe close to her face glistened with putrid grease. The stench nauseated her. Despite her dangling position, she was aware that he was by far the tallest of them all.

She gasped as understanding hit her. *These must be the Giants Curon had warned me about! Oh no!*

She took a deep breath trying to calm her rising panic.

Focus. She tried to recall all she could remember of the mythical creatures in the stories told to frighten Clan children. *What are their weak points? They are so big. They kill so easily. I must survive and escape! How will I ever get away?*

The realization that these were Giants, shocked her. She shuddered as she remembered the weird stories from her youth. The old feeling of fear and horror came back. But there was no parent to dispel the alarming images with a warm embrace. No soothing fur draped around her as she sat before a blazing fire. Now she felt completely isolated. How she longed for her Clan and her father! She even missed Alena, who had comforted him and became his life-companion after her mother's death. Tears ran down her cheeks as she remembered life with her Clan.

If only I had stayed with the Clan and not accepted the honor of advanced training at the Dynasty. If only I had not allowed the Dynasty's secret ways to upset me as much as it did. I should have heeded Curon's warning. I should not have climbed the mountain slopes to this isolated grove; I could have considered the new information Usux revealed, somewhere safely within the Dynasty valley.

Remembering weakened her. She had to know what the Giants were planning, where they were taking her. With an effort, she forced herself to concentrate. She twisted her head as far as possible to survey her surroundings but could not see where they were going. All she could see were the three other males following close behind.

I must try to recognize geographical features, to memorize the route. If only I knew this area near the Dynasty valley as well as I know the area around my own Clan valley. Such knowledge would help me.

Questa was still dangling face down. She was bruised and uncomfortable. The strange mode of travel made it difficult to think, impossible to trace their route.

She started hitting whatever part of her captor she could reach, yelling: "Leave me alone; I'm with the Dynasty! They will punish you. My father will find and kill you! He is an important Clan Chief."

The Giants looked at her strangely, making gruff noises, but her captor just tightened his hold. They did not understand her and neither could she make out the meaning of the sounds they uttered.

She had heard terrible tales of what happened to the victims of Giants and feared that there was substance to those stories.

I must differentiate facts from myths. I must stay calm and regain control, she thought and then started to murmur the calming mantra of the Oracle-Healers repeatedly: "I am strong. Fear weakens me. Panic paralyzes me."

#

The Giants moved quickly and nimbly up the mountain towards the snow line, where they soon joined another group of Giants, both male and female. The entire group formed a circle around Questa while her captor left her suspended from his arm. They all looked at her, pointing and uttering excited guttural sounds.

Their protruding mouths must restrict the range of sounds they make and limit them to those ugly noises. Their language grates on my ears!

The strangeness overcame Questa's resolution to remain calm. With eyes tightly closed, she tried to shut off her emotions, to suppress her rising panic. She shuddered involuntarily.

A loud command from her captor interrupted the Giant's chatter. They started up the slope until they reached a clearing, high up on the mountain. Her captor dropped Questa with a gesture indicating that she had to stay put. A few of the Giants moved around to block her possible escape routes.

The futility of escape was clear. Tears ran down her cheeks as she remained on the ground, rubbing her bruises. The cold air stung her nose with every breath. The panic and cold caused her to shiver uncontrollably but the Giants, unaffected by the cold temperature, did not even bother to adjust the skins slung over their shoulders. She crouched in a small bundle, folding her arms around herself to fight the cold, secretly peering at the Giants. She slowly maneuvered, until her back touched the trunk of a nearby tree.

For the first time, she could inspect her captor. As she had thought, he was huge, even bigger than his mates were. She found him extremely ugly.

He is wearing a kaross made of the skin of a... what is that? She could not immediately identify the animal, until she saw the head hanging upside down on his back behind his thick, short neck. It was a kaross made of the skin of a saber-tooth tiger, complete with head and massive teeth, which she surmised would frame the Giant's face when it functioned as headgear giving him an even more frightening presence.

That tiger must have been huge! Just for a moment, Questa could imagine the impressive sight of her captor wearing his headdress. *To see him wearing that would be terrifying!* She felt the cold shivers creeping down her back like icy fingers tingling her spine as she imagined the terrible sight. She turned her face away and watched the others. Her abduction was causing a great deal of pointing and noise. The Giants gestured and babbled with excitement.

I don't think they are going to kill me, I'm not sure they even intended to kill those Clansmen. They are just so powerful, a single blow can kill.

Dangling from the Giant's arm with her head nearly touching her knees had been painful and disorientating. It had made rational thought difficult, but now she could focus and organize her thoughts despite the cold.

I did not notice anger emanating from the Giants as they stormed forward to confront the Clansmen. They just tried to stop their advance... What else can I remember?... One of the Clansmen managed to get away. He'll tell the Dynasty what happened and then they'll come to rescue me.

Hope returned.

#

Her captor occasionally pointed at her, uttering noises, his tone aggressive. A female Giant stared at her menacingly, causing another chill to run down her spine. She concentrated hard, trying to interpret body language, to read the expressions of the troupe while looking at the different reactions of individuals. The feelings she could faintly Sense were unlike those of the Clansmen, but there were similarities, enough for her to form an impression. She could make out blame, anger, confusion and—fear. It was hard to isolate the emotions of individuals, but she could interpret the group feelings. She concentrated on the strangeness. She was sure that the ability to Sense individuals would become essential for future self-preservation and escape.

The Giant who kidnapped me must be the leader. He clearly rules the group. Then there is the female, in some way attached or belonging to the leader. I should concentrate on them to Sense their strangeness as being typical of the strangeness of them all.

The body language and gestures, coupled with what she could Sense, gave her some understanding of why the Giant was so upset. *He also thinks the Dynasty will send rescuers.*

The Giants continued up the slope of the mountain to where the forest and woods ended. In the shade, patches of snow remained. The days were warming; the snow was still retreating up the mountain after the cold season, with only flattened grass left between the trees.

She looked towards the mountain, *We are near the snowline, no wonder I'm cold. No escaping up the mountain here.*

The cold did not seem to bother them, her captor least of all. He even picked up snow from a shady spot and rubbed it into his hair, as if to cool his head.

I have to study the Giants and find a way to escape, Questa thought. *Know your enemy!*

The enlarged troupe moved on, carrying short stabbing spears. They had not bothered to collect the long throwing spears of the slain Clansmen.

They clearly have no use for our spears, which the hunters in all the Clans typically use.

Questa's captor tied a thin leather strap around her wrist with the knot pulled hard and tight. He handed the other end to a Giant who walked in the center of the troupe.

They are taking me with them, she realized. *They are not going to kill me immediately.*

The Giants selected routes through wooded areas near the snow line wherever possible. They moved swiftly, leaving little trace of their passing. It was already midday; the exercise kept her warm enough and the sun warmed her right cheek.

Secretly she tried to untie the knot, but her fingers were not strong enough. She noticed the creatures jeering at her futile attempts. She realized that with their strong fingers they were able to pull knots in rawhide thongs much too tight for any Clan-member to untie.

Counting the valleys they passed, helped her keep track of their route, but this part of the mountain range was not familiar and their destination was unknown.

If I manage to escape, I would have to find my way back to the Dynasty valley by myself, despite the increasing distance.

The stepped cliffs that towered over the headwaters of the Clan Valleys had already vanished. Above her, the individual peaks rose out of the thick snow covering the mountain range.

The streams were flooded, fed by the snowmelt from glaciers at higher altitude. She struggled through the waters, afraid that the strong currents might wash her away. The Giants were heavy and they waded through without effort, pulling her along by the leather cord, hurting her wrist.

Surely, by now the Dynasty must know what had happened. They must already have started a search, she mused. *I trust they know that the Giants are huge and probably very dangerous. In a fight, the Giants will injure many Clansmen or even kill them. They will certainly kill me when the Dynasty attacks. I will have to escape and hide until the rescuers arrive.*

She paid attention to every possible detail that might help her escape, but no opportunity presented itself. The Giants kept on glancing backward, careful to leave few signs of their passing. Where the Giants had moved through the woods and bushes, she saw only slight signs of disturbed branches and broken twigs in the undergrowth.

Are they worried about possible rescuers from the Dynasty or are they watching out for Primitives? She wondered, then realized, *No, they would not find Primitives a threat.*

To make it easier for any Clan expedition to find them, Questa left tracks in mud or sand and broke twigs wherever she could. The Giant behind her called out something in their guttural language, pointing to some of the signs she had left. The leader gestured to one of the males who unceremoniously threw her over his shoulder and continued on his way, not even noticing her weight. Questa was already bruised and sore from the way the leader had carried her and found the additional bruising excruciating.

"Let me go!" she yelled, indicating with gestures that she had learned her lesson, that she would not leave any further marks.

The Giant put her down.

The leader angrily gestured his displeasure and indicated that the one holding her by the leather cord had to walk directly behind him. He gestured to the others to watch her for any further tricks.

The Giant female she had noticed before, remained near the leader and therefore close to Questa.

She could Sense that the female was jealous. The implication filled her with dread.

The Giants walked fast with a rolling gait, taking turns holding the cord. Despite the hindrance, Questa kept up easily, accustomed to long treks in the mountains. Questa was sure that she could outrun them on a sprint in the open and could keep going faster and for longer distances. However, in the woods where she would have to force her way through the undergrowth, their strength would allow them to catch her easily. If only she could get a chance, but the Giants were careful, not allowing her to prove her agility.

The Giants wore furry skins draped around their shoulders and they tied the skins down with leather straps. An apron hid their private parts. The huge penises of the males occasionally became visible as the overlaps of the skin mantle swung open. Questa noticed that different Giant males glanced at her well-formed body and gave her lecherous looks.

Then making it even worse she realized, *If one of these huge males rapes me, it would kill me. No Clanswoman could survive such an assault.*

She was terrified at the thought and could not imagine the horror. The thought made her glance involuntarily in the direction of her captor's private parts, briefly revealed as the apron and skin mantle swung open. It was a huge and terrible sight. She paled.

Her captor had noticed and he smirked, highly pleased with himself. Questa had to block her Sensing ability quickly. What she had momentarily Sensed was terrible, fearful and it boded great evil.

The Giant female rushed up. She had noticed Questa's glance and forced herself between them. She grabbed the leather strap from the Giant's hand, jerking it brutally, forcing Questa into a position farther back, behind her. Her captor looked around, laughed, and continued at his fast pace, leading the troupe.

The female pulled Questa towards a Giant carrying a large bundle.

Questa held back. *What will she do to me?*

She exhaled deeply as she realized that the female had simply extracted a worked antelope skin. She draped it around Questa. It completely enveloped her, she could use it as a kaross. She understood the gesture, though apparently friendly, was instead an attempt to hide Questa's voluptuous young body and well-formed breasts. Her nipples prominent and high. The covering would hide her features from the leader's lustful glances.

The female prominently showed off her own bodily features whenever the leader was near, but her stocky build could not compete.

The animal skin covering Questa was much too big. It crawled with insects but it helped against the cold and, more importantly, it became a refuge, a place to hide as much of her body as possible.

The lascivious expression on the leader's face promised agony in the near future. She heard that Giants, Primitives, or other Clan-similar groups had assaulted Clan women in the past. Usually, the female's body rejected the deformed fetus as it developed and aborted it spontaneously. However, what would be her fate without the help of Sensitives or Healers? If born alive, the Clan-similar creature would be sterile and a Clan woman would probably not survive the birth of such a baby.

#

Darkness forced the Giants to look for a safe place to spend the night. They tied the strap to a sturdy tree, the knot pulled too tight for her to undo. She had to adapt herself to the available space, her arm outstretched. Wriggling, she managed to pull the skin over her until nothing showed.

After the Giants had eaten, her captor threw her a piece of meat and placed a gourd half-filled with water on the ground within her reach. The Giants made themselves comfortable all around her while two remained on guard.

The ground was hard and she was frozen and bruised. In the quiet, she concentrated hard, hoping to hear or Sense approaching rescuers. *Nothing!* She concentrated harder until she descended into an intense Sensing state. To fully enter the Abstract state was dangerous. One could lose control. She did not risk it. All she could Sense, faintly, was the strange vibrations Usux had spoken of. As if nature was holding its breath, in anticipation of some great event.

The biting insects, and the fear of an assault, caused a long night of suffering. How she longed for the comforts of the Clans. There they slept wrapped in furs infused with insect repelling herbs, on thick layers of soft fern bedding covered in softly worked skins. She cringed and made herself small whenever she heard a Giant move. How did she land in this terrible situation? Now her actions and irritations with Usux appeared petty. She fell into a slumber, reliving the start of the day, remembering what it was like in the Dynasty's Habitat. There her worries were not as serious. There she did not expect to be assaulted or killed at any moment.

Chapter 2 – The Dynasty

In her imagination, Questa relived the start of her day. The slight murmur of gently waking life filtered through the tunnels, breaking the silence inside the Dynasty's cave complex, announcing the beginning of a new day. It was the time for introspection, the time for reflection, the time for planning the day's activities.

The chamber had a musty smell. The walls near the entrance had been worn smooth by the hands of generations of Sensitives entering and exiting. The quiet time before dawn was a special time for sitting with the mentors to absorb new knowledge.

The more Questa contemplated the content of the training session she had just received, the less she liked it. It shocked her to learn that the Oracle-Healers had to keep secrets. Others in the Clans knew little of the abilities they perfected during their intense training sessions. She hated subterfuge and secrets. Most upsetting was the fact the Oracle-Healers accompanying the Dynasty's patrols misused their powers, specifically the gift of Sensitivity. She had always known about the patrols, which protected the Clan valleys from the aggression of the Primitives, but had not ever wondered how they managed to repel the overwhelming hordes. Now she knew that the Oracle-Healers project emotions whenever they meet Primitives, instilling a permanent fear of heights and closed spaces in them, which explained why the Primitives avoided the mountains and seldom tried to enter the Clan valleys. That type of manipulation was wrong, even though it increased the Clans' safety. It would have been much worse if the Oracle-Healers had manipulated or increased the Primitives' natural fear of other life forms. That would be intolerable!

Usux, her mentor, had been watching her.

She immediately strengthened her control. *I must not allow my thoughts to emanate.*

Too late! She realized Usux had noticed her anger, "The content of this session has upset you. You will have to keep many secrets once you return to the Clans. The dangers to the Clans and the situations you will have to face are much more complex than you realize. You will need the knowledge and exceptional abilities we are teaching you, when unique actions are required. Now is the time to share your thoughts and opinions. You must allow us to respond and to analyze your strengths and weaknesses."

He had detected much more than she ever intended to show. She was proud of her abilities and control. *How did he notice so much? Must I become a tool the Dynasty can use as a puppet? Never!*

Usux continued watching her. "You do not have proper control of your emotions as yet. You might as well let it out now. Emotion withheld during training will make it more difficult to teach you how to discover, use and control all your Sensing abilities. The last and most difficult exercises in ultimate control are still to come. We must begin soon."

Questa's blue eyes flashed as she stared at Usux, "Yes, I will tell you. Surely it is immoral for you to keep secrets, to manipulate the Clans without our knowledge and without permission. And instilling fear in Primitives—surely that is wrong!"

Usux sighed, but the expression on his face remained friendly but pensive, "We do not instill the fear, but only stimulate a pre-existing fear of heights and closed spaces. Your grandmother—"

She interrupted, "My grandmother would not have accepted these manipulations!"

With effort, she swallowed the rest of her word explosion.

"You are wrong... in thinking that." His self-discipline prevented the condescending addition of 'my girl,' which would have caused a final break.

Her eyes lit up. She guessed the meaning of the pause. *Even the self-control of Usux, the great mentor, can slip. Yet, he will not get the better of me! I will not relinquish loyalty to my Clan!*

She clenched her hands. With her temper now under control, she looked down, allowing him to recover and continue.

"Your grandmother, Chiara-the-elder, was an excellent Oracle-Healer. She also questioned many of our secrets, taboos, and traditions. However, in the end, when the reasons became clear, she agreed with the necessity to keep secrets and always honored them. I only teach to impart knowledge. Once you have completed your training, before we reveal the most startling secrets, you will also have to make the choice, like your grandmother. Then you may argue with our leaders here at the Dynasty. Preferably, with the younger Orrox present. He should have returned with his acolytes by then. They are visiting and exploring different Clan valleys. With his background he will understand many of your objections. I expect him to be elected as the Council leader soon."

Questa did not wish to hear. She was tired and had failed to hide her feelings. She wondered about this Orrox scion. *What is he like and how will he convince me?*

"My grandmother did not like the Dynasty. She did not like the Orrox scions. She was the best Oracle-Healer of our time and she hated deceit!"

Usux noticed the faint shaking of her head, "You must listen to me. We of the Dynasty have studied you since your mother died, when it became clear that you were a strong Sensitive. You have the potential to become an outstanding Oracle-Healer, like your grandmother. That is what our training can do for you. Your grandmother taught you control but you still have much to learn. You must also learn to control your emotions better."

He paused, allowing her to absorb what he just said.

She closed her eyes and bowed her head. Realization nearly overwhelmed her, *The great Sensitives of the Dynasty can read my emotions, my most private feelings about anything and everything.* She felt naked, completely exposed, *I have been so naïve and dumb.*

"Yes, we respect you and all the Clans too much to Sense private emotions without permission, but we have that ability. However, we can read body language and you are not hiding your true feelings well. That is part of what we'll teach you, if your training continues."

Questa shifted uncomfortably in her seat. She had thought she controlled both her body language and emotions well, *Apparently not! Talking so fast is also a definite giveaway. I will have to control my speech more carefully.*

A light, teasing tone crept into Usux's voice, "We are on the same side. You have been concentrating for many days. Go out into the open and look at the groves and fields, which also contain a few secrets that we will discuss later. The weather is good and the valley beautiful. There is much to learn.

"While there, try to Sense and interpret nature's strange indications. Try to distinguish the tremors from our local volcanos, from other indications. Natural forces are lining up for some great long-term event. Our experts are combining their abilities to Sense beyond our natural environment, trying to predict what is brewing. It might be a major storm, a long-term drought or something else. They say it is not local. The origin is far away, in the sunrise direction. We might experience, whatever is approaching, in a few days.

"Also consider your options. You will have to decide whether you are going to continue with your training. It would be a great waste if you decide to quit!"

Is there a threat in his words? What if my continued opposition frustrates Usux until he doesn't want to train me further? Then I will never become a great Oracle-Healer, like Grandmother.

She longed for the safety of her Clan but dared not give up her dream. She had much to consider. The slight moldy smell that had not bothered her before suddenly became oppressive. The caves were old and many of the Clan Sensitives had passed through and trained in these chambers. Their ancient presence tangible. The flame of the oil lamp flickering in the slight draught threw grotesque shadows on the cave walls, contributing to the mysterious atmosphere of the setting. A studious atmosphere dominated; it was not the place in which to allow prejudice to take over.

I will not allow my irritation to show again. Yes, I must go out into the fresh air and think. I will continue my training. I will be the greatest Oracle-Healer of all time!

#

As Questa left the training chamber, she noticed the general dilapidation surrounding her, which she had ignored in the first excitement of arrival, when the size and complexity of the Dynasty Habitat had so impressed her. She remembered her grandmother's warning, "The Dynasty has become degenerate, trusting on traditions to keep the system going, with little initiative or renewal allowed."

After leaving the cave complex, she headed towards the palisade entrance and walked out. She took a few deep breaths of the fresh mountain air. She smelled a tang of pine mingled with the pleasant odor of the awakening earth. Birds darted through the newly green leaves, sharing the joy of the rising sun with to and fro calls, competing in beauty and complexity.

She looked around, wondering where to find a place where she could relax and consider her options. She had not yet seen much of the valley of the Dynasty, where the Orrox descendants dominated. She suppressed all thoughts of them, concentrating on her surroundings. All was so peaceful. The sun was warm, removing the last vestiges of winter cold and leaving only the white snow sparkling on the high peaks. It was a beautiful day, perfect for exploring the valley.

Questa turned to the left, towards the woods. A clear path led through the dense undergrowth, leading up the slope of the foothills of the home volcano called Kajaban. She was convinced that she was safe, confident that her physical training and special abilities were enough to handle any unexpected situation.

The well-trodden path snaked uphill, avoiding steep inclines. Grass grew on the edges, adorned with colorful butterflies visiting the drops of dew still glistening along the stalks. A gecko on a rocky outcrop lazily raised its head and did not bother to dash away. The familiarity of nature made the climb even more enjoyable.

She inhaled deeply as she climbed, giving her additional stamina. She followed darting dragonflies, enjoying the cold, fresh air after the mustiness of the cave.

At a clearing, a few Clansmen from the Dynasty were tending some young trees. Large grains, similar to those she had often collected in open patches in her own valley, lay on a slab of rock nearby. A few of the Clansmen were munching the seeds as they worked.

She picked up some kernels, tasted, and smiled. They were bigger in size and better tasting than any she had ever collected. How was that possible?

I must find out more.

She turned to a Clansman directing the others, "Greetings Clansman! I am Questa from the Second Valley. Please tell me about these grains and the different trees you have here."

The Clansman was clearly proud of his work and spoke to her as an equal, "Greetings, Sensitive! I am Curon. The grains are grown down there, but surely you recognize many of these fruit and nut trees, which also grow in different Clan valleys. Our valley has areas where each of the types flourishes. Look, those that yield these nuts grow over here."

He showed her a variety of nuts, which he lifted out of a skin bag on the ground near him, and pointed out from which tree each was taken.

"We select them for different properties here. Some of the fruit trees are still in bloom up there, where it is colder and the climate and soil suit them the best," he pointed up the steep slope, to the right of the volcano. "They will bear fruit much later than these down here,"

Questa looked up to where a white patch stood out against the green and grey. "Is the splash of white the blossoms?"

"Yes. It is a beautiful location. But please don't climb up there. There have recently been reports of dark movements in the woods near the ice field. Now, we only venture up there when necessary."

Questa considered his words but remained curious. "My mentor, Usux, recommended that I look at the various plants and trees that grow in the valley. I would really like to see that grove up there. He didn't mention any possible danger. I'm sure I will be safe."

Curon replied, "Usux is not as knowledgeable about this side of the valley, nor has he ventured this way recently. There might be danger now. Please allow me to share more with you about these trees. If you wish, go down the valley to where we grow grains displaying other qualities. You will find much of interest there."

Questa had been irritated when she left Usux in the chamber. When she saw the seeds, larger than any growing in the Clan valleys, it seemed to confirm that the Dynasty was keeping the best for itself. She did not inquire further or heeded Curon's words. She felt her frustration return then realized, *I should not show my feelings.*

Careful to control her speech, she insisted, "I'm sure Usux would have warned me of any danger. Is there a path or do I just climb towards that patch of white?"

Curon sighed and nodded in resignation. "There is a path, Sensitive, starting between those two trees. I recommend that you do not linger. Please come back as soon as you have inspected the grove."

Questa felt slightly ashamed for ignoring Curon's advice, noticing his sudden formal tone, but she set out stubbornly, *At the grove, I will calmly consider my options.*

#

Curon turned to three of the Clansmen with him, "She worries me. She does not know this part of the mountains nor our valley. Please follow her at a distance and make sure she does not see you. Take your spears. Look out for her. You can clear the weeds while you are up there."

As they left, he thought to himself, *Those disturbances in the woods might have been the shadowy movements of Giants. I wish the young Orrox would return. We need his guidance. He would be able to communicate with any Giants, should they be here. Oh well, they are seldom aggressive and must be far away near the snow line!*

Curon watched his Clansmen follow the path Questa had taken with growing concern.

#

The slope was steep and the route not as well defined as the path she had followed before. The trees and undergrowth remained dense. She could glimpse the white patch only when she passed through a clearing or crossed a rise. At first, a few birds flittered away as she walked, but as she climbed higher, they disappeared.

At a rocky outcrop she stopped to look up. High above the white patch the trees thinned. There firs and spruce replaced oaks, chestnuts and elm, then disappeared leaving the high peaks bare and white with the wind blowing a plume off an isolated pinnacle.

The snow-covered peaks of the Great Mountain chain reached into the dark blue sky. High up the wind blew puffs of white cloud and snow into an ever-moving, glittering veil. Tall rock columns guarded the crater where the home volcano, Kajaban, regarded as dormant, released spirals of smoke. The slight tremors that the living mountain sometimes created had scared her when she first entered the Dynasty's cavern complex, but now she barely noticed them. The crater was the Dynasty's friendly companion, never threatening, never spewing lava in anger. The only outward sign of volcanic activity, was the occasional burp that released small quantities of grey ash.

It is cold up here. Questa shivered as she continued her climb, happy that she was already near the grove. She was out of breath by the time she arrived at the blossoming trees growing in a clearing where a few terraces broke the steep gradient of the mountain slope. A big boulder on the edge of the lowest terrace invited her to sit down.

The beautiful view is just what I need to distract myself until I am ready to reflect on my options calmly.

The air was clear. From where she sat looking down, Questa could see most of the broad valley. A meandering river twisted and turned on its way through the fertile plain, with sunlight flashing from its rippling surface. Her gaze followed its route where it encountered the surrounding cliffs. A dark gap was all that was visible of the gorge through which the river plunged, the only connection between the valley and the plains and marshes beyond.

A movement in the bushes below attracted her attention, *There is something in the shadows!*

She could hear the noise of sticks breaking. A big rabbit was scrambling from some unseen danger.

Questa strained her eyes to discover the threat. There was a different sound coming from behind her. With a gasp she twisted around, *What is that?*

Great wings came swooping down at her.

She cried out, ducked and covered her face as a *huge* wing slammed against her head, knocking her down the hill. She rolled and clawed and kicked, desperately trying to get any sort of traction to stop her fall. Crashing against sticks and brush, she finally managed to arrest her descent down the mountain.

Still dizzy from the spinning fall, she knew she had to find cover before the bird returned. She scrambled to a nearby rock and slumped against the cold, hard surface.

She tasted blood. Her eyes watered. She tried to focus and rubbed her eyes. Dirt on her hands, smeared her face and made things worse.

With tears streaming down her face. She touched her tender nose to find blood on her hand. *You're alive Questa. Be calm. Think.*

She could feel her heart thumping fast and breathed deeply to try and regain control. She hurt everywhere, but nothing seemed to be broken.

She looked up to see a *huge* eagle slowly beating its giant wings up to the sky. Its sharp talons sunk into the body of the rabbit. She heard the rabbit's death screams and realized, *Those could have been my screams.*

The eagle leisurely gained height.

A second eagle released a battle screech as it attacked, trying to steal the bleeding rabbit, grabbing at the limp body. The air vibrated with the loud shrieks of the two eagles.

Without waiting to see the outcome of the fight and with adrenaline still pumping through her veins, Questa crawled up the slope. She managed to regain the relative safety of the terraces. Panting and still feeling her heart hammering, she cringed behind the boulder.

Resting with her back against the cold stone with eyes closed, she felt her heartbeat return to normal. She hoisted herself onto the rock, whipped the blood away with a soft skin and carefully inspected her immediate surroundings.

A noise, the crack of a stick breaking, made Questa glance fearfully at the other side of the clearing. Three Clansmen carrying spears watched her from the concealment of the woods. They started to pull up weeds when they saw her looking at them, keeping their distance.

I hope they did not see my performance, she thought. *That would be so embarrassing.*

Questa felt comforted by their presence, *If they keep that far away, they won't bother me. I should thank Curon for worrying about my safety—even though danger does not come from the mountains. Danger lies on the plains below, in the marshes where the Primitives roam. It must be safe here. After all, the Dynasty's patrols keep the valley free of dangerous predators.*

With a smile, she reassured the Clansmen that she accepted their presence. *They must know that I am new at the Dynasty and don't know this part of the mountains.*

She allowed her thoughts to return to the dilemma of the early morning. The arguments with Usux filled her mind. Familiar myths and actions suddenly had complex and disturbing meanings.

She knew, *In order to become an Oracle-Healer, my thoughts must be clear and uncluttered. However, it is unreasonable to reveal the truth behind the myths suddenly and then to expect me to keep silent, ignoring how that truth affects my Clan and others.*

The implications of what Usux had revealed still disturbed her. Taking a deep breath to relieve tension, she relaxed, to consider his words carefully.

I must talk to grandmother! She must explain! Why must Oracle-Healers keep secrets? How dare they misuse their powers? Did grandmother also keep secrets, never telling us? How did she manage that? Maybe I misunderstood! Then she decided, *I must visit grandmother.*

A faint tinkling sound revealed the presence of a small brook in the bushes behind her. The climb and fall had made her thirsty.

I'll have a drink and wash the blood of my nose before settling down, she thought.

Some edibles would have been welcome, but she did not bring any, she had been too upset when she left the Dynasty's cave complex.

What a pity that the fruit on these trees are still far from ripe.

She got up and pushed away branches until she saw the sparkling water of the little stream. The silence, the absence of bird and insect noises, should all have been a warning, but only the lay of the land registered. Thickly wooded undergrowth grew up to the edge of a small pool. She washed her face and then, with cupped hands, she quenched her thirst. The water was cold and refreshing. Even another rustling in the forest nearby did not alarm her. Ignoring the sound, she subconsciously assumed it originated from the scurrying of some small animal.

Questa's training and her natural ability kept her aware of her surroundings, but she was at ease though irritated. A faint movement taking the shape of a figure in the shadows finally attracted her attention. Certain it was one of the Clansmen, she turned her head away, ignoring the figure. A bad odor registered. *There must be a dead animal nearby. I hope it's not in the stream.*

A feeling of strangeness, intermingled with curiosity, finally alarmed her.

All was so peaceful when her life became unbearably horrid.

<><><>

Chapter 3 – Heropto

During her pregnancy, Heropto's mother already knew she was carrying an extraordinary baby.

"Look big stomach!" and "She walk like duck!" The other females in her troupe gestured and whispered gutturally, mocking her behind her back, saying, "She think she better than we" and "Hope baby not big, not strong."

Then, frowning, "Who she mated? I kill my mate if it be him!"

When she felt the first birth pains, she asked an elderly female to accompany her to the place she had prepared, away from the troupe. Reluctantly the female followed her, and then gestured for other females to help. They knew that the females of all the roaming groups, similar to themselves, needed assistance when giving birth, unlike other mammals that give birth alone and seek isolation, away from even their own. They also knew their own code required females to assist one another in childbirth.

We must help. But if little one look like my mate, I make big trouble, they each thought.

Squatting, Heropto's mother pushed, but he was too big to enter the world easily, reluctant to emerge. His large head pushed through his mother's inadequately sized pelvis and he was stuck there. She yelled and groaned. However, the females were not concerned. They simply pushed forcefully on her stomach until he popped out, with fatal results for her, but no female mourned.

"Our mates now safe from that one," they whispered the thought.

Heropto was a strange baby. He had the typical Giant features of a large brow ridge with a horizontal trough above the eyes, just where his head sloped backward. The only anomaly was that his occipital bulge, at the back of his head, was unusually large.

"That make birth difficult!" the females pointed, accompanied by the rasping sounds they used as speech. "We call baby Heropto. Him big head kill ma."

The males said, "Look bulge on back of head. Him be quick, fast running, fast moving! This one fighter, if him live."

Each of the males knew that the strong baby could well be the result of his own escapades with Heropto's mother and secretly admired his size, hoping that the baby would grow into a strong Giant.

Thus, Heropto emerged in a hostile world without motherly care, not knowing who his father was. Although none of the males claimed him as theirs, they all instructed their respective females to give him breast. Under the male threat, the females took reluctant turns to feed Heropto. While nursing him, a female noticed that his head was abnormally hot, as if he had a fever. She dipped a soft chamois skin in an icy stream and covered his head. The baby stopped fidgeting and no fever developed. Scared of male reaction, the females soon learned to keep the baby's head cool, the only way to keep him calm.

#

Heropto's first memories were of hunger and escaping into the forest. His other memories, which sometimes visited him in his dreams, were of females yelling at him, clutching their young ones tightly to their breasts. He had already learned the best way to still his hunger, was to grab food from the other youngsters and run. When the mothers hid the food or tried to protect their children, he learned to bully them until the mothers gave him a portion in desperation.

He enjoyed hiding in the forest after grabbing food from enraged mothers, swerving through the trees fast enough to evade even the fathers. Although he avoided many well-deserved spankings, he remembered those he did receive well. Even as a toddler, barely able to walk, he never submitted without a fight.

In his dreams, the females threw food at him, food that grew in size enormously, overwhelming his small body. Alternatively, the females changed into horrible monsters pursuing him. He sometimes woke up in a sweat after such a dream and knew from the ugly looks of those near him that he had yelled out in his sleep. He learned to sleep away from the others, often covering his head with wet moss to keep it cool. His loneliness and feelings of rejection grew with time.

What I care they not like me? I better, I stronger. They weak ones!

The other children, even the older ones, gave way when he approached, avoiding eye-contact.

You will fear me more, you see!

To prevent Heropto from grabbing food intended for their children, the parents started setting aside a portion for him. He soon learned the delicate balance of demanding enough for his wants without the troupe shunning him.

Heropto grew to become heavier and stronger than his peers, and so did his spears and clubs, with which he became an expert. He craved meat to quiet his ravenous hunger. Despite his size, he could move silently through the woods and bushes of the Giants' territory and proved to be an excellent hunter, killing more prey than the combined effort of the rest of the troupe. He claimed twice as much meat as any of the others, as much as he wished. None dared to protest.

"Him kill, him take!" the hunters muttered, to hide their fear.

#

Heropto acquired many skills through watching the more skilled troupe members at their tasks.

"What you look? I give you nothing," the selected Giant often indicated, using their guttural language supported by gestures, as Heropto silently sat watching.

"I just look. Why you not make like this...?" He stopped making suggestions after the adept one angrily chased him away. He soon learned that he understood things better than the others did. With brilliant flashes of insight, that gave him excruciating headaches if he did not cool his head, he conceived better ways to ambush prey or make weapons.

"You not change how we do! I do like pa," members of the troupe often told him, resenting his skills. They were not stupid, but believed in the traditional ways of their ancestors. They did not like him and detested him for not honoring the ancient traditions.

The attention of young females compensated for his loneliness and the enmity of the males. Even the older females changed their attitude as he developed into a strong young Giant.

"I think him beautiful. Him face flat, not pull forward," the females whispered, believing that a flat face was the ultimate sign of ability and therefore extremely attractive—a thought they never shared with the males.

When Heropto was old enough to show interest in the young females, the males became even more hostile, hating the willingness of the females to offer the tribute of food he so often demanded.

An older female who had always been friendly took Heropto aside to instruct him. "You ready make plenty female happy! I teach you. You strong. Large muscle in leg and arm. Other places too! You strong all over!"

She looked at him admiringly.

"We females carry babies on hip until big. Even when we hunt! Must not have baby soon. We know trick. Male must help. I teach you!"

Privately, she thought, *Your ma knew well! I glad she not use trick—glad she got you!*

Then aloud, "Female must keep pebble between knees."

Heropto was young and even though the female was old and he did not find her very attractive, he was curious and enthusiastically accepted the lessons.

At last, the old female had to admit that Heropto had perfected his technique, "Now I teach you make baby. I too old for make baby. We not like animals. They make babies even when old."

The lessons ended abruptly when a group of females, both young and older, discovered the hiding place while a lesson was in its practical phase.

"You old whore," they gestured and yelled, adding many more gestures and gutturals. After that, the old female was not allowed the opportunity to offer anymore lessons.

\#

In his loneliness, though still young, Heropto often wandered far away from the troupe. He would stay away for several days, finding comfort in the closeness of the forest. He enjoyed lying on his back, sometimes with his head in a pool of icy cold water, looking up into the highest trees, searching for glimpses of the dark blue sky or the white clouds peering through the boughs. He learned to love the forest, where he spent his best times. He gained intimate knowledge and could survive indefinitely on mushrooms, herbs and roots, squeezing enough moisture out of moss to quench his thirst or cool his head.

He was inquisitive and wanted to know more about his environment. He continually asked questions but the other Giants ignored him or sent him away angrily, "Him pest. Why him question? Him give trouble!"

Unloved, Heropto lived off his wits. He watched the others and learned their skills by imitation and theft. When still very young he secretly borrowed a lump of obsidian from the troupe's stone worker. In the light of the full moon, he chipped off a few shards for his own use before returning the remainder.

In his hiding places in the forest, he practiced until he was an expert in forming stone spear points. He made one for himself that was bigger than any the troupe's expert had made. It was teardrop-shaped with a depression at the blunt back to fit into the end of a stout sapling, thereby creating a lethal stabbing spear. He used the sharp shards to smooth and carve away at the sapling so that he could perfectly seat the point. Proud of his achievement, he looked at it from all angles, held it in his hand, and tested its weight. The idea grew in his mind that the shaft should be in balance with the size and weight of the point. He chipped away the few remaining uneven protrusions of the spear-point and trimmed the sapling until he had a perfectly balanced stabbing spear, heavier and better balanced than any in the troupe. It was the first possession truly his own.

He practiced alone, improving his skills, even throwing it short distances to test its balance, but he did not intend to use this skill. To use a spear without physical contact with your prey was unthinkable. Even Heropto, who rebelled against all the Giant traditions, would never consider such a cowardly deed. He would hurl a club to stun his prey, but the kill must come from physical contact.

Strutting into the clearing where the troupe had erected their shelters to stay for a few nights, he waved the new spear in the air, showing off. The females were impressed but dared not show their admiration. The males tried to ignore him but could not avoid looking. When a male wanted to feel the weight, Heropto pushed him away.

The next day Heropto, with gestures and grunts, dared the males to follow him for a hunt. He danced and pranced leading the hunters until they got close to their prey. Silently Heropto crept nearer, then stormed the last few steps, wrestling the antelope to the ground before raising his spear high, sinking it deep into the animal's breast and finding the heart. None had ever witnessed such a feat.

"Single spear kill big-big buck, one jab! We never before see that!"

Heropto felt his heart swell with pride. He looked askance at the others. "My spear not fear anything. Not Giant, not animal. I say: you listen!"

The troupe's males trembled in fear.

"What will he do next?" The females whispered amongst themselves as they did their chores, "That spear come from spirits under full moon. See him use it! Club also. Him throw farther than all. Never miss. Spirits help him. Spirits protect him!"

Filled with fear, the members of his troupe avoided him. They did not disown him and were too afraid to expel him. Grudgingly they allowed him to grab the best food and choicest meat. They did not even shun him, that most cruel punishment, which small groups used against those who did not fit in. However, the reality was nearly as bad. They still acknowledged his existence and followed him on the hunt.

He always killed the largest prey, but refused with contempt to carry it back to the camp. They looked away when he was near but did not avoid all eye contact; they merely ensured that he could not interpret a look as a challenge.

Sitting apart from them, he listened to the troupe's stories and interpreted their gestures from the side. He learned that Pale-Others lived beyond the dry plains, on the far side of the great mountain chain. "The Pale ones have knowledge. Their females are small but beautiful, with soft flowing hair. There are valleys where sweet fruits and large nuts grow, edibles better than any of those in our own forests. The Pale-Others who live there chase Giants away with their dangerous magic."

He decided to see for himself.

At a time when his troupe was at peace, an elder from an adjacent troupe warned him. "Stay this side of mountain. No go to side where sun bake in midday. Magic of Pale-Others very bad. They evil eye you." He regarded Heropto with a serious face.

Heropto looked interested enough for the elder to continue, "Primitives on plains and swamps. Other side mountain. They small, angry, they fight. You easy kill them, one hand. Plains or swamps hot. Not cold like mountain. Food no good. Place no good. No go there!"

#

Near the forest where Heropto's troupe hunted and gathered, the great ice wall started. Heropto questioned the elder about it.

"Ice everywhere, here to where it dark. There sun not strong, weak," he said. "Ice high above, there dangerous. No go there."

The challenge was too great for Heropto to ignore. He wanted to test it for himself and managed to climb up the great ice wall where a deep crack allowed access. He kept his great spear, now fitted with a long shaft, with him. Unknown dangers might await him.

On top he identified with the white emptiness, stretching out to the horizon. Here, he was the only living thing, master of all.

He moved forwards, carefully at first, clutching his spear in his right hand. Then he rushed ahead, curious to inspect the great expanse of ice, covered with a thin layer of snow.

The ice gave way suddenly and he tumbled into a crevasse. As he dropped into the void, he instinctively tightened the grip on his spear.

The spear got stuck horizontally across the crack, nearly jerking his arm out of its socket. The pain almost forced him to let go. With his other hand he grabbed the spear handle and saved himself. For the moment he was safe.

I not die!

With both hands holding on, he tried to find purchase for his feet. His feet, wrapped in animal skins against the cold, slipped on the vertical ice and made the spear slither sideways. He got tired. His heavy skin kaross dragged him down.

Groaning and with muscles aching, he hoisted himself straight up. He maneuvered his left elbow over the spear shaft which slipped further. He hung on one armpit. Still holding onto the spear with his right hand.

I not fall now!

Carefully he worked his right arm up and across until he was hanging with both arms across the shaft. He raised one foot onto the ice. Working against the sliding direction of the spear, he managed to crawl out of the crevasse, kicking and panting.

Exhausted he lay on his back on the cold ice. His head burned like fire. Scooping some loose snow over his head relieved the heat.

When his heartbeat returned to normal, he continued exploring.

By moving carefully, testing the snow and ice bridges with his spear, he learned to safely negotiate his way across the ice field. He developed an eye for danger and found the risky crossings exhilarating. On the ice he could test his skills, pitch his abilities against nature, and, after the exertion, cool down his flaming head.

The older Giants spoke of the ice wall slowly creeping towards the midday sun. Ice had already swallowed pools— even hills—they had known as children. Heropto's exclusive icy domain was expanding. It pleased him.

He liked the freshness of the air and the open vistas. Also, the sight of the blue sky reflected off the ice in lighter blue hues, where the cold wind cleared the snow. But best of all was the forest, which he loved.

When he returned to the troupe after long explorations, none of the troupe indicated they had missed him or had even noticed his absence. Their indifference added to his growing bitterness.

#

The young male Giants wanted to copy Heropto's most risky feats, but few dared. Many admired his strength and the way females looked at him. The young males discussed and exaggerated his prowess with females.

His arrogance grew in line with his following.

Reluctantly, the males of his troupe had to admit that he always seemed to know where the prey would be and he was therefore able to plan a better ambush.

With his spear ready, Heropto was the first to see an opportunity. He could anticipate the movements of prey, think fast, and act even before they moved. He was the first to jump onto the prey. Only then did he allow his followers to join him and sink their spears into the creature as well. Afterwards he mocked their performance, while soaking his overheated head. When the males, still following the troupe's leader, were unsuccessful in their hunt, he would throw his trophies in their midst with disdain and clear contempt.

Heropto was the only one prepared to face the wild boars with their quick movements and dangerous tusks, which soon became his preferred prey. As a special favor he sometimes shared this delicacy with his most trusted followers. A couple of the younger Giants carried out his instructions unquestioningly. The instructions soon changed to commands.

The older Giants did not appreciate him or his skills. They did not treat him with the respect he felt he deserved. Despite his prowess, they never invited him to join in their banter around the evening fires, but ignored him when possible. When Heropto broke the neck of a large gazelle with his bare hands, without using a stone axe or club, the young males were impressed. But the older Giants warned, "Heropto bad influence on young."

Heropto retired to the forest and brooded in his loneliness. To force the troupe to give him the recognition he craved, he decided that he had to perform a feat never achieved before. His chance came when hunters reported they had seen the tracks of a sabretooth tiger near a stream. It led to a rocky hillock. The information caused the troupe to panic and relocate, erecting their shelters far away from the threat.

Heropto's eyes gleamed; a sabretooth kaross would be just the token he needed to force recognition. Without asking the hunters for more details, he started off in the direction from where they had come.

One of the young males noticed Heropto's reaction, and gesturing to his mates, they followed him at a distance. They saw him finding the spoor near a stream.

Heropto was pleased to see them. He needed an audience to witness his prowess but he ignored them, as if unaware of their presence.

They whispered together excitedly, "See size of spoor! Paws huge," and "He not follow! Dangerous," also "We keep together. More safe." They followed at a respectful distance.

Heropto tracked the spoor to the tiger's hideout near a hillock.

The tiger growled a warning when it became aware of the intruders. When Heropto ignored it, it stood menacingly, pacing about its territory and growling even louder.

Instead of running away to become easy prey, Heropto remained where he was.

The furious tiger walked in a large circle around Heropto, roaring and shaking its head, stalking its antagonist.

Heropto provoked the tiger even more, by throwing stones and a thick wooden stick at it, while inching closer to within striking distance with his spear.

The furious tiger stormed and leapt, slashing at anything that moved. Heropto ducked and lunged to the side, anticipating every move. A giant claw drew blood from his arm. When the tiger hesitated, Heropto leaped onto its back. Using his immense strength, he stuck his spear deep into the predator's thick neck.

The tiger reared and clawed at Heropto and the spear. Bucking and roaring—mad with pain—he tried to dislodge Heropto, who used the spear as support.

He pushed the spear deeper, hoping for the kill.

The young Giant males stood back from the battle, horrified.

The tiger tried to get rid of Heropto. It stormed at the nearby thickets where the young Giants hid. They scattered, screaming. Two of them were unable to get away.

The tiger focused on killing the young males, tearing them apart, biting and slashing. The colossal beast's roars echoed in the valley.

The pause was long enough to allow Heropto to withdraw his heavy spear and strike again, sinking it into the sabretooth's heart.

With a final roar the tiger collapsed on top of the mauled remains of the two youths.

Panting in quick gasps, Heropto pulled out his spear and jumped to the ground.

There he stood, his arms and spear raised to the heavens. "All creatures bow to me!" He roared, imitating the sabretooth's challenge to the world. "I kill all!"

After the excitement of the fight, while dousing his head, he resolved, *I strongest. This tiger prove me mighty! Me force troupe obey.*

The youths stood to the side, staring at him with ashen faces and large eyes.

"You help. Pull tiger," Heropto commanded.

Trembling and with clammy hands, the youths obeyed, grunting as they tried to pull the massive tiger off of their dead mates.

Arrogantly, Heropto sent the surviving young males away with the corpses, to expose these in the time-honored way. He stayed with his prey. The giant fangs were as long as his forearm. He stroked the dead tiger's fur, admiring the powerful body and caressed the mighty muscles, now void of life.

He skinned the tiger alone and worked the skin until soft, keeping the head with attached teeth as a headdress.

Wrapped in the magnificent pelt he returned to the troupe. The enormous tiger head towered over his own, huge teeth framing his face, reaching down to his shoulders. He walked into his troupe's midst in his arrogant way, expecting adoration.

The older Giants moved away but secretly admired the trophy from a distance. One of them looked carefully and then whispered to a companion, "The Pale-Others beyond the mountains preserve skins better."

Heropto heard and stopped in surprise. Angry at their lack of praise, he looked at them for a moment before turning around. With his huge head held high, he left the troupe.

The troupe blamed Heropto for the unnecessary death of the young males. The troupe displaying fear and anger instead of the respect Heropto had desired and expected. Led by the youths' mothers, fury grew in the troupe. Heropto's followers had to choose between the troupe and Heropto. Finally, all ignored and finally shunned him.

\#

The idea of the Pale-Others haunted his thoughts.

With growing bitterness, Heropto decided to make his move. He will cross the mountains and see the abilities of the Pale-Others for himself and force adoration.

With growing bitterness, Heropto decided to make his move. He will cross the mountains and see the abilities of the Pale-Others for himself and make his name.

Heropto's closest followers couldn't stay away. They found him at the edge of the woods, in the direction away from where shadows fall in the middle of the day.

Deigning to notice them, Heropto said, "You follow me. We do big things. Giants tell of us. Till all Giants go to earth."

He could not express all his thoughts in the rudimentary language of the Giants, but his thoughts were clear, "Me know more. Troupe do what me want! I force all Giants give me, best herbs, best roots, best meat from all hunts. Also those with me. We share when I master of all forest."

To consolidate his powers, he needed to meld his followers into a tightly knit group, who would obey him unquestioningly. Then they could dispose of the nearest troupe that regularly infringed on his own troupe's territory, serving as an example to other troupes and spread the fear he wanted to instill in his followers.

The first step in Heropto's plan was to force his followers to join him in a dangerous and outrageous feat. To visit the Pale-Others who controlled the areas on the far side of the great mountain range, was ideal. They were strong, dangerous and unforgiving and the route to them was long and perilous. If he could show that he had defied and outwitted the Pale-Others, all Giants would fear him and follow his orders.

The strongest young Giants and a few admiring females assembled at the edge of the woods when the days lengthened and warmed. Heropto exuded charm as he explained the planned adventure with many gestures and grunts. His followers would be dependent on him and his leadership during the adventure and he would teach them to obey him unconditionally.

"We cross the plains and go to Great Mountain Range. We cross to side that face sun when sun highest. Far side of mountain. Pale-Others grow good fruit and nuts in valley. There we eat. We come back. We show fruit and nuts to Giants."

Heropto and his followers left the Giants' wooded forests. They crossed the dry plain and reached the mountains in a few days. Crossing the mountains was more difficult than he had anticipated, but Heropto's knowledge of crevasses and snow bridges allowed them to ascend a large glacier. He was pleased with the difficulty and noticed how lost his followers were in the unknown environment. He grunted and made sure they knew, without his leadership, all would have died.

At the top of the glacier, Heropto ploughed his way through the ice field covering the apex of the high pass, making a path for the rest to follow. At the far side, they descended another glacier and experienced the heat of the direct sunlight on the mountain slopes facing the sun.

He demonstrated his abilities and strength, reinforcing the loyalty and fear of his followers. A young female attached herself to him. Using the skills the old female had taught him, he satisfied his urges even though he felt as little attachment to her as he had to the old female.

Following the edge of the snowfields in the sunset direction, they approached a volcano surrounded by rocky pinnacles. At the upper end of a valley, below the volcano, they found trees with sweet fruit and many different kinds of nuts. Heropto wanted to taste more of this abundance.

"I go down in valley. You, you, and you also come. You others stay," he ordered.

One young male dared to warn him, "Pale-Others have magic can kill. We not disturb them in valleys! Can kill us from far."

Heropto slapped the rebel hard, "You fear Pale-Others? You think Pale-Others strong like me? You think me not more strong? You think me not think good?"

The youth hung his head in shame, "No, no! You strong."

Near a little stream, Heropto noticed a Pale-Other female. She was skinny and seemed weak. She had a face even flatter than his. He liked the color of her hair. Long and golden, her hair flowed softly onto her shoulders, shimmering in the light of the sun. It was nothing like the tangled hair of the Giants, which was thick and red, unwashed, sticky and smeared with fat. He wanted to touch that hair, feel its texture, but she cried out loudly when she saw him, forcing him to silence her with his big hand.

Then things happened over which Heropto had no control and his life became too complicated to handle.

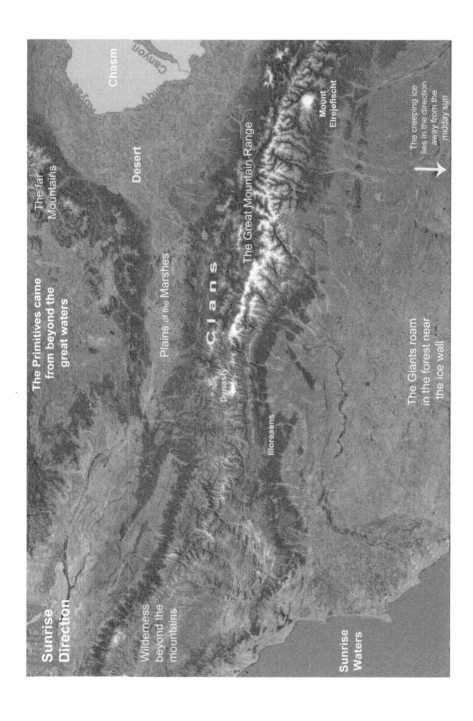

Chapter 4 – Captive

Questa woke up in a daze. She did not know where she was. She was sore and tired.

Prickling feelings in my hand.

She flexed her hand to get the blood flowing.

What is restricting me?

She tried to move her arm. Movement brought back memories. The leather thong tied around Questa's wrist had cut into her skin.

Giants! I am a captive.

She remembered suffering an uncomfortable night. She had tried sitting up and lying down, always with her arm extended towards the tree, around which the Giants had fastened the other end of the leather strap.

The realization exhausted her emotionally. Unaccustomed to the hard, rough ground, she did not fall asleep until exhaustion overwhelmed her. Frightened of cramps, she moved her legs. They felt like lead.

How will I manage to walk?

It was just light enough to see and the fresh smells of dawn filled the air, but she hardly noticed. Birdsong did not soothe her, while she massaged her wrist.

A Giant approached, loosened the cord slightly before brutally dragging Questa towards where the others had already started.

Questa stumbled, trying to scramble to her feet, bruising a knee while being pulled along the ground.

A few turns around a wrist ensured that the Giant did not accidently let go. They joined the others who rushed up the slopes towards the snowline. There they hurried along, following the line of the mountains in the sunrise direction. By following a twisting route, they managed to keep within the wooded areas, nearest to the snow line, whenever possible.

After a while, another Giant took over the responsibility of restraining her with the strap. It felt like someone stabbed her fingers with needles, warning her of limited blood circulation. She pulled at the restraint and flexed her hand and fingers frequently to keep blood flowing. Soon, her forearm muscles cramped from the constant flexing, but she forced her arm to obey, fearing the loss of her hand. Questa could barely keep up with the fast pace. Her knee hurt and her legs cramped. Each step caused a flash of pain, which occupied her mind. Slowly the exercise warmed her and the stiffness and pain decreased.

#

Plans to escape took precedence in her thoughts. She watched carefully, hoping that whenever her guards changed responsibility for holding the strap, she could yank loose.

Surely, I can run faster than any of them, despite my bruised knee. Their clumsy gait, when trying to run fast, must make them slower than I am. I should be able to get away. But we'll have to be in the open.

However, the Giants were careful. They kept her in the middle of their column when walking and only handed over the leash while surrounding her in a clearing within thick bush.

Questa listened carefully and observed their gestures.

If I listen at the sounds they make, I might pick up words and understand their meanings.

This soon became intolerable, the males kept gesturing and looking at her while speaking. Even worse, while she was concentrating on them, they managed to catch her eye before she could look away. Her future fate became clear, too clear. She understood that many of the words she heard were lewd. They even argued about what would happen to her after the leader had finished, whose turn it would be to use her if anything worthwhile was left over.

She kept her eyes downcast, listening to the sounds only when they were not discussing her. Whenever the group rested, allowing her to sit down, she crouched within the Giant's skin and hid her face behind her hands. She concentrated hard, peeping between her fingers to follow the gestures. She made sure she never raised her eyes to face level and avoided all eye contact.

When not trying to understand the Giant's language, she worried, *How did they catch me so unawares? How is it possible that I felt angry and insecure at the Dynasty where I was safe and never threatened? I had no idea what real danger and suffering were, I should not have been so ungrateful!*

#

Despite the cold, Questa perspired during the fast hike. She longed to tarry at one of the streams they passed, long enough for her to clean. She felt uncomfortable and damp, but the Giants did not allow her to stop. She desperately missed her daily wash. It was clear why the Giants stank.

A highlight of her day was when a female noticed her scratching and gave her some grease that smelt of putrid fat. Friendlier than the others, she indicated with gestures and uttering guttural sounds, Questa should smear herself. By the evening, the grease smeared on Questa's body was old and sticky.

If only I could get hold of an obsidian shard. Then I could use the sharp cutting edge to get rid of this horrible strap and run. But how to get one without the Giants noticing?

The pools that formed behind lava-flow barriers had transformed much of the molten rock into obsidian deposits. She pulled towards each pool they passed, indicating a wish to fill the gourd the Giants had given her. She splashed water on herself to show that she wanted to wash. Always searching for a useful shard.

If only the Giants would utilize a few of the pools we pass every time we cross a stream, she thought.

But the Giants ignored the water pools. They only filled their gourds at small waterfalls, never washing themselves, ignoring the layers of putrid grease and sweat on their bodies.

That must be how they compensate for the cold climate they live in.

At night, she shivered until she was dry. The offered grease proved effective against insects and an additional protection against the cold. Even though the feeling of grease on her skin was irritating, she smeared it on liberally. She lay down to sleep feeling sticky but the itching was gone. She never thought about the warning of a looming natural disaster, expected by the Dynasty. She never tried to Sense in the Abstract mode to analyze the environment. There was nothing to gain by exposing herself to the risk and exhaustion accompanying that state. Much better to concentrate on the Giants.

#

Questa slowly adapted to the rough trek and uncomfortable nights, and she even got used to the odor of the grease. Nevertheless, the combination of always feeling cold, the hard ground, and the irritating leash around her wrist, left her sleepless at night. She imagined her escape and planned the details.

I will get my chance, if they relax their vigilance! What are their weak points?

Remembering details of the myths surrounding the Giants, she tried to understand what had happened. As far as she knew, the Primitives living in the marshy plains below the Clan valleys were the only serious threat facing the Clans. Neither the Giants nor any of the other Clan-similars living far from the Clan valleys, ever posed a serious danger. She remembered tales of a Giant having kidnapped a Clanswoman, but that had not happened within her father's lifetime and must have been very long ago.

She remembered overhearing a bard telling her father that an inquisitive Giant occasionally visited the head of a valley, near the snow line, raided a grove of fruit and nut trees and then disappeared.

I thought the Giants were peaceful beings.

Then she recalled how the conversation continued in a whisper. "Long ago some Giants had caught a group of hunters that had crossed the mountains and hunted near the Giants' domain. The girls in the party were rescued, but only after having been assaulted and raped. Many died in childbirth and a few deformed children were born."

The bard did not know what happened to them.

Her father only said something about the offspring being infertile.

Have the Giants changed? Are they a new threat to the Clans? She wondered, adding another concern to her thoughts. *The Dynasty must know that the Giants have abducted me. Surely,*

Clansmen from the Dynasty will save me! But I cannot wait. I will have to escape.

Yet, she found no opportunity for escape. She was always tied up and hated it. Her only chance would be to find an obsidian shard and cut off the strap, probably during the night. Then creep away until she reached open country and could run.

#

Thanks to the jealous female, the Giant leader kept away. Despite their gestures and threats, the Giant males did not dare to challenge or anger the leader by harassing her. Questa was still safe, but the leader was getting irritated with the female and the danger of an assault was increasing daily. She was scared.

She tried counting how many valley-headwaters they had crossed. However, it was impossible to keep track, some streams converged before flowing into a valley and others formed gullies lower down, while the Giants remained in woods and trees, following a circuitous route. Even orientating herself relative to the mountain peaks that she could glimpse through the trees, whenever they crossed over open ground, was difficult.

One day, a tall mountain peak, taller than any of the others, became visible beyond the nearer range. It had to be the hallowed peak the Clans called El-El. Her heart gave an excited leap whenever the peak showed itself through a gap between the peaks closest to them, a peak shrouded in myth, where Oracle-Healers collect secret herbs that grow in its dark ravines.

She remembered how the bards had described the peak, *Where the Spirits of earth reach up to touch the Gods in heaven.*

Near the peak, they passed through patches of dense mist. Lush plants grew in the moist soil with large, almost translucent green leaves, dripping moisture. Questa recognized several edible plants and herbs, which grew taller and had larger leaves than those she knew. The mist moistened her skin below the strap and made her itch. The strap became a symbol of her captivity, the equivalent of a prison.

If only I manage to escape, I can find edibles and medicinals here. Surely, the spirit of EL-El would watch over me, allow me to find a sharp obsidian shard to cut myself loose one night, she thought, reverting back to childish superstition.

#

In an attempt to find an alternate escape plan, Questa used her training to interpret the sounds as the Giants argued and conversed. Analyzing and taking note of their gestures and body language, helped. More and more sounds acquired meaning. She carefully kept her growing understanding to herself, hoping for useful information. She interpreted certain sounds and gestures as indicating the leader. Her nearest rendition of the name was 'Heropto'. He was markedly different from the other Giants. There was something feverish about his head, which reflected in his eyes.

He has a fanatical streak and seems much more intelligent than the rest of the troupe, she thought.

Her interpretation and understanding of a lively discussion accompanied by wild gestures lessened her fear of an immediate assault. *Heropto is going to parade me as his prize before all the Giants when we arrive at their destination. Until then I think I'm safe.*

#

The dexterity of the Giants amazed Questa. Only slightly taller than the average Clan-man, but adapted to the woody environment, the large, lumbering bodies moved silently within the woods and undergrowth. They left few tracks, if any. In this environment they progressed faster than any member of the Clans could.

Questa understood that in the dense foliage, where they could fight hand-to-hand, they were invincible. Nevertheless, they tried to make tracking difficult, probably afraid of the Dynasty's revenge. By watching and copying the movements of those ahead of her, she managed to keep up and avoid scratches.

Sometimes at dusk when the Giants prepared an encampment, one of them, usually Heropto, arrived late carrying a deer or some other prey. She was always given a portion. And he always doused his head in water afterwards.

From the gestures and utterances of the Giant who kept watch, she guessed that rescuers from the Dynasty might be following them. However, she never got a glimpse of rescuers. When the troupe stopped for a quick meal, she looked back in vain, imagining any movement to be rescuers, but they never came. Then she noticed the amused expression on the Giants' faces and hope disappeared.

One morning her Captor and a few of the males stayed behind. They concealed themselves in a wooded copse with moss-covered boulders, dragging Questa along. When those that had stayed behind caught up, there was blood on their hands, clubs, and spears. They looked pleased and Questa guessed that they had ambushed rescuers from the Dynasty. Interpreting their gestures and understanding a few words, her fear grew until she convinced herself that they had killed all the rescuers. Her last hope of rescue disappeared. She considered her options, escape was impossible. The best Questa could hope for... was a quick death.

#

They were already far from the Clan valleys when the Giants paused at a brook with a few small pools. A deep gully surrounded by cliffs and topped by a waterfall, blocked all escape routes. The Giant holding Questa's leash looked around and released the strap. Questa massaged her wrist to get the blood flowing again. She carefully moved upstream, watching the Giant from under her eyebrows. When he did not react, she climbed higher, to a spot near the waterfall, where she could wash unseen.

Splashing in the water, making sure no Giant followed her, she was grateful for the opportunity.

It's amazing how the smallest concession can make me happy now.

She smiled as she enjoyed the feeling of water washing away the grease and sweat. Then she found a few sharp shards deep in the pool, she could barely suppress a laugh. Warmth radiated through her body.

They must not know!

She sat down beside the pool and took deep breaths to help her calm down. Dipping into the pool again, she felt confident that

she could hide her feelings.   Before she returned to where the
Giants were relaxing, she managed to hide the shards underneath
the Giant's kaross. The opportunity for a night-time escape had at
last presented itself. With difficulty she managed to hide her
excitement.

Soon thereafter they turned into a ravine and followed it
upstream. It was deeper and broader than most of those they had
previously crossed.

Escaping that same night became critical. Once they enter the
snowfields, escape options would disappear. That night they slept
at the edge of the snowfield, above the tree line.

*If I can escape here, I'll be on open ground and will be able to
run. Starlight reflecting off the snow will allow me to see enough to
get away. Tonight I must cut myself loose. It might be my last
chance.*

As usual, the Giants found sleeping spots around her, except
for two on guard.

Questa waited until the position of the stars indicated that
half the night had passed. The Giants had already changed guards
and she was sure that even the guards were sleepy. All was silent
except for the sounds of small insects, the occasional hooting of an
owl, and the scurrying sound of a mouse trying to escape. The
guards were looking towards the tree line, not watching her. The
strap was attached to a peg. She lay curled around the peg, hiding
it with her body.

She cut the cord quickly, then turned over slowly, as if in her
sleep. Pulling her legs in underneath her, she waited a moment,
identified a gap between the sleeping Giants, and crawled silently
through the gap. She dared not look up. Looking at the Giants
might register through their sleep. They might react.

She was already past the last Giant and ready to jump up and
run when she became aware of Heropto towering over her. He
picked her up, grabbing the kaross and shook her. He laughed. All
the Giants were awake, laughing and mocking and taunting her.
They had obviously guessed her plans all along.

Heropto shook her until the shards fell to the ground. Then
he released her. He kicked the shards towards the fire in disdain
before tying a new strap around her wrist. Questa cried through

the remaining night while the Giants not on guard went to sleep, ignoring her.

The next morning, Heropto grabbed Questa by the arm and dragged her back down the ravine. He pointed out the bloody corpses of Clan warriors, surrounded by their broken spears. Questa's face turned ashen, then she started trembling uncontrollably. The smell of blood made her choke.

Heropto grunted a warning and dragged her back to his troupe, a satisfied expression on his face. She understood, he would kill rather than allow her to escape.

Chapter 5 – Apocalypse

At the Valley of the Sparkling Waters, Anja left the Clan-Habitat with a light skip in her step. Loving eyes followed her lithe figure, noticing how the pretty girl was maturing into a great beauty. She was excited, elated. Although she tried to suppress the outward signs, she couldn't quite contain a slight smile, or the spring in her steps. She passed through the opening in the palisade and turned to the left, towards her special place near the stream. She inhaled deeply, enjoying the cool fresh air. *How beautiful the view!*

The glistening white snow-caps on the highest peaks cut into the deep violet of the mountain sky, accentuating the beauty of the mountains and filling her with joy.

Beyond the stream, out of sight of the cave that formed the Habitat of the Clan of the Sparkling Waters, Anja made herself comfortable. She had the whole day to prepare herself for the ceremony at sunset.

Thinking of the honor bestowed upon her made her heart jump with excitement. She still found it hard to believe that the Clan Chief had selected her to lead the initiation ceremony. In the quiet of the dawn, she prepared herself, rubbing the gourds and pouches hanging from a leather belt around her waist, the symbols of a Healer. The woody feel of the gourds contrasted with the smooth leather of her pouches and the soft fur of her mantle. She remembered her own initiation and the significance of the occasion, three years ago. Tonight she would have to conduct the required rituals.

Anja allowed her five primary senses to sharpen, allowed tranquility to fill her being. She focused on the beauty of the surroundings, only sub-consciously aware of extraneous sounds or movements that could reveal the presence of a predator, the only possible danger that might interrupt her meditation. She felt safe and secure, loving the smells and sounds of the early morning. The air vibrated with birdsong and the noise of insects. As the increasing warmth allowed the flowers to release their perfumes, the fresh scent of dawn filled the air.

The rising sun emerged, peeping through a gap between the distant mountain peaks and highlighting the red-gold streaks in her long blonde hair. She ignored faint tremors and a vibration in the air. Land-shakings were not uncommon in the great mountain range. There was no other indication or warning of an impending Catastrophe. Her grandmother was deep in the cave, isolated from nature's hidden indications, only discernible in Abstract Sensing mode. There was no warning. Anja was so happy, it felt as if her heart would burst.

#

When the sun was about two hands above the horizon, well above the rim of the valley, Anja heard the rumbling.

The sound originated from somewhere in the sunrise direction. She jumped up, looked down the valley to determine the source of the sound. The horizon was blurred. A strange buzzing sound vibrated in the air, getting louder. She strained her eyes to focus better but could not locate the origin of the sound.

Moments later the earth shook violently. The heaving earth threw her to the ground. The shock of the fall stunned her. She tried to sit up, but the moving ground made it impossible. She rolled onto her stomach with legs apart for stability, desperately clutching at the soil.

Wave after wave of shaking continued, accompanied by deafening rumbles. She clamped her hands over her ears, trying to lessen the noise, still too stunned to be scared. In her mind, an eternity passed before the rumbling sounds, like continuous thunder, rolled away in the sunset direction.

Anja remained motionless, her eyes tightly closed, too frightened to move. When the great noise had abated somewhat, she sat up slowly, with trembling lips and chin.

Looking up at the mountains, she could see rocks trembling, shaking loose. Huge boulders tumbled down the mountainside, gyrating in a chaotic display. The whole mountain was alive with movement. Whole areas of vegetation, like floating islands, slid down the slopes. The smell of dust filled her nostrils. She cried out but her mouth was too dry for any sound to emerge. Trembling, Anja took a few deep breaths that ended in sobs. Despite her resolve to be brave, her tears flowed freely.

Dust rose from the ground enveloping boulders and bushes. The sound of rocks rolling down the slopes penetrated her awareness.

This is dangerous! She realized. *Even the very big land-shakes were never like this. It is much more intense and very different from any I have ever heard of.*

Trembling from shock, Anja took a few deep breaths that ended in sobs. She tried to recover her nerve but failed, her cheeks streaked with involuntary tears. Eventually she felt better and tried to get up. To her surprise, she found that she was not seriously hurt, only bruised.

The cave! I must reach the cave!

With an ashen face she hurried towards the cave Habitat.

The well-known path was blocked. Trees and boulders had created obstacles, difficult to climb over. In a panic she scrambled around the debris. Dry sobs escaped her throat.

Before she had reached the cave site, the second series of shock waves hit. The noise had never fully ceased, but she was so dazed that she did not notice an increase of the rumbling sounds.

Anja collapsed and rolled herself into a protective ball. Whimpering with fear, she called for her grandmother. Grandmother was always there in a crisis. She kept her eyes tightly closed, expecting the soothing sound of her grandmother's voice.

There was no warning, no way to protect herself when the third shock wave hit. This time she was hurt. Small boulders, catapulting over larger ones, struck her. A tree, tumbling down the slope above her, pinned her to the ground, twisting her ankle. She cried out in pain, squeezing into an even tighter bundle. There was nothing else she could do. Blackness creeped in at the edges of her vision, she tried to take the pressure off her twisted ankle, but could not. Then the dark consumed her.

#

The three distinct types of shock waves, originating at the site of the Toba Super Volcano's eruption, propagated around the world and caused volcanic and land-shaking activity everywhere. Anja knew nothing of this greater picture, but only experienced the local Catastrophe.

She lost consciousness... When she came to, she saw the sun was already at its zenith, a red sphere without heat. Her throat and mouth were dry. The taste in her mouth was bitter from crunchy dirt. Dust blocked her nose. Some time passed before she understood the enormity of what had happened. She was shaking uncontrollably. She had to calm down.

First escape from under this tree.

She pushed with both arms, groaning loudly with the effort. Her movements were jerky and without power. She waited, taking deep breaths before trying again. Then she pulled up her knees as far as she could and kicked. A sharp pain shot up her leg, making her cry out again.

Despite the pain, she kicked again. The tree moved slightly. Biting on her lip, she ignored the pain. She pushed and squirmed and heaved. Bit by bit she succeeded to move the tree to the side.

She lay still. Her eyes closed. When she recovered, she crawled out from under the rubble.

I have to return to the cave. There grandmother will put a poultice on my ankle and I can clean up.

With her chin lowered to her chest, she lacked the energy to get up. Slowly she focused on her surroundings. Wiping tears from her eyes, she looked up at the mountains towering over her. They always inspired her. The sight must give her strength. Ice dust twinkled in the sky high above, diffusing the sharp outline and features of the well-known peaks. Massive snow slides must have occurred. The mountains were suffering with her. There was no stimulus there.

She could not make out any detail but she could hear ominous sounds, things were still sliding and rolling down the mountain. She felt no emotion, just a lump in her throat and the pain from many bruises. Her ankle was sore, blue and swollen. She tried to get up but nearly fell down. It was impossible to put weight on her left foot.

In a daze, she concentrated on one thing only, *I must get back to the cave! I must get past the rubble. Something terrible has caused the massive shakings.*

\#

She squinted, peering in the direction of the cave, the Habitat of the Clan. There was little to see. Dust obscured everything.

Anja put all of her weight on her good foot, dragging the other, using it only for balance. She was forced to take a detour. Her bad foot caught on a branch causing sharp pains to shoot up her leg. She reflexively pulled the leg up and fell off balance, landing on some rocks. The pain was unbearable. She pulled her knees up to her chest, curling up, tears causing dirty streaks running down her face.

Crawling forward she found a broken branch, long enough to use as a support. Scarcely recognizing any of the features around her, she slowly hobbled on. She had to move around fallen trees and rocks. Snow and mudslides created additional blockages.

Why is no one from the Clan looking for me?

Anja felt very much the young girl again. Not at all the self-assured young woman who the Clan had singled out for an exceptional honor.

Injured, she wanted Grandmother to comfort and soothe her. Near the cave she called out, her voice hoarse and pained. Someone had to help her into the cave.

At the cave site, just where she was sure the entrance must be, she saw only snow and debris.

This cannot be! Where is the cave? Where is everyone? Where is grandmother?

She shook her head, *Concentrate! The cave must be here. It cannot be gone! There must be another reason why I cannot see the cave. Maybe I'm at the wrong place.*

She looked around to re-orientate herself, her eyes widening.

She shook her head again, *How can I be wrong? These cliffs have partly collapsed but the remnants look just like those surrounding the cave Habitat. The dust obscures everything. I must have lost my way. I must find the cave!*

Her ankle screamed for attention. She slumped and tenderly examined her ankle and foot. Each touch sent a shock of pain through her leg.

Why is nobody out here? They must help me. They know I must attend the ceremony! They must be looking for me at the stream.

Anja looked around absently rubbing her arms. There was no visible sign of the cave, nor any indication of remnants of the cave, only a large depression breaking the line of the cliff-face. The broken hulks of trees stuck out of the mixture of snow and mud, showing where parts of the cliff had collapsed. The gnarled forms torn from the mountain, stripped of newly budding leaves, looked like dark arms with outstretched fingers pleading to the dusty sky for rescue. Many were still moving, slowly toppling over or quaking while settling in new resting places. In her imagination, they were also reaching for her, threatening and scary in their unsteady quivering.

A roaring vibration in the air made Anja cringe again. Far away, a smoke column was expanding above the peaks.

A new danger? Maybe one or more of the local volcanos are waking up. I thought they were dormant.

She did not have enough energy left, could not isolate herself from her immediate surroundings to allow her to Sense what was happening. The earth shook. Fearfully she waited for more convulsions, but nothing happened. Finally, she looked up.

All movement had stopped and she could think again. She tried to reassess her surroundings, searching for clues where she might be in relation to the Clan cave.

I'll go to the stream and search back to the cave from there.

She struggled upright to retrace her steps. Choosing a roundabout route without obstacles, she hobbled along, sparing her ankle. She reached the stream and sat down, gasping for air through her sobs. Her ankle hurt. She mumbled aloud, "They must be here, by now someone must have missed me and is looking for me."

She immersed her ankle in the cold water. Eventually she calmed down and looked around searching for landmarks. The dust had settled somewhat and the noise of rolling boulders had lessened. She knew exactly where she was. Then she slowly returned to the cave site. Many known boulders were displaced or missing but she could recognize a few trees standing at strange angles as those she had climbed as a child. This was the cave site.

Still, there was no sign of the cave or of life — she sat down; her brain uncomprehendingly blank.

Realization of a great loss filtered through her muddled brain, surpassing the pain. She tried to fight the need to retreat into the darkness of denial but reality intruded and her thoughts cleared. The only sign of where the cave used to be was the broken cliff-face, half swallowed by snow and mud.

This is impossible. My friends, my grandmother and the others, they must be somewhere!

However, there was no sign. Despair overwhelmed her and she fell into a swoon.

Chapter 6 – Orrox

Orrox and his acolytes sat in a circle on a small rise at the head of a fertile valley. The bulk of the great mountain range loomed above them. Their discussion centered on the necessity for stability in the Clans. Orrox held his hands in front of him, fingertips touching. He was asking questions, encouraging responses and then evaluating the logic.

The two recently mature Clan-girls argued against secrecy while the two boys had the opposite view. Orrox looked at Bronnox, encouraging him to start.

He was taller and slightly older than the other acolytes. Smoothing his long brown hair, bound back from his large forehead, he tried a rational analysis: "If secrecy is required to stabilize the happy lifestyle, satisfying the needs of the Clans—"

Camla, who had been silent and deep in thought, interrupted, "What is happiness? Are the Clans happy? I can imagine..." Then, realizing she had interrupted Bronnox, she smiled apologetically, "Sorry! Please go on!"

"You take a strong view, Bronnox. And trying to define happiness, Camla!" Orrox said with a slight smile. Then, more seriously, "The Council and Dynasty take the view that fulfilment of expectations and a purposeful life are the true sources of happiness. As stated by a wise sage: 'Happiness consists in seeing one's life in its entirety as meaningful and worthwhile'... But what about the Cave of Secrets? Does it contain necessary secrets?"

Lonna made a face, but said nothing.

"Yes, Lonna?" Orrox prompted.

"I want to think about this a little longer but I have some questions: Who decides what must be kept secret?"

"Some things are dangerous if abused. Only a Healer should be allowed to have that knowledge," Bronnox grumbled.

Lonna crossed her arms and frowned, her lips pressed together.

A soft expression crossed Bronnox's face, but Lonna did not notice. With her back turned, she was talking to Camla.

Interesting, Orrox thought. *I'll have to watch those two.* Then, *My acolytes are thinking clearly and discussing options and possibilities rationally. It is time to show them more.*

Out loud he said, "The Oracle-Healers know all the secrets. That will include you. It is time I show you what the Oracle-Healers hide in the Caves of Secrets. This cave services the Clan whose Habitat is lower down, the Clan of the Second Valley."

The acolytes leaned forward; they had been waiting for this.

"I have shown you the type of secret clues the Oracle-Healers use to direct one to the hidden cave within each valley. It is different in each valley. Ammox and Lonna, see whether you can find the cave. Wait for us there. Bronnox, you and Camla can do the same when enough time has lapsed."

Ammox and Lonna crossed the valley slowly, eyes peeled, searching for clues.

The three who stayed behind relaxed where they were.

Orrox had his own issues to deal with. He had grown up in the Clan of his grandmother and father, always with the knowledge of his dynastic obligations and of the Dynasty expecting him to move to the Dynasty Valley. He was not sure how to handle the responsibility he felt, and had towards the Clans once he took over the Council leadership.

Oh, well, he thought, *at least training the acolytes is a good start.*

His thoughts returned to the acolytes. Bronnox was rational and the best tracker of the four. Lonna analyzed difficult questions while Camla tended to project friendly emotions easily. She was more concerned with healing than any secrecy issues, while Ammox always had original thoughts. He tended to envisage amusing or unusual alternatives.

Orrox Sensed small tremors. Not from local volcanoes, not a local land-shaking, something unusual. Whatever it was, it has been present and increasing for some time.

What can it be? he wondered.

While mentoring the acolytes, he had not entered the Abstract state to Sense the wider environment. That would be much too dangerous without another trained Oracle-Healer present. He would teach and demonstrate that technique when they all return to the Dynasty Valley.

A rumbling sound came from below, where the valley turned in the sunrise direction. The ground was moving. Over the flat marshy area that drained into the valley proper, the ground was rising up, looking like the crest of a wave rolling towards them. Orrox did not know what it was. He cried out, "Lie flat on your stomachs and protect your heads!"

The two acolytes obeyed immediately, turning around to face one another, legs apart, hands covering their heads.

The earth shook and they felt the ground rise and fall with a deafening noise and loud explosive cracks.

When the twisting, rolling motion subsided, Bronnox looked at Orrox with large eyes. "What was that? It was huge! What was that noise?"

"I don't know!" Orrox said. "Where you hurt?"

"Only scared." Camla said.

Orrox looked at them both critically, then to their right where the Cave of Secrets lay. "Where are Ammox and Lonna? We must find them!"

The cave was invisible, not only hidden by the forest nestled against the cliff face, but also by piles of rock. The only entrance was an obscure crevice some way up the cliff face.

He jumped up, "Follow me! We must see how those two fared!"

They had felt ground tremors and even intense land-shakings before, but this was way more intense than anything they had previously experienced.

"There may be follow-up shakings. I think the sharp sounds were the roots of trees snapping."

The rumbling sound continued, but with less intensity.

Bronnox called out, "Look at the mountain!"

Boulders were rolling down the mountain slopes, leaving a wake of dust and destruction. A whole section slid down the steep face to tumble over edges like a huge waterfall. Trees were swept away in the landslide, slowly toppling over. Fractured rocks released the pungent smell of sulfur. The sound of avalanches roaring down the mountainside filled the air.

They were halfway across the valley, when the continuous rumbling noise increased again. "Down, down! Lie flat again!"

This time the shaking was even stronger. They experienced violent side-to-side and vertical jerking. After the intensity decreased, more powerful shaking resumed, which changed to big, slow sways that gradually faded away.

They remained down on the ground, silent, too frightened to speak or even to think.

Orrox rubbed the back of his neck. He knew he had to find the other two. Despite his greater knowledge and longer experience, he felt numb, exhausted, as if his brain would not function. The two acolytes stared at him, waiting.

With an effort, he sat up, "Careful! I expect follow-up shakings. The other two went in the right direction. Let's find them."

They entered a wooded area at the same place they had seen the other two disappear. He selected a route away from the path loose boulders might take.

"Call out! They cannot be far."

He had barely uttered the words when a growing noise forced them to fall down again. Intense shaking loosened boulder around them.

When the earth had settled once more, they called out loudly, but received no answer.

"The Cave of Secrets is hidden in those cracks in the cliff. I hope they reached it before this last shaking," Orrox said, pointing. He clenched his fists tightly. Only the whites of his knuckles proved how anxious he was.

Boulders and broken trees blocked their path as they approached the cliff, forcing them to clamber across or around obstructions. Twice more the rumbling noise frightened them, but they reached open ground before the next tremor hit.

Fresh scars on the cliff-face showed where boulders had bounced down the cliff face.

"You stay here in the open. It is relatively safe. I'll check whether the cave is undamaged and stable."

Orrox soon returned. "Some boulders have fallen into the crack. It's quite a scramble! The cave is undamaged but dusty.

Come with me. You'll have to stay in the cave till I return. I must find Ammox and Lonna."

"I am a good tracker. I should go with you," Bronnox said.

"No. You stay with Camla. In the cave you are protected. I will be back soon."

There was a knot in Orrox's stomach as he left the cave. The three shock waves were all massive and intense. The effects of any one of the three, might have killed his missing acolytes.

Sending out the acolytes, two at a time, is normal and an essential part of their training. I may not blame myself, he thought. *But, surely they are safe! They must be safe. I must find them.*

Clenching his jaw, he took control of himself and resorted to reason.

How would Ammox and Lonna have handled the danger? They must have noticed the approach of the first wave. They are clever, they would have quickly moved into the safest area they could find.

Orrox followed the line of the cliff downhill. He called out as he went, "Ammox! Lonna! Are you safe?"

At last, he heard them answer.

"Whew!"

They both lay flat in a shallow cranny against the cliff where they were protected from rolling boulders and loose debris.

"We knew you would find us. We decided that it is safer to wait here until the land-shakings had ceased. Had you not come, we would have continued to search for the cave and waited for you there."

They both managed brave smiles.

The smell of sulfur surrounded them. Lonna used a flaxen cloth to cover her mouth and nose.

"What a nasty odor!"

"Careful! Everything is loose. We will most likely experience more of these local tremors. Come with me. Bronnox and Camla are in the Cave. I believe the worst shakings have passed. Land-shakings produce only three main shock waves. The cave is very similar to those in other Clan valleys. It is a natural hollow in volcanic rock up a cliff, hidden behind boulders and trees. It is stable and safe. Not like many Cave Habitats that are situated in soft loess cliffs, easy to enlarge and adapt."

At the cave the four acolytes embraced one another, smiling and laughing.

Bronnox stroked back his hair and kept looking at Lonna while Ammox said, "Surely you were not worried. Just a little tremor, we hardly even noticed!"

Bronnox and Camla pounced on him.

"Just a tremor! You probably fell down trembling in fear with the first wave."

"I bet you were as scared as we were!"

Lonna smiled, "We were really scared, but luckily we found a safe spot. Then it was not too bad."

Orrox looked around and inspected the various areas. Herbs and ointments, strips of pliable bark, flax fiber and soft leather as well as containers with salves, powders, potions, syrups, and clear water, collected from various fountains, were all stored and carefully marked. Dried edibles were stacked on a rock shelf.

"Bronnox and Ammox, please make a small fire just inside the entrance. Use dry logs. We don't want smoke to pinpoint the position of the Cave of Secrets. Primitives are at their most dangerous after any Catastrophe, when they believe the Clans are vulnerable"

Soon they were drinking a hot herbal drink.

A follow-up shaking interrupted their quick meal. The acolytes looked at Orrox with large eyes but he did not seem concerned, "Like the previous few, this latest shaking must be of local origin, after-effects of the original shockwaves. Since they did not damage the cave, I believe we are safe in here."

Orrox had to distract them. *They have to think rationally.* "This was not an ordinary land-shaking, but something much bigger and originating from great distance. Think! What did you notice?"

Bronnox reacted first, "I noticed the multiple shakings you mentioned. They were big, not like follow-up shakings."

Ammox leaned forward, keeping eye contact with Orrox. He could not hide the trust he felt of Orrox's ability to keep them safe. He said, "Yes. There was a delay before the second shaking started, furthermore the second shaking was different. The first rolled towards us and the later ones jerked us around."

The others nodded their heads in agreement.

"Yes. Very good. You must not allow fear to impair your ability to observe. Even though it was so intense, the delay between the different shaking-phases indicates the distance of the source. Whatever it was, it is very far away and huge! It might be a very large volcanic eruption, of immense proportions."

Orrox was convinced the catastrophic effects must have been widespread and all encompassing, seriously affecting all the Clans. *The Dynasty Valley is at risk. My dynastic responsibility will soon include them and all the Clans.*

He had to arrange aid wherever needed. For now, the safety of the acolytes must take priority and they have to see whether the Clan in this valley needed help. *Members of the Council as well as my Orrox cousins must handle the crisis and arrange assistance for those Clans in need, until I can join them.*

Looking at the acolytes he said, "There must be damage everywhere."

He sat in silence, thinking of the layout of the mountains and the Clan valleys before continuing, "We must go down to the Habitat of this valley's Clan to see what occurred. After such an intense shaking, Clansmen or children might be injured. We must hurry. You are still in training but you can already treat lesser injuries and wounds. I rely on you to also treat complex wounds, but just refer to me first. I know your individual abilities and am proud of your progress. You will soon have to prove that your training was effective."

They gathered the necessary salves, strips of bark, bindings and other medicaments quickly.

#

They slowly descended into the valley proper, searching for a way around and over the many boulders and obstacles. Orrox led the way. He continuously looked for possible safe refuges in case of follow-up shakings.

Ammox started teasing Camla, daring her to jump from boulder to lower boulder, laughing as their feet barely touched the support before flying on to the next boulder, lower down. Orrox had to rein them in, "We are not safe yet! Many boulders are now loose.

And please, not so loud. Should the Clan have suffered, your laughter would be insensitive."

He was relieved that they had not been hurt. *Their exuberance proves that they have already overcome the traumatic experience. How wonderful to be young!"*

As they descended, Lonna fell between two boulders and was trapped under the broken trunk of a tree.

Bronnox reacted immediately, "Are you hurt? I am coming."

With Ammox's help they moved the trunk. Lonna was only bruised and managed to climb out of the hole.

Orrox heard a noise, an intense rumbling, which gave him adequate warning. The noise rose in pitch. Looking in the sunrise direction, he saw a dark, brown-grey wall rolling towards them at great speed.

He had noticed what seemed to be a safe location under an overhang. Large boulders against the cliff face gave additional protection.

"Hurry! Follow me!"

They reached it just in time. The sound of a powerful storm exploded upon them. The narrowness of the valley and the trees helped dampen the overwhelming whistling of the wind.

The wind hit the cliff with a deafening roar, dumping detritus, sand and a layer of fine yellow-grey dust.

"Quickly! Cover your faces with cloth or a skin. Breathe through that and protect your ears."

They sat with their backs against the cliff, pulling worked skins over their heads and covering their ears.

The cliff protected them from the worst flying debris. Yellow-brown dust seemed to penetrate everywhere. It burned Orrox's lungs and made it difficult to breathe. He knew the acolytes were suffering too, but he could do nothing to help them.

At least they are supporting each other.

The whistling wind flattened nearly everything in its way. Strong gusts followed, storming up the valley, hitting them with shattering force, as if trying to lift them out of the valley. The winds swirled around, coming from unexpected directions, suffocating and exhausting them with unrelenting blasts of sand and dust.

\#

When the wind finally subsided, the acolytes were gritting their teeth. The intensity of the unfolding Catastrophe escalated dramatically, spiraling beyond anything they could ever imagine. Orrox could see they were scared, fearing sudden death.

Orrox Sensed the panic that emanated from them, their previous exuberance forgotten. The yellow-brown dust slowly settled, then swirls of wind scooped up the dust and moved it up the valley.

The wind eventually died down, followed by an eerie silence. The setting sun disappeared, leaving an all-encompassing gloom that darkened the valley.

"We're lucky to have survived," Orrox said but a faraway rumble made them cringe against the cliff again.

What more is nature planning to throw at us?

He listened carefully, "A nearby volcano has erupted! That has not happened in a generation. We thought they were all dormant. Perhaps it is Mount Bubis, located halfway between us and the Dynasty Valley. It might even be far away Erejefischt. If so, it is huge."

That would devastate a Clan near the volcano, he thought, *What can I do! What can I do! In the future, when I am the Council leader, the safety of the Clans would be my responsibility. But there is nothing I can do about that now. I have to concentrate on the local issues. The acolytes and the Clan living in this valley.*

He had to suppress his concern. There was no point in upsetting the acolytes even further. He had to reassure them.

"It's getting late and we'll not be able to find our way in the dark. Let's make ourselves as comfortable as we can and eat a little. We'll have much to do tomorrow," Orrox said.

Orrox lay awake long into the night, he could not stop worrying. Finally he woke Bronnox and said, "I must Sense what happened. I will be unconscious for a little while. If I don't wake up within double gracia heartbeats, force me to waken. Slap me hard if necessary. Count carefully."

He closed his eyes and forced his exceptional Sensing ability into an intense Abstract mode. He concentrated on Sensing life and nature. He had to limit the time he spent in the strange state. It is easy to lose your way while observing and analyzing within that expanded reality.

Orrox could not Sense anything useful. All of nature was in chaos. All indications were continually changing, as if boiling in a huge cauldron. The Catastrophe swamped everything. There was nothing else to Sense. With a jerk he forced himself out of the strange state.

Bronnox was counting his own pulse, looking worried.

"Thank you. I'm fine. Don't tell the others. Mentors at the Dynasty will teach you this Sensing ability once we're back. I must think."

The night was darker than Orrox had ever experienced before. The darkness was so intense, he could discern no difference whether his eyes were open or closed. He shivered involuntarily. Everything was wrong and terrible.

#

There was only the slightest hint of light when Orrox got up, certain it had to be morning. Soon, the others stirred too. Soft murmurs indicated their uncertainty.

Ammox spoke first, "I'm sure I have not slept at all but I'm tired of lying down! Let's make a fire and ask Orrox questions. I'm positive I can quiz him until he begs us to stop— "No more questions!" The last spoken in a good imitation of Orrox's voice.

The suppressed laughter showed they were awake.

"A fire is a good idea! Who will start it?" Orrox said.

Ammox had no choice but to volunteer.

The girls were the first to show their anxiety. While waiting for the water to boil, they asked, "Orrox, are our Clans safe? Did they also feel the shakings and wind?"

Orrox would have liked to reassure them but truth must always prevail, "I believe the effects were felt in all the Clan valleys and everywhere else as well. We have to be strong and concentrate on what we can do together."

The intensity of the shakings and the wind fascinated Ammox, "Can you imagine the size of the eruption that could cause the effects we experienced here? It must have been *huge*."

"This is all speculation, but the answer probably is: It is bigger than any ever remembered or imagined. Its origin is very, very far away. We know that because of the long time it took for the later shakings to follow the first one. It certainly is a Catastrophe such as the Clans have never experienced before!"

"I'm sure it must have been a huge yellow fire monster that crawled out of the mountain in which it was trapped. It shook its body three times scattering lava all over and then exhaled. That explains the shock waves as well as the little breeze we experienced," Ammox said with a straight face. They all laughed and the concerned expressions on their faces relaxed.

"You are so stupid," Camla said with just a hint of a smile, bumping him with her shoulder.

#

Despite the deep gloom, Orrox decided it was light enough to resume their descent. The sky and mountain still melded in obscure darkness, making it difficult to see.

"We must hurry, eat something, then we must go."

They ate some nuts and seeds and drank a brew of herbs and honey.

While they ate, Orrox said, "The land-shaking and storm-wind might have caused great hardship for the other Clans. We'll have to use our provisions sparingly. We do not know where and when we'll be able to get more."

They proceeded down the valley towards where Orrox was sure the local Clan lived. The going became very difficult. Debris and even whole trees were stacked against the larger boulders that blocked their way. They had to make their way around or clamber over obstacles that had not existed the day before.

The trunks of larger trees had pieces of bark hanging loose, with deep gashes where boulders had come flying down the valley; the wind had torn even thick branches from the trunks. Splinters covered the ground and the smell of sulfur still stung their noses.

Orrox remained silent, noticing the damage. His concern grew as they descended. The steep sides and surrounding vertical cliffs had made this valley unusually vulnerable. Boulders near the edges of the cliffs had all tumbled into the valley and the valley itself had acted as a chute, concentrating the storm-wind and causing even more damage.

The sky remained dark, the gloom and debris made it difficult to find stable ground to place their feet. Occasionally an exclamation indicated that some debris, covered in dust, had collapsed to scratch their legs or twist their ankles. Soon even Orrox had scratched and bleeding shins.

"I wonder what happened to the Clan of this valley," Bronnox said. "Look at the devastation around us. The Clan Habitat must have been damaged too."

Chapter 7 – Alone

At the Valley of the Sparkling Waters Anja's reason slowly returned. She remembered with a shock, *All the members of the Clan were inside the cave when I left.*

Yet her brain rejected reason and she desperately clung to hope, *Surely they must have escaped. There must have been a warning. They could not have all been inside!*

She called out as loudly as she could. Her mouth was dry, making her voice sound feeble and faint. The dust smothered the sound further so that not even an echo from the nearby cliffs answered. She swallowed hard, trying to moisten her throat. Then she cupped her hands over her mouth to amplify the sound. Trying to Sense the presence of any Clan-member, she called and listened. Surely, someone must hear her, but there was no response. She called her grandmother's name, hobbling back and forth, near where the cave had been. No answer! She started calling her friends by name, one after the other. All she heard was the mountain groaning like an injured animal as broken trees and rocks still broke loose, rolling down slopes until caught in mud traps. She continued to call until the dust and dryness of her mouth prevented further shouting. Still, there was nothing, not a sound or any indication of life.

Exhausted, Anja collapsed, holding her head in her hands. She tried to remember details. The members of the Clan would have just awakened and would be preparing food or already be eating. Preparations for the Clan induction rites and the subsequent feast would occupy them all for the rest of the day.

Nobody would have gone hunting or left to collect foodstuffs. Anja could imagine the easy discussions and wanderings from one cooking fire to the other. It all happened within the cave. She had to concede, *No, nobody had any reason to leave the cave.*

Her mind again rejected what she knew was true. Spurred by a desperate hope of finding a survivor—*any* survivor—Anja imagined possibilities. *Maybe they needed water or something else and sent some child or an adult to fetch it.*

She looked around. The landscape had changed into something barely recognizable. The cliff had collapsed in many places. Mud and snow slides covered the mountainside, filling the troughs and gullies. The worst damage was at the cave site. Trees near the cliff-edge hung upside down, suspended by exposed roots. Others slipped down the slopes in massive mud-islands. Only broken branches or twisted roots protruded above the rubble. Boulders crashing down from above had splintered or uprooted even more trees. The clammy smell of freshly overturned soil mixed with the woody scent of torn trees. The sulfurous odor of shattered boulders hung over all.

Anja's sprained ankle became cold and painful, making it difficult to move. Ignoring the ache, she dragged herself along to inspect the heaps of rubble and slush. Hoping for a response, a sound, anything, she called out again, her voice ending in sobs.

Tearing at the branches and boulders, digging with her bare hands, she tried to remove the rubble covering the area where the cave had been. She could hardly move the branches trapped in the ooze.

She finally gave up, drained. After resting a while, she hobbled towards a rise. Very little rubble rested on the flat surface, leaving visible most of the collapsed cliff. She sat down on the ground in despair, looked up at the mountains with their beautiful peaks. It provided little comfort. Instead, they possessed a gloomy, threatening appearance with the snowfields darkened by the murk, dust, and mud. Glistening ice-dust hallows encircled the peaks, accentuating their blackness against the brilliant white.

Melancholy thoughts, mingled with feelings of rejection, mulled through her brain. *My mother died at my birth and my father gave me to Grandmother to raise, abandoning me. He allowed my sister to stay with him; he did not love me! Now the entire Clan has abandoned me. They did not come to look for me. Even the cave has shunned me and disappeared!*

Then the overwhelming thought, the realization: *Grandmother is dead.*

She struggled to accept this greatest of tragedies.

She had lost everything, but the worst of all was the loss of her grandmother. Hunched into a bundle, hugging her knees, she sat, feeling that the world had turned against her, rejected her. She was unable to face the reality of her loss.

A sudden blast of chilled air blowing down from the high peaks slammed into her. Scared and cold, she pulled her soft skin garments tighter around her. Driven by thirst, she limped towards the little brook on the far side of the rise. Although the water was too filthy to drink, she tried to wash her hands and face, turning the dust to mud. The coolness of the mixture brought some relief, but no hope. The chaos surrounding her initiated a deep despondency. A sticky darkness dominated Anja's thoughts, whirling through her brain. It was as if the dark dust swirling around the mountain peaks had descended to take hold of her complete being. She remained sitting next to the stream, her head in her soiled hands.

She had always been proud of her ability to think rationally and to be in control of her emotions. With great effort, she forced herself out of depression, out of the negativity that was threatening to paralyze her. A feeling of shame forced her to start thinking rationally. She had to find her Clan, or any Clan-member, any who survived. *Maybe Grandmother did survive! Someone will know.*

#

Her grandmother had taught her that one of the joys of being a female herbalist, even a very young one, was the ability to select and choose colorings and aromatic herbs. Anja valued her ability to help beautify the other girls. She had left the cave with her hair plaited with the softly worked skins of small mammals and rolled in a bun on her head, which conveyed her status, while loose locks fringed her face. She knew she was pretty and wanted to look her best.

Now Anja's appearance had changed. Her crouching, collapsed form masked her tall, athletic build. Dust and mud matted her hair. The soft skins that her grandmother had lovingly used to decorate her plaited hair, hung loose and no longer indicated status or accentuated her beauty. She looked ragged, neglected, her face streaked with dirt and tears. Her easy smile now a thin, quivering line.

Scared and exhausted, she had to force herself to move. She hobbled along in her search until she found a nearly uprooted tree, which she recognized as the tanning tree. It was still upright but leaned over at a crazy angle.

Hunters had tanned and hung a few animal skins on the tree to dry. A heavy boulder tied to long leather strips and broad pieces of skin still remained hanging from a thick branch. The men had often cut the skins into lengths and then rotated the boulder, winding up the cords to their limit. When released the boulder would spin, winding the cords in the reverse direction, to be caught and wound up again. Anja remembered how they repeatedly twisted the lengths of skins, infused with selected barks to soften and preserve them. They continued until the leather became soft and pliable and could be cut into thin leather thongs and thicker straps, or put to other uses. They scraped and softened larger skins in the same way. She could identify fox, hare, beaver, badger, and marten skins, but the softest was the skin of the beautiful chamois.

A huge skin, the fur of a cave bear, brought tears to her eyes as she remembered how brave the hunters had been, how they had killed the huge and dangerous animal, defying death.

Anja kept the soft pelts of silver foxes, to keep her warm, as well as squares of chamois skin. Stroking the bear pelt, she placed it under branches, in a safe place out of reach of scavengers. Of these foxes and wolves were the worst. Although still in a daze, she collected and hid the other skins and leather straps, partly out of habit but also from an instinctive desire to organize and remove the signs of destruction. A nearly finished pouch, sewn together using sinews, hung on a nearby tree where one of the women had carelessly left it the previous evening, with the bone implements and obsidian shards hanging in a smaller pouch nearby. A gourd that had spilled its content rested next to the stone seat the seamstress had used.

Anja thought sadly of the woman, Sewjen, who often sat there to watch the men at work. The memory of Sewjen and the damaged tree brought her loss into clearer focus. With tears streaming down her face, despondency overwhelmed her again, a feeling that all was lost, that no one had survived.

It was nearly dusk when Anja returned to the rise. She did not encounter a single survivor of her Clan, no recent tracks in the dust, no sounds, nothing. The realization that she was all alone frightened her more than she had ever felt fear before.

How could life get any worse?

Then she heard a new, very loud rumbling disturbance, growing ever louder. At first, she thought the sound came from one of the volcanoes. Listening carefully, she recognized, it came from the sunrise direction, the direction away from the great mountain range. It was not a volcano erupting. The sound rose in pitch, until it became a shriek hurting her ears.

The intensity grew until the sound surrounded her, coming from all sides. She clamped her hands over her ears, but to no avail. The noise hammered and pulsed inside her head, continuing relentlessly.

With head bowed, she closed her eyes tightly. A change in tone made her look up. A dark wall, like a monstrous moving cliff, rolled towards her. It obscured the valley and surrounding hills, reaching up to the heavens.

High overhead, far above the peaks, long yellow streaks, like fingers with horrible claws, reached out, moving towards the sunset, where the sun was still visible. An even higher pitched screech accompanied the dust-laden storm wind that hit Anja. It flung her violently to the ground, rolling her over, until it pushed her into a recess between two huge boulders, at the edge of the rise. The devastating roar of the wind blasted through her protecting hands, with which she covered her ears, which suffered from the relentless attack.

Anja was too tired to cry and it felt as if the storm would lift her up and blow her away like chaff in the wind. Despite her injuries and pain, she wriggled in between the boulders for protection. Airborne particles blasted her skin, until it was raw. Loud, cracking noises filled the air as branches and whole trees blew past. A tree branch pierced her leg. She screamed in pain, but couldn't move the leg to safety.

After losing everyone, it seemed impossible that things could get worse, but she was wrong.

Anja knew she was going to die. She even welcomed the thought and closed her eyes as darkness overwhelmed her.

<><><>

Chapter 8 – Escape

The Giants followed the ravine up into the snowfield. There a channel in the snow led uphill. Questa saw large footprints on the trampled snow, coming from the opposite direction. Proof that the Giants had used this route when they came from the far side, crossing the mountain range.

The temperature dropped as they ascended, forcing Questa to pull the large kaross tighter around herself. All hope of rescue disappeared. She wanted nothing more than to just drop to the cold ground and freeze to death. *The Giants are going to kill me anyway. Why are they even dragging me along? There can be no good reason. Rape. Torture.* She shuffled along, head down, eyes drooping, not caring where she stepped.

As the snow got deeper, the Giants made a channel in the snow, as wide as their torsos.

The channel reminded Questa of their amazing strength as they lined up in single file. They forced their way through the snow, which sometimes reached up to their shoulders. No Clansman would be able to copy such a feat. Looking back, she saw the last Giant in the row swiping snow from both sides into the track, closing the channel behind them. The closed route made it nearly impossible for any rescuers to follow them. Their route led upward and deeper into the mountain range, in the same direction as shadows fall in the middle of the day, the direction the Clans called, "the direction away from the midday sun."

Questa's footwear was not nearly adequate to protect her feet from the cold and snow. Her feet became extremely painful, and then just numb. Frostbite was a real threat. She wanted to die, but she knew the Giants wouldn't allow that.

For now, she had no choice but to live. In fear of losing her feet, she yanked at the leather strap the Giant in front of her held, until he stopped.

Turning her back to the nearest Giants, she tore off a piece of the garment she was still wearing underneath the large kaross and tied it around her feet. Her footwear was already scuffed and disintegrating.

The Giant holding the leather strap laughed, probably amused by her dejected demeanor, still persisting since they had outsmarted her, when she had tried to escape. More amiable than usual, he threw two pieces of skin covered in fur on the ground near her and indicated with gestures that she should tie these around her feet, with the fur inside. He added a few leather cords. The line of Giants stopped and several laughed again.

She copied the way the Giants had tied similar pieces of skin around their feet. They waited for her until she was ready. Her black mood made it impossible to appreciate the gesture.

Heropto snarled an annoyed curse as he waited impatiently, showing no concern for Questa's wellbeing.

The Giants had tied a strip of long-haired skin over their foreheads and peered through the fur with half-closed eyes. The Giant threw a strip of these at Questa's feet. Even though the Dynasty had more sophisticated eye protection for use in the snow, Questa was grateful for the fur. It blocked the worst glare of the sun.

When night fell, the Giants stopped below a hollow cliff clear of snow. It was just in time. Questa was exhausted. The skins on her feet were too big and forced her to shuffle along, dragging her feet to keep the skins tied to her feet. She struggled to keep up.

El-El, towering to the right, was now clearly visible. Strands of fog hid the valleys and encircled the mountain slopes in loose fronds. The towering peaks covered in snow were etched against the darkening blue of the sky.

Looking up, Questa saw the beauty, but it did not touch her. Her mind was numb, associating only with the dull black rocks in their contrast to the bright background of white snow.

#

The next morning, Heropto led the group up a glacier with deep crevasses. He tested the snow bridges with his stabbing spear and crossed with confidence. The danger did not seem to bother the Giants and they all followed. They crossed many crevasses before they reached a saddle between two peaks where the descent to the far side of the mountain range began. The slopes faced away from the sun and the cold increased. They were already far removed from the sunny Clan valleys. Each day, the distance between her and her home in the Clan valley grew as more of the mountain range interposed between their position and those valleys where the Clans lived.

Questa suffered from the cold and, despite a growing lethargy, massaged her feet and wrist deep into the night, flexing her fingers. The skins the Giant had given her, although much too large for the purpose, saved her feet. The cold did not bother nor affect the Giants, but Questa shivered in the huge kaross.

They finally descended below the snowline, onto a lightly wooded slope. It was still cold but the danger of frostbite had passed.

When they reached the woods at lower levels, her captors slowed down and pointed towards a mountain outcrop. They remained concealed within the woods.

Questa looked carefully but saw nothing deserving attention.

The Giants crouched down or crept from one hiding place to the next.

Heropto yelled at them, angrily pointing forward.

In front of them, a grassy plain stretched as far as she could see, disappearing over the horizon. Low shrubs marked the occasional depression that broke the continuity of the plain. The new season's young grass was just pushing through the older stems, shimmering in emerald green. On her left, a gully descended onto the plain, creating a greener line that disappeared into the distance.

From the Giants' body language and gestures, Questa understood Heropto's command, they must cross the plain quickly.

They are scared of being in the open. Strange! We are now so far from any Clan valley that no rescue is possible. Why all the anxiety?

In the dark, just as a half-moon appeared over the horizon, they started crossing the plain, moving fast. The Giant holding the strap, impatiently yanked Questa along as she struggled to find her footing. The sky was clear. Starlight provided just enough glow to enable her to discern larger obstructions. By daybreak they were already far across the plain, hurrying along without resting.

Questa remained aware of her immediate surroundings. She saw a few plants with edible seeds, roots, and leaves, growing within a clump of scrubs near a dry gully. *Water must collect there when it rains,* she thought.

Questa noticed a suppressed excitement in the tone and tempo of the Giants' speech. She tried to interpret the gestures and the few sounds she could understand. The leader pointed forward with a satisfied look on his face and the other Giants, who had often looked back, now focused on the horizon far ahead. Whatever danger they seemed to fear, had passed.

Somewhere beyond the plain, we will enter the Giants' wooded forests. That's their home. There they are safe and I am lost.

A few of the Giants again spoke excitedly, looking at her and then, with lewd gestures, at the leader. She understood their meaning all too well. The leader's female companion reacted furiously whenever a male Giant drew their leader's attention to Questa, especially when they pointed at or touched her. Questa knew that when they reached their destination, she would be doomed and would probably die while they assaulted her. She looked away, trying to ignore the realization that a competition had started to determine who would get a turn once the leader had paraded his trophy and had finished with her, should she survive his attentions.

In their relaxed mood, the group slowed down to eat and drink sips of water from the gourds they carried. Without actually stopping, they continued until the sun was low and they had already left the mountains far behind.

That night was the worst Questa had experienced as yet. She couldn't sleep. Images of her fate haunted her. All hope was lost! Suicide became an option, perhaps her only solution. She searched for ways she could end all of this, to end her life.

#

The next morning they delayed, starting late. The Giants had spread out, leisurely making their way across the plain when the land-shaking struck. That and the follow-up shakings surged across the plain like massive waves. The first wave swept the group off their feet. They were all floundering on the ground, while Questa, Sensing their fear, remained lying down as quietly as possible. The Giant holding the leather strap, let it go, forgetting about her. A second wave hit and then a third wave approached, preceded by a rumbling sound. The heaving ground came rolling towards them across the plain.

The Giants jumped up and fled in different directions. The heaving earth quickly overtook them, tossing them like the skins they had thrown at Questa. Bodies flew in every direction.

Questa remained where she was, lying down. The shaking had left a heavy cloud of dust hanging over the plain. Under its cover, she managed to crawl away and conceal herself in a depression between a few shrubs. Ducking low, she reached a dry gully, then she sprinted up the gully.

The hated leather strap swung wide and caught in some of the shrubs, before tearing loose. She wrapped it around her arm and clenched the end in her fist, as she ran. The big kaross was another hindrance, which she nearly discarded but decided to keep for as long as possible.

She struggled on as fast as she could. One hand clutching the kaross and the other the leather strap. The bottom of the gully was rough and uneven, impeding her progress as she stumbled over obstacles, still trying to remain concealed in the shallow riverbed. Crouching while keeping her balance, slowed her down even more.

She heard the Giants call out and looked over her shoulder. The leader chased her. He ran at an angle to intersect the gully at a point in front of her. There was no further point in trying to hide.

She clambered out on the far side of the gully, heading for a few deep crags she could just see. It was far away, where the mountains reared up to the nearly invisible sky, obscured by dust. She sprinted on the even ground. The dust made it difficult to breathe as she gasped for air, running for her life, ignoring the dryness of her mouth and the shrubs scratching her.

The heavily built Giants ran with their swinging gait and could not match the fast pace that she held, despite the antelope kaross. The leader of the Giants was much faster than the rest and succeeded to keep up at first. But when he understood that he could not catch her, he stopped to wait for his troupe.

Questa kept looking back. The pursuers were losing ground allowing her to slow down to a speed she could easily maintain. She kept that speed until the Giants were small specks in the distance.

There was no point in trying to hide her tracks. The Giants had the reputation of being adept at tracking, even better than the Primitives. They would be able to pick up her trail, no matter what she tried.

Panting, she sat down on a boulder to plan the rest of her escape and to catch her breath. From there she could keep an eye on the Giants who had resumed their pursuit. The unknown flank of the mountains, facing away from the sun, showed no obvious route to the other side, where the Clan valleys lay. Her only chance was to retrace the same route the Giants had taken from the Dynasty Valley. Looking ahead, she searched for features to show where they had left the woods and mountain slopes and had descended onto the plain.

She inspected the nearly invisible mountains obscured by dust. If she missed the route and entered a dead-end, the Giants would certainly catch her. The Giant female would undoubtedly kill her. How to negotiate a passage through the deep snow was a problem she left for later, realizing that the shaking must have caused avalanches that probably made the snow passages inaccessible.

To die in the snow is a better outcome than to let them catch me again, she decided, fighting the feeling of despondency. *Better to continue until I fall and die than be tortured, raped, and killed by the Giants.*

Rumbling sounds, like thunder, echoed in the gully. Questa could feel the air vibrating. Far off beyond El-El, black smoke rose above the mountain range, just visible above the layer of dust and the higher peaks.

Is that a volcano? she wondered. Then, ignoring the sight, she concentrated on her immediate problems.

The Giants were quickly reducing the advantage in distance she had gained. She would have to start running again. She quickly collected a small stock of edibles growing near the edge of the gully, roots and seeds she had noticed before. She missed her pouches but used the leather strap around her wrist to tie her finds into a fold of the kaross.

At a steady trot, she aimed towards the mountains. The ground rose steadily. She repeatedly crossed ridges and gained height. The gully to her left became deeper as she progressed. Where it broke through the ridges, small pools appeared before the water disappeared underground, only to reappear lower down. She was sweating profusely. When she was sure the Giants were still far enough away, she went down to drink and filled a gourd the Giants had given her. She remembered being told that Giants did not like heat and always avoided over-exertion and sweating, which could be fatal in the cold climates where they lived.

They will suffer and that might help me, she thought.

She kept looking back. The Giants were only visible as far away specks again.

She saw the dark wall of grey-brown dust when it first appeared as a faint line on the horizon. It was coming from the sunrise direction. The dust-wall increased in height until it filled the sky.

Something terrible was approaching at great speed—nearly upon her. She had to find a safe place to hide. At the last moment, she found a spot.

Huge boulders stacked loosely against the low cliffs, where the gully broke through another ridge, formed gaps through which a small body could crawl. Storm waters had deposited a clean floor of roughly grained sand in the cracks. Wind had created a maze of tunnels.

The dust cloud hit the Giants first, blocking them from sight and allowing her to dash into the gully unseen. The storm wind hit just as she crept into one of the gaps.

She wriggled deep into the protective shelter up to where the boulders rested against the smooth gully wall. The earth shook with the fury of the wind. Grains of sand swirled through the tunnels, nearly choking her.

Surely the Giants had not reached a good shelter. They were still on the open plain when the storm reached them. If I'm lucky they'll all be killed. If they survive they will certainly be injured.

She remained quiet and completely still in her hiding place, hoping the Giants would not be able to pursue her anymore. The wind was fierce. At last, the storm passed.

Even if the Giants did survive, the wind has definitely wiped out my tracks. They must have lost sight of me after the dust cloud engulfed them and can't know in which direction I ran or where I am hiding. This is a safe place to wait.

Sand and dust had accumulated against the boulders obscuring the tunnel entrance. Even so, she crawled to the farthest end, carefully removing all marks behind her and taking the time to smooth the sand. To create an impression that the sand had never been disturbed, she fashioned false insect tracks with a twig. Carefully placing sticks and leaves in a natural arrangement, she made wind hollows behind them.

If the Giants should search the stack of boulders, they will not suspect that I am hiding there. And they are too big to crawl between the boulders.

The openings between the boulders gave her fine shelter, with enough space and a comfortable floor of clean sand to lie on. Her gourd was full and she had food to survive for a few days, if she used it carefully. The tunnels were gloomy and dark, but she felt safe.

Questa remained where she was for two days, barely moving except for flexing her fingers and trying to undo the knot in the leather strap on her wrist. The seeds and roots she had collected were nearly gone and she used the balance sparingly. She still had a little water but that would not last long either. When taught the techniques of the hunt, she had learned patience. She could sit immobile for extended periods, waiting for prey. However, alone in her hiding place, it was different and she had to fight loneliness. She longed for her own Clan, her father and all the other Clansmen.

In my own Clan, I never felt lonely. I always knew where all the other Clansmen were. How silly resenting my stepmother now seems, she thought. *My father needed a new companion. It wasn't Alena's fault that my mother had died. Alena was always good to me, and always welcomed Anja and Grandmother with a smile, when they came to visit. To blame Grandmother for taking only my younger sister to stay with her in the Valley of Sparkling Waters is unjust too. My father loves both Anja and me and would have suffered even more had both of us left.*

The trauma of her abduction and loneliness, brought the resentment she had been carrying into sharp focus, and she was able to analyses and forgive. Still, she felt that it was a pity that her grandmother had not been able to spend more time training her. Her sister, Anja, was already an accomplished Oracle-Healer.

In her hiding place, Questa thought of her training as a Sensitive and Oracle-Healer. Despite her irritation with Usux, she was thankful that her training at the Dynasty included exercises to enhance memory and perception, patience, meditation, and mental preparedness, all of which came in handy now.

Questa sat still, tears washing away old resentments. She remembered Usux's words, the Dynasty experts had Sensed the indications that a great disaster was eminent. They did not know what and where, except that it would come from the sunrise direction. This was it. The Catastrophe. She concentrated to Sense, but dared not enter the Abstract mode. The recent events dominated everything. She sensed nothing more.

Finally, she exercised her ability of control and started doing memory exercises to keep herself focused, reconstructing the route back to the Dynasty Habitat, preparing herself for her future flight. She knew that the route back was going to be difficult. However, the relative security of her hiding place had a soothing effect.

When the faint light in the tunnel indicated morning, Questa moved cautiously, climbing up a shaft formed by a few boulders. She peeked just over the top to look at the surrounding area.

She saw a transformed landscape with no sunlight, just a deep gloom with dim light penetrating a yellowish-brown sky. A layer of similar colored dust covered the gully and the plains for as far as she could see, obscuring the leaves of plants. Its weight collapsed the shrubs. There was even a layer on the tops of the boulders. It swirled in the air at the slightest disturbance. All was silent and the earth gave up no smell, not the fresh earthy smells of the new season nor the dead smells of decay, as if the earth had moved beyond death to an ultimate end. Moving towards the mountains on the plain would stir up a dusty cloud visible from a distance as well as leave very clear tracks.

Questa had to fight the overwhelming feeling of despondency again, concentrating on what her immediate actions should be. She looked for the best route towards the mountains, somewhere safe to hide there. Then she returned to her hiding place to think. She must leave few signs.

Her provisions would not last long. There should be water in the gully, but fetching that would also leave clear tracks. The best strategy would be to move at night, when she could gain distance before her movement and tracks became visible in the light.

Emerging again near the top of the boulders to plan her route, Questa inspected the gully. There should be edibles and small pools under the ridge and she would be able to fill her gourd in the last light, before setting off.

When the gloom deepened, indicating the approaching night, it was time to start. With her eyes just above the top of the boulders, she looked around. There were no Giants anywhere. Climbing back down she emerged from a crack at the bottom of the gully, leaving clear tracks as she sped towards where she expected to find water. All she found was yellowish-brown mud and a layer of dust on the surface of a small pool. She pushed it aside and scooped up some water. It tasted acidic and sour, undrinkable.

The dark of night was approaching fast. She had to find drinkable water urgently, before the last light failed and she started towards the mountain. Suppressing anxiety, she searched desperately. *There has to be a place where the water seeped out directly from underground.*

The gloom darkened as she searched the gully near where it broke through the ridge. Fighting her rising panic, she finally found a spot where seep-water had collected in a small depression. After she removed the mud and repeatedly scooped the water out of the hollow, the water cleared and lost its bitter taste, allowing her to suck up a little bit. By sucking and spitting she managed to fill her gourd. She had not yet found any edibles when the darkness made a further search impossible. Her effort left clear marks of her presence, making her hiding place useless.

She had to move on. Fighting panic, she decided to stay near the gully, keeping it on the right as she moved up to the mountains. The gloom had progressed to darkness with just enough visibility to allow her to cross the ridge and get going.

Soon it was too dark to see at all. The darkness was more intense than she had ever experienced before. The yellowish-brown atmosphere blocked all light and there was nothing to guide her. In desperation, she veered right, trying to find the gully again. Questa felt the slope under her feet and scrambled down, until she again felt the upward slope on her right-hand side.

Trying to stay in the center of the gully, she struggled upwards, tripping over shrubs, stones, and boulders, feeling her way. The sloping sides of the gully her only guide.

She dared not stop. When light came her tracks would be clearly visible. Logical thinking abandoned her. She did not even consider how she would negotiate the mountains. Her all-consuming thought was to keep on. Just go. The farther she went, the better her chances of outdistancing the Giants, once they picked up her trail.

At last light came. The mountains were still far away. Moving at night had been a mistake. She was exhausted and had not made as much progress as she had hoped. She forced herself to continue.

The light allowed her to climb out of the gully and to pick the easiest route. She crossed the terrain at a faster pace, keeping the gully on her right. Too tired to look back, she just kept on going without thought. The ground became steeper, rising to the foothills. She did not notice the change but trudged on until she collapsed.

Exhausted, she took a drink from her gourd and looked back. A dirty dust cloud rose from the plain, much too near, following her tracks. In a panic, she looked around to orientate herself. She was not sure which direction to take.

Questa remembered the Giants had used a route quite high up on the mountain. But in the gloom, everything looked different. She had to continue. Towards the mountains. Either that or be recaptured.

Questa stood up and tried to run. She took a few steps, tripped over a bush, fell down, and lost consciousness.

Chapter 9 – Second Valley

The floor of the valley was a chaotic tangle of branches, boulders, mud, and trees. Continuing down the valley was more difficult than Orrox expected, and he could see the acolytes tiring, but he pushed on relentlessly. Their faces lit up when Orrox stopped at a small area clear of debris.

"It must be nearly midday. Let's rest and discuss what to expect when we reach the Clan of this, the Second Valley. We must pay our respects and find out whether they need any assistance. It is a proud and ancient Clan. A member of the leading family of this Clan has been the Chief for many generations. The Clansmen are very fond of their Chief and strongly support him.

"Be careful not to give offense. They have specific preferences of how a visitor is supposed to respond to their greeting. They appreciate a visitor who gets it right. Pay attention—there are always hints of how a Clan expects a stranger or newcomer to behave." Orrox looked at each of the acolytes in turn, who nodded their compliance.

"Good protocol requires we stay for at least the night but then we must hurry to the Dynasty Valley. I must find out how much damage the Catastrophe has caused and assist wherever possible.

"The fastest route is across the plains of the marshes. The Primitives who roam there are dangerous, but it is our only option. We will do our best to avoid them. Should we encounter them, we will protect ourselves from any aggression. The alternate route using the high ledges skirting the mountain is still snow-bound and is not viable. The land-shaking and storm wind probably loosened material. There is a great danger of avalanches."

"Well, I'm glad you will allow us to stay at least the one night at this Clan," Ammox said, keeping a straight face. "I'm sure the many pretty girls we will find there will be absolutely heartbroken when I have to leave them so soon."

Camla poked him in the ribs with her elbow, "Be serious. They might have suffered from the Catastrophe."

Orrox just smiled without rebuking him.

After eating, they made their way through loose tree trunks and branches scattered around. Broken boulders and the smell of sulfur emphasized the devastation in the valley.

#

The Clan cave came into view on the right-hand side, as they descended the valley, between a series of overhangs. Below high cliffs, it made a pretty picture. A few terraces stepped down to the level valley floor. Down the middle, a meandering brook flowed from pool to pool. On the far side of the stream, the wide valley remained level up to the cliff face. A strong palisade, the entrance closed and tied shut with flax ropes, enclosed the cave and highest terrace. Weeds grew on the terraces. Rocks and boulders lay scattered all over. Part of the palisade was splintered and flattened.

Orrox called out loudly as they approached, but there was no answer. Through the remnants of the palisade, he could see weeds were removed near the entrance. He saw no shelters.

"The place is abandoned, but still seems to be maintained," Orrox said. "See, the construction is solid and strong. The land-shaking and wind did not destroy it, falling rocks probably caused the damage. The Clan must have moved before the Catastrophe. Look, part of the cliff is unstable. Many of the rocks and boulders must have fallen from there."

The acolytes looked up at the crumbled rock face.

"This area is dangerous," Bronnox said. The others nodded in agreement.

"We'll look for the Clan farther down," Orrox said as he led them away from the palisade. The shock waves, wind, and resultant Catastrophe caused much more damage than he had expected. The high route to the Dynasty Valley was definitely not an option.

The valley narrowed with cliffs towering above as they descended farther. Boulders, which bombarded the valley during the land-shakings, lay strewn across the valley floor.

Orrox looked up, checking for further instability. Beyond the cliffs, only the gloomy sky was visible. The acolytes followed Orrox's glance and kept silent, the smell of dust and sulfur in their nostrils.

"This is a dangerous place during any land-shaking strong enough to dislodge those boulders," Ammox commented, for once not in jest. Reality subdued his tendency to jokingly point out ridiculous alternatives to words or situations.

#

The first sight of the area where the Clan now lived, came as a shock. All was chaos. They could make out the layout of the Habitat area from the remaining wreckage where the Clan had built their shacks. Only the remnants of a strong palisade still stood. The binding vines and flax, lay draped around large boulders. Torn and broken skins and posts, remnants of shacks previously inside the palisade, hung on the branches of trees. No-one was in sight, no Clansmen nor any injured either.

The acolytes stopped short, gaping at the damage. Shock registered on their faces.

Orrox moved forward and looked around, "Spread out. We have to find survivors and treat any wounded. Let's search the whole width of the valley. Bronnox, go look beyond those larger heaps of rubble, see if you can find anything! Ammox, search to the right, Lonna and Camla, to the left! Then follow me lower down."

Orrox climbed onto a large boulder, from where he could see farther and called out. When he heard nothing, he moved farther down the valley and tried again. After repeated attempts, an answering call came from the direction of a hollow cliff.

A large, rather brusque figure with penetrating blue eyes appeared, clambering over branches and smaller boulders. As he came forward, he raised his right hand, extended to the side with a bent elbow and open palm. Orrox copied the gesture and, after a glance from Orrox, the acolytes followed his example. They waited, showing respect.

"I am Jupex, the Chief of the Clan of the Second Valley. Some of my Clan are injured. We're busy making our wounded comfortable. We cannot afford you any hospitality now, neither can we accommodate or help you immediately. You will have to wait until we're ready to receive you."

Orrox felt ill at ease. *This is unusual. He must know who we are. I expected a better welcome. The destruction and injuries must be extreme.*

However, he kept quiet.

They all knew the Clans prided themselves on the hospitality they showed visitors from other Clans. They usually received an Oracle-Healer, especially those who were from the Dynasty, exceptionally well.

Orrox glanced at the acolytes, signaling them to stay back and behave as meekly as possible. He expected the normal ritual, a Look-Out would approach them to find out who they were and then formally announce their presence to the Chief and the rest of the Clan. For the Chief to approach them himself was strange, indicating disorder.

Before Orrox could act or reply, an attractive woman with shining blonde hair joined them with the same gesture of greeting, her green eyes tired and sad. She spoke haltingly, evidently tired and under great stress: "I am Alena, Jupex's life-companion. I apologize for his abrupt greeting. We're concerned with the wellbeing of our Clan."

She paused and gave Jupex a worried look before continuing, "I remember a message from an Oracle-Healer who sent greetings and requested permission to spend time up the valley with a few acolytes for training. A great land-shake and storm have destroyed our palisade and shelters. Please allow us to delay proper hospitality, until we have recovered. We have all sustained injuries and we're still looking for a few of our Clansmen who are missing.

"We have already found some bodies and laid them out there, below the cliff. Those of us who are not badly hurt, are looking after the seriously injured. Our Healer, my stepdaughter, left for further training a couple of moons ago. We're short on provisions and will not be able to receive you until we have retrieved our stores."

Orrox decided to continue formally, thereby reducing the awkwardness of the meeting. "I am Orrox of the Orrox Dynasty and I know of you, Jupex, Chief of the Clan of the Second Valley. It is an honor to know you, Alena of the Second Valley. These are my acolytes: Bronnox, Ammox, Lonna, and Camla. We came down the valley to see whether we can be of assistance. We are unharmed.

We do not expect your kind hospitality since we have experienced the Catastrophe ourselves but still have some provisions.

"Please forgive me any discourtesy. I have instructed my acolytes to search for Clansmen in your area before you replied to my calls. We do not wish to violate your hospitality or area. I'm experienced in healing and my acolytes are Healers in training. We wish only to help and will then leave. Please allow us to assist with treating your wounded."

"I thank you and know who you are, Orrox," Jupex said, glancing at Alena. He whispered in a low voice, "He is "The Orrox" of the Orrox Dynasty. You know, after whose ancestors the Dynasty was named."

Turning back to Orrox, he replied, "I know the Dynasty well."

He paused before continuing, "My people have been badly injured. I'm afraid more will die. We have no trained Healer, and I don't know how we will be able to treat all. We would welcome your help. Please come to where we have found some shelter."

Alena said, "We're grateful you are here. We need the help of trained Healers, even though we all know how to use common herbs."

Orrox and the acolytes followed Jupex to the hollow under the cliff.

"My first life-companion was a very famous Oracle-Healer but she died long ago," Jupex said. "Alena is now my trusted life-companion and comfort, but not a trained Healer. My daughter, Questa, is a Healer. She is highly gifted but not here."

Alena added, "Jupex has another daughter, Anja, who lives with her grandmother's Clan, the original Clan of my predecessor. Although young, she is an exceptionally talented Oracle-Healer. I wish she was here to help."

They all scrambled to the hollow cliff where Clansmen cleared a relatively flat area from debris. They were scurrying back and forth, helping wounded and comforting a few frightened children. They glanced at the newcomers without stopping while Jupex announced loudly, "This is Orrox and his acolytes. They are Healers and will help you. We will observe the formalities once all our injured have been treated."

The Chief towered over his companions, his blond hair gathered to form a waterfall on top of his head, accentuating his height and even towering over Orrox.

Many of the Clansmen suffered from bruises but Orrox noticed a number lying on woven mats with flax or soft skins covering wounds, which still seeped blood.

"How did this happen? What caused the bleeding and wounds?"

Alena answered, "During and after the land-shaking, large rocks tumbled over the cliff's edge and bounced or chipped into shards as they hit boulders inside and near the palisade. The boulders and the splinters hurt many. The largest splinters caused deep wounds. The sound of rocks splitting was so loud it hurt our ears. While we were treating the injuries, stopping blood, a storm wind blew down the palisade and our shelters, causing many more bruises and opening up many wounds."

"Orrox, please attend to those nearest the cliff. Their injuries are the most serious," the Chief commanded without further acknowledging or announcing Orrox's status. "You acolytes go and look after the other wounded. Orrox, will you then check on how your acolytes are doing?"

Orrox accepted the Chief's instructions easily, even though they both knew, visitors from the Dynasty rated special deference. Orrox knew the conceit of his predecessors occasionally damaged the relationship between the Dynasty and the Clans and kept a humble profile, signaling to the acolytes to do the same, to ignore the Chief's brusque style.

The Clans treasured their alleged independence and Orrox did not intend to challenge their beliefs. He knew the proceeds of hunting and gathering were not enough to support the comfortable existence of the Clans. The healthy lifestyle with its exhilarating challenges, the good life all Clansmen enjoyed, depended on the Dynasty. Without the organization and redistribution of goods, their standard of living would immediately decline. The clay oil-lamps, the Dynasty distributed and so widely used in the Clans, were only one example of the improvements, which brought about such a high quality of life. The Clans assumed the manufacture of the devices and the techniques to improve life and health, all originated at the Dynasty Valley.

Orrox had attended many of the training sessions conducted at the Dynasty. Those for Bards and Oracle-Healers were his favorites. Sophisticated knowledge was incorporated in the Bards' tales, songs, and demonstrations. All Clan children absorbed these as they listened to visiting Bards. Women continued teaching the children and reinforcing the techniques between visits. The Healers and Oracle-Healers did the same. In appreciation, the Clans regularly sent meat and other provisions to the Dynasty.

Alena walked up to where Orrox was busy and said, "Jupex is under great stress. The suffering of the Clan affects him even more than the rest of us. Thank you for helping us."

"Certainly! We're pleased to do so."

Walking over to Jupex, who was bending over one of the injured, Orrox said, "Jupex I believe it would be better to move the more seriously injured to the sheltered area over there, where they are shielded from the others. What do you think?"

"Please. Go ahead."

Carefully, under Orrox's supervision, they moved the patients and made them comfortable, far enough for their groans to be out of hearing of the rest of the Clan. Orrox moved from one to the other, inspecting injuries and dressings.

"Camla, Lonna! Come and help me treat these wounds. Bronnox and Ammox, go help Jupex repair and organize the Clan shelters and protective barrier. They can erect a palisade later. Also, tend to the lesser wounds and injuries."

He removed the rudimentary dressings applied by the Clan's women. The wounds were clean. Then he expertly applied healing ointments and redressed the wounds using the salves and special mixtures they had retrieved from the Cave of Secrets. Camla and Lonna did the same. The quality of the salves and new dressings significantly reduced pain and comforted the injured.

A baby who had been crying incessantly, started sucking his thumb and fell asleep, while a wounded mother felt good enough to comfort her clinging child.

"Jupex, your Clansmen did a good job in helping your injured. I think they are now doing well."

As the pervading gloom deepened into night, Orrox called the acolytes to him, "We should stay here as long as our services are needed. This will be a hard night for the injured. Our supplies are nearly gone. Bronnox, you are the strongest. Go with Lonna at first light to fetch more medicines and salves from the Cave of Secrets. You two know what we'll require. Ammox and Camla, you two can continue attending the wounded."

#

In the morning, Jupex sent a few Clansmen to dig out grains from the storage holes, still situated under each of the original shelter positions, outside the abandoned Habitat cave. A few of his stronger Clansmen, careful not to cross avalanche paths, fetched meat, fruit, and vegetables from the ice caves high in the mountains.

Orrox was with one of the seriously injured. Although he gave him a sip of a strong healing potion, the injured lost strength quickly.

He signaled for Jupex to approach and said in a low voice, "Please call his near relations. I cannot do anything more. I'm so sorry."

A pretty woman, clearly also injured and leaning on a grown-up boy, approached slowly, dropped on her knees and embraced the still warm body. Tears flowed freely. A girl, younger than the boy stroked her mother's hair, crying too.

Jupex put an arm around the boy who, like his sister, was uninjured. Alena was still busy comforting another family, who had lost a mother and two children. Those of the clan not nursing the injured surrounded both families, making soothing noises.

"These deaths touch us all," Jupex said. "We all look after one another, you will never be alone."

After that, no more Clansmen died and the other injured improved quickly.

The next day, the Clan built a funeral pyre near the stream.

Jupex and the whole Clan were in mourning. They brought the bodies to the funeral pyre and with help from the acolytes, they washed them, using fresh mountain water from a spring bubbling from underneath a nearby cliff face. They made the deceased as presentable as possible. Then the acolytes brought the injured, those who could be moved, to a level area where they could hear and see the funeral rites. Orrox and the acolytes remained with the injured while the Clan-members each passed by in a last farewell.

Jupex led the ceremony. He recalled the good times and experiences shared with each of the victims, before lighting the pyre. "With deep affection, we take leave of each of you. Even though you have been taken from us long before your time in old age, we celebrate your lives and the experiences we have shared."

Each Clan-member added kindling and dry branches to the fire, recounting an incident they shared with each of their dead companions. The acolytes helped the injured reach the pyre, before helping them back to the area under the hollow cliff. They placed some kindling on behalf of those of the injured who could not safely reach the pyres.

The rest of the Clan stood in a circle around the pyre with bowed heads while Jupex lit the fire. Only a few of the Clansmen remained to guard the fire until only ashes were left. Assembling the Clan again, Jupex performed the final rites. He picked up ashes in both hands and threw them in the air, crying, "We honor you, beloved ones. Add your ashes to the soil and fertilize our valley. Allow plants to grow and nourish us, who stay behind!"

The remaining Clansmen were sad but satisfied, singing a sad lament as they spread the ashes.

That night Jupex sat with Alena, who was leaning against him for comfort. He turned to Orrox, "Thank you for your assistance. We were a small Clan and are even smaller now. We now number far less than the gracia limit. Usually only the very old, approaching gracia years, depart this life, without suffering, allowing us to celebrate their lives with happiness. Now we said farewell to many who died in pain and in the prime of their lives. Our Clan is much weakened!"

Orrox agreed with Jupex, "Yes, I agree. I believe we should request the help of the Dynasty and of other Clans to help you reestablish your Habitat and erect your palisade."

Silently he thought, *Yes, you are weak and the damage to your valley is immense. A Primitive attack would be disastrous.*

Orrox continued aloud, "I'm worried about the safety of all the Clans and must return to the Dynasty as soon as possible, and, if you agree, summon help. Will you be able to attend to the injuries until we return?"

"Certainly! You have left enough medicaments for our women to bring all the remaining injured back to health."

Orrox wanted to consult with Council members at the Dynasty. *I must leave as soon as possible. The acolytes are worried about their own Clans and should come with me,* Orrox thought. *They need not remain to help here, Jupex is managing the situation well. We must arrange help and protection for this Clan. I am sure Jupex and his Clan will be safe.*

Chapter 10 – Jupex

Jupex first saw Chiara during the Vigil of the Fires. He was young and too shy to approach her, or even try to find out who she was. During every assembly, or when the young ones gathered around the fires in the evenings, he was always aware of her presence, and noticed what she was doing or what young man maneuvered to sit near her. On his way back from the Valley of the Fir Trees, where the ceremony was held that year, her image kept popping up in his mind.

At MaXiox, his best friend's challenge, he aimed his spear at a scurrying rabbit and missed the easy target.

"What's wrong with you?" MaXiox asked, surprised.

"Nothing! I can still beat you to that tree on top of the hill, the one above the cliff. Come on, no cheating! We must go straight up."

Some of their birth-group, a third of whom also attended the ceremony, joined in the race. Soon the girls and boys were scrambling up the broken rock face to collapse out of breath beneath the tree. MaXiox just barely beating Jupex.

"How did MaXiox manage to defeat you?" Alena asked. She was one of the few girls of his birth-year who was not a cousin, not even once or twice removed. "You seem to be distracted. You always climb faster than MaXiox. He can only beat you when you are racing on level ground."

Jupex had not slept well and dared not tell the truth. Images of the girl whose name he did not even know, haunted him all night. "I allowed him to win," he declared pompously, provoking skeptical hoots from the others.

He and the whole of his birth-year group were doing their compulsory three years of service and training. Their duties included maintenance as well as patrolling the valley and surroundings, cutting up the carcasses of animals killed during the hunts, carrying that and additional foodstuffs to and from the ice caves high up in the mountain. They also went on expeditions into the desert to collect salt, flint, and other necessities not found in the valleys. They were too busy or tired to seriously consider romantic relationships, and Jupex seldom had time to think of the girl.

They were all inducted into maturity at the initiation ceremony, which was the second Rite of Passage of any Clan-member, when their service years had passed. The group of the next birth year, three years younger, had to do all the preparation for and work during the ceremony. After the ceremony—always held at the beginning of the growing season—they all had leisure time.

"Hey, MaXiox," Jupex said, "let's go on a tour to visit the other Clan valleys and get to know them."

He had not been to another Clan valley for two years.

"I think you are looking for the girl we saw during the Vigil of the Fires. But yes, let's go. We can take our time and stay a few days at each valley."

Jupex had not realized that MaXiox had noticed his fascination with the girl.

"By the way, her name is Chiara and she is from the valley of the Sparkling Waters."

Jupex ignored MaXiox's teasing.

Enjoying himself, MaXiox continued, "With your luck, she has already chosen a life-companion and this whole expedition will be for nothing!"

Those of their birth-group who had attended the feast, remembered and started teasing as well, "So, you are ready for your third Rite of Passage, are you? Looking for a life-companion?"

Jupex, the attractive son of a Chief, and probably the future Chief of his Clan, was a desirable life-companion, but he was not likely to choose one of the girls from his own Clan. For Jupex, the girls of his own birth-year felt too much like sisters for him to consider them in a romantic light. The girls of the next birth-year, three years younger, were still too young to attract his, or the attention of the other boys in his birth-group. Furthermore, the too close family relations between many within each valley, limited the choices.

As if he had not heard, Jupex turned to the others, "Who will join us?"

They would have to break up in small parties if they all wanted to visit the Clans. No more than half-doucia members could visit a Clan simultaneously and they will be expected to join in the Clan activities, helping with the same duties that they had performed during their service and training period. Only two girls and a boy volunteered to join them.

"You should take it easy like the rest of us," their peers continued to tease. "You're just looking for potential life-companions. There is no hurry to find one yet. You can wait for many more years."

"Unless you can find yourself a beautiful Oracle-Healer, Jupex," Alena said. "The whole Clan would benefit from that. Just make sure she is pretty."

It was not all teasing. Jupex's mother, Riana, had been the only qualified Healer in the Clan. Although she came from a family and Clan of strong Sensitives, her Sensing abilities were weak, just strong enough to help her when healing or looking after the injured.

Jupex ignored the teasing and started preparing for the trip. He filled gourds with fresh water and pouches with edibles, including some herbs, an obsidian blade, a club, a spear thrower, and a few spears.

The five companions of his birth-group set off together, similarly prepared. They decided to visit the valleys in the sunset direction first and then turn to the valley in the sunrise direction, where the Dynasty Valley was also located. They planned to return before reaching that. A visit to the Dynasty Valley required a special invitation, difficult to obtain.

Their route traversed the mountains by means of the high passes and narrow ledges in the cliff faces. They had memorized details and markers that should lead them to each of the different Clan valleys.

The Clansmen at each valley received them warmly, often allowing them to stay for the duration of a complete moon cycle. By the time they were ready to leave, they had learned details of the valley and its surroundings as well as the best route to the next valley. After visiting the single valley in the sunset direction, they reversed their route and crossed two high mountain passes to reach the valleys in the sunrise direction.

The third valley they visited, after negotiating a route following exposed ledges high up the cliffs, was the Valley of the Sparkling

Waters. As they approached the Clan cave, a shiver of excitement ran down Jupex's spine as he remembered the girl.

MaXiox looked at Jupex with a twinkle in his eye and Jupex had to suppress a smile. His friend knew him too well to be deceived.

A warm welcome again greeted them. A striking woman of about the same age as Jupex's mother approached, "Our Chief is out on a hunt and it falls on me to welcome you. We have heard that you were on your way to our Clan to visit," she said calling each by his or her name. "I am Chiara, and this is my husband PreTox. I know your father, the Chief of the Second Valley as well as your mother, who grew up in a valley not far from here. As girls, we knew each other well and even visited each other's Clans. Come along, I will show you where to stay."

The Clan had a large and comfortable Habitat cave in the cliff face with many extensions cut into the soft loess walls, each with a ventilation shaft to the slope high above.

"This material is quite soft, not like the hard rock of our Habitat cave. Is it really stable?" Jupex asked a Clan-member.

"Our cave has withstood many land-shakings. They occur as often here as in the other valleys. Water dissolves the soft material easily, but we have built channels to divert any flood waters away from the cave and from entering the shafts."

#

That evening the Clan gathered around the communal fire comparing different versions of Clan myths. Soon the talk changed to boasting, comparing the exceptional properties of their respective valleys.

Jupex, remembering MaXiox's words, wondered whether the girl that he remembered was really from this Clan. He watched Chiara looking for similarities, thinking that the girl he remembered was possibly Chiara's daughter. He had seen the girl only on that one occasion, two years before. He couldn't remember all the details, but he still thought that he recognized similar features.

MaXiox watched him with an amused smile and broke the silence, "We were at the Vigil of the Fires when it was held in the

Valley of the Fir Trees. I seem to remember that members of your Clan were also there."

"Yes, a few of our Clan was there. PreTox and I did not go but my daughter did. So, you were there? Did you see my daughter? She is also called Chiara."

"Yes, I believe we did. We were still busy with our three years of service and training. Is your daughter here?"

"No, she is still doing her years of training and will only be initiated next year. She has gone to the Dynasty for advanced training as an Oracle-Healer. We really miss her."

The conversation then turned to other matters, songs and stories taking precedence.

Jupex continued thinking of the girl, Training at the Dynasty! They only choose the most talented for that honor. She must be an exceptional Sensitive. Too good for me.

Before he fell asleep that night, Jupex confessed to MaXiox, "I was fascinated with what I remembered of the younger Chiara. Thanks for finding out more. She is clearly destined to be the life-companion of some great Sensitive. I will have to forget her. Let's enjoy the rest of our visits."

They stayed with the Clan of the Sparkling waters for a full moon cycle before moving on, but Jupex did not forget the image of the girl he had seen only once.

#

Chiara-the-elder was not only an exceptional Sensitive, she also had excellent people-skills. She became aware of Jupex's interest in her daughter and started inquiries about his lineage. She consulted the Sensitives of the Dynasty as well as those from other Clans. Together they came to the same conclusion, any female issue of Jupex and Chiara-the-younger would bring together several lines of Sensitive talent, including those lying dormant in both Jupex's father and mother.

"We cannot force the match, but just think of the talent and abilities should those two conceive a daughter!" They all agreed and started to coordinate the matching of Jupex and Chiara-the-younger.

"In another year the girl will be initiated and the two can meet. We must somehow keep them from choosing another life-companion until they are both ready to meet and choose."

After several discussions, they devised a strategy: "It should be easy to keep Jupex interested, the young Chiara is beautiful, and he is one of the few boys who would not be intimidated by her talent and intelligence. We will just have to make sure that all visitors to his Clan mention her beauty and achievements," they said. "Chiara, if you agree to this match, you should tell her of Jupex's visit to your Clan."

"Yes, I will. I like him, and I believe my daughter will too. He made a strong impression on the rest of my Clan. We can occasionally discuss him, his Clan and his personality. It should work. My child has not yet formed an attachment and is not impressed with most boys, especially since they tend to be intimidated by her intelligence and abilities."

#

A year later Jupex and Chiara-the-younger met again at that year's Vigil of the Fires. MaXiox had already decided on a possible life-companion from another Clan and did not attend.

"She is even more beautiful than I remember," Jupex told MaXiox after his return to the Second Valley. "Golden hair, the bluest of eyes and a fantastic figure. You would not think that she would have anything to do with me, coming from a Clan without its own Sensitive Healer. Even though she is super intelligent, she is quite humble. We were able to discuss any topic. She always had a well-considered opinion. She is wonderful. She said she would not mind if I visited her Clan."

"So, are you going to visit her Clan? When? Don't you think her mother will become suspicious?" MaXiox said with an amused grin.

That was a new and worrying thought. Chiara-the-elder would certainly have a great influence on her daughter.

She is the most famous Sensitive in all the Clans, thought Jupex. Her daughter... The image of the beautiful girl dominated his thoughts. He shook his head. Chiara has inherited the strong Sensitive ability of her forebears. Her mother will influence her choice. She will choose a great Sensitive. How could she even consider me? Although I am a Chief's son, her heritage and therefore status is so much more. We don't even have a Sensitive in our Clan.

Dejected, Jupex performed the routine tasks expected of him but often isolated himself whenever he could, sitting alone, staring into nothingness. He didn't know what to do, but desperately wished to see Chiara again. Then he would continue with whatever he was doing, struggling to concentrate.

"There is no point in worrying," MaXiox said. "I know you. You are thinking of the girl all the time. Go to her Clan and see how they react. If she rejects you, at least you will know where you stand. You are useless here, you might as well leave!"

"Yes, but if her mother rejects me, I'll have no reason to live anymore!"

"Oh, good grief, Jupex. Don't be so stupid. You are too dramatic. Her mother received us well at their Habitat. The girl also has a say. And if she doesn't like you enough to withstand her mother, you might as well overcome your infatuation and forget about her, instead of feeling sorry for yourself and making us all miserable."

"Yes, but last time she wouldn't have guessed that I am interested in her daughter," Jupex was angry with his friend but had to admit the rationality of his advice. He was sure that he would never be able to forget the girl and finally decided to face the dreaded mother. He left for the Valley of the Sparkling Waters soon afterwards.

That first visit was a frustrating experience. Chiara-the-elder was friendly but cool while the girl at first ignored him or found excuses to disappear with her friends. Then she would sit with him around the Clan fire and they had long talks, as good as when they had been at the Vigil of the Fires, a few moons before. The next night she sat with her mother and except for a friendly smile, ignored him. Then they had intense and intelligent discussions and just when he thought he was making progress, she would ignore him again, all her attention on the girls of her birth-group or on conversations with members of her Clan.

During a friendly talk, she mentioned that she had heard of the soft leather obtained from the chamois goats in the mountains above the Second Valley. When he asked her whether she wanted a worked chamois skin, she changed the subject, asking about the beauty of the crags in the mountains above the Second Valley.

Chiara-the-younger was fascinated with the young son of a Chief but knew enough to keep him interested without betraying her own partiality. He was very accomplished, but she wanted him to prove himself before committing. She was quite cool as he took his leave.

Chiara-the-elder closely watched the two and became amused at her daughter's feminine guiles. Her offspring was definitely interested, without any prompting.

She noticed how Jupex looked hopeless and unsure of himself. Alarmed that her daughter had overplayed her feminine trickeries, Chiara-the-elder was friendlier and asked him to give her regards to his mother. "We were good friends when we were small. Remind her of the conversations we had when visiting each other. I heard that she makes a very good ashcake from chestnut flour. Please ask her to send me the details."

Back at his own valley, Jupex's mother, Riana, accepted the friendly message, thought for a while, then asked him all the details of his visit. When he had finished, she smiled and told him to attend to his tasks. "You've been away and there is much to do."

For half a moon, Jupex was very active. He helped others with their tasks when his own was completed or dared the young ones of his peer group to race or respond to dangerous challenges. But at night, was even more despondent than before. His mother approached him, "I'm going to prepare some chestnut-flour delicacies for my old friend Chiara. Won't you please take them to her when they are ready?"

Excited but unsure of his reception after such a short time period, Jupex felt that he had to have a special present to give when he again appeared in the Valley of the Sparkling Waters.

He went in search of his friend, "MaXiox, do you remember the large chamois bull we've seen in the high mountain. I'm going to kill it for its soft leather. Will you help me?"

"Sure. And why do you need such special leather? Is it a present?" he asked with a knowing smile.

Jupex ignored him, "The bull was last seen on the ledges up there," he said, pointing.

Without wasting time, the two set out on the hunt. Following and clambering from ledge to ledge, MaXiox coaxed the bull in Jupex's direction, who took chances to intercept the animal. Risks he normally would have avoided. On the edge of a high precipice, he managed to spear his prey.

Jupex took his time preparing the soft chamois skin, working and fantasizing until the skin was perfect, a present worthy of the beautiful girl. The skin was soft and ready by the time his mother's delicacies were ready.

Chiara-the-elder greeted Jupex warmly, pleased with the edibles he brought and the details of how to prepare them using chestnut flour. Chiara-the-younger was friendly and accepted his gift with a brilliant smile. They talked each day and grew to know each other better.

#

After the visit, Chiara's eyes sparkled whenever anyone mentioned Jupex's name. Her thoughts turned to the future. She wished to have two children, as was the norm in the Clans. She wanted the first to be her own entitlement, and would be a daughter, of course. The second one would have to be the entitlement of some man, but not any man. Maybe Jupex. It must be a man worthy of her and her children, someone worthy to be her life-companion. Not like some girls who managed to have more children by enticing more than one man to allow them to carry each man's entitlement child.

Chiara knew that men usually wanted a son. She had accepted long ago that she would probably have a daughter and a son, the son being the choice of her life-companion. But secretly she still hoped for two daughters.

#

During regular visits, their relationship grew to the stage where they could discuss their ideals. She was surprised when Jupex told her that he did not mind if the child that he was entitled to, was a girl. All changed. Two daughters were a possibility. She was delighted, threw her arms around Jupex's neck and kissed him passionately. It was their first kiss.

"If our daughters are as beautiful and talented as you are, I can ask for nothing more," Jupex managed to say while returning her kiss. "But please, you must join my Clan. We need your Sensitive ability."

The agreement to become life-companions followed automatically.

#

When Questa was born two years later, their happiness compensated for the sorrow accompanying the death of Jupex's father, who had sustained an injury during a hunting expedition. Jupex became the Chief and Chiara-the-younger proved to be the Oracle-Healer the Clan needed, an excellent Chief's wife, and then mother.

Chiara-the-elder, happy with her daughter's life-companion, was there during the birth. Reassured that the girl was healthy and well looked after, she returned to her own valley. She was there again when a second girl was born three years later. Despite her talents as Healer and Sensitive and the help of other excellent Healers, she could not save her daughter's life when complications set in.

Jupex was devastated. He could not believe that he had lost the wife with whom he was so deeply in love. Questa was only three and did not fully understand what had happened, not even when her father could not stop crying and hugged her close.

Chiara-the-elder took care of the new-born girl, Anja, using all her talents and abilities to keep the baby well fed and healthy. She did not neglect Questa but helped her to cope with the loss of her mother. Her love for both girls was abundant and evident.

After a few days, Jupex started functioning again. He was strong and managed to contain his grief. One of Jupex's birth-group, Alena, helped Chiara-the-elder to care for the girls. When

Chiara was convinced that Alena loved and cared for Questa and would look after Jupex, she spoke to him, "I must return to my Clan. It would be best if I cared for the baby. After all, I am her grandmother. I would like to care for Questa as well, but she is already old enough to stay, if you insist. I can see that the women of your Clan will take good care of her and I will come to visit regularly."

With difficulty Jupex agreed to the arrangement and fixed his love on Questa, always remembering and missing the baby who he saw at least once a year as she grew to be a beautiful girl and then a young woman.

It took a few years before he realized how well Alena had looked after his beloved Questa and as the fourth Rite of Passage, a minor one this time, he committed to a second life-companion. It was Alena's third Rite of Passage, the first one being her birth and the second her induction into the Clan.

Chapter 11 – Survival

Anja came out of a state of semi-consciousness. She knew she had died and could not understand why being dead was so painful.

Surely, pain disappears with death!

Anja did not know how she survived the dreadful night. She could not even remember when the wind had died down.

She tried to open her eyes, but found her eyelids stuck together. Yellow dust had crusted her eyes closed. She wiped her eyes with the back of her hand, making matters worse. Her mouth was dry and clogged with bitter tasting mud. She loosened her gourd and removed the stopper to wash out her mouth with large amounts of water. With closed eyes, she felt around until she found the soft chamois skin and threw some water on it. Dabbing her eyes, she managed to unstick her eyelids. They stung, causing painful tears as she opened them. She wiped her face while her eyes streamed with tears. Finally, she could see.

Dawn had come. No, not dawn, just a gloomy light.

A layer of the fine powder covered everything. As she sat up, her movement launched it into the surrounding air. She inhaled, choked and coughed. Forced to inhale again, an increasing cycle of coughing resulted. Grabbing the pelt of a silver fox, she buried her face in it, fur inside. She choked again, this time from the dusty fur. It only helped after she shook the finely worked skin vigorously, covered her mouth and nose and could breathe normally. The familiar animal smell was reassuring, a smell she had often disguised with aromatics when using fresh skins in the cave.

Her mouth was dry and clogged with bitter tasting mud, while her eyes streamed with tears. She loosened her gourd and removed the stopper to wash out her mouth with large amounts of water.

Her left leg was badly scratched and bruised. It throbbed with pain and her ankle hurt even more. She used the last water in her gourd to clean the scratches and soothe the bruises.

I must get more water.

Thirst forced her to limp and crawl towards the stream. Moving carefully, trying not to disturb the dust, she managed to reach the stream. Thick mud had replaced the water and yellow-brown sediment had formed a hard crust on the surface of the little depression. Working the thick porridge-like mixture away to the side and repeatedly scooping away the sludge, allowed the rocky bowl to fill with clear water. She rinsed her mouth again, drank and refilled her gourd.

Exhausted, she collapsed occasionally drinking and splashing her face. The realization grew, *I am alone!* Then, *I must do something.*

In despair, she stumbled towards where the cave had been destroyed, seeking something familiar, a link to the past.

At the remnants of the tanning tree, she clung to the trunk, the rough surface scratching her cheek, a link to the time that had been. She gathered a few digging sticks nearby and recovered the bearskin. Not only as a kaross, but also as a reminder of better times. A sturdy length of thick root with a knobbed end, was the only weapon she could find. A useless weapon, not quite a club. But it helped, she felt safer. A long and painful effort brought her back to the knoll. She dragged the bearskin behind her while clutching a few more skins and tools in her arms. She hid these treasures between the boulders and covered them with branches. Then she started another search.

As she moved, her muscles warmed and became less painful. She saw no signs of life, neither in those areas where the women had lately gathered roots and plants, nor in the direction where the men had laid out their traps. She found two small rodents and a hare dead in the traps and brought them to the knoll.

Anja needed fire. At the stream, she selected a smooth, straight hardwood stick. A piece of soft, dry wood served as a base. Using an obsidian shard she had found at the tanning tree, she made a small hole in the soft wood, ending in a triangular slit. Fitting the rounded end of the stick in the aperture, she started to twirl it between her palms, pressing it down. As she twirled, wood-dust ground loose and heated up to form a red-hot coal. It dropped through the slit onto a small bundle of dried grass. Protecting the grass in her cupped hands, she blew softly on the coal until a little flame sprang to life in the grass.

A satisfied smile crossed her face. She placed the burning grass bundle, in a protected corner between the boulders. By feeding the flames with sticks and finally wood, she created a fire and much needed comfort. She used the obsidian shard to skin the animals and to cut the meat into strips. Suspended on a green sapling over the fire, she grilled some of the meat to still her hunger and smoked the rest for preservation.

Safety in the form of a shelter was the next priority. She fashioned a roof between the boulders with the trunks of young trees to form beams, then covered them with skins. With an entrance closed by thick thorn branches and enclosed at all the other sides and above, she felt safer. She dragged dried logs, firewood and sticks towards the fire. There she broke them up into useable lengths, until she had a large supply of kindling and wood. With the fire and enough skins to keep her warm, she had a useable shelter and could ward off predators. For the threat of Primitives, she had no solution except to hide.

As Anja's anxiety diminished, her loneliness grew as the high peaks remained invisible. The sight of the peaks became an obsession, their obscurity a sign that her familiar world was gone.

The darkness and cold increased as night approached. She remained in the relative safety of the shelter between the boulders and rolled herself up in the bearskin. With the fur against her body and her nose and face buried in the pelt of the silver fox, she felt soothed by the soft, tickling sensation.

The sky darkened until she could see nothing, all was black, darker than the darkest night she had ever experienced.

She fell into a dreamlike state in which the clear white snow-caps on the peaks were again etched against a dark blue sky. In the dream fragments of wind-cloud surrounded the highest peaks with the air sweet and clean. In a fitful reverie, she recalled her youth.

#

Anja's first memory was of her grandmother singing a little song she had made up. Her grandfather was sitting nearby humming an accompaniment. Anja was not the only one who thought Grandmother had a beautiful voice. Others of the Clan were listening to the pure sounds too, while slowly continuing with their various tasks.

She was only four years old then; it was the evening before her first remembered visit to her father's Clan, the Clan of the Second Valley. Grandmother had told her that she had visited him twice before, but she was too small to remember him. Fearful that she would not know him when she saw him, she clung to Grandmother. How would she know who to greet? Grandmother would be so ashamed of her if she made a mistake!

Her grandfather was finding excuses to remain near them, hugging them both. He was not going along on the visit, *He's going to miss us!* She knew he loved Grandmother and Grandmother loved him too. *But not as much as Grandmother loves me!*

"Are you sure she will be safe? Her Sensing ability is still so delicate. Anything unusual can hurt her brain. Lightning can kill her. It might strike anywhere, unexpectedly. If she Senses the impulse, she will be hurt," Grandfather's expression showed his concern.

"I will know of danger long before she's hurt and can make her sleep and block her perception," her grandmother replied.

Grandfather kept silent but gave her a huge hug.

Grandfather loves me too! He worries about me. But Grandmother will keep me safe.

They were in the corner of the cave reserved for her grandmother and grandfather. Grandmother had pulled back the skin partition that provided privacy when needed.

They seldom visited the deep cave extensions where the Clan stored enough foodstuffs to last for a year and where her grandmother separately kept all the salves, ointments, potions, and other items that visiting Oracle-Healers brought for use and safekeeping. Grandmother was the Clan's Healer and always attended to badly hurt hunters but, when a fierce thunderstorm threatened or raged outside, all her attention was focused on protecting Anja and keeping her safe deep inside the cave complex. The headache that Anja always developed in a storm disappeared there and Grandfather sat with her, soothing her. Anja remembered this corner as the center of the home where she grew up. Other experiences only left fleeting memories.

The cooking fires were near the entrance. They were all burning brightly, creating yellow images dancing on the cave walls. Anja imagined them to be pretty young girls, swirling in the thinnest of garments with yellow hair swinging wide, golden hair identical in color to her own. The color her grandmother said her own hair had been, before it became lighter and turned white. She knew that her sister had the same hair color. She wished she could remember what her sister looked like. However, she was to see her soon! Anja remembered that she had felt a tremor of expectation, somewhere below where her heart was supposed to be.

With nostalgia, she remembered how most of the Clan sat around the cooking fires talking. The men telling stories of their latest hunt while the women compared ways to prepare food or the best herbs to use for seasoning. As a young girl, she found the women talking about pigments and aromatic plants extremely boring. They discussed the different mixtures and how they got the men to extract oil from plants.

In the end, she became the one who advised them how to make themselves attractive. She smiled at the recollection, *As a small girl, all the talk seemed so silly. I was content.*

She was then still small enough to fit into the large bathing basket, so tightly woven that no water escaped.

As long as I smelled fresh after bathing in lukewarm water, I was happy, joyful thoughts.

To meet her father, she was going to wear a skirt made of soft chamois skins, worked until soft and nearly translucent, a skirt that swung wide when she twirled around.

She remembered all in detail, "May I show my skirt, Grandmother?" she had asked.

Receiving a smile and a nod, Anja picked up the small, flimsy garment. She ran to her dearest friend, a little girl of her own age, who sat in a similar alcove with the skin curtain open.

"Look at my skirt, Kala! They say the men are collecting more chamois skins to make you a full dress for your birthday!"

The two girls had giggled together and rushed from alcove to alcove to show off the skirt and tell about the expected dress. They demanded attention and admiration at each cooking fire, forcing conversation to stop.

The Clan happily indulged the two girls, considered especially 'sweet,' the more so since there were only the few children of each birth cycle in the Clan. Anja remembered vaguely what Grandfather had said, "With the latest babies who were born, the Clan has again reached the magic number of gracia (144) members."

She did not know what he meant but she had understood that all was well. The other two children of her own age were boys who she and Kala usually ignored. She remembered that at the time there were four new babies. She and Kala had often watched and wanted to play with them, but they were too small. However, the three older girls often played with her and Kala. Still older were three boys and two girls. Her grandmother had helped at all their births. She had known from the start that Grandmother was very important.

Older children had been of no interest. Even the group that was going through initiation with the related ceremonies had not concerned her or Kala. She knew the small boys of her own age showed interest in the hunting techniques of the initiates but it was so typical of boys to do boring things.

Anja did not remember much of the travel to her father's Clan in the Second Valley, except that she was scared of the great heights and the narrow ledges. She did remember that her grandmother carried her over the most frightening parts. She also remembered meeting her father and that his face was familiar. He wanted to pick her up but she hid in the folds of her grandmother's garment. She had her special skirt on but forgot to twirl and let the folds swing wide. Her sister looked older than the girls she normally played with at her own Habitat. Only when her sister knelt and smiled, did Anja overcome her reticence and showed off her skirt.

She could not remember how long it took before she sat on her father's knee and started loving him too, but never as much as she loved Grandmother. And she always loved her older sister, named Questa. She remembered them playing together continuously until she had to leave amidst a flood of tears. After that, all the visits to and from her father and sister became mixed in her memory and she could not separate one occasion from the other.

And then her father's life-companion, her stepmother. She had mixed feelings about her, even though she was always friendly and gave her, Anja, sweet treats when she was still a small girl.

#

Further recollections of Anja's youth were filled with happy memories. She grew up in the safety of the Clan. Babies came regularly every third year, never fewer than two of a gender. There was always a grandmother, past childbearing age, to help the mother.

She remembered grandmother's living mother and grandmother, famed Oracle-Healers in their own Clans. She did not see them often. The many generations within her Clan were all strong, often reaching an age of gracia years. They told stories or memories and experiences. They often explained the complexities and responsibilities of a Clan Healer. With shame she recalled how she regarded them as teaching aids only. Thinking back, she can now appreciate their love and dedication, proud when she was quick to understand or remember.

She had to learn the use of tisanes, potions, medicaments, and the other techniques to keep the elderly strong and fit. When their bodies indicated that they were ready to pass on, the old ones refused further invigorating draughts, participated in a farewell feast, and went to sleep painlessly, never to wake up.

As they grew up, Anja and Kala drifted apart as their interests diverged. Anja was interested in healing and helped her grandmother whenever she could, while Kala took great interest in boys.

With a slight smile, Anja recalled how a boy of her own Clan once kissed her. And twice there were boys of other Clans who kissed her during the ceremony of the Vigil of the Fires, the feast during the longest night. It was quite exciting, but she was more interested in watching Oracle-Healers dispensing medicine.

Grandmother first taught her to block out the pain emanating from the patients she treated and then to carefully share and absorb some of the pain. The most difficult was to block out the effects of a thunderstorm. They often discussed symptoms and solutions until late at night. Her fondest memories were sitting with Grandmother, practicing or demonstrating what she had learned. Grandfather usually hovered nearby and sometimes corrected a mistake.

Now she had to accept the finality of her loss, *Grandmother is dead! And Grandfather too.*

#

Anja remained in a semi-slumber until the howl of a predator woke her. It came from the direction where the cave had been.

The smell of decay must have summoned them, she thought. She realized that during her slumbers the far away cries of wolves had registered in her semi-conscious but she had not reacted. Now they were much nearer with no one from the Clan to chase them away with firebrands.

Suddenly wide awake, she listened to the whines as the wolves followed her smell towards the knoll. Soon the wolves were sniffling and yelping around her shelter. One jumped onto a boulder and pushed its nose down between the protecting branches and the boulder. Its drooling saliva dripped on Anja's leg.

Its head pushed the skin cover aside. The reflection of the smoldering embers reflected off yellow eyes, excitedly staring at her. Huge fangs appeared behind snarling lips.

The hungry wolf smelled food: Anja.

She scrambled back into the farthest corner, grabbed a broken branch to use as a club and threw a log on the fire.

The wolf forced its head through the protective branches spanning the gap between the boulders, shaking its head and scratching with its legs.

Bit by bit the creature's frenzied actions created room for it to descend, slowly entering Anja's shelter.

Half of its body appeared past her branch and skin roof. The wolf snarled and growled baring its huge teeth, ready to bite.

She felt the boulder wall behind her. There was nowhere to go.

In desperation, Anja grabbed a log from the fire, the end burning brightly, and pushed it into the creature's mouth.

With a loud yowl, the wolf backed up, shaking its head.

The disturbed embers flared up, lighting the shelter. Smoke and sparks swirled into the wolf's eyes.

It yelped again and reversed, whining and squealing all the way, scratching its way up and over the boulder. In its effort to escape, the wolf's flailing claws cut deeply into Anja's forearm. She managed to stick the sharp end of her digging stick into its neck before it disappeared over the boulder.

Anja heard the wolf pack tearing into their wounded mate, savagely ripping it apart. She noticed a stream of blood sliding down the boulder wall, glistening in the fire's light. She must have hit an artery in the wolf's neck.

Despite her pain, Anja hastily added more logs to the fire. She trembled with shock. Listening to the wolves feasting on their companion, she kept the fire burning.

The deep scratch on her arm pulsed painfully. She knew she needed to rinse the dirt and decay left by the wolf's claws, before the gash festered. But getting to water was impossible with the wolves prowling close by in the darkness.

She fed the fire. Her sole defense was a longish log, the one end glowing red hot. She kept it ready to fight off another attack, occasionally pushing the end into the fire to keep it smoldering or burning.

She peered through her damaged shelter roof, listening intently. Expecting the wolves to return for her. Finally, the dark receded somewhat. She sat motionless in her corner, wondering why the dark did not make way for the dawn, but the gloom endured. She clasped her head between her hands, willing the pains in her arm, leg and ankle to the background, focusing her thoughts.

She had to think clearly. Of utmost importance was to protect herself, to make sure that she would be safe from another attack. If only she could find survivors of her Clan. They could chase the wolves away and search together for other nearby Clans.

Her thoughts jumped back to the present. No sun was visible in the sky, not high up or low down and it was still getting colder. She had to find survivors but could not expose herself to danger.

Getting rid of the wolves was her first priority. Brandishing another fire-log, she made a second fire at the entrance to her shelter. The wolves retreated growling. After a few more mock charges, the nocturnal creatures skulked down the valley and disappeared in the woods.

Her wounded arm needed urgent attention. It was painful and already red and swollen. Red streaks ran up towards her shoulder. If that continued she knew she could develop a fever, lose her arm, and probably die. She tried to wash it with the little water left in her gourd. It did not help. She sucked at the injury, trying to clean it with her tongue. It tasted foul. The dirt would cancel the effect of the few healing salves in her gourd. A waste of the precious resource.

She had to reach the stream and clean the wounds. Keeping her eye on the woods, ready to dash back into the protected cover, Anja collected sticks and branches. She found enough pine resin to make torches to carry with her.

She limped to the stream carrying a lighted torch. How she would fend off an attack by more than one wolf, she did not know.

She had no choice. It was better to die quickly while fighting than die slowly rotting from within She had to continue.

At the stream, she surrounded the little fountain with fires. In the relative safety, she rinsed the wound on her arm. Biting on a stick, she used a sharp obsidian shard to cut out and scrape out the dirty material surrounding the scratches. Groaning from pain, she continued cutting, scratching and washing until the wounds were clean.

She rubbed healing herbs and salves into the gashes, then attended the other injuries, including her arm, sore leg and ankle. Listening and looking around, she decided it was safe enough to return to her shelter and then limped back.

The painful wounds, bruises and sprains kept her awake that night while she restlessly mulled over her fate, worrying about the possible return of the wolves or an attack by Primitives. They might be attracted by the smoke of her multiple fires. The night was eerily silent with few sounds. She heard the howl of the wolves far away, getting softer as they moved farther away. The silence became a threat, a chance that it was the presence of Primitives, which kept the night creatures away. Despite her fear and pain, pure exhaustion overwhelmed her. She fell asleep with images of physical danger alternating with visions of past days, transforming into nightmares less frightening than reality.

#

Anja's wounds and bruises healed slowly as she limped from place to place, always on the lookout for any sign of life other than the occasional small rodent. She kept hoping that some Clansmen had not been in the cave during the Catastrophe, had survived and would return to the cave site. She knew that she should not linger near where the smoke of her fires betrayed her presence, but she had nowhere to go and could not bring herself to leave the area, which triggered so many memories.

At last, she accepted that all members of her Clan had died. She had to prepare the funeral rites and conduct the accompanying ceremony. She would be the lone attendant. The collapsed cliff and mudslides had buried her Clan companions, making a funeral pyre unnecessary. She needed very little preparation. She sprinkled some dried powdered herbs on the rubble, where the cave used to be. Tears streamed down her cheeks as she performed the rites her grandmother had taught her.

Ignoring the potential danger of remaining near the cave site just a little longer, she said her farewells, remembering the special times they had spent together. Anja took her time naming and remembering each one of the Clan, even the youngest babies, ones she had recently cuddled or heard crying. She remembered her peers, her birth-group. They had played, served and learned together, sharing initiation, joys and hurt. Anja tried to remember specific incidents and feelings they had shared, taking all day to remember, sometimes crying and sometimes laughing.

That night, sleep eluded Anja again. She rolled around restlessly. Only danger remained for her here in this Valley of the Sparkling Waters, where she grew up and which she had known so intimately before the Catastrophe. She thought of the layout of the area the Clans occupied: the high mountains with the fertile valleys draining onto the plains with their bogs and marshes, lying beyond the mouth of her valley. There the Primitives roam. They would kill her if they can. That route is impossible.

As is the mountains. They are always dangerous. And, since the Catastrophe, the slopes and cliffs are clearly unstable.

She could not remain in the valley but there was nowhere to go and no way to safely exit the valley. Wondering what to do, uncontrolled tears ran down her cheeks.

What is to become of me?

She feared the future.

Chapter 12 – Origins

Jupex sat thoughtfully watching the fire. He stretched and looked up, first at Alena and then at Orrox.

"I quite understand your need to visit the Dynasty urgently, but, before you go I would like you to look at our Clan cave, which we have abandoned despite its better location. I believe the cave brings bad luck and caused the death of my first life-companion during childbirth."

Jupex looked down, lips trembling. He took a deep breath before continuing.

"Areas within the cave have always smelled bad. After a land-shaking the odor increased, becoming noticeable everywhere. Despite the efforts of visiting Oracle-Healers who tried to get rid of the smell, the stink remained. Two women recently died in childbirth, as if we were back in primitive times. I believe whatever causes the stench, is to blame."

Jupex stared sadly at the fire, stretching out his hands to warm them.

He continued, "I decided to move down here, to set up a Habitat in this protected corner of the cliffs. We have kept the cave-palisade intact to keep cave bears out. I've informed the Dynasty of our troubles. We must determine whether we could make it safe again. Because I value your opinion, I would regard it as a great favor if you would inspect the cave."

The sound of a baby crying made him pause.

"I have not been up there for some time and many Clansmen avoid it too. The lack of a cave Habitat has inhibited us from growing our Clan. The valley is fertile enough to sustain a full Clan, a Clan containing gracia members. However, without a safe cave, the Council is reluctant to allow members of our Clan to have additional children and our numbers have declined. This Catastrophe will make it worse! My Clan is slowly getting smaller; births are not replacing deaths."

"I'm quite prepared to inspect the cave and share my opinion. I'll tell an expert from the Dynasty what I have found when I'm back there," Orrox answered, while he thought to himself, *A delay of a single day will not make any difference.*

Then he added, "But as far as growth of the Clans is concerned, you know the traditions and taboos."

"Yes, we know they came from long ago, and there are good reasons for them."

Looking at the fire, Jupex continued, loud enough for all to hear, "We would be honored if you, as an Orrox scion from the Dynasty, would tell the young ones the tale of the origins of our Clans and our traditions and taboos. It is always a popular subject when a bard visits, but they know little of how the Sensitives and the Dynasty fit into the story. To hear an Orrox tell it, would be a rare treat for all of us and would take our minds off the experience of the Catastrophe."

Orrox nodded in agreement, and began, "It really began at the time of the Inter-Clan Devastation, which is also sometimes called the Deadly Strife. Before that time our forebears lived a chaotic life. Our male forebears often sired many children with different females, believing their offspring would look after them in their old age. Even though most children died in infancy, the numbers of our forebears grew steadily."

Orrox pretended not to notice their sudden interest. He studied the fire and slowly sipped a draught Alena had previously poured for him and Jupex.

Jupex found it difficult to suppress a smile.

Orrox paused until the patience of the younger ones was at the breaking point, then he continued in a dreamy voice, as if not aware of his surroundings. "Ollionox was the first of the great Sensitives. He started as a recluse. Living in the loneliness of his cave, he discovered his gift and the power it brought. He developed the methods we still use to record our experiences. His Clan abandoned him in the mountains when he was still very young. Before his time, the Clans regularly left deformed, unwanted or misunderstood young ones in the mountains to die."

His audience gasped in horror.

"Yes, it was a primitive time. To make it more real, close your eyes and imagine Ollionox's experiences."

Orrox emanated images as he recalled the history. The projection was so clear, the acolytes and the Clansmen could visualize the times of the Deadly Strife, as if they themselves were Ollionox:

Ollionox sat outside his cave looking down at the forest below him. The location suited him well. A nearby fountain of scalding hot water gave him an unlimited source of heat. Because of the distance of the areas where the Clans roamed, he felt safe of the taunts he remembered all too well: "Another one of those who is 'sensitive to storms!' They are all mad! They hide or yell during storms and they hear things and see things that do not exist. They even claim to know how we feel! They are crazy!"

During the years of his isolation, he had discovered his ability to be aware of the life surrounding him. In the depths of the cave, where no other life was present, even insect life registered. Larger animals were easier to detect and the few times he had watched Clansmen from a hiding place, awareness of their presence was strong. He could guess their feelings and create the same emotions within himself. By concentrating hard, he saw them react to the sentiment.

After intense exercising of this ability, he developed headaches. While massaging a specific area on his temples to reduce the pain, he found he could make the pain disappear by flexing certain facial muscles, affecting his temples. As his skill to exercise the muscles improved, rubbing his temples with his fingers, proved that he was controlling blood flow through certain arteries. By flexing the newly discovered muscles and much practice, he managed to stop or enhance his awareness of life.

One day a far-off rumbling attracted his attention while he was contemplating the implications of these discoveries.

A thunderstorm is threatening! I'll wait it out at the back of the cave.

He could already feel the impulses of the distant lightning affect his awareness of life. Ollionox moved to the back of the cave, shielded from the effect of the storm's lightning flashes.

Today I'm going to test how much of the storm's effects I can block, he decided.

At the height of the storm, Ollionox slowly moved to the mouth of the cave. By tightening the muscles in his temples, he blocked out all impulses of the lightning, which previously would have caused intense pain or even a seizure leading to possible death. All his awareness of life was also blocked out.

Exhausted, feeling the muscles cramping, he retired to the back of the cave.

For many seasons, Ollionox exercised and strengthened his abilities and the muscles he used to block awareness or create an emotional state in others. As his ability improved he named the skill *Sensing* and the projection of feelings *Emanating*.

It is time to visit the Clans. I can help those who have the Sensing ability and do not have control. I can teach them, Ollionox thought.

As he descended towards the plains he passed through a forest teeming with life.

I can recognize the presence of different animals.

He sat down under a large tree and emanated friendliness. Squirrels and other small animals approached him without fear. While feeding a squirrel he Sensed the approach of a large lifeform.

What is that? I Sense aggression.

It was very different from the weak emanations of the surrounding life. Definitely a predator.

Ollionox strengthened his friendly projections. He could not quite synchronize his projections with the animal.

What can it be?

Too sure of himself, he stood and scanned the surrounding forest.

A huge cave bear appeared, sniffing the air. Detecting Ollionox's smell, it reared up and stormed with a roar.

Ollionox's tried to use his projections to stop the attack, but it had no effect.

He spun around when the bear nearly reached him and hurriedly climbed the tree. The heavy bear followed closely. It could not match Ollionox's climbing speed.

Ollionox continued until he reached the thinnest branches near the top, where they could barely support his weight.

The bear gave up when it realized the weaker branches would not hold its weight. It climbed down and sniffed at the scent left by Ollionox's presence.

Letting out a sigh of relief, Ollionox watched the bear as it circled the tree, until, at last, it retreated. When he could not Sense the presence of the bear anymore, he slowly descended.

Ollionox remained in the forest for another year, Sensing different life forms and when possible, emanating friendliness to the small animals and strengthening his ability to project feelings. By the end of the year, he could identify different predators as they approached, giving him enough opportunity to escape.

Observing animals and birds, while collecting roots, herbs, and plants in the forest and on the mountain slopes, allowed him to become an expert on natural resources.

When he felt ready to face Clansmen, after years of isolation, Ollionox entered the well-watered plains below the mountain range, where the loosely organized Clans lived.

Meandering streams, fed by the many fertile valleys, were fringed with trees bearing fruit interspersed with large grassy areas where antelopes, aurochs, and other game roamed.

Ollionox approached the first Clan and was afforded hospitality. He joined the Clan's medicine woman, called AllVoir, while she treated the sick or injured. They shared knowledge and different methods of curing the sick or injured and of applying healing powders and herbs. The Clan called her the *Sage* since she was also the Chief's main advisor.

During long nights, Ollionox conversed with AllVoir and realized she had life awareness. She was a Sensitive.

"How do you survive thunderstorms and the stress of Sensing pain?" he wanted to know.

"Oh, we Sages in the different Clans excuse ourselves and hide in the deep recesses of caves when the weather becomes threatening. We tell the Clans we need contemplation time."

Ollionox taught her the methods of control and blocking he had discovered.

AllVoir convinced the Clan that Ollionox had superior herbal knowledge. Accepted as a Sage and advisor, Ollionox moved from Clan to Clan where many had a medicine Sage with life awareness in attendance. They often told Ollionox how difficult it was to survive. Many babies, suspected of having the ability, died young. Others were prone to fits, hiding in caves when thunderstorms threatened. They were also taunted with the label, 'Sensitive to Storms.'

Orrox paused and the emanation of Ollionox's life faded away. He looked at his audience with a slight smile, "As I said, individuals within the Clan soon became aware of Ollionox's powers and accepted him as a Sage and advisor. That was the beginning of the Sensitives' role in Clan-life."

Many in the audience sat as if transfixed, looking at Orrox with large eyes. Some put a hand over their eyes and then swept it back over their brows and hair, as if to change their perspective from the imaginary world to reality. They had forgotten their injuries and pains while absorbed in Orrox's projections.

"Projecting my imagining of Ollionox's early life, is very tiring," Orrox said. "I hope it helped you forget the trauma of the Catastrophe. Give me a moment before I continue the tale of our history."

Orrox took a few deep draughts of his drink. His audience was quiet, waiting.

"After Ollionox's time, possibly due to the improvements in health his legacy created, fewer children died and our forebears grew in numbers. The loosely organized Clans burned the woodlands, to encourage new green shoots to grow, making it easier to hunt their prey. They ignored the wise reprimands of the Sensitives, as the healing Sages were already called.

"Fires burned uncontrolled, until the grass and forests retreated and the plains changed to the scrublands and marshes we now know. The Sensitives were concerned. They warned the Clans against slaughtering too many young fawns and calves before maturity, before they calved. All the concerns, including a warning that the Clans were becoming too numerous and that the game was in danger of being hunted to extinction, were ignored and ridiculed.

"As if to confirm the warnings of the Sages, a great drought, lasting many years, reduced the remaining grasslands to dust. The rivers and streams dried up and the game disappeared. The only resources left were in the valleys, but there were too many Clans with too many Clansmen for the remaining forests and woodlands to sustain them all. Insufficient amounts of foodstuffs remained, while over-exploitation destroyed the little there was. Because they could Sense and feel the suffering of the hungry Clans, the Sensitives developed symptoms of headaches, depression and worse.

"The hunger and want drove the Clans to compete for the remaining edibles and the previously peaceful Clans became aggressive. Dissatisfied Clansmen ignored their Chiefs and started rampaging in small groups, stealing, fighting and finally killing to get food. The fighting destroyed whatever was left. As suffering in the Clans increased. Pain throbbed through the Sensitive's minds. Those who managed to suppress or block their Sensing abilities and therefore the agony, were able to remain with their Clans but could not fulfill their traditional roles of healing or advising. They used all their energy blocking their awareness. In others the reflected suffering from the hungry Clans overwhelmed their Sensing abilities, causing irreparable damage to their minds. Only those who could move far away from the suffering were not affected."

Jupex and many Clansmen nodded.

"The suffering of those near an untrained Sensitive can drive the Sensitive out of his or her mind. When the Sensitive Sages experienced the mass suffering of those near them, they cringed and hid, causing the Clans to accuse them of cowardice or even causing the suffering. The Clansmen did not understand even though Sensing and Emanation often helped them through pain and sickness."

Orrox's listeners remained silent. In the silence, Orrox noticed the absence of the usual night sounds.

Glances confirmed his audience's awareness of the superior abilities of both Orrox and his acolytes. They were Sensitives who managed to block the reflected pain of the injured while they helped them, even though the acolytes were still in training.

"Sensitives already lived in the valley, which we now know as the Valley of the Dynasty. Others tried to reach its safety. At the time of the Great Drought, the forests in the Dynasty Valley were spared the ravages of the other valleys and were not burned. The Sensitives of the Valley were already rescuing, receiving and training young Sensitives from the Clans. They taught them the methods Ollionox first devised, methods greatly refined and expanded since then. The Sensitives were powerless and could not even move out onto the plains, because the agony of the fighting, hatred, and pain was so intense, it overwhelmed their ability to control and block what they Sensed. Even in their isolated valley, far from the fighting, the Sages could still Sense the suffering. Some, with superior control, managed to venture out onto the plains, trying to convince individuals to stop fighting, but they found that a new culture of vengeance thwarted their efforts. Each Clan-member who lost a companion, made an oath of revenge. Revenge was always greater than his own loss. Killing and even torture escalated until no Sage who tried to help, appease or defuse the situation, was safe. The Sensitives in the valley did have extra provisions, but not nearly enough to save the Clans. They hid some food in places where young mothers could find it to feed their offspring, thereby ensuring the survival of the strongest young Clansmen."

Orrox got up and stretched. Alena passed him a fragrant draught before he sat down again.

"The drought lasted until the Clans were reduced to a small number of individuals, wandering around without any Clan affiliation. Predators found the unorganized individuals easy prey in their weakened state. This reduced their quantities even further.

"A little rain fell allowing grasses and plants with edible roots to grow and a few of the smaller game returned. The few surviving Clansmen were widely scattered, frightened, and traumatized. They were at the point of extinction.

"The sad fate and actions of the survivors deeply troubled the remaining Sensitives. Many mourned lost relatives. In their valley, they carefully nursed the available plants and game. With the returning rain, they were able to produce a surplus of edibles.

"They organized a gathering of all the remaining Clansmen, choosing the days surrounding the longest night, symbolic of a change to a better future. Although the survivors feared the probable slaughter, the Sensitives convinced them to gather under an oath of peace. Under Sensitive guidance they deeply repented their misconduct. Even the greatest enemies renounced vendettas. The Sensitive's control over the food available at the gathering probably contributed to the peace. The hunger of the Clans won out over fighting.

"The surviving Sensitives, Healers, and the few remaining Clan Chiefs met. The Clans had to reform, but subject to rules, which could become traditions, supported by taboos. They agreed that a Council with a selected Council Leader would permanently support Clans and Sensitives with training, knowledge, and medicaments. The first Leader was an outstanding Sensitive, an offspring of Ollionox. Of whom I am a direct descendant.

"The wisdom of those first Council members still endures and is reflected in our lifestyles. They realized the fine balance required to create a stable society, which must last for innumerable generations, but must still remain dynamic and adaptable. Growth must be in abilities and even comfort, not in numbers.

"The new Council suggested techniques to improve Clan-life and reduce the risks of lean years. A new rule was that a surplus of edibles would be gathered and stored in ice caves high up in the mountains. They decided on methods and procedures to ensure that the new Clans could grow to an ideal size, a size dependent on the fertility and other factors existing in a valley. The methods helped to ensure sustainability of life and resources in a stable Clan environment. They decided on an absolute upper limit of gracia Clan-members because they knew through experience, how factions and discord destroyed the tranquility of larger Clans. They established the rules, which became traditions. Including the tradition that each Clan-member had the right to one child only.

"All the Clans and their members made a pact that they would uphold these agreements as traditions and unbreakable taboos and would teach them to their children. We still comply with the pact.

"Eventually the rain returned and even though we have experienced serious droughts again, we have all lived comfortably through those and many other crises, under the benign guidance of the Council at the Dynasty Valley.

"Copying nature, we all live a comfortable life, but due to our ability to analyze, we avoid nature's tendency to overpopulate, sometimes causing extinction or community collapse. The Council continually stay aware of changes, which could affect Clan stability and take the required measures to protect the Clans. The Catastrophe is such a threat and the Council has much to consider.

"My ancestors established the Orrox Dynasty. My forebears have often brought forth a Council Leader, always a Sensitive, who qualified after intense training and education. The Council Leader always takes the name of Orrox, if he had not been so named at birth. The Council still meets annually at our Dynasty Valley Habitat. When the time comes, they choose a new Council Leader whom they unanimously consider worthy."

Orrox finished the tale and the whole assembly clapped their hands.

Orrox took the opportunity to add a few thoughts. "You must all realize how comfortable our lives have become since that time. Much has improved. We have found medications and herbs that allow the Oracle-Healers to cure most illnesses and have developed methods to ensure the healthy births of our babies, even a gender of our choosing. We are so accustomed to the good life that we forget how short and brutal life was before. Our food has improved with larger and improved fruit and other edibles. We enjoy nature and keep fit by hunting and hiking in the mountains, visiting beauty spots. Games and educating our children keep our minds sharp.

"We have only to look at the Primitives of the Plains and Marshes to get an idea of how hard life can be. It is difficult for them to adopt better life-style, given their smaller brains and slow thinking ability. Their continuous squabbling, fighting, and killing render any joint venture impossible. Their numbers grow whenever there is enough food to feed their many offspring. They are again too many, reducing the plains' fertility, in a similar way to what we did so long ago. The Council, during their meetings at the Dynasty, is still discussing what we should do for them should a disaster strike, one which they might not survive. The consensus tends to be that we should not interfere. To do only what is possible without endangering ourselves. However, arguments continue."

Jupex thanked Orrox for telling the tale. The Clan-members moved away allowing Jupex to ask privately, "Do you think the Clan will be safe here? What is our future?"

Orrox kept his answer to himself, *It is still cold even though we're already in the warm season, the season of plenty. The dust remains, blocking the sun. Without the sun, it will get even colder and the Clans will suffer terribly. I fear for the future!*

<><><>

Chapter 13 – Illoreaens

The sound of voices slowly penetrated Questa's consciousness. Fear gripped her. She cried out in despair, believing the Giants had caught her again.

A voice made soothing noises, calming her. She couldn't understand and tried to concentrate. The sounds were friendly and not guttural. Slowly she recognized the language. It was the language of the Clans. Although colored with a strong accent, it was still her language.

She irrationally thought the Giants had somehow learned to speak like the Clans. Something sweet dripped on her tongue. She swallowed and opened her eyes to see male figures, but not Giants. Except for their garb, they could have been from any of the Clans. One held a container with sweet liquid to her lips while the others were looking down the slope in the direction from where she came.

Questa concentrated hard to understand the strangeness of their speech. She understood when one of them said, "The Giants are approaching and seem very agitated. What should we do?"

The one bending over her ignored the question but said, nearly without accent, "You are safe. We will protect you! We are the Illoreaens." He handed her the container. "Drink some more. It will give you strength."

She swallowed a huge gulp.

"Do you feel better now?"

She shivered, not only from the cold but also from the sudden release of tension. She drew the Giant's kaross tightly around herself and nodded. His speech was vaguely familiar. She had heard a similar accent when she spoke with Curon, back at the Dynasty. The stranger looked inquiringly at the kaross and then at Questa's face. She couldn't help herself, she started crying, sobbing in relief.

He handed her a cloth made of an unknown substance, "Please! We have to act. The Giants are near!"

He turned to his companions, using the strange pronunciation again, "We must warn them. If they continue coming, we'll have to defend ourselves. Let's move to the small cliff up there, the one with the boulders on top. We must prepare ourselves!" Looking at Questa he added, "I believe the girl can walk if we support her."

Questa suppressed her sobs and dried her tears with the cloth.

These strangers seem friendly. Will they harm me?

The stranger helped her up, supporting her as she stumbled. With his assistance, she managed to follow the others up the ridge, where they gathered at a pile of huge boulders. Some stood with their backs against the bigger boulders while others crouched on top. Here they waited calmly for the approaching Giants.

The leader addressed Questa again in the more understandable accent, "I am JaYan. We are the Clan living in the Valley of Perpetual Shade. Despite the damage during the great land-shakes, our Look-Outs remained vigilant. They saw your escape and how you hid in the gully before the wind engulfed everything. We looked for you during the days after the windstorm, despite the difficulty to see in the dark and gloom."

Questa did not understand. *How could they have seen me, been watching me? Surely the distance was too great for me to have been visible.* She did not Sense danger, just friendliness and a bit of amusement at her bewilderment.

"We will explain later. Now we have to deal with the Giants."

She massaged her wrist, tugging at the hated leather strap.

The stranger, JaYan, looked down, "Should I remove that?"

She nodded. He swiftly cut the leather strap loose with an instrument she did not recognize. She rubbed her wrist looking down. An excited, thrilling sensation welled up inside her.

Free at last! Then, *I am safe!*

Set free from the imprisoning leather strap caused her to momentarily forget the threat of the approaching Giants.

When they were within hailing distance, JaYan called out, using the Giants' own guttural language. Questa heard friendliness with an element of challenge in his voice. The Giant leader answered in an aggressive tone.

The leader... Heropto was it? Yes! That's him!

A further exchange followed, ending in JaYan speaking in an authoritarian tone, issuing a command.

He turned to his companions, "Be ready, they might attack. We will have to use flyers. Make sure we retrieve all of the flyers!"

The Giants were still under the ridge, each carrying a knobbed club and a short stabbing spear.

Questa watched as Heropto gestured wildly, yelling at his troupe. Intense dread slammed down on her like a great weight. She fell to her knees. The female, the one she remembered as Heropto's jealous companion, yelled back.

Questa could see the anger in Heropto's face. When the female persisted, he hit her in the face with his fist. Questa was sure no ordinary being would be able to survive such a blow, but the female just shook her head and continued arguing.

Heropto positioned himself on a large boulder from where he could watch his enemy. With gestures, he commanded his troupe to split into two attacking groups. They climbed the ridge on each side of the Illoreaens' location.

Questa remembered how, at close quarters, the long throwing spears of the Clans were useless against the strength of the Giants.

She yelled, "Careful! They are very strong! They will ignore your spears!" Her face turned ashen as she cowered against the protective boulder. She closed her eyes and covered her face with her hands.

I cannot watch these Clansmen die. It's like what happened at the Dynasty. They died while trying to protect me!

She started crying again, petrified, certain that disaster awaited them all. She closed her mind. Scared of again Sensing and experiencing the pain of Clansmen being killed.

The Illoreaens concentrated on the Giants, ignoring her.

She heard JaYan shouting, trying to persuade Heropto to turn back. But Heropto concentrated on his troupe.

Heropto will never give up. When I was captive I tried to understand what drove the Giants. I must listen and interpret. My knowledge might help my rescuers. Questa thought, overcoming her fear with great effort.

JaYan called out one last time in the Giant's tongue. *Clearly a warning!* Questa recognized.

The Giants, both males and females, hesitated. However, on a shouted command from Heropto, they ran forward, but halted out of range of the Illoreaen spear throwers. The Illoreaens were ready, their spears fitting snugly in their throwers, ready to launch as soon as an enemy came within striking distance.

JaYan called out, "There are too many! We will have to use our bows as well. Remember all flyers must count and be recovered!" Then, as if to himself: "We could really use MaGan's expertise right now."

JaYan gave another command, then to Questa's surprise, the Illoreaens threw back their coverings to reveal curved sticks. They grabbed them in the middle. Multiple long straight saplings were attached to their plaited leather belts. A strange sight, unlike anything Questa had ever seen before.

The Giants surrounded them on three sides, remaining out of reach of throwing spears. Heropto moved cautiously over the ridge to a new vantage point.

Individual Giants took a step forward, shouting, shaking fists, stomping their feet, and making faces. The Giant then stepped back, allowing another to demonstrate his aggression.

JaYan listened intently, an expression of interest on his face. Heropto cursed. His impatience grew with every word uttered during each Giant's lengthy demonstration.

Questa Sensed the aggression emanating from the Giants despite not concentrating on them. Then curious about the strangeness, a peculiarity she had also noticed while she was still a captive, she allowed more of the Giant's emanations to register, concentrating on their minds.

Their emotional state, which reflected their intentions, was too horrible to endure. The emanations deviated in so many respects from those of the Clans that, if encountered in a Clan-member, she would have diagnosed a sick brain. Then she completely closed her mind, blocking off all emanations.

Heropto moved forward, shouting threats. He yelled a command and the whole troupe attacked simultaneously.

JaYan called out a final warning in the Giant's language. When the Giants ignored his warning, he turned to his companions, "We have no choice but to kill if they ignore our first volley. I shall aim at the leader. Killing or even hurting him should discourage the rest!"

The female Giant aggressively headed straight for Questa. Even through her closed mind, she could Sense the focused hatred of the female. It rose above the general aggression of the other Giants and the calm determination of the Illoreaens.

The Illoreaens used their spear throwers to launch their spears accurately, hurting but not killing the Giants. They switched to using the strange curved sticks, which JaYan had called 'bows.' They did the real damage, launching the saplings accurately and at great speed.

The bows fascinated Questa. She forgot her fear.

This is new!

The saplings flew straight, one after the other, killing or hurting Giants.

JaYan, in whose hands a bow had also appeared, launched a sapling at the leader, half-hidden above them. It hit him above his thick brow, but, instead of penetrating, glanced off into the air. He yelled out in pain, the wound bleeding profusely.

Blood blinded him as it streamed down his face. When he yelled, the Giants hesitated. They saw their leader bleeding and retreated in panic.

Some of those capable of retreating fell, stumbled and fell down the ridge in their haste, rushing down towards the plain, leaving their dead behind. The female, forgetting Questa, ran to the leader, trying to stop the bleeding. The leader pushed her aside, yelled threats and then followed the others as quickly as his powerful legs allowed.

Not a single Illoreaen was hurt. The Giants never got close enough to use their clubs or stabbing spears.

"A bad aim. He moved just as I released the flyer, only part of his head was visible," JaYan said calmly. "Amazing how thick their skulls are. Imagine a flyer not penetrating but just glancing away!" Then, turning to his comrades, "Make sure we get all our flyers back. The Giants must not learn the use of bows and flyers. They are intelligent enough to replicate them if they ever see complete examples."

Questa relaxed the full blocking she had to apply to reject the emanation of pain during the battle. The Illoreaens spread out to retrieve the saplings they referred to as 'flyers'. She Sensed the mixed delight and sadness of her rescuers but also the strange feeling of pain emanating from the injured Giants and the shock of death as the victors plucked their flyers from the bodies of two lethally injured Giants. Three more were dead. All the others were able to scramble away.

Questa experienced the strange ecstasy again and quickly closed her mind, blocking all Sensing, even though a full block diminished her ability to function effectively. *Enjoying horror can be addictive. A danger all Sensitives must avoid.*

JaYan kept a close watch on the Giants who were still moving away. He looked at Questa and said, "It is better to kill than to maim. Giants have no sympathy for their wounded or disfigured. For them, it is a much better fate to die quickly in a fight than to be abandoned to die slowly from injuries or be eaten alive by scavengers."

He faced his companions, "In addition to my ineffective shot, two of you did not hit your targets either. You know who you are. MaGan will be unhappy. We must practice when we return. Let's go!"

They moved up the slope towards the mountain. JaYan indicated Questa should stay near him, "Shall one of us support you? Do you feel well enough to walk?"

"I feel much better, thank you."

"I'm sorry you witnessed that. We hate suffering and believe a quick kill is preferable if we have no choice and have to defend ourselves. I hope the Giants will return to collect the bodies but I believe they will just leave them. We will talk later. We must get you to safety first. Here, have some more of this potion, it will give you strength."

Questa was still in shock, not only from what she saw but also from what she Sensed. She would have to consider it all later.

She accepted the draught. Even though she carefully rolled the liquid around in her mouth, she could not identify the taste, despite indications of familiarity. There was no distinctive smell either. She regarded herself as an expert in drugs and herbs and asked, "What is this?"

JaYan glanced at her, "As I said, we will talk later."

#

Frustrated and curious, Questa followed the group of Illoreaens, one of whom followed far behind, keeping a lookout. They moved fast, heading straight for the mountains.

Questa kept up, staying near JaYan. Nearer the mountain, the open grass of the plain gave way to steeper slopes and a series of high ridges, ending in a long yellow sandstone cliff. Behind the cliff, the mountain sloped steeply upwards, disappearing in the persisting gloom.

Despite the bad light, Questa noticed differences. Each ridge contained areas of different rock types. The properties of rocks and soils have always interested her. A passion she shared with her grandmother.

I will inspect it later. Grandmother would be so interested.

Before darkness fell, they arrived at a broken palisade obscuring an opening in the cliff, one just large enough to allow two to pass side by side. Members of the Clan were busy repairing the palisade. She saw others with the strange curved sticks keeping guard, half-concealed behind boulders. High up on the cliff more guards sat in recesses, holding tubes to their eyes, seeming to look towards the plains. The face of the cliff was smooth except for the dark holes.

JaYan stayed with Questa as the group hurried towards the opening. The entry was a tunnel, which made a few switchbacks before ending in a large cavern. Questa could see many openings through which figures moved constantly.

This must be part of a vast cave complex within the mountain, she thought. *It is dug out of this soft loess rock from which the Dynasty's Habitat cave is formed.*

She looked at the smooth wall surfaces, *But the surface is very smooth and hardened. And here there is so much space! This is amazing!*

She watched the activity around her. Groups were busy organizing and repairing partitions. They were neither of skins sewn together with sinews, nor of wood, but were made of what looked like square rocks, all the same size. Steady flames without smoke lit the cave, much brighter than the Clan's fat and oil clay burners. The brightest were contained within translucent spheres.

She had noticed the brighter burners the Dynasty used, but these were very different.

Questa froze in place, realizing her mouth gaped open in amazement and quickly closed it.

Work stopped as they entered. A crowd gathered around in curiosity, all speaking together, looking at the Giant's kaross with surprise but keeping their distance. Questa Sensed only interest, no aggression.

"How pretty she is! You can see she is beautiful; despite the dirt and the horrible skin she has wrapped around her." Questa overheard different remarks, it made her feel more confident.

Amazed at the strangeness of all she saw, she tried to Sense answers, making sure she did not read their individual emanations. Their minds were familiar.

They are all of Clan-origin.

JaYan spoke up, "The Giants were aggressive and attacked. We were forced to kill five. Please continue with your work. She's very tired after her grueling experience. Let her eat, drink and sleep. We can hear her story tomorrow."

He turned to Questa. "Just tell everyone who you are."

"I am Questa, daughter of Jupex, Chief of the Clan of the Second Valley, everywhere renowned for his bravery and hunting skills. My mother was Chiara-the-younger. Originally from the Clan living in the Valley of the Sparkling Waters. I am the Healer at my father's Clan."

"Welcome, Questa of the Clan of the Second Valley!" JaYan said, "Welcome to the Illoreaen Habitat. You must have many questions. We should wait until tomorrow, after you have eaten and rested, before sharing more."

Questa couldn't help herself but continued looking at the amazing sights in the Habitat. Horizontal surfaces made of wood stood at the far end of the hall. There was a similarity between those used in the Clan caves, but these were wider, smooth, and flattened on both sides to a thickness the length of her thumb. Some young women, wearing translucent, nearly transparent garments of the same strange cloth she noticed before, placed wooden bowls on the surface. A lovely smell made Questa realize how hungry she was.

"Come and sit on the bench at the table and eat, then a good sleep will reinvigorate you. But first, allow our women to exchange this horrible Giant's skin with something more suitable," JaYan said and left.

The danger of the Giants was still foremost on Questa's mind, but before she could call JaYan back, two young women led her away. Questa was ashamed, she knew she stank. The putrid fat mixture still covering her body made her smell as bad as any Giant.

The girls seemed to understand her embarrassment and wiped off the worst dust and grime before allowing her to wash properly. When she was clean, they gave her a covering made of the same soft cloth they were wearing. It was soft and warm.

The Illoreaens wore coverings thinner and lighter than the softest worked skin she had ever seen, held together with shiny clasps and belts. The belts were made of an unknown cloth. They resembled flax but with a much smoother and more flexible texture.

She felt more secure and comfortable than she had felt for a long time and returned to what the Illoreaens called a table. Meat and boiled grain kernels lay ready. Fresh fruit and a wooden mug containing a fruity liquid completed the meal. The food tasted better than any she had ever eaten at her Clan or even at the Dynasty. She tried to figure out what it was made of.

Someone showed her where she could sleep, a comfortable nook in an adjacent area with soft skins to lie on. Before she settled down behind a drape, a friendly female approached and took away the dirty skins.

"We'll clean these and give you new garments." *Yet another unfamiliar word.*

Questa recognized many of the words they used as old-fashioned, words seldom remembered in the Clans. She understood the reference to tables and benches as a disused grand term for the much rougher items the Clans normally referred to as surfaces and seats.

The bedding felt unexpectedly soft and comfortable, in contrast with the hard, cold earth she laid on during so many nights. The coverings were strange and soft too.

I would like to inspect them later. My first priority must be to share everything I know and have learned about the Giants. The

Illoreaens must plan a defense. I'm sure Heropto will return with his troupe. He is not one to give up easily.

She stretched and curled herself up in the gentle luxury, intending to think, but fell asleep immediately. She slept well without nightmares.

#

The next morning, dim light entered through openings high up near the roof. She washed in lukewarm water available in a washing area, giving special attention to her hair. She arranged them handsomely. A belt and coverings of a strange consistency lay in wait. A little experimenting, remembering how the women draped the soft material around them, allowed her to dress attractively, showing off her figure. After another good meal and feeling refreshed, she looked for JaYan to seek answers.

Everything is different from what I am used to. Clean, smooth and well arranged.

She walked towards one of the openings in the partition in the great cavern, which she heard called a hall. With friendly gestures, an Illoreaen indicated she was not allowed to go there.

Soon JaYan arrived. A crowd gathered around, conversing softly.

"Let's hear her story, JaYan said. "Then she'll want to know about us too. Let her speak!"

The voices fell silent, allowing JaYan to continue. "As I told you, we are the Illoreaens. We are related to, but different from the Clans. We have heard your name, Questa of the Clan of the Second Valley, but we do not know how the Giants managed to kidnap you. Please tell us."

"Yes, I will. But please, the Giant's leader is very dangerous and is fanatical. You must be prepared. They killed a Clansman with a single blow. I learned a lot during my captivity and must help you against them."

JaYan smiled and answered, "Don't be concerned, we know the Giants. You are safe here and we can protect you. Now please tell us what happened."

Questa told her story briefly and then she answered many questions and gave more details to satisfy the Illoreaens. They seemed to know all about how she escaped from the Giants, hid, ran through the night, and then collapsed.

Questa's acute hearing, sharpened during her training, overheard whispers, not intended for her ears, "I told you she was beautiful, but did not expect how beautiful. What a transformation. No wonder JaYan looks at her the way he does. I think he is smitten with her beauty!"

JaYan did not hear, "Your fate would have been terrible, had you arrived in the Giants' woodlands," all the others nodded their heads in agreement. "I'm sure the Dynasty did not expect trouble. They never considered the possibility of the Giants abducting a Clan woman.

"I have heard of the Giant who abducted you, they call him something like 'Heropto' in their tongue. Stories about him have reached us before. He is intelligent and has great ambitions. We know he is dangerous. He is aggressive and dominates most of the Giants. They are afraid of him. He has surrounded himself with a gang of the most aggressive Giants. You were intended to be a show-piece, a trophy to strike fear and create adoration in all the Giants."

At the thought, Questa shivered and turned pale. She experienced the offensive odor of the Giants again, the horror she had Sensed during her ordeal.

One of the women turned on JaYan, "How can you be so insensitive?"

Another wiped Questa's brow with a damp cloth and gave her a draught to drink.

JaYan continued, "I am sorry for being so blunt. We started planning and preparing a rescue as soon as we noticed you in the troupe. We understood how difficult rescue would be. Impossible once they reached their woodlands home.

"We had new hope when you escaped. We followed your progress until the wind struck. We saw the wall of dust appearing on the far horizon in the sunrise direction. A Look-Out kept watching and saw the Giants disappear in the dust cloud and how you scrambled into a gully before the dust-cloud reached you. We kept watch from then on. The Giants managed to creep into the same gully in which you hid during the windstorm, but lower down. They stayed there until they noticed the dust you raised yesterday morning."

"You spoke to the Giants before they attacked, didn't you?" Questa asked.

"We have to communicate with the Giants to avoid conflict. A few of us have learned their language. They are Clan-similars, not apes. They live near the great Ice Cliffs far away in the cold, wooded forests, in the darkness direction. There they hunt by ambushing prey. They are much stronger than either the Clans or the Primitives and more intelligent than the latter. They regard Clan women as beautiful. Leaders have occasionally captured Clan women before, trying to enhance their stature. But not recently. The women rarely survived. If they did not die during the regular rapes, they often died during childbirth. Surviving children are usually sterile and seldom live to maturity. We always do our utmost to save abducted Clan women. The Giants are scared of us."

They fell silent while Questa considered his words. *Why would the Giants be afraid of the Illoreaens? They were no different from the Clans, all blond with a touch of red in their hair, lending it a golden sheen, not dark red as those of the Giants, nor black, the Primitives' coloring. She glanced at JaYan; he was attractive with a strong face, not quite square, his eyes widely set and piercing.*

"Although I saw your abilities and the strange devices with which you repelled the Giants' attack, I am still scared." Questa paused.

With a smile, JaYan waited for her to continue.

"I heard you calling the curved saplings, which work like throwing sticks, 'bows' and the small spears they throw, 'flyers.' They are very different from the spears and the throwing sticks we use in the Clans. What are they? And those tubes your members put to their eyes, what do they do? And what is the cloth you wear?"

A few of those surrounding Questa hid their mouths in their hands, suppressing laughs at her unfamiliarity with their devices. Others had a concerned look.

JaYan answered, "There is much about us you don't know, even hidden from the Dynasty. We keep our devices secret and the Orrox encourage and support us in the secrecy. We have used devices we normally would not show, to save your life. I must, therefore, ask you for a pledge to keep secret what you see and hear, and not to reveal this to any of your Clan, not even your Chief, mother, father, or siblings. Do I have your pledge?"

Questa said, "Of course! You saved my life and I give you my word even though I'm opposed to selective secrecy. I'm doing advanced Oracle-Healer training at the Orrox Dynasty. I'm a Healer and sworn to keep confidential whatever I learn when treating Clansmen. Although it is different, I swear to keep your secrets also."

JaYan hesitated, looked at his companions, who now all looked concerned. "So, you are a Healer, and also an Oracle-Healer, whatever that might be." He paused and glanced at the others.

Those surrounding them stared at her with unreadable expressions. A few brought a hand to their cheek while others changed weight from one leg to the other. Questa Sensed a sudden cooling of the emotions emanating from them.

They have turned aggressive. What is going on? What changed? It must have something to do with Oracle-Healers. But what? Questa thought, not showing she noticed the change.

"Well! We'll investigate that later." He paused again, looking down. At last he looked up and continued, "You might as well know. There is a reason for our secrecy. We often search for, experiment and develop remedies or medicines or look for solutions to various problems. We have learned early not to reveal when we are trying something new or strange. We only show results when we have proven utility and effectiveness."

JaYan hesitated. He looked at a companion standing next to him, who nodded after looking at Questa, frowning.

"As you obviously know," JaYan continued, "the Council only allows the inhabitants of the Dynasty Valley to distribute items that will improve the quality of life of all the Clans, without disrupting their lifestyle or well-being. We create all those. The fat burning lamps the Clans use, is an example. They are adapted to the resources available in the valleys. The light emitting quartz you see here, is another of the successful results of experiments to give light within our halls. They are exclusively used here because they require many resources not available in the Clan valleys."

Questa crossed her arms. Her eyes narrowed. *What is this? More secrets kept from us! We always believed the items the Dynasty distributes were developed by other Clans.*

JaYan looked at her and frowned.

He must have noticed something.

Questa uncrossed her arms and relaxed. *I must hide my feelings!*

JaYan looked at his companion again before continuing in a soothing tone, "The Clans have a life, stable since ancient times, since the time of the Inter-Clan Devastation, the time of the Deadly Strife. The Clan culture allowed the Clans to survive countless natural disasters, floods and droughts. It is a proven, sustainable, and beneficial lifestyle. One producing contentment and happiness."

The Illoreaen standing next to JaYan continued, without introducing himself, "Surely, you as an Oracle-Healer must be aware that the Dynasty discreetly distributes those developments they believe are suitable to the Clans, based on their available resources. They usually use the Healers and, I assume, you, the Oracle-Healers. The Council insists on doing it this way."

He paused, looking straight at her, "If our results and failures were widely known, or even our existence, our activities would be compromised and improvements would stop."

JaYan glanced at his companions with a worried look. Questa was sure they were hiding much more than they revealed. Noticing her skepticism, JaYan continued, "You must have heard rumors of great feats with wonderful devices and occurrences. The Council, through their Orrox leader, always dismisses the rumors as myths or flights of fantasy. Yes, we keep other things secret as well. You will see many of these at our Habitat. I must therefore repeat, insist, you must not reveal what you might see, not to anyone. We have your pledge. I assure you there are good reasons for our secrecy."

Questa took a deep breath, "I was not aware of your existence," she paused. "I sometimes get new medicaments or small implements from the Dynasty and sometimes wondered about their origin, but never knew. I have given my pledge of secrecy and I will respect your wishes. You have saved my life and

I owe you that." She shook her head, exasperated. "But I would have kept your secrets, even without owing you my life."

JaYan looked surprised, "You did not know! I should not have revealed so much. I was sure a highly trained Healer—or did you say an Oracle-Healer from the Dynasty—would have known much more. Thank you for your discretion and your pledge to keep our secrets. You will surely learn and finally agree to the wisdom of our selective policies."

She managed to suppress her irritation, *I don't understand what is going on. I must return to the Clan valleys. I must get back to Grandmother and ask her advice. Once I'm back at the Dynasty, they will not deny me the opportunity to return to Grandmother and to continue my training afterwards.*

She looked from JaYan to his companion. JaYan was friendlier, but she could Sense something was bothering him. The other regarded her with scorn.

Questa decided to ignore their reaction.

"I told you the Giants are dangerous but you seem very confident of your ability to handle them. I assume your confidence is based on more secrets. The Clans expect Oracle-Healers to form an opinion and advise on strategies. I cannot do that here. I need knowledge and can perform the function only if you trust me and request help.

"But I am very concerned about the Giants. It would help my peace of mind if you would explain those weapons you used against them, when rescuing me."

JaYan became serious, "All we are prepared to reveal now is that the bows and flyers are examples of self-defense research, using materials available in our valley and area. According to the Council, the Clans hunt well enough without them. However, the Dynasty's specially trained protectors are trained in their use and have access to them. But for defense purposes only. I understand the protectors patrol the valley entrances against Primitive and predator intrusion. The bows are kept hidden and only used in emergencies. They are strictly not used for hunting."

JaYan's speech became more heated as he continued, his tone more intense: "We keep the existence of this weapon secret since its use in the wrong hands can disrupt the society of the Clans.

Can you imagine the danger if the Primitives got hold of bows and flyers and learned to copy and use them?

"Heropto concerns me too. He has now seen our use of bows and flyers and might have figured out how we managed to repel his attack. I too am concerned about the safety of the Clans!"

Questa could see the veins in his neck throbbing with irritation. Questa took care to block her Sensing. To Sense his emotion would be unforgivably rude.

Chapter 14 – Lone Traveler

The earth shook only once during the restless night Anja endured. The shaking made her freeze up in fear, but the shock was light. The thoughts of how dangerous it was to stay in the valley, continued to cycle through her mind.

The smoke of my fires might have attracted Primitives and there is no way I could survive an attack from a larger wolf pack. I have to get out of the valley and find another Clan.

The morning light revealed white frost instead of glistening dew. Despite her bear fur, she remained cold and sat near the fire. An idea slowly formed. There were only two routes out of the valley, through the plains and marshes below or into the mountains above.

Anja remembered how her Clan assembled a strong group before using the lower route. They took along adequate provisions and had the ability to defend themselves against the Primitives. Because the marshes where the Primitives roamed were too dangerous, they had remained in the foothills. She thought of the gullies they crossed, climbing down the steep sides and up the other, through tangled and sometimes thorny shrubs. They moved from one defensible position to the next. Her grandmother stayed nearby, not allowing her to walk on her own, holding her whenever she was scared. She knew the ferocious Primitives were the main danger but their group was strong and vigilant and she could remember no encounter.

Descending to the plains on my own is death.

The high passes were out of the question—fields of snow and ice, as well as glaciers with dangerous crevasses, blocked any possible high route until late in the season of plenty. She had heard avalanches roaring down the mountain during and after the land-shakes.

No, the high mountain passes are impassable. The mountain ledges are the only way to escape the valley. Yet they are dangerous in themselves.

She remembered accompanying her grandmother on a visit to her father's Clan. She visualized the route up towards the mountain and the broad ledge that narrowed as it traversed the high peaks dominating the valleys. The height used to terrify her but she later climbed without fear. That was a dangerous route to follow. She was confident her abilities were up to the challenge. At least there were no Primitives and less danger from predators in the mountains.

I will have to be agile.

Anja stood and walked a few steps. She could walk with only a slight limp. She looked at her arm. The wound was red but not too painful.

That will not hinder me.

She sat down on a boulder and looked to where the nearby spurs leading up to the mountains were just visible through the polluted air. It did not look good. She lowered her head in her hands, trying to recall details of the route and to consider its difficulties.

I'm sure I can find the route leading up to the cliffs. There I'll have to identify the correct ledge to follow. The one giving access to the valleys to the left.

She had often used this route in visits to her father's valley, which lay in the sunset direction. She was not sure of the similar route leading to Clan valleys to the right. Her face crumpled in a frown.

If I miss the connecting ledges I'll be in trouble. They peter out or end in sheer rock faces or vertical drops. I'll have to find the important markers on the route.

She pictured each leg of the route in her mind.

The gloom and dust will hide the faintly trodden paths and indicators. But I'll find them!

Memories flooded back of hunters recounting their adventures. They always gave details of each of the ledges on the routes they used. Groups visiting, attending meetings or communicating with potential life-companions, tended to be even more specific.

Anja planned the trip. She would visit the nearest Clan Habitats first and continue with their help. The less known route and ledges leading to the right, the sunrise direction, passed by the erupting volcano.

Passing by the volcano will be dangerous. I have no choice. I have to use the ledges to the left, leading in the sunset direction. Towards father's Clan Valley.

She selected a digging stick and skins to take along, not enough skins to make a proper shelter, but as many as she could tie around her waist and shoulders. The bear fur was essential, but she discarded and hid the remainder of the skins, pouches and leather straps. She placed a few sharp obsidian shards, medicinal herbs, dried roots, nuts, and edible leaves in different pouches.

It should be enough to live on for a few days, or even twice as long if I keep to a strict ration.

After another restless night, Anja rose early, washed her face and topped up her gourd at the seep. She looked around. There were no familiar smells, no sights to remind her of the valley that had been. Reluctant to leave the remnants of the valley of her birth and life, she took a few deep breaths. It helped her overcome her uncertainty. She was scared and on her own.

I have always been with company when leaving the valley before. But, here goes!

She ascended a spur. Only the faint indications of the path leading out of the valley showed, a route pioneered by different animals moving up and down the valley in search of food. A grey layer of ash still covered the trees, bushes and grass. The ash had combined with frost to form a hard crust, which reduced the dust clouds that originally rose wherever she walked.

#

Anja started at a slow trot, ignoring the many dangers one could encounter in the mountains. Her light tread, softly sweeping her forward in the running style of the Clans, still punctured the crust, compressing the ash to form clear tracks as she went. As her leg muscles warmed, the remaining pain and limp disappeared. The steady rhythm had a hypnotic, soothing effect. She ran on without the overwhelming anxiety she experienced before.

The path led up a ridge where Anja had to find the start of the crossover ledge, leading to the next valley. It was harder to find than she expected. The ridge ended in a narrow knife-edge with the sides falling away sharply on both sides. The top was nearly clear of the yellow dust. She reached the cliff where she clambered over broken and semi-vertical slabs, until she found a familiar ledge.

I'm sure this is it.

Loose rocks and a number of large boulders partly blocked the ledge. Others had gouged out sections as they tumbled from above. She negotiated her way past the boulders, progressing well. The ledge slowly narrowed but she moved easily, even when forced to shuffle along the edge of the vertical precipice with her back against the cliff face. In front of her a heap of rubble, stacked against the cliff at a steep angle, blocked her path.

If I take care, I can cross that.

She crawled over the mixture of soil, ash, and rock. The whole mound moved. It slid until part of the pile gave way and tumbled over the edge. She heard the echoes of rocks hitting and bumping over lower ledges.

She saved herself by flinging herself upwards against the sliding rubble. Her weight stabilized the sliding mass. Carefully, bit by bit, she moved back. The detritus shifted again. She lay still, too afraid to breathe. Maneuvering slowly, she eventually reached the stable part of the ledge, exhausted. Still lying on her stomach, she took a big gulp of air.

She turned over carefully, managed to sit up and slowly moved away from the precipice, letting out her breath with a whistling sound.

"Phew!"

Using her hands she came to rest with her back against the rock face. With a blank look on her face, she registering nothing. A tremor shook the mountain, noisily dislodging rubble. It added material to the blockage causing further slippage and covered her with yellow-brown dust. She returned to reality.

What now? I have to pass the blockage.

In despair, she started moving rocks and scooping soil and ash with her hands. It was futile.

She crouched with her face between her knees, hands behind her neck.

What do I do now? There must be a way.

She crawled to the edge of the ledge. Looking below, the rubble made lower ledges even less of an option. She knew of no other ledge that would allow her to continue.

In the gloom and enveloping dust, she could hardly make out the slopes far below. From previous trips, she remembered seeing the steep slopes, deep gorges and dense thorny growth at the bottom of the cliff.

She was desperately lonely, short of supplies, and tired.

There must be other usable ledges.

She slowly retraced her steps, looking down, searching for a break in the cliff face.

A male chamois on a lower ledge looked down, watching for danger. The deer never looked up and did not see her as she quietly watched him, wondering where his mates were and where they browsed in the unforgiving mountains. His presence was a comfort, an assurance that life still existed after the Catastrophe. After a while, the deer moved on, jumping onto a small projection before disappearing around a corner, taking a route only a chamois could negotiate.

#

Twice she followed a break in the cliff-face, down to lower ledges and shelves, only to find a vertical face or precipice blocking the way. She followed ledges but was always forced to turn back, exhausted from climbing, and struggling over rubble.

Returning from another failed attempt to descend, she started back to her own valley. She passed a gap in the rock above the ledge. In desperation, she climbed up and into the crack, pushing her back to the one side with her feet on the other. Slowly she edged upwards, moving her feet up a tiny distance, one at a time, then pushing back with her hands allowing her back to wriggle up. She did not look down. The precipice was ready to swallow her should she fall. After a long vertical climb, she emerged onto a broad ledge. The ledge ended in a vertical cliff in the sunrise direction but continued in the sunset direction for as far as she could see. It was bounded by vertical rock faces above and below. She decided to follow it.

At nightfall, she slept in a hollow portion of the cliff where the ledge was nearly horizontal. Scared that she might roll over in her sleep and fall off the ledge, she pressed against the cliff. An explosive sound rose her from a fitful slumber. A tremor had dislodged rubble, debris, and a huge boulder. The overhanging cliff projected it all into the air, clearing the ledge except for the boulder, which had hit the edge and shattered. Trembling with fright, she folded the bearskin more tightly around her.

When light allowed, she continued along the ledge. She struggled over rubble and debris until the ledge narrowed and then petered out underneath an overhang. The only option was to retrace her route. Maybe find a way down and reach the original ledge, the one on which she had started out.

She passed two vertical fissures, looked at them and passed on. A third slight break in the cliff below was more prominent, she hesitated and nearly passed by, not wishing to tire herself even more. She looked over the edge and saw a ledge, some way down. The descent was exposed, but easier than she expected. Facing the cliff, jamming her hands and feet in the fissure, she found projections and grips to support herself. She was aware that if she slipped or lost her grip, she would fall and disappear into the gloom below. Fortunately, she could not see the bottom. There her mangled body would end up, should she make a mistake.

She reached the ledge. Blockages made it impossible to go back in the sunrise direction. Towards sunset, in the direction she wanted to go, the ledge had collapsed. The continuation of the fissure opened up to form an exposed crack lower down.

Her supplies were nearly gone and she was tired out.

I have to continue descending.

She clung to protrusions with hands and feet. Slowly she wormed her way down. Exhausted, she entered a trance-like state, thinking only of going down, going down. She never looked up, unable to see the bottom, not knowing where the crack was leading her.

The crack narrowed to a point where it forced her onto the rock-face. She lost her grip, slipped and fell.

<><><>

Chapter 15 – The Dynasty Valley

Despite his impatience to leave, Orrox followed Jupex up the valley, to the cave. *If I don't do this for Jupex, he will be unhappy and our visit a failure. Yet I should not delay unnecessarily. I must arrange aid for Jupex's Clan. At the Dynasty, they would know the extent of the damage caused by the shock waves. They will know how many other Clans suffered and what had happened to the acolytes' respective Clans.*

They stopped in front of the still, mostly functional palisade, and looked around. The palisade protected a large area in front of the cave entrance. The magnificent location overlooked the fertile valley, now in chaos.

Jupex had not been to the Habitat since the land-shaking, "It is hard to believe, but only a short while ago, this was the most beautiful part of the valley."

Orrox nodded sympathetically, "We passed by here on our way down and saw the broken palisade. We stayed clear when we found the site abandoned."

Surrounding cliffs enclosed the valley with the stream meandering nearby. Although hidden in the gloom, Orrox could imagine the views. Downstream the distant plains would have been visible through a gap in the cliffs and upstream the snow-covered peaks that towered above them, would have been visible as they stood guard. He admired Jupex for making the difficult decision to abandon this beautiful site.

Jupex ignored the flattened parts of the palisade, but loosened the leather straps and opened the entrance barrier. Stepping through he said, "We'll repair the damage to the palisade soon. It will not take long."

As they approached the cave, a smell of rotten eggs attacked their nostrils. Holding a soft chamois skin to his nose, Orrox entered the cave. The strong odor became overwhelming.

"This is dangerous. No wonder you had to abandon the site."

Jupex hung back, watching, pinching his lips together.

"We recently noticed that the stench became stronger after a land-shaking. The smell was never as strong as this. The land-shakes must have opened something. We decided to abandon the cave."

Jupex prepared a torch, but before he could light it, Orrox called out, "Stay back! Do not light the torch!"

Orrox came out of the cave, took a few deep breaths and entered again, clamping the skin tightly over his nose and mouth. The cave was high and roomy, big enough for a Clan with many members. At the back, tunnels led into darkness. Orrox moved forward carefully to where the smell was noticeably stronger.

What a pity, he thought. *It is so difficult to find suitable caves. At least the gas might prove to be useful.*

Moving towards the source of the smell, he listened, advancing cautiously, then took a small shiny container out of one of his pouches. He captured some of the gas escaping from a fissure, before restoring it to the pouch.

"I can hear a soft hissing noise," Orrox called as he rushed back to Jupex, "Was the smell always there?"

"Not always. It started some years ago, but was faint. We tasked some of the young ones to wave branches and skins. It helped to dissipate the smell."

"I saw the opening through which the gas escapes and I think I know what it is. Move back, away from the cave mouth, before you light your torch."

Jupex looked at Orrox strangely, not understanding the need. Without saying anything, he lit the torch and handed it to Orrox.

Orrox ran to the cave entrance and threw the torch deep inside, then jumped back.

The torch whirled in the air. Before it reached the ground, a flash of fire lit up the cave with a resounding boom. A blast of hot air rushed out of the entrance.

Orrox looked in carefully. The torch still burned on the ground. Deeper in, at the fissure, another flame burned steadily.

"I thought it might be flammable gas," Orrox said. "The flame will burn away the gas and give light to part of the cave, but it still does not make the cave safe. If the flame should die, the gas would be dangerous and lethal. I think a knowledgeable member of the Dynasty will be able to block or even contain the gas. If they succeed it would make everything safe and give you permanent light and fire as a bonus."

Jupex clasped Orrox's arm, "You believe the cave Habitat might be saved? Thank you!"

"I would not recommend use of the cave while any smell persists, and the gas is not controlled. It is usable as a place of safe storage only. I will ask the Dynasty to send someone with knowledge to visit soon," Orrox said, putting a hand on Jupex's shoulder.

"Let's return with the good news. We all feared we would have to abandon the cave to the cave bears."

It was common knowledge cave bears inhabited good caves, hibernating in the season-of-shortage. Clansmen could only steal a cave from the huge and dangerous herbivores when the bears left the caves to browse during the season-of-plenty. They would erect a pre-built palisade as soon as the bears left, strong enough to withstand the furious attack when they returned. The only alternative was lingering warfare, killing the bears as they entered or left a cave. Such a war usually claimed one or two Clansmen. To make a valley safe, a Clan had to chase the bears from all the caves in the valley and erect palisades to keep them out, a continuous and dangerous task.

They scrambled over the loose material, working their way down the valley towards the Clan's new Habitat.

"It is difficult to protect the Clan without a cave. We will be able to handle smaller predators, even wolves," Jupex said. "But, will your patrols be able to protect us, should a group of cave bears enter our valley or if the Primitives manage to move into the valley?"

"I'm glad you brought it up. The best solution would be if we could somehow contain the gas and allow you to move back," Orrox answered. "But until then you are not safe enough. I will strive to arrange the Dynasty's help and protection immediately upon my return there."

#

The Clan expectantly waited for Jupex and Orrox's return: "Can you fix our cave? Will you report what you have found to the

Council?" "Are we safe without a cave? Should we return despite the smell?"

With the whole Clan assembled, Jupex said, "We are honored to have you and your acolytes with us, Orrox. Our special thanks for your assistance."

"We are pleased to have been able to lend a helping hand. Thank you for receiving us, but now I need to visit the Dynasty Valley. There I can arrange the support you require."

"I understand your urgency. I believe you must follow a route via the marshes and plains, despite the danger of Primitive attacks. The alternatives, through the mountains, are dangerous and the ledges unstable or blocked, probably impassable. Snow still blocks the passes and there is the danger of avalanches,"

Alena agreed, "I hate the idea of you meeting Primitives on the plains or getting caught in the quick-sands of the marshes, but the mountains are even more dangerous," She turned to Jupex. "Only this morning, MaXiox tried to fetch provisions from one of our storage caves above the snow line. He reported that the cold is re-freezing the lower ice fields. The slippery ice, combined with unstable snowfields and loose boulders, made all the paths dangerous. He just managed to reach the cave and you know how good he is in the snow."

"I agree, the bottom route is the only possibility. But I think we should be safe," Orrox said.

Jupex frowned. "But I don't think the five of you are strong enough to travel alone across the plains."

"The Primitives have been peaceful. When did you last need the Dynasty patrols? It's been a long time since they had to confront the Primitives."

"Still, you and your acolytes are only five. I think I will accompany you with a few of my strongest companions."

"You don't have to worry. The Primitives must have their own problems coping with the Catastrophe. Even though I think we should be able to avoid them, we would welcome your company."

Jupex turned to his life-companion, "Alena, you must organize the Clan, while we're away. Everyone must collect and store as much provisions as possible. Orrox believes the cold and dark will last long. We'll hunt on the way for additional meat. The women are better at looking after the remaining injured, therefore the men who remain will have to help with collecting herbs, as well as hunting."

"Yes, I'm afraid it might become difficult to find food," Orrox said.

#

Few of the Clan had ever seen the Dynasty valley, which lay beyond all the Clan Valleys, far in the sunrise direction. A visit was an exciting idea, widely discussed. They were curious and excited.

"Only a small group of expert hunters can go. They must be strong, experienced and fully recovered from any injuries," Jupex warned.

A group of strong male Clansmen assembled, offering to accompany Orrox, Jupex and the acolytes. Discussions continued until late at night before Jupex settled the matter by selecting four of the strongest and most able. The company would consist of Jupex, Orrox and his acolytes as well as MaXiox, JuroNox, CroBal and StuDol.

Early the next morning, when gloom replaced the dark of night, they set off down the valley. Each carried enough provisions to last the journey. They armed themselves with heavy knobbed clubs as well as sleek spears, made from strong saplings.

Orrox admired the workmanship of the Chief's spear; it was well crafted and tipped with a tear-shaped flint point of great value.

"We dip the spear points in a mixture made from the crushed bodies of poisonous beetles, diluted with animal blood and made sticky and hard with the poisonous sap of the Kamasi tree. The mixture is a Clan tradition and is much more potent than anything available from the Dynasty," Jupex said, looking sideways at Orrox.

"And our spear points are better than those we have seen anywhere else," MaXiox declared confidently, while his companions nodded their agreement.

Orrox kept his doubts to himself but spoke to the acolytes when they were alone. "We know better spear points and poisons are available at the Dynasty. But please do not contradict them. Clans should be self-sufficient and innovative, whenever possible.

Particularly if their methods are good enough to ensure a good quality of life and no taboo is broken. It is even better if the innovation creates a new, beneficial tradition."

He paused, "You will find tools in which users believe, work much better than ones they don't trust, even if the latter is superior. What is more, they will seldom trust an alternative suggested by an outsider. Never introduce a new or different tool or method to a Clan, without first convincing a few leaders to adopt it. If they like it, the entire Clan will adopt the idea. Otherwise, let it be."

#

Their winding route down the valley following a stream zigzagged around boulders blocking the path. Eventually, they emerged onto the plains, where the stream changed into a marshland with wide meandering channels.

"We need to make sure the Primitives do not detect our presence," Jupex said. "They hate intruders into what they regard as their territories. We'll have to find a safe area to sleep, where they can't surprise us."

The sky remained murky. Without the mountains to serve as a guide or reference, it was difficult to find the way in the gloom. Nevertheless, Orrox always found the best route.

As light faded the group selected a set of large boulders, made a small fire in a protected nook and surrounded the area with broken branches for early warning and protection. The night was black and dark with no starlight or moonlight penetrating the dirty sky.

Orrox and Jupex woke up regularly to arrange, change or relieve the two on guard. They both possessed an uncanny ability to estimate the passing of time, without reference to stars or moon.

Orrox did not sleep well; he worried about the Dynasty, the Clans and the danger of the Primitives, *How much damage did the Catastrophe cause?*

All was silent, without even the normal night sounds when MaXiox jumped up with a loud yell, "What was that?"

Orrox and Jupex immediately reacted and stood ready, their backs to the group, their spears ready. The acolytes joined, standing shoulder to shoulder. The four Clansmen saw what they did and joined in. Without breaking the circle, they slowly retreated towards the boulders. Soon they stood with their backs against the boulders, spears pointing out. Only MaXiox remained where he was.

"What happened?" Jupex asked.

MaXiox admitted, "Something ran over my face. It was followed by a hard blow and searing pain. Look, blood!"

"Yes, there is a scratch on your cheek," Orrox said. He threw some kindling on the fire and looked around. "See. An owl with a mouse in his claws. Up there! I'm sure the mouse ran over your face and then the owl followed, chasing the mouse."

A flush crept across MaXiox's face. The group teased him mercilessly, "You scare easily!"

Orrox allowed them to continue for a moment before interrupting, "You responded well. Remember how we formed a protective circle. Do not let false alarms affect your quick reactions."

#

After a long night, the darkness changed into the dull greyness of morning.

Orrox said, "We'll have to stay near the foothills to avoid the marshes. Each of the Primitive bands regards a different area of the plains and marshes as their domain. Once they see our tracks they might become aggressive."

None knew how Orrox orientated himself. He occasionally made the group wait in a protected spot while he and the Chief went on to explore. They disappeared silently. While they were away, the Clansmen looked around nervously. Every rustling sound caused them to tighten their grip on their spears and clubs. The acolytes were more relaxed, trusting in Orrox's ability to warn them of any looming danger. Suddenly Jupex and Orrox were with them again. They had returned so quietly that no one heard their approach.

"We saw something strange," Jupex informed the group. "The areas in and near the marshes have become very treacherous with bogs everywhere. Trees are down and partly swallowed, as if the ground had turned into liquid and then solidified again. We found a few animals ensnared in solid ground, as if the ground partly engulfed them." They displayed an antelope carcass without legs. "This antelope died trapped in the ground and the cold has preserved the meat. We had to cut off its legs to extract it. The legs were trapped in congealed mud as hard as rock."

"I'm always sorry for any animal trapped in a snare. It must have died a horrible death," Camla said.

"At least when we put out snares, a hunter soon visits them to put a trapped animal out of its misery," Lonna said. "But did you see any sign of the Primitives? Are we safe?"

"No, we did not any. If we knew where they were, we would be able to choose a safer route. They usually hunt together in small groups. I wonder what happened to them. I'm sure they will not trouble us—we're a large group and they have too many problems of their own. Even so, I don't think it is safe to enter deeper into the marshes. Many new bogs have destroyed the routes the Primitives use. We followed a specific series of their route markers with well-trodden signs of regular use. They led us into a nearly invisible new bog. The route is dangerous. We'll have to be very careful," Orrox said.

Jupex's four hunters skinned the antelope and divided the meat into portions for each to carry.

Orrox led them unfailingly from hideout to hideout, always staying near the foothills. Despite his concern for the fate of the Clans in the valleys, below which they passed, he hurried on, resisting the temptation to see how those Clans had fared.

#

On the fourth day, the group approached the valley of the Dynasty. A steep path wove into a deep gorge. The noise of rushing water got louder as they descended. Orrox kept looking upwards into the gloom. As they approached the stream, he shouted. The sound of the stream drowned his voice. He called out again. There was no answer.

"The Look-Outs of the portal should have confronted us. Something is wrong," he said, stopping at the stream's edge.

Jupex looked questioningly at Orrox, who explained, "There are only two approaches to the Dynasty Valley: this one through the gorge, which we call the portal, and the other, at the head of the valley, through the mountains and skirting the volcano. The gorge is well guarded against Primitive intrusion. The Look-Outs always signal to let the Dynasty Habitat know when visitors arrive."

Orrox still peered into the gloom, inspecting the gorge. Huge boulders partially blocked the stream. The tops of the cliffs high above were nearly invisible. Orrox looked around, called out again and scrambled onto a large bluff. He looked upstream to where the stream forced its way through a narrow cleft in the rock face.

"There is a narrow ledge on the other side of the stream. It leads up into the gorge. The sentinels stay on a higher ledge, which is hard to see from here. Look there! I can just make it out. But, where are the guards? The shelter on the ledge is also missing." He paused, "Look, the flood marks! There must have been a huge deluge. Even the grass and ferns have been flattened. The water rose higher than the Look-Out ledge! Surely, they must have escaped in time."

"Will we be able to enter the gorge and find your relations?" Jupex asked, looking at the mass of water behind the boulders blocking the stream. The water stretched from cliff face to cliff face, filling the gorge.

Orrox inspected the watercourse, opaque with ash and swirling, unsettled mud. "I think I can wade along the cliff face if the ledge, which used to be above water level, is still there. It could not have collapsed. It's of the same hard rock as the cliff itself."

Without hesitating, he clambered over the boulders and carefully dropped down into the flood. The water rose to his waist before he found secure footing.

"The ledge is here but very slippery, covered in mud!" he said as he shuffled forward, the water churned brown behind him.

"Wait here until I return," he called over his shoulder. He cautiously moved forward, sometimes slipping, but always recovering his balance. He soon disappeared around a corner.

When he reappeared he said, "It is slippery but manageable. Follow me, but be careful!"

The rest followed and soon emerged from the pool and stood on a muddy strip below the cliff. Upstream the gorge widened.

The acolytes had previously seen the entrance to the Dynasty valley, but for the Clansmen, the first sight of the valley was an impressive surprise. Where it widened, the cliffs on both sides retreated and rose higher and higher, encircling a huge fertile plain with the stream meandering down the center. Nearly dry rivulets formed tiny waterfalls, the only remnants of the torrents that used to fall down the cliffs to form pools, before disappearing into the fields of fern.

Orrox sat down on a boulder at the side of the stream. This view used to be his favorite. He remembered the first time he saw it as a small boy, accompanying his father as they entered the gorge.

His father had sat looking up the valley, with the young Orrox leaning against him.

"The most beautiful view in all of the mountains," his father said and Orrox still agreed, remembering the view as it was, before the Catastrophe. The high cliffs rising to the incredibly blue sky while the green valley stretched away towards the faraway line of yellow overhanging cliffs, into which his forebears had carved the Habitat. The palisade used to be just visible if one strained one's eyes. From there a nearly vertical slope rose up to the mountain peaks. The flat top of the snow-covered volcano showed white at the back. In summer, the snow reached the line of the ridges containing the storage caves. In winter, the snow line was much lower, but well above the Habitat, basking on the sunward slope.

The remembered view was not visible. He only saw boulders scattered over the valley floor and other marks of the destruction left by the Catastrophe. The murky sky obscured not only the mountains but also the far end of the valley.

Jupex also remembered the beauty of the view. He had seen it before and waited in silence until Orrox came out of his reverie and started up the valley.

Boulders, branches and even blown-over trees, obstructed their route up the valley.

Orrox sped ahead and the others struggled to keep up.

"This is not good. Look at the mud, it covers the entire floor of the valley. See how high the marks of flotsam and debris are! There are always Clansmen from many Clans learning skills here, but I see none. I hope they are safe!"

They passed a level area, where only a few stalks of grass remained, the rest flattened by the mud. The surviving stalks held large seeds.

MaXiox collected seeds by sliding his partly closed fists along the stalks as they walked, wiping away a covering of dirt. "I've never seen seeds this large anywhere," he said.

StuDol, JuroNox, and CroBal followed suit.

"They taste better than those we can find in our valley," one of them said.

Orrox noticed them collecting, "Yes, they are edible and taste good, even if not cooked. But we have no time. We can try to collect some later."

Here was something new and Jupex needed time to explore the implications, *On my previous visits, I remained on a path farther from the stream and these grasses. My escort probably kept me away on purpose!*

The Clansmen looked at Jupex in surprise, concern registered on their faces but the Chief, whose face briefly showed a similar expression, did not react, not even with a glance.

A smell of sulfur became strong, but there was also a smell of smoke. They clambered over obstacles as they followed the path near the stream. The valley widened to form a large, clearly fertile, meadow.

Rounding a corner, they all gasped at the view before them. Charred skeletons of tall trees, fringing the cliffs on both sides, were all that remained. Blackened stalks indicated where grass previously covered large patches of ground near the stream. The mountainside glowed a dull red. Columns of smoke rose from the steep slope.

As the plain sloped upwards toward the cliff, Orrox hurried forward. When they came nearer, he started to run towards where a mountain of rubble blocked and partly covered the loess and chalk cliff at the head of the valley. Patches of dirty snow mingled with the detritus.

The group could just discern a drenched slope with water oozing onto the heap, making its way down many separate rivulets.

It formed a muddy stream where the mass of mud and rubble petered out. Steam rose from the water, further obscuring sight.

Orrox clawed his way into and up the debris. He did not get far before he sank into the muck. Jupex intervened and gestured to his followers; they extracted Orrox from the mud and allowed him to collapse. Through sobs he said, "There was a waterfall near the entrance to our Habitat. Look! Half the mountain has collapsed into the valley! The Habitat is gone!"

Looking up they could just make out the scars where a huge expanse had broken loose from the mountain's side and poured snow and mud over the cliff's edge. Black ridges ran down the slope like so many evil fingers. Their cracked surfaces glowed bright red. Wisps of steam rose wherever the lava touched moisture. Clumps of red-hot lava were still falling over the cliff from the end of a shiny-black lava flow.

"The volcano erupted and melted the snow," Jupex muttered softly, but they all heard.

The splash of the stream was the only sound breaking the silence.

Orrox sat staring at the muddy stream. Dry sobs escaped from his shaking body.

The Chief and his Clansmen stared at him.

Orrox said, "This heap of snow and rubble is where the Habitat of the Dynasty was. There is nothing left! Many must have died!"

The acolytes went to sit next to Orrox. After a while, the acolytes returned to the group, leaving Orrox to sit alone, after he accepted the calming emotions they emanated.

Orrox sat with his head slumped to his chest, his hands on his head. Grief overwhelmed him, The Dynasty will not be able to help the Clans. The Dynasty does not exist anymore. What now?

"We should first start searching for survivors and then create a shelter," Jupex stated. He faced the acolytes. "Each of you start searching in different directions. You know the area better than any of us do. One of my Clansmen will join you. It's better to search in pairs." Turning to his Clansmen he continued, "Many may have escaped. My daughter Questa was in training here. We need to find the place where the mentors and trainees stayed. We must find her."

The search started in four directions with the smell of decay and the pungent stench of rot, strong in their nostrils. They found no life.

But Jupex would not give up hope of finding his daughter.

Chapter 16 – The Valley of Perpetual Shade

Questa heard a murmured conversation between some Illoreaens, "Look how easily we killed the Giants with our bows and flyers."

"They don't even know how early our Look-Outs saw them approaching."

"They cannot ever overcome any of our methods of protection."

"The Giants are too dumb. They will never understand all our safety devices."

Fear gripped Questa, *The Giants are not stupid. I Sensed them during the whole time of my captivity. The Illoreaens ignore the Giants' strength and brutality. They are dangerous. JaYan has confirmed their intelligence. Surely, they will be back using new strategies.*

She told JaYan of her concern, "Their leader is very intelligent. I fear him. Are you sure we are safe? How can I return to the Clan valleys? Can we avoid the Giants when I leave?"

JaYan introduced his friend as MaGan. They were both annoyed and renounced their companions. "Don't underestimate our adversaries. They are not stupid. They are dangerous, and now very angry! Heropto has lost face and will not accept defeat."

JaYan's speech betrayed serious concern. Questa could see he was worried and she wanted to know more. "What if the Giants attack? Can the Dynasty help? Will their fighters have bows and flyers? How do the tubes help?"

"Yes, the bow and flyers are ready for the Dynasty's fighters to use. We can withstand any attack until help arrives. We have methods to signal the Dynasty if necessary. They will come and you can accompany them when they leave."

He hesitated, looked at one of two Illoreaens whom, from many small indications, Questa recognized as senior to the others. She noticed the slight nod, which allowed JaYan to continue. "The vision tubes allow us to see details of things far away. They are another thing we created. We do not share details about them, because we can only construct a few. Not enough to distribute to the Clans. The Dynasty will not allow selective Clans access to our devices. They will not distribute items hinting of our knowledge and existence. Knowledge of better weapons, including the bows and flyers, is more critical and kept very secret."

It was MaGan's turn, "Yes, the Clans only need weapons for the hunt. The Dynasty's patrols protect them. They do well enough with what they have. To further satisfy your curiosity and to reassure you as to our ability to protect you, I will tell you more about the bows. They were originally made of the wood of specific trees and originally called 'tensioned saplings.' We used to pull the two ends of a thin, straight branch or young tree trunk together with a string making a 'bow.' Instead of such thick saplings, we now use a combination of antlers, horn and special wood to make the bows stiff, though flexible. For the strings, we originally used plaited sinews and tendons of specific animals, but we have now developed better strings. One of the Illoreaen families transfers the knowledge of how to make the bows from generation to generation.

Questa could see MaGan's pride in the weapon.

MaGan continued, "We teach the youths the safe and accurate use of the bows. Bows are not throwers but launchers. A flyer launched by a bow can be lethal at longer range than a throwing spear, even one thrown with the help of a spear launcher. It can even penetrate the hide of an auroch."

"May I inspect them?" Questa asked.

MaGan was hesitant. He looked at the others for a moment and decided: "You have seen many used, so you might as well look at them more closely."

One of the onlookers disappeared and soon reappeared, handing Questa a bow with several flyers in a round quiver, a sheath made from bark.

The sheath was different, more primitive than those she saw hidden under the Illoreaens' mantles and revealed during the attack. She was sure the bow she saw JaYan use during the attack was similar but more sophisticated than the one handed to her. She decided to say nothing, *I am not going to make my ability to notice details obvious. Otherwise, they will hide even more secrets. I need to know much more. I must evaluate their abilities and weaknesses. In the future, I might have to advise them on how to counter an attack.*

The flyers were similar to a throwing spear, but thinner and shorter, the length of an outstretched arm. A flint shard, the size of a thumb, created a sharp point at the one end. Feathers were attached to the sapling at the other end. Questa pulled on the string of the bow and found it stiff, hard to move.

"Only experienced and practiced users can pull the string far enough for the bow to be effective," JaYan said.

An Illoreaén took the bow and one of the flyers, held the sinew in two fingers of his right hand and placed a flyer's end on the sinew. Using great force, he pushed the bow away from his body with his left arm, until the bow nearly doubled over. With a *twang*, the sinew released to propel the flyer so fast, Questa could not follow its path but only heard the sound as it struck a wooden pole at the far end of the hall.

She could not refrain from calling out, "Wow! That is incredible!"

The onlookers laughed, pleased.

MaGan straightened his back. With a satisfied look he said, "With every generation, we improve our methods and abilities. We often receive requests to supply special aids for advanced Healers to fulfill their function. They are in the form of powders, potions, draughts, and materials."

He might be boasting. Is he trying to impress me? Questa wondered.

"We also distribute tools, the use of which requires special training that only selected Healers may use." MaGan paused, "You said you are training at the Dynasty. We know of the secret hierarchy of Healers with more secrets revealed as they rise in knowledge and ability. You called them Oracle-Healers, I think. And you are training to become one?"

He must be wrong! How could he know these things if I don't? Questa believed his words but wondered, *Who decides which developments would benefit the Clans and who have access to secrets?*

She fingered the bow and held her head down, hiding her shock, saying nothing, *The less I know about anything controversial, the easier it will be to keep my pledge of secrecy. A hierarchy! Again, a new and upsetting secret. I must discuss this with Grandmother. Does she know?*

She kept on looking down at the bow, in deep thought, aware of the implements and devices Oracle-Healers used.

I have often used potions and powders, which helped me in healing different maladies and injuries as well as tools to remove splinters or other objects from wounds or to stabilize a broken limb. I also know that, as my ability and training progressed under Usux's mentorship, I will be taught how to use more of these aids... The mixtures I sometimes drink, help me to focus and create the right atmosphere to analyze trends and recommend actions. What the Clans call divination. I always assumed all these came from the Dynasty. I never guessed the true source.

She looked up, noticing a few of the senior Illoreaens looking uncomfortable, their eyes on JaYan. He extended a hand, waiting for her to return the bow.

Possibly members of an Illoreaen Council, she thought. *He has probably revealed too much. Secrets surround me! I hate secrets.*

Despite her long silence, JaYan did not seem to have noticed her shock and continued, "We develop and give these special devices to the Dynasty in exchange for special soils and rocks gathered by the Clans. They also give protection and supply us with foodstuffs from their Habitat and we advise them on how to improve the foodstuffs they grow. We regard ourselves and the Dynasty as working in close interdependence. You'll now have to excuse me. I have matters to attend to."

Questa could not think of what could be so urgent. *At the Clan, there was always time but here there was an atmosphere of purpose, a slight discomfort in her presence. How can the Dynasty and the Illoreaens work so closely together? They are physically so far apart; the whole mountain range lies between them.*

To use her Sensing ability to try to solve the mystery, would be impolite to her hosts and she refrained.

#

Questa's curiosity spiked. She walked around inspecting the drapes and screens and the smooth planks and walls. She noticed more than the Illoreaens wanted to reveal. They could not prevent it. At least she had promised to keep everything she saw secret.

In the very few areas of the cave where she was allowed, she inspected the unknown materials of which the walls, tables and benches were made. It was impossible to guess where they came from. She could hear activity inside many areas and was curious and a little irritated. Although food and drink were always available in the central hall, she was denied entrance to the area where they prepared the food. She liked to try new combinations with the plants, herbs, and roots she collected and preparing them to make tasty food. She could not understand why the Illoreaens kept her from helping. *How can the cooking area contain secrets I may not discover?*

The only distraction was the game of Clan-life as played by many. JaYan told her how his father developed the game as a present on his half-doucia birth celebration.

He and MaGan remained the ultimate master players in this game, which simulated the lifestyle of the Clans, so different from that of the Illoreaens.

"The children all love the game. We grown-ups play at a much deeper level. It helps us understand how the Clans live. We can then focus our efforts to find items or methods useful to the Clans," JaYan said.

Questa soon became an expert too. She knew the reality of gathering herbs and avoiding dangers in the valleys and she was surprised at how realistic the game depicted Clan life.

#

JaYan came to her when the gloom deepened into darkness, "You will have to stay with us for a while; we expect courier-messengers from the Dynasty soon. They will bring fresh food and the supplies of meat we store in the ice caves. You can return with them. We have ways of sending messages. We have tried to inform them you are safe but have not received a reply. They will be glad to see you."

"I don't have any choice, I'll just have to wait," she said and went outside, hoping for sunlight, her shoulders slumped. She stood within the area enclosed by the palisade. The gloom and suppressed hostility of many Illoreaens, had a depressing effect.

What can possibly have antagonized them so?

A flyer came hurtling past her and lodged into the palisade wall at an angle. It had come from one of the inspection holes. She spun around, but there was nobody at any of the Look-Out points and the guard on duty had clearly noticed nothing.

She was not surprised. The Illoreaen on duty visited each guard point and hall only once or twice during his patrol.

There were two choices: hide behind the palisade wall, on the outside, where she was exposed to dangers hiding in the nearby woods, or cringe against the cliff near the entrance, where she was not visible from any of the Look-Out points. She chose the latter and rushed towards the cliff. She stood with her back against the cold rock wall, arms spread out to be nearly invisible from above. Everything was silent. Only the slight creaking of the breeze blowing in the woods reached her ears. She remained in place, wondering what to do.

Suddenly, with loud shrieks, several children rushed out of the Habitat entrance, yelling, "Torturer! Torturer!"

They ran to the palisade and grabbed the flyer and surrounded her, danced around, still screaming abuse. Then they disappeared as quickly as they had come.

In shock, she stood frozen. After a while, she entered the Habitat and retired to her sleeping cubicle. She had no idea what had happened and why the children tried to scare her.

Why did no one respond? She wondered. Then realized, *The cave walls are too thick to transmit sound. No one heard anything.*

She did not sleep well and stayed in her cubicle until hunger drove her to look for food. She looked around carefully when she reached the hall, nobody looked unfriendly. Their body language did not reflect the expected enmity. She did not try to Sense where the aggression came from, but remained on guard.

Questa felt increasingly uncomfortable. Her eyes had lost their luster. She analyzed her feelings.

I miss the openness of Clan-life. The limited number of Clansmen ensures that all members know one another well. No Secrets. I don't like the huge numbers here. It was the same at the Dynasty. They know nothing of one another! I'm a stranger.

She knew she overstated the case in her mind and could not help ridiculing herself.

I'm angry. Why? She examined her thoughts for a moment, *I detest the Illoreaens' assumption of Clan inferiority, their belief that the Clans cannot be trusted with Illoreaen know-how. The Illoreaens' excuse of why they do not share, does not convince me.*

The irritation she had felt when Usux, her mentor back at the Dynasty, told her of the secrets she had to keep from the Clans as an Oracle-Healer, grew. She blamed JaYan, even though she knew he was not solely responsible. It felt like a lifetime since she had left Usux.

Since then, she had suffered days of terror and weirdness.

#

JaYan noticed Questa's silence and approached MaGan, "We will have to find her something interesting to do."

"Yes, I noticed how she wanders from place to place. We can ask her to help mix and package herbs and infusions. As a Healer, it should be her expertise. I believe she would find it interesting and we might learn from her. The Clans know a lot about the properties of different plants and herbs. Of that, there is no knowledge we need to keep secret."

"SkepTan will never agree with you. The biologists don't like to share. He believes his group knows everything there is to know about plants. And, of course, of animals as well."

As the two approached Questa, JaYan said, "We supply the Dynasty with many medicinal powders and potions. Will you help us select and package them?"

At last, I can use my expertise, she thought. *Maybe I can teach them something while I wait for the Dynasty to fetch me.*

"I'd like that," she said after a moment's thought.

Questa was escorted to an adjoining hall where different herbs and solutions were collected on flat surfaces. She recognized many, but others were unknown to her and reminded her of her sister, *Anja might recognize many more. She collects pouches full of different herbs and receives many more from grandmother. My own hoard and knowledge are so much more limited.*

Markings on flat surfaces called racks were associated with each. Questa learned the meaning of most of the pictorial representation or the series of symbols by concentrating hard and asking questions. Each mixture was clearly identified with its recommended usage. The Illoreaens stored mixtures in correctly marked pouches or gourds and discussed cases where the drug was exceptionally effective. She found them to be very skilled.

After a while, the work slowed and her workmates seemed at a loss on how to proceed. One of them intercepted JaYan as he passed. They both looked at Questa as they conversed quietly. JaYan called MaGan and they left together.

JaYan returned after a while, "There is another secret you must not divulge. We store our mixtures in special containers. They are very different from the pouches and gourds you know. Those you have been helping with are being prepared for the Dynasty to take along when they come. The rest will go into our own long-term storage; we store them in Transparent formed into containers, as you will now see."

From an adjacent area, her co-workers brought forth a few containers with round bodies, each with a long neck ending in a round lip and a stopper of similar material. The objects looked like obsidian, but were not dark. They were light and she could see the inside clearly. They glistened in various colors.

"What are these made of?" she asked.

"We call the material, 'Transparent'."

A perfect description, she admitted to herself.

The novelty triggered Questa's interest. JaYan watched with satisfaction.

"These are the most beautiful vessels I have ever seen. They look a bit like obsidian, don't they?" Questa asked, her eyes bright.

"They are similar to obsidian, which is sand and rock molten by the heat of volcanoes. We heat a special sand mixture until it is pliable, which allows us to make these and many other things, including the essential parts of the vision tubes. These containers are unique and the mixtures we store in them will not go bad. Using them is a much better way to store things. Much better than using pouches and gourds."

Questa picked up one vessel after the other, admiring the beauty and properties of each. "They are heavy. I'm sure they are much more difficult to make than just heating sand."

Questa was quick in understanding and perception.

JaYan quickly glanced at her. "You are right," he said but did not explain further. An Illoreaen overhearing them looked worried and glanced at JaYan.

She later overheard him saying, "She is too quick in understanding and perception."

Questa frowned in frustration, *The Illoreaens' excuse of why they do not share the use of the beautiful vessels made of Transparent, or bows, or vision tubes, is not good enough.*

#

MaGan observed Questa's knowledge and ability when working with the herbs, mixtures, and potions. He was ultimately in charge and allowed her to continue on her own, allowing her co-workers to pursue their own interests.

He saw how she referred to a set of runes and numbers displayed on a flat surface on the wall, while she mixed and filled the different vessels with different powders and fluids. The symbols indicating the content which she had to use to mark each stopper, if not already marked. When she occasionally called on MaGan for help, because she did not understand or know the specific remedy, he was pleased to share the information. Often she knew more than he did and he learned from her. He soon found she had already learned all the symbols and knew in which vessel each concoction belonged. He learned to trust her.

While filling Transparents, she ran out of vessels of a specific size and form and sent a passing Illoreaen to tell MaGan what she needed. She had seen the others disappear into a specific corridor to collect vessels before. When MaGan did not appear, she went to fetch them herself, without thinking. She found a chamber filled with containers of many sizes and shapes.

Relaxed while selecting the vessels she needed, she had no reason to block her Sensing. Walking back carrying the required vessels, she passed an opening and suddenly, overwhelmingly she Sensed emergent life—life in the earliest stages of development; life at its most vulnerable. Developing human life without mothers.

Strange! In a panic she reacted, *Life needs help!*

Assisting embryonic life and ensuring its healthy development was her duty, calling, and expertise.

She rushed into an adjacent chamber, passing through some hangings. She Sensed multiple lifes, but no couches, no females.

Only MaGan was present. He wore coverings of white cloth. Different pieces covered his face, hair, hands, and feet. Behind sheets made of the same transparent material as the vessels she worked with, she saw small open containers. The multiple lifes that she Sensed were in these receptacles.

"What are you doing here? Get out!" MaGan yelled, pushing her out of the Chamber, "You will contaminate the chamber. This is not for you! Go back!"

Questa ran out of the chamber in total bewilderment. She was pale and her eyes wide. The Illoreaens in the chamber of herbs ran away when they saw her storming in. JaYan and MaGan soon arrived. She sat with her head in her hands, gasping for breath.

She looked up as they entered, "What was that? I can help. I am a healer. Something is dreadfully wrong."

MaGan's face was flushed, "You trespassed in a totally restricted area! Forget whatever you saw. We must limit your movements. You may not enter any area beyond the central hall. Promise you will abide by this decision. You will not be allowed to help with herbs or food anymore."

She tried to explain and ask questions but they silenced her, MaGan was furious and JaYan looked sad but determined. Now there was nothing to do except to wait for the group from the Dynasty to arrive and take her away.

If only they come soon, she thought as tears flowed.

#

Questa spent more and more time outside the Habitat, not caring about danger or whether she would be accosted again. She wandered up and down the Valley of Perpetual Shade.

Groups of young Illoreaens worked in the valley, in the mining pits or otherwise performed a variety of tasks. She estimated their age to be about a doucia-and-a-half (18) and was surprised at how hard they worked. Sometimes, when they practiced with bow and flyers, they asked her to keep away, but otherwise they were friendly. At other times, she saw them running up steep slopes or carrying provisions from the ice caves.

She assumed they were doing something similar to the period of training and service, which was required of all young Clan-members. Explaining the duties of the youths in the Clans to a supervisor, she asked whether they used the same system.

"Yes," he explained. "They are the young inductees doing their Illoreaen service lasting a quarter doucia. I don't know about the arrangements in your Clans, but here we all go through this service period before we settle down as mature Illoreaens."

Again, a tradition similar but still different to the one she knew.

Questa could feel the tension wherever she went. She knew the Illoreaens did not trust her—she did not belong. Her being an Oracle-Healer in training influenced even the children to regard her as evil. Her own irritation with the lack of trust and the secrecy surrounding her increased and she irrationally continued blaming JaYan. Her training made it possible to hide her feelings and she was convinced none of the Illoreaens knew of her anger until she could not contain it any longer.

"JaYan! You have luxuries and comfort but keep the Clans ignorant. I cannot forget that you deny the Clans the luxuries you take for granted."

"Yes, we live a comfortable life, but so do you in the Clans. Luxurious is too strong a word. Through the generations we have managed to avoid the trap of either the Clans or the Illoreaens competing for what you called luxuries. Certain items, like light cubes, heating and special cloths make our knowledge search easier. According to your Dynasty Council, these items are not strictly necessary for the Clans in their pursuits and could disrupt your meaningful lifestyle. A wise one of old said, 'A meaningless life is a terrible ordeal, no matter how comfortable it is.' ..."

"I don't accept that. However, I have pledged my silence. I want to return to the Clans. You said the Dynasty is sending a group with supplies. When will they come? When will I be able to leave? I want to leave now!"

<><><>

Chapter 17 – Losses

A heap of detritus was all that remained of the Dynasty Habitat. A sickening smell permeated the area. Even though the search parties held soft skins and bundles of flax in front of their noses, the stench overwhelmed them.

As the gloom deepened into night, the search parties returned. Jupex had already moved some of the rubble to create an open area away from the cliffs, where he built a rudimentary shelter. They assembled around a fire looking downcast.

MaXiox reported first, "I searched with Ammox. He doesn't know where the Dynasty mentors train the Oracle-Healers. We have no way of knowing where Questa was when the Catastrophe struck. We searched around the heap of snow-and-mud. It is heavy going! At the stream, it is soggy. Elsewhere the mud has dried to a hard consistency. And farther on there are ridges of still hot lava. We don't even know where the Habitat entrance was. Branches, ferns, grass, and even whole trees are mixed together with the lava. It is impossible to move or dig effectively. The mudslide blocks the stream in many places, to form pools of mud. We tried to climb up but had to abandon the effort. Ammox sank through up to his armpits. You can see how the branches in the slush have scratched him."

The other search teams gave similar reports.

Ammox and Bronnox compared what they saw and shared their thoughts, "The water flowing down the mountain is hot, nearly boiling. The shock waves must have triggered a huge eruption and melted the snowfields, which turned into flash floods and drowned the valley.

The other search teams gave similar reports.

Too many days had passed since the Catastrophe for any hope to remain that anyone inside the Habitat survived.

Orrox sat alone on a boulder beyond the stream, staring up towards the hidden peaks. The acolytes joined him for a while, without speaking, and then returned to the others.

At Jupex's questioning glance, Camla explained: "We were able to use our empathetic emanation as a group to soothe him but now he wants to be alone."

Jupex quickly suppressed a frown. Their explanation showed Sensitive powers and easy use greater than he ever imagined. Meanwhile, his concern for Questa grew but he convinced himself that she was safe. That she was elsewhere when the Catastrophe struck.

Orrox remained alone during the long night. The lone vigil allowed him to regain control of his feelings. In the morning, he took initiative again, "I believe the flood and lava killed everyone inside the Habitat and palisade very quickly. I trust they did not suffer. We must find other survivors. There must have been many in the valley lower down."

After a light meal, the companions climbed up an opposite rise to get a better perspective of the volcano and the valley. Between the lava-flows, the mountain slope was clear of snow but soggy. Wisps of steam rose from hot spots. There was no sign of life or any survivors.

Orrox, observing the mud, the snow slides and the cliffs, pointed out the main features, "The main Habitat was there, below where the yellowish portion of the cliff is still visible. There is a deep over-hang in the softer rock, extending from there to there. A massive stone wall, built just outside the edge of the overhanging cliff, further protected the main Habitat. To enter one had to ascend from below."

Jupex looked more carefully at the heap of rubble. He could now see a depression where the wall had trapped the water and mudslides, directing it all into the Habitat. A flash flood must have filled the whole Habitat with water and slush. "Survivors would surely also have rescued anyone trapped inside after the mudslide."

Orrox agreed, "I'm sure they are all safe somewhere. We must just find clues of their whereabouts."

The search broadened to encompass the entire valley. Late in the day, they found a single survivor, a grown-up boy, approaching manhood. He was overly thin, hungry and barely alive, laying underneath a bush, high up a spur, near where a little stream flowed into the valley. At the shelter, Lonna and Camla nursed and nourished him, applying salves and ointments to his scratches.

Orrox and Jupex both wanted to ask many questions, but the boy was too weak to speak, "We Sense internal injuries. We'll have to wait until medication and sleep have given him some strength."

By the next morning, the boy had recovered slightly. He was able to tell his tale, at first incoherently, but later continuing with many pauses.

"Great shaking. Things fell from the roof, baby killed." His eyes filled with tears, "Many hurt, women screamed."

Orrox bent over the boy, whispering softly, trying to calm him down. He stared at Orrox with large, frightened eyes.

"I intimidate him. Camla, you try to get him to speak clearly. A feminine touch is called for. Some soothing might be appropriate."

Camla held the boy in her arms, her lips moving as she uttered soft sounds. The boy rested his head on her breast and spoke softly, in longer sentences. "Women gathered round baby. Crying, screaming. Such shaking. Much worse than before."

The acolytes and Clansmen could just make out his words. The boy spoke with an accent and used the old-fashioned words of one of the fringe Clans. Slowly an image formed of his experience of the Catastrophe. However, before he could tell what had happened, he fell silent, too exhausted to continue.

Lonna gently stroked his hair.

The boy's heavy accent thickened when he spoke again, "The mountain fell over cliff edge. There, above!" he paused, frightened. His eyes stretched wide. "Much dust, smoke!" He pointed, "Snow come down. I run."

Orrox and Jupex tried to find out more, "Do you mean the mountain exploded?"

"After the shaking, before wind. Before dark. Smoke. Mountain give burning rocks. All snow came down."

He paused out of breath and became agitated again, "Clansmen from valley run away. Many inside. Mud kill Mother and Father! Me struggle. Me get out. Whole mountain come down!"

He started crying. Lonna and Camla soothed him, stroking his hair. Between sobs he whispered, his eyes large, "Forest gone. Trees in air. Fell on me. Everything dark. Later. Boom! That side. Hot, very, all trees burn. I lie in water behind rock. Snow and mud come down mountain. Mud cover me. Water everywhere. Much water. Valley fill with water."

They had to locate the survivors.

Questa must be with them, Jupex thought.

He questioned the boy further while Orrox stared at the boy intently but the boy got less coherent as he tired.

"Let him sleep." Orrox said, "He's badly hurt and needs rest."

"The poor boy," Camla said, a tear running down her cheek. "Imagine his fear and confusion. He lost everyone he loves."

Lonna sighed and the two males bent their heads, closing their eyes momentarily.

Orrox continued after a short pause, "I've managed to form a picture of what happened. After the Catastrophe and the gale, the volcano erupted. Later the whole side of the mountain exploded, releasing a heat storm, charring all the trees in the valley. Great lava flows would have melted the snow and he remembers how a flash flood submerged the Habitat and transformed the whole valley into a lake. It probably took days to drain away through the gorge. I'm sure that's what happened."

Jupex looked at Orrox strangely and even the acolytes stared with wide eyes.

Orrox sighed. "Yes, I did Sense his memories while Jupex questioned him. Yes, our code prohibits reading thoughts except when life is at stake. And yes, I do believe this is a life and death situation. We must find out what happened to those who were in this valley during the Catastrophe. Finally, yes, I am expert enough not to cause him any damage by probing his mind this deeply. I only managed to get a reflection of the images as he remembers."

The acolytes seemed satisfied but Jupex frowned.

"As long as you can find out where Questa is, do whatever is required," he murmured.

When the boy woke again, he tried to sit up and cried out in pain. Lonna, who had remained by his side, heard him and called Orrox, "Careful! I Sense inner bleeding."

Orrox emanated a soothing emotion. "Yes, so do I. He's not in pain when he lies still, but the injuries are serious."

The boy looked at him with dull eyes and tried to speak.

Orrox and the acolytes could Sense his desire to share his experience.

Lonna, who was holding his hand said, "I think he will find relief in telling what happened."

The boy was calmer now and much more coherent.

"Everything shaked. Something hit me. Hard! Then I know nothing."

"And when you woke up?"

"I cover in mud. And branches. I struggle get out. I call and search. No one."

"How far did you search?"

"I wait for water go away. Then I go down. To place of my father. For food. He has seeds. Seeds of plants we grow. Down there."

He pointed downstream, took out a few heads of barley and a few grains of wheat from a pouch he carried and showed them.

Then defiantly: "We may eat seeds. Orrox allow us eat seeds. We not show them outsiders." He did not recognize Orrox.

Jupex picked up and inspected the grains, "I know both these grasses. Their seeds are normally not as large as this."

He looked at Orrox strangely again, who simply said, "Let's put them away for now. There are more important issues to discuss."

The boy clutched his head in his hands mumbling, "I look everywhere. Everyone gone!" He broke into sobs. Camla moved to his side, joining Lonna. They tried to console him.

Jupex had taken over the questioning, "Did you go to the valley entrance? What did you see?"

"There was mud. I climbed up side. No shelters, no Look-Outs. Nothing! Nobody. All washed away!"

"What happened before we found you?"

"I tried go to Habitat. Strong wind threw me on ground! Big noise and wind hurt me. There is nothing. Only mud and water. Then you here."

Orrox was still busy with his own line of thoughts, "I don't think he saw what happened to the Dynasty members. Those Clansmen and guards who saw the destruction of the Orrox Habitat, the collapse and muddy avalanche flowing off the mountains like water, must have been terrified. They probably fled through the portal in terror and must have escaped before the flood."

Under Orrox's critical eye, the acolytes gave the boy a potion to suppress pain and infection and then allowed him to sleep.

When the boy woke again, he was much more lucid.

Orrox again tried to extract important details of the Catastrophe, find out who was present and where they were, but the boy had been absorbed in his daily tasks and did not notice much.

Jupex asked, after looking at Orrox, "A girl from my Clan of the Second Valley, Questa, my eldest daughter, was with the Dynasty for training. Did you see her?"

The boy had a clearer memory of what happened before the Catastrophe than of what happened afterwards. "Me sorry! The female of your Clan? Your daughter? So sad! Forgive me, I tell sad news."

The boy collapsed in wretched silence.

Jupex could barely contain his impatience. However, he had to allow the boy to recover before pressing him for details. "I am sure it is not of your doing and you are not to blame," he said, trying to calm the boy.

Orrox glanced at his acolytes. Together they emanated soothing feelings. He nodded to Jupex to continue. Gently, Jupex coaxed the boy, "Come, tell us all you know."

"I saw female. She spoke to me. We sleep inside palisade. She nice. My father tell of seeds and grasses. We know grasses. We look after them in valley. Everything! Washed away!" He paused, thinking, then continued, "She ask of trees in forest. We not know. We only pick fruit and nuts when ready," he paused again then continued defensively, "She speak others of trees."

He seemed to have lost the thread of his tale and could not be hurried.

"She go to forest. Clansmen follow. They carry spears. Good Orrox spears."

They all knew what he meant. The light spears with teardrop shaped flint or shiny points, were well known to be the best available to Clansmen.

All waited for the boy to continue. He slowly became more lucent, "They went to forest. Many go there when they here. She go alone."

As he paused again, Orrox looked at Jupex and softly explained: "Your daughter must have gone by herself to inspect the trees we grow. In various areas of the valley, different trees grow more vigorously, and we can advise in which area of a Clan valley each kind of tree will flourish. Oracle-Healers need to know the different uses of all the plants and trees, their anti-insect, medicinal and edible properties, and where they grow the best."

The boy took a drink from a container Lonna handed him and continued. "Fennox come back. He tell of Giants. They capture Clan female. He and others try protect her. They three," he showed three fingers. "Giants kill two. Fennox came back alone. We afraid of Giants."

Jupex paced up and down, shaking, his hands clutching his hair. He had refused to believe Questa could have been in danger. Now he knew and was devastated.

Orrox quietly continued to question the boy for a few moments and then approached Jupex. "I know the Giants' habits. Scaring Questa probably amused them. I imagine they started teasing her. They sometimes do that, unexpectedly appearing around trees, laughing and touching a victim's hair. I know of them doing this in jest and, after having amused themselves for a while, they leave."

He paused to look at the group. "They are normally harmless despite their strength. As far as I can make out from the boy's tale, and yes, from Sensing what he remembers, she reacted violently, and the Clansmen sent to guard her, attacked. Our light throwing spears are useless in the forest and no match for their heavy thrusting spears.

"Yes! Yes! But where is Questa?"

"He does not know what happened to Questa. The Clan sent out a search party but found only the two bodies. There was no sign of either Questa or the Giants. He doesn't know what happened to a second search party."

"We must find Questa. Anything could have happened to her. We must go now!"

Orrox tried to calm Jupex; "As you know, even in the open we have to keep well away from the Giants, regardless of special spear points. We're too few to search for Questa, the more so since she has been gone for such a long time. No tracks would have survived the Catastrophe. We need help. Let's search for survivors first and take them to your Clan. There we can assemble a strong search party and ask other Clans to join the search."

Jupex was not comforted; he walked away and sat down on a boulder with his head in his hands. "Questa, my beautiful girl. We have lost Questa!" he moaned, rocking to and fro.

#

It got colder at night and frost covered the ground. The mood of the group deteriorated even further.

Orrox knew they needed to act; to find out what happened to his Clan, to the other Clans, to find Questa, to simply survive. Both he and Jupex had to suppress their grief.

He hid his nagging concern from the others. *What about the Primitives? They are aggressive and unpredictable cannibals, who find pleasure in killing any stranger who trespasses into their hunting area. What if the survivors came across a troupe of Primitives; what if they did not stay together for protection?*

Their own immediate safety and survival were the most urgent.

Under Orrox's guidance, they scoured the valley for seeds, herbs, and edibles. They found large seed kernels above the flood line. These were dry and ready to fall off their stalks, making them easy to gather. Despite the havoc of the floods, mudslides, and avalanches, they managed to collect enough edibles, not only for their journey back to Jupex's Clan, but with more to spare.

After inspecting the dangerous slopes above the valley to ensure safety, they extended their search into the mountains where patches of trees and plants had survived the fires.

Following Orrox's specific instructions, the acolytes went in search of the expected troves of edibles. They hoped to find dried fruit and meat as well as already roasted nuts stored in the freezing cold of storage caves high up the steep slopes, above the snow line. They found it very difficult to scale the mountain. Fissures releasing lava had melted the snow, leaving only mud on the slopes. They did not recognize any features or find any markers to lead them to the caves. The gloom had not yet darkened when the acolytes returned from their search.

Jupex strived to fight a deep depression caused by his realization of Questa's fate and probable death. He forced himself to function effectively again. He joined Orrox when the search groups returned to report, "We have found no sign or footprints of any survivors, nor of Giants or Primitives. The environment is in chaos, all the annual shrubs and plants and even some perennials are dying. Fruit trees dropped their blossoms and the perennial trees have shed their leaves."

Camla had stayed with the boy, who was very weak. On their return, they found her in tears, "His slumber deepened into sleep. He gave a few jerks and died without waking up. He did not suffer much. I was so sorry for him. It felt as if we had formed a special bond."

Lonna went to sit with her and stroked her hair. Camla nodded in recognition, but continued sobbing uncontrollably. When Lonna handed her a skin, she buried her face in the skin, clutching it with both hands.

Still stroking Camla's hair, Lonna said, "Just think how lonely he would have been and how he would have suffered from his injuries, had he lived. He knew you and you helped him."

"I was afraid he would not last long," Orrox said, controlling his emotions, along with the others.

After Camla managed to regain control of herself, they all sat together silently for a while. Then they performed funeral rites for the boy, built a pyre and watched mournfully, as it burned.

After the ritual, Orrox wanted to search for the ice caves himself, but the acolytes warned: "Don't go. Don't take chances. We need you."

Jupex agreed, "We have enough provisions to see us through. You must not risk your life. You might be the last of the Orrox Dynasty. You carry unique knowledge that we all need. The avalanches and eruptions have probably destroyed or covered the caves. A further search is senseless."

Orrox bowed under the pressure. "We can come back when things have stabilized. Jupex, I think the best is to return to your Clan and get reinforcements. What do you think?"

Jupex agreed. "Once we return, I can organize a group to search for the Giants, to follow them unseen, and find Questa."

"Yes. But on our way back we must search for those who fled the valley."

They collected various kinds of nuts. They even found some medlars fermenting in a protected space against a slope, amidst some over-ripe and rotten fruit and berries. Dust covered them all. Only the medlars were of any use.

"The fruit was probably stored in one of the ice pits up there," Orrox said, pointing to the mountains still obscured by the gloom, "My Clansmen regularly bring down stored fruit during the cold season. Help me to clean off the rotten meat of all the fruits, except the medlars, and bring the stones and pips along! They might be useful. Only the medlars are still edible."

The acolytes and Clansmen gathered up the fruit and carried them to where they washed the dust and ash off the over-ripe fruit. They ate some and did not receive any sympathy from either Jupex or Orrox for the resulting stomach aches they experienced later in the day.

#

Orrox was always able to discern the onset of a new day, despite the gloom. The valley and all of nature were eerily silent with no sounds of nocturnal insects or prowlers, or of their prey. Even though no birds were announcing the break of day, Orrox got up, joined Crobal who was on guard and added wood to the fire. They exchanged a few words and then woke the others, "We have far to go and the visibility remains bad and gloomy. Get up." They draped their individual fur mantles or karosses over their shoulders to keep off the chill, tying them down with thin leather straps.

"Be ready for anything! We don't know the dangers we might encounter or how the Catastrophe has affected predators. We must keep together and always have our spears at the ready," Orrox said, while continuing to keep his worries about the Primitives to himself.

"Hopefully several survivors managed to flee the valley before the flood and wind and stayed together. They must have used the same path by which we approached the gorge. It is the only way out."

With full pouches, some hung around their waists and others slung over their shoulders, the companions left the Dynasty Valley. They passed through the narrow gully and found themselves up to their waists in the water again.

Jupex and Orrox followed the path away from the gorge onto the plain, where tracks on wide patches of sand allowed a picture to emerge.

"It looks as if they fled into the plains individually. They are in extreme danger," Orrox said. "They do not know the marshes or the treacherous routes. If the Plain Primitives discover them, they will be tortured and killed. We are too few to do anything to help them. Let's hasten back!"

I wonder whether any are still alive, he thought, hiding his fear from the others.

Chapter 18 – Hidden Valley

Anja desperately searched for a better handhold as she slipped, her feet seeking traction on the smooth rock. All in vain. The last possible protrusion was moist and muddy.

She fell, slipping down the rock face. She jammed a hand into a narrow crack. The rough surface took the skin off her hand and arm, without stopping her fall. She slid faster and faster down the nearly vertical cliff, her skin grazed by protrusions and the rough edges of the crack.

The rock face ended in a steep scree slope. Bushes on the slope broke her fall. She partly rolled and partly slipped down over and through ever-thicker undergrowth.

When the ground levelled out she came to rest. With her last strength, she drank the water remaining in her gourd. Different parts of her body screamed at her brain. Everything hurt. Tears ran down her face. Then she fell unconscious.

Anja woke in complete darkness. None of the usual night sounds gave any clue about her surroundings. An eerie silence pervaded the night. Sliding on the loose stones, she crawled to the bottom of the scree, orientating herself by touch. Knowing she was easy prey for predators.

There are trees here!

Painfully she passed over dead detritus and branches she searched for a safe place, until she found a hollow under the roots of a very big tree.

This might give some protection.

She marginally improved her safety by covering the entrance with a nearby branch. Despite the danger, she fell asleep again, only to wake up in gloomy light, not knowing where she was.

She stretched and experienced the pain of her new bruises and scratches, but these were not nearly as bad as the injuries she had endured during the Catastrophe. She picked up a short digging stick as a rudimentary weapon. Holding it ready she crawled out of the hollow. Standing up painfully, her skin stretched over the abrasions and congealed blood. There were no threatening sounds, only the creaking of the great boughs of the massive tree, the protective roots of which had afforded rudimentary protection.

Suddenly a loud shriek slammed into her ears, followed by softer repetitions reverberating through the surrounding forest.

Ignoring her painful bruises, Anja dove back into the protective hollow. Stretching an arm out through the roots, she dragged two more branches to increase her cover.

Then, silence.

Another squawk, now from far away.

Oh! It is the screech of some large hawk, she realized, but she remained in her hideout, still shivering from the scare. She closed her eyes to calm herself and to focus on sounds.

A long time later she heard the far of howl of wolves. Not near enough to pose a threat.

I cannot hide here forever. I will have to see where I am. Carefully she scrambled out from under the covering of roots and looked around.

A cliff face, with tall trees growing up to the edge of a steep scree slope, rose up above her. Boulders had tumbled down from above, splintering and mangling the nearest trees. Yellow-brown dust still covered the trees but only in a thin layer, not as thick as elsewhere.

The gurgling sound of water revealed the presence of a nearby brook nearby. She selected a sturdy branch. After breaking away twigs and foliage, she had a rudimentary club. She dared to approach the little stream. The sunken valley and dense foliage had protected the water from the heavy pollution she had encountered in her own valley. After repeatedly scooping a mixture of mud and ash out of a hollow below a small fountain, it filled with clear water. She drank her fill, replenished her gourd and ate a little of her reserves. Movement warmed her limbs and she managed to ignore the pain.

Anja looked around, wondering what dangers might be lurking in the trees. Her priorities were survival and safety. Then she could continue the search for other Clans.

She enlarged the hole under the roots into a reasonable place to stay. While continuously scanning her surroundings for danger, she carried sand from the edge of the brook to create a better floor in the cavity. She created a barrier with many broken branches and could block the entrance should she have to quickly retreat to comparative safety. It was the best she could do for now. The hollow cavity was her best option.

Sitting down inside her nook, she reviewed her situation. The bruises and scratches were painful but did not hinder her too much. She expected to hear forest inhabitants, but she only heard the trees creaking whenever a breeze moved their tortured shapes. No rumbling from the high mountains, nor any other sound, not even from the birds she expected here: no snow-cock, no grouse, no finch, nothing. Nature seemed to have died.

In Anja's immediate vicinity, she recognized some plants with edible roots, and farther away, a nut-bearing tree. Using a few leather straps, she tied a strip of fur around her shoulders against the cold. Holding her club ready, she approached the rivulet before venturing into the trees. She found and collected an abundance of edible roots and plants and even some nuts. The herbs and leaves were still green and not as wilted as they had been in her own valley. Coming back, she sat with her back against the trunk of the giant tree, continuously looking around and listening. She twirled a hardwood stick in a softwood base between her palms, to start a fire, as she had done many times before. Despite the painful abrasions on her arms, she continued until the glowing coal ignited some dry material and then dry wood. Carefully avoiding smoke, she added dry wood.

No need to attract unwanted attention. Stay vigilant and hide if I Sense any danger!

She had created a protected hiding place, had collected food and water and had made a fire, those were the essentials.

That's all I can do. Now for a meal.

The Clans often used heat-retaining stones for grilling and roasting or to line fiery holes in the ground, forming an oven. They collected them from the desert: round stones to heat and drop into gourds filled with water for boiling and flat slabs heated for cooking.

Usable stones and reeds were abundant at the creek. She roasted some of the roots and nuts to detoxify them and stop germination. If she could later snare small animals or catch fish in the brook, she could smoke the meat and fish to preserve them.

There should be rock-salt somewhere. Something else I need to look for, she thought.

Having eaten, Anja grabbed her club again and continued her inspection. She walked carefully, trying to be as quiet as her injuries allowed. Cautiously, always keeping a climbable tree in mind, she followed the brook up to its source, a crack in the cliff.

I'll climb that, if I hear or see anything!

The heights of the cliff face disappeared in the gloom. The ledge she had followed the previous day was not visible from below. Discoloration showed that rain could transform the brook, now just a trickle of water, into a raging torrent below a waterfall.

Many small fountains increased the flow and added clean water. Lower down the stream had already begun cleaning itself. She followed the stream down to where it dropped over a precipice and disappeared in the dusty gloom far below. Vertical cliffs extended for the whole width of the valley, up to the rock face in the sunrise direction, down which she had fallen.

She scrambled up the scree slope through the bushes and inspected the rock face. It sloped steeply and then became vertical, forming the crack higher up. It would be a very difficult and exposed climb to return this way and would not improve her chances of finding other Clans.

Scrambling over detritus and fallen boulders, Anja spent the rest of the day following the line of the cliffs, passing the crack where the brook started. She was in a small valley high up in the mountain range. Walls of rock surrounded the valley on three sides, with the sheer drop at the lower end. She heard the screech of a hawk, echoing from cliff face to cliff face, only once more.

I wonder whether it is the same one. Where is its prey? She strained her eyes to see, but saw nothing.

In the sunset direction, the ground sloped up from the stream to where the cliff was more broken. Near the corner where the rock faces met, a series of deep cracks with vertical sides penetrated deep into the adjoining spur. It presented the best promise of a possible exit out of the valley. The direction was also good, leading towards the sunset. There she might find one of the Clan valleys.

She looked for signs of dangerous predators but saw none, the valley was too small for even deer to survive. The only tracks and droppings she noticed were of rodents and other small animals, prey for hawks but too small for any bigger predator. No life stirred.

Anja felt relatively safe in her retreat, which she thought of as the 'Hidden Valley.' There were enough food and plenty of dry wood.

I might as well stay until I have recovered my strength.

She built a large fire in front of her hiding place. For the first time since the Catastrophe, she slept well. Her bruises did not keep her awake and she slept without dreaming, soothed by the warmth of the fire, only waking twice to add firewood.

Anja slept late to allow her body to recover from the hardships she had endured. Late in the day, she started searching and collecting, managing to store and preserve enough edibles and medicinal herbs to last for several days.

Tomorrow I can continue my search, she thought, relieved to have survived the ledges and the fall.

The next morning, when light allowed, she again filled her gourd and pouches with as much provision as she could carry. Then she started out towards the cracks. Should they lead nowhere, she could return to the cavity between the roots, which she blocked with many additional branches and where she left some herbs and edibles behind, enough to keep her alive in case of a quick retreat.

Though broken, the cliff was high and vertical. Huge scattered boulders lay around with a rock tower standing detached from and hiding much of the face. Cracks and gullies penetrated deep into the mountain spur.

She started at the nearest gully and entered each in turn, but they all petered out to become narrow slits under overhanging rock faces. None looked promising.

There must be another way out and I will find it, she thought as she returned to the safety of the big tree.

The next day she tried to climb the waterfall, but the constant flow of water had polished the rock, making it too smooth to climb. Each day she tried another escape route, including the precipice where the valley ended. She avoided the small fissure above the scree slope, down which she had fallen into the Hidden Valley, until no other option remained. When she finally tried the route, she managed to climb no higher than the treetops before it became too difficult and she nearly slipped.

She clung to small protrusions, just big enough for a few fingers on each hand to hold on, her feet getting little purchase on the rough surface. With her right cheek pressed hard against the rock, she froze. She had to move. She slowly leaned away to turn her head to the right. The slight movement nearly dislodged her. Her right hand had to find a lower handhold. Letting her hand slip slowly down the rough rock, she found something better. A vertical crack into which she could jam her hand.

She repeated the movement with her left hand. Now off balance she carefully found a better stance for her right foot lower down and then one for her left foot. Climbing down proved very difficult. Fearful of falling again, she decided not to climb open rock faces again.

Anja was exhausted and slept well, which helped her heal. She collected roots and herbs every day, much more than she required, and stored them safely. With no sun, moon or stars to help her keep direction, she relied on the growth of plants and mosses for orientation. Although there was much less dust than in her home valley, it still covered everything. She often removed ash, or dusted tree trunks, before old moss growth became visible.

Near the giant tree, she found a pleasant pool. Sweeping the surface with branches helped clear the remaining ash. She threw off her coverings and waded in, stirring up mud. She had not washed properly since the Catastrophe, even a mud bath would be welcome. The brook flowed strongly into the pool over a series of smooth slabs.

Anja crawled up the wet slope, washing off much of the mud. Then, turning on her back, she allowed the water to flow over her. Though cold, the bath was very refreshing. Working her way to the side, she stood up on the slabs, legs apart for stability. She was young with well-formed breasts, the nipples high, prominent and hard from the cold. While stretching, she allowed the drops of water to run down her body. She felt better than she had since the Catastrophe.

Things will work out, she thought. *I will find a Clan and survivors.*

She shivered. The soft skins she used for drying were still at the tree. Quickly wrapping her wet body in her fur mantle, she hurried back to her tree and a warm fire.

Later in the day the pool was clear, allowing for a much cleaner bath.

The Clan of the Second Valley, my father's Clan, must be near here. If only I can reach it! I must find a way to climb out of this valley, which gives me a chance to rest in safety.

The only option was to inspect the cracks again. She remembered each of the gullies she had inspected and decided on one near the top of the valley where the cliff turned back in the sunrise direction.

The bottom of the gully sloped upwards. A few large boulders lay jammed in the narrow crack, mostly near the top where they transformed parts of the gully into a dark tunnel. Bushes and even trees, many broken by falling boulders, grew on some of the stone bridges, blocking more of the light and heightening the gloom below.

Farther on the gully widened. A vertical wall divided it into two corridors. The crack to the right soon narrowed further and then came to a dead end against a smooth funnel, polished through ages of storm deluges. She went back to the split and tried again. On the left-hand side, the gully also narrowed and then veered right. The slope steepened, until it ended in a vertical crack with boulders jammed here and there. She was desperate to find a way out and managed to work her way upwards, sometimes using the jammed boulders as handholds or stepping-stones and sometimes wriggling herself upwards.

She emerged out of breath, to find herself near the top of a mountain spur. She stood on a horizontal slab, split by several deep parallel cracks. Clearly the tops of adjacent gulleys, none of which allowed an alternate escape route or entrance into the Hidden Valley. She placed three gourd-sized rocks in a triangle, then another rock on top to form a pyramid, creating a marker to identify the correct location of the fissure, which leads to the gully.

The mountain range rose to her right with ridges stepping up until ending in towering cliffs, the tops disappearing high above, in the enveloping gloom. In the distance, a grassy plain sloped downwards and then dropped steeply towards a valley, the form of which she could just make out. Behind her, the slab extended to where it fell away with a sharp edge into the deep valley from which she had just emerged, the valley she thought of as her 'Hidden Valley.' The wind-driven sand had sculpted weird forms from the weathered sandstone. They stood scattered around, as if on guard.

The valley before her looked habitable; it could be a Clan valley. She sat down pleased with herself, drank from her gourd and ate well, convinced she would be able to replenish her supplies soon.

The spur led up to the mountain, where it merged with the top of the valley and the roots of the mountain chain. There was something vaguely familiar but she could not be sure. In the gloom, everything looked different. If this is the valley she remembered, there would be a connection with the ledge traversing the mountain, where a path led down into the valley.

She got up and followed the spur upwards. At the top, she turned in the sunset direction, climbing down onto a swampy area above the valley. She descended slowly, still hiding her tracks from possible danger. She made her way through some marshy ground. On reaching firm ground, she walked faster, entering the valley from the top.

The valley and mountains were familiar; she recognized landmarks and became excited. She knew the valley; she was sure of it! Her spirits rose in expectation of seeing familiar faces and of experiencing the presence of ones she loved.

She saw familiar tracks in the dust. It was the final proof. Clansmen had walked here. These tracks were made after the Catastrophe. The dust layer was disturbed and compressed. She made her way down as fast as she could. She saw more and more footprints. Her steps were light, she felt like dancing. The darkness that lay on her mind, the pessimism that had nearly overwhelmed her, the shock of losing her Clan, disappeared. She felt happy, cheerful for the first time since the Catastrophe.

She was making good progress when she heard yells and shouts reaching her from lower down. She stopped to listen. The gloom concealed the source of the noise and she could see no movement. Frightened, her joyful mood disappeared. With instinctive caution, she hid behind a few boulders in a clump of bushes, watching through drooping leaves, wondering what was happening. The noise increased. Fear impinged on her Sensing. Cries of distress and terrible yells reached her ears. Anja cringed in her hiding place, making herself as small and invisible as possible, blocking any perception or Sensing of pain.

Then the horror was upon her.

Chapter 19 – Return to the Second Valley

Orrox wanted to return to Jupex's Clan immediately. He wanted to arrange a search party urgently. They had to find the survivors who escaped the disaster in the Dynasty Valley.

Jupex's only concern was the fate of his daughter. During murmured discussions, the acolytes slowly assembled near Orrox while the Clansmen moved towards Jupex. Orrox, noticing the movement, repeated his request, "We are too few to search effectively for either your daughter or for the Dynasty survivors. We must go back to your Clan for reinforcements."

Jupex did not agree, "We can also split up. My Clan is weak after the Catastrophe. You can request help from any of the Clans while we start our search for Questa. Two of my Clansmen can go back to get more help."

The Clansmen near Jupex looked worried. This was not a good time for the two leaders to argue.

"I fully understand your wish to immediately start searching for your daughter, but consider! The mudslides and avalanches have erased all signs and tracks in the mountains. Those, combined with the lava flows, make it very difficult for anyone to traverse the mountain slopes. Better to hike quickly on the plains and face the danger of coming across Primitives. The Giants are probably on their way back towards their woodlands, which are far away. They have to cross the mountain and travel much further. They live where shadows grow long, and days are short, in the season of scarcity.

"If we hurry back, a large group from your Clan can start immediately. They will be able to move fast over the plains and through the mountain chain. When they catch up with the Giants, they will save your daughter. As we pass the mouths of each Clan valley, I can summon help from that Clan. I believe many of the Dynasty's survivors took refuge there, and we will find them." Orrox paused to catch his breath. "Come on, Jupex! It is our best option."

Jupex looked away while Orrox spoke, he did not want to listen to Orrox's arguments. His Clansmen looked down and did not look at Orrox either. Despite their great respect for the Orrox, their ultimate loyalty belonged to Jupex.

"Think about it. Together we are much safer while we cross the Plain." Orrox said and sat down with his acolytes. The Clansmen were silent for a while before starting a discussion. Orrox saw MaXiox talking to Jupex. He looked serious.

After a while, Jupex approached followed by his companions, "I agree, you are right. We have to keep together and all return to my Clan quickly."

Orrox reached out and squeezed Jupex's arm, "Yes. Let's go!"

The companions started immediately. They hurried along until they came to another little brook where they found a few gazelles nosing at the ooze, too weak to run away.

"The water is sour and clogged with dirt." Bronnox started to clear away some of the mud and ash allowing fresh water to seep in and form a pool. Lonna was the first to help. Soon the Clansmen also joined in.

"We can create a few places where the animals can drink as we go. Clear water will soon form near water seeps and we might help a few to survive until then," Orrox said.

With an additional task to distract the group, they forgot their differences and progressed quickly across the plains, with short stops at each stream they crossed. Everywhere they looked, signs of devastation haunted them.

#

As the gloom deepened, Jupex and Orrox worked together to find a safe spot where a fire would not be visible from the plains. Near a creek fed by a fountain, where they were able to clean a depression and collect sweet water, they prepared to spend the night. They made a fire between some rocks where the trees would hide any reflection.

Orrox took an oak branch the length of his arm and carved one side flat, forming a wooden slat to write on. He then carved lines on the wooden slat.

One of the Clansmen, StuDol, watched with interest.

"We must keep track of how many days have passed since the Catastrophe," Orrox said. Then, glancing at Jupex, he added, "I believe the Catastrophe will prove to be a turning point in the life of the Clans. We need to keep close count, we cannot lose track of when we must have our feasts or perform rituals. For example, the Vigil of the Fires is held in the season-of-shortage on the shortest day, when the days start to lengthen again. In this gloom, it will be harder to determine the day."

"Yes, that is my favorite feast," MaXiox said. "Jupex met Chiara, his first wife, at the one we attended during our service years. I love the ritual of keeping watch while many fires, surrounding the Habitat, blaze throughout the long night. When I was small, I believed the fires invited the sun and the long days to come back again."

The acolytes, who had joined them, laughed, "Yes, the same tale is told to the young ones in all the Clans!"

"There was also a tall tale of why the plants and trees start budding well before the warmth of the fruit collecting season-of-plenty sets in," Camla said. "It is the time of births and renewal, a sacred time, the time when men must obey us women and do whatever we want."

"As if it is different at any other time!" Ammox grumbled to the amusement of all.

Bronnox, ever the observant hunter, was concerned and serious, "We may well laugh, but this should have been the time of renewal. The grazers are struggling. The young shoots have died, and ash covers the old grasses and the leaves of the trees. Things are bad!"

#

The next day, they passed the mouth of a valley. "Even though a strong Clan lives in this valley, high up near the mountain range, I think we must continue to your valley," Orrox said. "Assemble a larger group to start the search and only then summon help from the different Clans, as we pass their valleys again."

As night fell, Orrox and Jupex identified a spot to stay for the night. "Now that we are in the Primitives' territory, we must constantly remain vigilant. They might even discover that the regular patrols from the Dynasty have ended, leaving the Clans unprotected. Sleep with your spears at hand. If anything happens, retreat with your backs against these boulders, with your spears to the front. Two of us must always be on guard. We'll take turns. We must sleep in protected hiding places."

They ate some nuts and dried meat from their individual pouches. The Clansmen, all experienced hunters, proved their ability at concealment. Even the acolytes disappeared. Only the red glow of the embers was visible, shedding just enough light for those on guard to watch the immediate surroundings. They stood with their backs against the boulders and shielded their eyes from the glow. The night was again pitch dark with no light from stars or the moon penetrating the blackness.

With the first glimmer of light Orrox rose and approached MaXiox, who was on guard, "Did you see or hear anything?"

"No, nothing."

Jupex was awake and greeted MaXiox before leading Orrox away from the others.

"We need to talk," he said in a hushed tone, "All of us in the Clans have great respect and admiration for the Orrox Dynasty. We believe the services the Dynasty renders are essential to our well-being." He frowned, "Few of the Clans, except us Chiefs, of the Clans, and Healers in training, ever visit the Orrox Dynasty's home valley. What we saw in your valley and what I deduct from my observations upsets me. Things none of us Chiefs know about. Secrets! My first wife and her mother were and are both highly respected Oracle-Healers. You know of them, Chiara-the-younger and Chiara-the-elder. They did not tell me you kept secrets from the Clans. I cannot believe my Chiara kept any disturbing facts from me. We loved one another and kept no secrets. Please explain what we saw."

He's expressing his frustration, Orrox thought. *Because we did not immediately start the search for his daughter, Questa. She is his only remaining link to the memory of his first wife. I'll have to tread carefully.*

Jupex continued, "It seems to me the Dynasty, of which you are a very important member—if not the most important—has broken our proud traditions. They have served the Clans well and ensured our survival since time immemorial. I'm not even sure you abide by the rules you so effectively recite! Even though you grow the best and abundant food in your own valley, you still require the Clans to contribute more! I believe you are wasteful and abuse your Sensing ability, breaking the strict rules set by the Council. You have broken the tradition of the Clans!" his voice rose as he spoke.

Orrox was silent for a while. "We should keep our voices down. Sound travels far in this strange quiet we are experiencing. You are only partly right and I can merely give you a brief explanation now.

"I must admit, when I first arrived at the Dynasty from my mother's Clan as a juvenile, I felt the same. I now fully associate myself with the Dynasty. The Dynasty, admittedly under Orrox guidance, does much more than you are aware of. What we do not share is special measures we are forced to take to ensure the wellbeing of each Clan. Each of the valleys must be able to nourish the ideal number of Clansmen. These measures are more complex than immediately obvious and differ from valley to valley.

"We cannot tell the Clans what we do to help individual Clans. The Clans themselves don't know either. Other Clans might demand the same things in their valleys, which is impossible or detrimental. The patrolling and safety of the Clans and the training of Oracle-Healers are even more complex. I will gladly debate this point with you later.

"The plants and trees yielding the grains you saw, and the fruit you did not see, are being developed for later introduction to those valleys where they will flourish best and yield abundant food. We do not introduce them in valleys where they will not grow as well. We do not introduce them in valleys where they will not yield abundant food. We also ensure that each valley has a few unique resources.

"There is much more the Orrox Dynasty does and has done through the generations that even you, the Clan Chiefs, do not know. We train Healers and supply the special powders and healing potions needed to keep all the Clansmen healthy and active into extended old age. The uncomplicated, high-quality Clan life you depict, is a gross simplification, an impossibility without the Dynasty's benign oversight, helped by the Oracle-Healers. I am concerned about how drastically the Clans' lifestyle and safety will be altered by the loss of the Dynasty's support and protection."

Orrox took a few breaths to curb the intensity of his speech, "We'll discuss this later; let's not argue but confront the tasks ahead together."

He looked at Jupex earnestly, as Jupex acknowledged the logic of the suggestion with a nod.

"One more thing. On my abuse of my Sensing abilities: reading the poor boy's memories, to discover the fate of my Dynasty, is one of my seldom used powers. We, the Orrox scions, are taught and trained in the use of great powers, but they are seldom used. As Sensitives, we are all under oath to preserve the privacy of each Clan-member. We are only allowed to use our powers when there is a clear danger to life, and then only when there is no alternative. You would have noticed how shocked my acolytes were when they realized I used my ultimate Sensing power. My communication with them was also at a much deeper level than you can imagine. They each evaluated my justification for themselves. I don't feel at all guilty for reading the boy's mind."

Before Jupex could respond or inquire further, MaXiox, still on guard, whistled, imitating the sound of a night prowler. A dark form was just visible in the glow of the fire. More forms stood etched against the lightening gloom of the sky.

Instantly, Jupex's hunters flanked him, all with their throwing spears in hand, standing close with their backs hard against the large boulders. Orrox threw some kindling on the hot embers, which flamed up. Several Primitives became visible, glowering at them, brandishing their heavy knobbed clubs and threatening with the sharpened saplings they used as spears. Orrox, flanked by his acolytes, stood nearby, each holding a Dynasty sourced spear. Ready to thrust or throw.

Orrox started communicating with the Primitives, using noises and low sounds coming from deep in his throat. They were interspersed with click sounds from the front of his mouth. He accompanied the sounds with hand and arm gestures and body postures.

Neither Jupex's group nor the acolytes could understand him, but they all felt the intensity of the sounds.

One of the Primitives responded but the tones were unfriendly and then became threatening, as the exchange continued.

Orrox's tone, which originally was soothing and friendly, became hard and threatening, but this did not seem to have the desired effect.

The Primitive yelled and moved forward menacingly. His companions joined him gesturing wildly, and attacked.

<><><>

Chapter 20 – Giants return

JaYan tried to appease Questa after her uncharacteristic explosive demand to leave the Illoreaen Habitat. She appreciated the effort, but they both knew she contained her impatience with difficulty. She longed for the opportunity to return to the Dynasty or, better still, to her own Clan in the Second Valley. Many days passed with no news of messengers from the Dynasty. JaYan thought the delay was probably caused by the difficulties they experienced in crossing the mountain range. Overcoming the chaos caused by the Catastrophe.

Wandering around in the few areas not off-limits to her, Questa often wondered about the embryonic life she had Sensed in MaGan's secret chamber. Although she made sure never to Sense the emotions of any individual, Sensing the presence of life was inherent to her ability. Something she could not easily, and did not wish to, block.

In keeping with her idea of good manners, she not only blocked the ability to Sense emotions, she even ignored much of the body language she observed. She did not hide her Sensing ability on purpose, but the subject never came up in conversation and she never mentioned it.

She was bored. Her one comfort was to withdraw to one of the female bathing cubicles. There she often soaked herself for extended periods in the warm water. Hot water from an underground spring flowed into separate sets of carved basins. Tightly woven baskets contained sufficient water to wash. These were exclusive for either male or female use, with a pre-wash area for each. Basins nearer the inflow were hotter than those situated lower down, and she could select the temperature suiting her mood. This was even better than the partition at the Dynasty or at the Clan Habitat in her own second valley, where men and women took turns to use a pool, also fed from hot springs nearby.

#

Questa remained aware of the danger the Giants posed and, when away from the others, she often tried to Sense their presence.

What if Heropto and his gang are still lurking somewhere unseen? If they are, how can the messengers approach safely? What will happen if the Giants intercept us during my return to the Clan valleys, accompanying the Dynasty's courier-messengers?

She perceived the Giants as a lethal threat, a danger which none of the Illoreaens seemed to care about.

Until the Giants appeared.

The trauma of abduction had attuned Questa's Sensing to the unfamiliar emotional patterns of the Giants, especially that of Heropto. Long before even the Look-Outs with the viewing tubes saw the Giants approaching, she vaguely Sensed the anger of Heropto, focused on her and the Illoreaens. She climbed to a high point, away from the interference created by any local minds and focused her Sensing. She concentrated on the characteristics of the Giants' minds. Yes, they were there! Adjusting her Sensing to attune to Heropto's mind, she concentrated hard and confirmed her fear. Heropto did not approach alone, many more Giants accompanied him. All emanated anger.

She hurried in search of JaYan. When she could not find him, she confronted a passer-by, "Excuse me! I'm Questa. Please call JaYan. It's urgent."

He gave her a strange look, nodded and hurried off. She did not even know his name. She waited patiently. Most of the Illoreaens never approached her or told her their names. Questa found them rude.

When JaYan finally arrived, he said, "I'm sorry, I have no news. We have been expecting the courier-messengers from the Dynasty for several days but they have not yet arrived. I'm surprised because they are never late. I know you are impatient to return to the Clan valleys. Damage to the difficult passes over the mountain range must have delayed them, but they will be here soon. Then you can leave safely."

"Yes, although I am thankful for your hospitality, I still look forward to leaving with them. However, it might not be possible, and it is not the reason why I asked to speak to you. The big Giant they call Heropto is approaching with a large group of very aggressive Giants. I Sense rage in Heropto."

"You, you – what? How do you know? What do you mean when you say you 'sense rage' in a Giant? How can you know? What do you know about Heropto?"

"I know Heropto. I was his prisoner and I Sensed the characteristic of the Giants' minds. Especially Heropto's. Surely you must know, all Oracle-Healers have Sensing ability, some stronger and others weaker. It is the only way to fulfill the complete healing and oracle functions. Surely you know! I am of the female line of Chiara, the line with the strongest Sensing ability of all."

"I have heard of the exceptional healing abilities of the Chiara line, no more. Sensing ability—what a disaster!" JaYan remained silent for a while, "Sensitive! Even worse if you are right."

Questa did not understand his response. She was confused, and felt insulted, "The issue is the Giants. You must prepare yourselves immediately!"

"A Sensitive! Excuse me," and JaYan was gone. He returned much sooner this time, accompanied by MaGan, who immediately confronted her, "How dare you claim Giants are approaching our Habitat? Our Look-Outs have noticed nothing."

"I'm a Sensitive and training as an Oracle-Healer. Of course I know! I was their captive and under their leader's power for many days. I concentrated hard to understand the strangeness of their minds. I can now partly Sense their emotional patterns, even though their minds are very different from ours. I could think of no other way to prepare for a possible chance to escape. Yes, it was futile then, but now I am able to Sense them. They are angry and in a frenzy, looking for revenge. They are emanating intense emotion. We must act quickly!"

Questa did not notice the strange looks on MaGan and JaYan's faces during her passionate explanation. They looked at her sharply.

"I don't believe you. Are you making fun of us?" JaYan managed to utter. His eyebrows pulled into a frown. Then he gave a sigh, raised his hand to his forehead and stroke back his hair before letting it fall limply to his side.

MaGan said nothing but stood with a furious expression on his face, his fists clenched.

She looked back, trying to convince them. "Of course not! I can emanate the truth but a Sensitive never emanates without permission... I see, you have never experienced it... I don't want to confuse you and detract from your ability to act. I assure you it is true. Please believe me!"

The two just looked at her, then at each other.

"Please, you must hurry! The Giants are dangerous! You must act now!"

The two stood in silence. JaYan scratched his head and at last, looking at MaGan, said, "You better do something."

MaGan turned around quickly. Over his shoulder he said, "We'll send out sentinels to see whether any Giants are really approaching before handling this matter...

"JaYan, you arrange protection for the Habitat. I'm going to send out sentries and arrange an ambush, just in case. I will send messengers to all who are outside. Should there actually be Giants, an ambush at each of the mineral diggings could have interesting results."

He walked away quickly, then suddenly turned around, facing Questa, "If this is a hoax, you will regret the day we saved you!" Then marched off.

#

Long before the Look-Outs noticed any Giants, the sentries confirmed their approach. The Giants avoided the open plain, but came slinking along the gullies and through wooded areas. Their stealthy approach allowed the Illoreaens time to prepare. Without Questa's warning, many would have been surprised outside the Habitat and lives lost. Now, with her early warning, they all retreated to safety within their cave system or placed themselves in ambush at the different approaches to the Habitat. At the diggings, the young ones excitedly arranged their own ambushes and means of protection.

Questa remained on watch in one of the Look-Out recesses in the cliff face. She focused on the Giants, then went to search for JaYan and MaGan. She found them arguing. "I have Sensed the emotions of the Giants. They still do not realize you know of their approach. They plan a surprise attack."

She wanted to add more but the two gave her a cold look and turned away. JaYan looked back once, quickly, hesitated, but then continued on his way. Confused and hurt she returned to the lonely recess.

By the time the Giants arrived, the Illoreaens were prepared and waiting. The young inductees at the diggings, away from the Habitat, regarded the threat as an exciting adventure. MaGan visited each of their positions and ensured they had enough flyers and throwing spears. The approaches to their protective positions were clear, affording open lines to launch their projectiles, with no hiding places or woods in which the Giants might take cover.

"Remember, if any Giant should succeed in reaching you, you will be helpless to protect yourselves. Your spears will have less effect than the flyers, the Giants are that strong. If they should storm, you must stop them all. Do not leave your protective positions under any circumstance and stay away from any wooded area!"

MaGan found JaYan preparing the defenses of the Habitat, "Our palisade works against us. It can give cover to any Giant from projectiles launched from our Look-Out points in the cliff. A few Sharp-shooters will have to remain outside the Habitat, hiding behind the palisade. We're making small apertures in the palisade through which they can launch their flyers. My main worry is getting them back into the Habitat should anything go wrong. The scrubland is much too close to the palisade for my liking. The Giants might be able to hide there." JaYan paused. "Do you feel comfortable with our young ones protecting the diggings and hiding at the ambush points?"

"I have explained the danger and ordered them not to expose themselves. They are a good crowd but excitable. They have heard of the Giants' horrible intentions for Questa. I fear they might lose their heads, leave their cover, and confront the Giants. They have no idea of how strong the Giants are, no idea how easily the Giants can kill with their bare hands. I tried to tell them but the exuberance of youth might cause fatalities."

The Giants crept up to the Habitat, keeping themselves hidden in the woods and scrublands, never approaching the ambush points. A few moved up the mountain, staying under cover of woods and brush-land, effectively surrounding the Habitat and the diggings. Heropto and the main body of his followers crept up to the Habitat, but stayed well outside the range of throwing spears and flyers. They waited for Illoreaens to appear, but neither group moved.

"I think they must have spied on us from within their hiding places and have seen no visible movement at the diggings, or here at the Habitat. They must know we were aware of their approach," MaGan said.

JaYan agreed, "What now? The young ones at the diggings and in the ambush points dare not leave their protective positions and dare not come into the Habitat. They will have to move through wooded areas, where the Giants will easily overcome them."

A stand-off developed. Heropto was too clever to attack over open ground and the Illoreaens were unable to drive the Giants out of the woods and thickets.

When the gloom darkened into night, the Illoreaens threw poles covered with a glowing liquid into the open spaces in front of the defenders. It gave enough light to see all movements.

A Giant snuck up to a protective position above one of the pits, where the young ones usually dug out shining quartz crystals. A young one called GerMa used his spear launcher and wounded the Giant in the leg. He yelled furiously and hurried back to the cover of the woods, amid the laughter of his companions.

Heropto was angry and impatient. He yelled at his followers. He assembled the whole group and attacked the defenders above the pit from all sides simultaneously.

One even managed to climb up the loose gravel at the side of the pit. Because the young ones had their backs to the pit, concentrating on the attack from all the other directions, he approached unnoticed. He grabbed the nearest defender by the leg and dragged him from the pit. They tumbled down the slope together, the Illoreaen youth screaming at the top of his voice.

The defending youths tried not to panic.

"I'll go after them!" GerMa yelled.

The Giant made the mistake of looking up as the two reached the bottom of the pit. GerMa, who was looking over the edge of the pit, launched a flyer at the dim outline, hitting the Giant in the eye. The Giant fell down screaming.

A second Giant chased the escaping youth, who hurriedly scrambled up the steep side. GerMa launched another flier, wounding the pursuer in the thigh. Limping, he hurried back to the protective woods.

As the rescued youth rejoined his companions, he turned towards GerMa, "Thank you. That was a near thing! But I was just about to tear out the Giant's eyes with my bare hands."

His friends laughed with him. Then, without losing concentration, resumed their defense with renewed vigor.

The dim glowing light was enough to outline the large forms of the Giants, making them clear targets. Obedient to MaGan's instruction not to kill unnecessarily, the young defenders aimed at legs and arms, launching multiple flyers.

The screams of the fatally wounded Giant at the pit reverberated through the valley. He scratched and pulled at the flyer that had penetrated his eye, but only managed to push the flyer deeper in, until it penetrated his brain. His screams continued until he died.

Instead of continuing the attack, the Giants stopped, then started to pull out the flyers still stuck in their flesh.

A new wave of flyers rained down on them.

The Giants quickly retreated.

The Illoreaens heard Heropto's loud abuse of his small group of companions. It continued until the light of day. He then climbed onto a prominent stone outcrop, facing the Illoreaen Habitat, and yelled his defiance "I kill you! Give back prize or you sorry! We now few, but we back. I take treasure and food!"

Few understood the gruff sounds but the aggression was clear. JaYan translated and the Illoreaens looked worried.

"I'm not very concerned. They have found the supplies near the diggings and are taking those. I think the treasure he mentions are the colored stones and quartz we have discarded in front of the quartz diggings.

"I wish to commend the bravery of our young at the pit. They showed great discipline. They even managed to retrieve all their flyers."

The young ones were treated as heroes and strutted around proudly, with GerMa in the lead.

The next day the Look-Outs, high up the cliffs of the Habitat, observed the Giants on the plain. They were on their way back to their woods and forests near the ice cliffs. Heropto paraded proudly, displaying handfuls of colored stones, which the Giants had collected without meeting resistance. It secured his status and reputation. The Look-Outs watched them through their viewing tubes, until they disappeared in the gloom.

Questa expected some recognition for Sensing the danger and giving the Illoreaens early warning, but she experienced the opposite. No one asked her to Sense whether the Giants were gone but ignored her and even avoided her. She did not understand their conduct. She had concentrated on the Giants while they were there. She Sensed they were gone, but nevertheless warned JaYan, "Heropto is in danger of being ridiculed for the way you saved me and defeated his troupe. He is very angry. He wanted to catch us by surprise. The looting was just an emergency measure to save face. I think he will be back. Next time he will be more dangerous and come with a new plan."

JaYan listened with a serious expression but did not respond.

MaGan sent out a patrol and put out sentries to make sure all the Giants were gone. Soon he brought in the young ones from their positions of ambush and defense. They were hungry, cold and, except for those who fought at the pit, disappointed. They never saw a single Giant and did not get the opportunity to prove themselves in battle.

JaYan spoke to the young ones, "The Giants are incredibly strong and dangerous. We are fortunate no one was hurt. Those at the pit were lucky to escape."

The young ones listened patiently but did not agree.

Turning to MaGan he said, "Your young trainees are a good bunch but they illustrate the old truth, until one reaches the age of twice doucia, emotions prevail and well-considered opinions or actions are scarce."

MaGan laughed, "We were like that too, remember?"

<><><>

Chapter 21 – JaYan and MaGan

Despite their different personalities and interests, JaYan and MaGan had always been close friends. They were cousins, born during the same birth cycle in the early Season of Plenty, with over three doucia other babies. Even so, they reflected the different interests of their parents. JaYan's parents were interested in devices, metals, and special substances while MaGan's parents liked group activities and excelled in hunting and sport; they trained youths and developed medicines, testing their effects on individuals.

At MaGan's, visitors regularly fetched medicine, shared experiences and grievances or told stories. In contrast, at JaYan's the occasional guests came to discuss new finds or the wonders of the starlit heavens, or to debate on how to construct a better viewing tube, or the possible solutions to some other technical problem.

For JaYan, logic and facts were all important. Yet for MaGan, an individual's perception of the effectiveness of a cure or medication was often more important than reality.

They played with the other children in their peer group. When they were six, they also played with the older children of the previous birth cycle, a quarter doucia older.

Generally acknowledged as the ultimate experts in their different fields, the parents of the two friends shared only family interests. However, the families each appreciated the expertise of the other and often consulted and used the other's abilities to further their own research. The two mothers, sisters who so greatly differed in interest, loved each other. They taught the two boys to play together, using their different abilities to enhance their games.

The two cousins celebrated a joint 'half-doucia' birth celebration. This was an important birthday. During three moon cycles, the different children in their peer group, all born in the same birth cycle, celebrated their birthdays. All the children from their birth cycle attended all the parties.

MaGan grabbed JaYan's arm at their party. "Come and see what my father gave me!"

Together they slipped out of the cave and through the opening in the palisade. They dashed through the woods until they were out of sight of the Look-Outs keeping guard in recesses high up the cliff.

From a hole under a boulder, MaGan extracted two sets of bows and flyers of reduced size. They were wrapped in soft chamois skins. "My father had one made for you too!"

MaGan jumped up and down in his excitement. "We can hunt rodents and birds. They work! My father showed me and said I may show you too. He said we're very responsible for our age! Here, this one is yours!"

JaYan picked up the bow. It was beautiful, smooth and shiny. MaGan grabbed a flyer and fitted it to his bow. He aimed at the soft trunk of a fern at the nearby stream. He let fly and hit the trunk in its center.

"How's that!"

"Good shot!" JaYan admitted, looking at his own flyers. They were made of straight saplings, as long as his forearm, with the sharpened point covered in a hard, shiny substance.

"My father painted this shiny stuff onto the points. He says it is nearly as hard as a shard!" MaGan said, looking at one of his own flyers. "He asked me not show these to other grown-ups, not until we're much older. He said that many adults will say we're too young to use even these sets. We must also pick up all our flyers and not lose any of them."

JaYan took aim at the trunk and missed.

MaGan was not finished, "My father says the messengers of the Dynasty carry all the meat we eat from their ice caves to ours. He feels we must get our own fresh meat, to be independent of the Dynasty. Therefore, we are never too young to learn to hunt. He calls it being 'self-sufficient.' He says fresh meat tastes much better than when first stored in the ice caves." MaGan stood up straight, looking very serious as he made this speech.

It took a few additional attempts before JaYan succeeded in hitting the trunk.

MaGan hit the trunk twice more before they collected their flyers and wrapped up the hunting sets.

"We have to go back! The party is for both of us and our whole birth-group is there. They will miss us. Let's hide our bows and flyers here, we can come and practice again tomorrow."

They returned to the Habitat where JaYan said, "Come and see! My parents gave me a game of logic. I can show you how to play it!"

In a chamber near where the children were gathered, JaYan's father placed tokens of different colors on an irregularly shaped board. A piece of pure quartz with many facets glistened in the middle of the board.

Some children were from JaYan's and MaGan's peer group, but others were from the older birth cycle. They assembled around the board.

JaYan's father explained, "This game is called 'Clan-Life.' It practices strategic thinking while forcing players to make allowance for possible threats which can destroy the best-laid plans. The game allows for two to six contenders to play, each using different colored tokens."

MaGan grabbed a red token, "This is my color! I'm the fighter."

"Wait! There is much more to the game," JaYan's father tried to contain MaGan's enthusiasm. "By manipulating the piece of quartz, each contender receives a random set of doucia attributes, each representing a hunter or gatherer with different abilities. On the resources board, we place markers upside down. Each marker is either blank or contains the image of a different animal or plant. The animals can be prey, predator or neither; and the plants can be edible, medicinal, poisonous, or provide cover.

"The purpose of the game is to collect provisions to keep your Clan well fed and healthy, without being killed by a predator or poisonous plants. Every player deploys his hunters and gatherers on the action board without initially knowing the positions of the plants and animals. You must deploy your strongest hunters in such a way, they protect the weaker gatherers, without interfering with their ability to collect edibles or process meat. Contenders can work together for protection but then they must share the resources of the area they can occupy and might collect less food and medicinal herbs.

Four movements of the quartz piece represent a game moon. The game ends when an agreed number of game moons have passed, doucia being the standard. Each contender must provide for his game-clan for the duration of the game. Like life, survival is a competition and the best players must have built up a surplus at the end. The other game-clan might not survive. If hunters or gatherers are injured or killed, they lose gathering or hunting time, to treat the wounded or move the body. The group thereby loses ability. At the end of the game, the game-clan must be safe and well provided for, otherwise the player cannot become a game-clan Chief. The best contenders receive honors as game-clan Chiefs."

To the gathered adults, he added, "Like life, the game involves multiple combinations of strategies, plus chance, with imperfect information."

JaYan's father joined him in playing the first game while his mother helped MaGan. Many of the children gathered around, watching closely. MaGan proved to be very good, but his game was aggressive. While JaYan proved to be a natural player.

As the two grew older, the game remained their favorite, typically playing a game spanning at least a game year. They learned to play on their own and often played to support each other's hunters and swept large areas of the board to collect provisions. When the two played together, not even players twice their age could beat them.

MaGan enjoyed the game but preferred to practice with his bow and flyers. He enticed JaYan to practice with him in exchange for spending long hours working out winning strategies in the game of "Clan-Life." The game proved to have many levels of complexity, which they discovered together.

The two cousins became more than relatives—they became best friends.

#

For Clan children, including the Illoreaens, their doucia birthday was the most important of all and their introduction to pre-adulthood. On the eve of their birthday celebration, the two were playing 'Clan-Life' with some of their peers. All the players were struggling to keep their game-clans provisioned but both JaYan and MaGan were individually slowly gaining on the others. JaYan was a far better player but MaGan was ruthless, eliminating JaYan's strongest hunter by pushing him into poison ivy and grabbing the valuable herbs, which JaYan's clan-team had discovered.

"You do not play fair! We should work together for the common good. There were enough resources for both our game-clans to share!" JaYan protested.

"Not really!" MaGan replied, "If we play the game right, our teams must each collect enough provisions within a moon cycle or a year, which gives us only a limited number of moves each. If we don't manage to collect enough, our game-clan starves. A win with a reduced clan or even with only your hunters left, isn't a very satisfactory win. A raid on your clan saved my game-clan. See, I play the grown-up version of the game. Realism!"

"I don't think I like your realism. I bet in reality, you would not take anything from me to save yourself."

"Only because we're part of the same team," MaGan laughed, "Come on I've won! Let's go and watch the preparations for the celebration."

One of the players, called SkepTan, part of their peer group, was even more upset with MaGan's ruthless play, "I think you are as barbaric as a Primitive! I like to play the game in such a way that my game-clan has enough provisions, without sweeping the plains and killing as many animals as possible, as the two of you do. The game allows enough provisions by concentrating on gathering in fertile areas and only occasionally supplementing the game-clan's food with meat."

"You are boring, SkepTan!" MaGan mocked him. "Go play with your plants and animals at your parent's living area. Your taste buds will wither away from lack of eating tasty fresh meat."

As they walked away, he commented, without bothering to whisper, "He's the most annoying of all in our birth-group. Instead of doing something like hunting or climbing or running he just watches his plants and small animals. Boring!"

JaYan disliked the MaGan's mocking insult, aimed at SkepTan. He glanced back to where SkepTan stood, downcast. However, JaYan soon forgot him in the excitement of the ongoing preparations and celebrations.

The incident would haunt JaYan and MaGan in future years.

<><><>

Chapter 22 – A Sensitive in our midst

The Giant's surprise attack was unacceptable, but what really upset the Illoreaens was the discovery that Questa was a Sensitive. Not only a Sensitive, but also one with the ability to Sense the presence of the Giants long before their own methods detected them.

The Illoreaens had several concerns. "What more can she detect? Does she read our minds, our innermost thoughts? Can she control us?" Addressing JaYan, one of them, surrounded by a few others, asked, "What is the Coordinating Committee doing about her? Are we safe? You are the Coordinating Speaker. It is your responsibility!"

Questa did not need her Sensing ability to be aware of the sudden surge of resentment. When she walked past any of the Illoreaens, they glared at her, putting up their hands in a shielding gesture before hurrying away.

The Illoreaens avoided her and she kept to herself, trying hard not to yield to the bitterness she felt. Eventually she approached JaYan, "What is going on? Why do you all blame me for warning you about the threat of the Giants? Surely the warning saved lives!"

JaYan looked at her with a troubled face, raising his hand to his forehead and sweeping it back over his hair. He sighed. "I'm sorry. We did not know you were a Sensitive or even that there are still Sensitives within the Clans. The implication is a great shock."

"All Oracle-Healers are Sensitives and we are well-regarded. I told you I am an Oracle-Healer in training, which must have confirmed that I am likewise a Sensitive. I have never hidden my ability! I owe you my life and I am grateful. But why this hostility?"

"We of the Illoreaen Coordinating Committee are discussing the matter and will explain soon enough, but we have to consider our options first, so please be patient."

"I have never been ashamed of my abilities. No, I am proud of them! What is the matter with you?" Questa withdrew into her resting place away from all activity, where she hid behind a drape, her back against the smooth wall. She avoided contact and ate her meals alone when the eating area was not busy.

An entire day passed before JaYan approached her. "Please come with me. We have much to ask and to explain."

Questa followed JaYan into the depths of the cave, into areas previously denied her. She looked around. She had been brought to a large cavity with smooth walls and ceiling. Comfortable seats surrounded a large circular table and a slight, musty odor proved regular but ancient usage.

This is an important place where decisions are made, she realized.

A few older Illoreaens sat around the table. JaYan signaled towards a seat, placed where all could see her. She could feel the hostility in the room without Sensing. *Their body language and faces show aggression,* she thought. *I will have to discover what I did wrong, and respond carefully. Was it my intrusion into MaGan's secret chamber of life that angers them so much?*

JaYan took a seat directly opposite her and started to speak, "Questa of the Second Valley, you know me and MaGan. We are members of the Coordinating Committee and I am the Coordinating Speaker. We have many tasks, which includes making recommendations and decisions on any matter concerning the Illoreaens' well-being.

"We owe you an explanation regarding the treatment and the hostility you are experiencing. Your trespassing into our fertility chamber already distressed the Committee, but discovering you are a Sensitive, is infinitely worse. Your claim that Healers within the Clans are often Sensitives, is hardly believable and a shock.

"If true, the thought of the Dynasty never divulging this information intensifies our astonishment and will affect the trust relationship we believe we have with the Dynasty.

"We would have to determine the truth and, if what you say is true, we must also discover if there is anything else the Dynasty has hidden from us. Please be very open with us and answer the multiple questions we wish to ask.

"Before we start, let us explain our position and concern relative to Sensitives. We also need a commitment from you not to use your abilities. I believe in you. I assured the other Coordinators you can be trusted. Do you agree?"

Questa's resentment of the treatment she received grew. She was upset, and it showed. "I'm an honorable Clan-member, a descendant of many generations of highly regarded Healers and Oracle-Healers, whom all the Clans trust," she said. Her face flushed red, "It is forbidden for any Sensitive to infringe on any Clan-member's privacy, if that is what you mean with 'using my ability'. I did not and will not do that!" She paused to take a deep breath, "I only focused my Sensing on the Giants when their focused hatred infringed on my awareness. I made sure there were no Illoreaens nearby when I intensified my Sensing of the Giants." Unconsciously, Questa leaned forward and then got up, raising her voice. "We never Sense without explicit permission, except in cases of immediate and imminent danger. Never! To abuse hospitality by Sensing one's host, would be extremely offensive. Worse, it would be unforgivable! No Sensitive would ever do that!"

Questa realized she was standing. Embarrassed, she sat down. "Of course, I will not use my Sensing ability if not specifically requested to do so." She shivered from the excitement and intensity of her emotions. Despite the chill in the chamber, deep within the cave system, she felt uncomfortably warm.

JaYan tried to soothe her, "We mean you no harm! We did not intend to insult you. I apologize. We are in unknown territory and must explore how to go forward."

To one of the others he said, "Let's get her something to drink and eat before we continue."

A Coordinator got up, said something to someone outside the chamber and then returned to his seat.

They all looked at her, many with less antagonism. Some even held expressions of melancholy. Their feelings emanated and penetrated her inadequately blocked Sensing. She immediately strengthened her control.

A young Illoreaen brought in a wooden platter containing some sweetmeats and a goblet with a refreshing drink.

Questa felt drained by the emotions she suppressed. She gratefully drank from the goblet and ate a few of the sweetmeats, noticing the subtle flavors, better than those she was used to. She slumped in her seat.

The youth looked around the table questioningly. None of the Coordinators responded, but JaYan indicated the youth should bring enough for all.

JaYan waited until the young Illoreaen returned and placed goblets and platters of sweetmeats on the table, then, with his eyes sweeping over the Coordinators to include them all, he said, "We'll need this before we're finished."

Turning to Questa again he said, "Let me relate our traditional history. Our shock on discovering the continued existence of Sensitives, and that you are one, arises from what history tells us about the Sensitives of long ago. Our abhorrence and fear of Sensitives originated during and after the Inter-Clan Devastation. You must know the history?"

"Yes, of course. It was when Sensitives settled in the Dynasty Valley."

Shock registered on all faces and a deathly silence descended on the gathering.

Then yelling and questions erupted. One voice—louder than the others—dominated, "Are you saying there are Sensitives at the Dynasty Valley! Even Orrox may be a Sensitive?"

Questa couldn't understand the reaction, "Yes, of course he is. The Orrox Dynasty scions usually have the strongest Sensitive ability of all."

Chaos broke out.

MaGan shouted, "Everyone calm down!"

With difficulty, MaGan and JaYan managed to restore order.

"Listen!" JaYan called out, "Questa is not concealing how widespread Sensitivity is in the Clans. She doesn't understand our reaction. We must find out why our view differs so radically from Questa's. We have already decided to research Sensitivity in depth."

It took time, but finally the gathering subsided and the members of the Committee nodded their heads, indicating he should continue.

"For the sake of comparison, I will re-tell the relevant parts. We expect you to disclose where you disagree. You might not know the part of the history which concerns us. It might be of interest to you."

"The relevant history begins with the Inter-Clan Devastation, also called the Deadly Strife..." JaYan continued to tell the tale of these occurrences, which Questa knew well.

She wondered why JaYan repeated the story but realized the group he refers to as the 'wise Elders' in his story, was the Sages who had warned the Clans of their excesses. *The Illoreaens don't know that they had already developed Sensing abilities and could read trends and warn against impending disasters, that they were the ones who became the first Oracle-Healers.*

The Coordinators in the hall listened attentively and JaYan continued without noticing that Questa already disagreed with a part of his tale.

JaYan continued recounting how the drought broke and the rains came again. His recollection confirmed the Illoreaens' knowledge of the taboos and traditions of the Clans, which originated at the time.

"The combined Council of Chiefs and Elders believed, just as the Clans, the Dynasty and we, the Illoreaens, still believe, stability is essential for ideal living conditions. The danger inherent in living this ideal, is stagnation. Therefore, the Clans have always had to preserve the ability to adapt to changed conditions and to keep diversity intact. This requires a fine balance and we have always encouraged originality. I assume this is knowledge shared by all? We at the Illoreaen Habitat provide for the unexpected and allow originality to flourish."

JaYan looked at Questa but continued before she could respond.

"Seeing you did not know of our existence, you would also not know of the decision to create three groups, each with different responsibilities. The lifestyle of each must ensure the well-being of the whole.

"The Clans would continue their essential lifestyle of gathering herbs and edible plants supplemented by hunting. However, the other two groups must ensure the Clans have the facilities and access to medicinals, and techniques to cancel the inherent hardship of such a lifestyle. Strict rules must make this possible.

Most of this effort must remain unknown to the Clans, to ensure stability and avoid the probable competition, where each Clan wants more for themselves than the others have. I understand the rules governing the Clans have not changed: Each Clan must regulate the number of its members to keep them within limits dictated by the number above which factions tend to form, i.e. gracia Clan-members and also by the potential yield of their immediate environment. Each Clan needed a Habitat from which to hunt and gather food.

"To eliminate cold and hunger and to increase comfort without affecting the stable lifestyle of the Clans, we, the Illoreaens were formed. Our mission is to develop means to enhance the quality of life of the Clans. I believe that no Clan has ever found themselves limited due to a lack of available resources. We must ensure, with the Dynasty's help, that each valley contains plants yielding adequate produce. The same with animals, which can be hunted for meat. These developments were intended to be in secret and the results to be discreetly distributed to all Clans, when ready.

"The new Illoreaen Clan consisted of talented Clansmen, from all Clans. Those selected were knowledgeable in edibles, coverings, torches and lamps burning fat. Others were skilled at flaking obsidian to create cutters or to improve hunting aids and techniques."

"Over and above their other functions, the Dynasty were tasked to monitor and to improve the yield of the naturally occurring grains, fruit and nut trees, by careful selection. They were also made responsible for collecting and storing enough provisions for distributing during times of shortage. The Clans must provide the necessities.

Turning to Questa he asked, "Do you agree with my recounting of our joint history?"

This is all nonsense, Questa thought. She looked down at her hands during most of the speech. Suppressing her anger with difficulty, she took a few deep breaths before looking up and answering as calmly as possible, "I never knew anything about the Illoreaens and I believe very few if any in the Clans know of you. Those you call wise Elders, we know as the Sages and there is much more than you are telling. But please, finish your tale. Then I will comment."

JaYan looked at her sharply, as if wanting her to explain, then said, "Calling the wise Elders Sages, is just a difference in terminology."

He looked at Questa but she looked down, avoiding all eye contact. After a short pause he continued, "To stabilize the whole, the Council of Chiefs and Elders would meet annually at the Dynasty Valley to resolve disputes and devise strategies to handle threats. The leader of the Council often came from the Orrox offspring of the wise Elders. The Dynasty has always acted as the link between us and the other Clans. The Dynasty acts as a central control to ensure the Clans never fall back into their bad ways.

"You must know the training of Healers depends on the medicinal remedies, potions, mechanisms, and methods the Dynasty receives from us, as well as the roots, barks and herbs collected by the Clans."

He paused. "MaGan, I believe you should continue."

MaGan, sitting next to JaYan, at what Questa recognized as the head of the table, stood up and looked sharply at Questa, "The rest of the history as we know it, differs from what we think you can tell us. I have learned how knowledgeable you are working with herbs and medicaments; my group and my ancestors have always experimented with remedies, potions and healing.

"We make extracts from plants and herbs and develop potions and powders. For instance, the painkilling powders you said you have used before, we extract and concentrate from poplar trees and the healing powders from specific fungi growing on milk. We also developed the methods to cut into the living flesh to heal or extract diseased tissue while a patient is rendered unconscious. We do much more and carry out extensive tests before releasing anything to the Dynasty for distributing to the Clans. You must have used many of these as a Healer.

"We explain new medicaments and dosages to a few very knowledgeable Healers. In their turn, these Healers discuss the effectiveness of the medicines, methods, and techniques with us. The Dynasty makes all the arrangements. We never suspected any of them to have Sensing ability. They might have hidden it, we do not know. We always understood that those whom we train, teach the Healers from the Clans in their turn. Those we met were always well-trained Healers sharing their latest successes with us."

The Coordinators around the table nodded their agreement.

Questa listened in amazement. She never guessed how the tutors at the Dynasty got their superior medicines and deep knowledge. She did not doubt the truth of the tale. *It is all so subtle, with just a few essentials hidden. Secrets surround me!*

"I didn't know! But why the shock and hostility towards me, and I assume all Sensitives? We have never done you any harm and our abilities are essential to the Clans."

JaYan responded, "We have supplied exploding powders, which burn or create smoke in different colors. Some of our powders and potions give illusionary effects of higher perception. We often worry about possible misuse of our innovations. The name Oracle-Healer has always bothered us. We were concerned they might use the illusions to make bogus predictions, call them oracles and use them to manipulate the Clans. However, the Dynasty has always assured us the use of these effects is only for entertainment during feasts. Now we understand, all Oracle-Healers and probably many Healers are Sensitives and can read the emotions, possibly thoughts, of other Clan-members. This means they may even be able to use our powders and medicines to manipulate other Clan-members. Mind control over time would certainly lead to misuse and eventually be used for evil means, creating havoc and warfare among the Clans. This, obviously, cannot be allowed."

Questa leaned forward. Her hands covering her eyes and forehead.

JaYan didn't notice, "The Dynasty told us, such use is an aberration, punishable by the strongest measures possible. They assured us, such a horror is impossible. We believed them! We find the idea outrageous! To my surprise, you easily admitted to being an Oracle-Healer. We tolerated you. You were pleasant, dependent on us and you would soon return to the Dynasty. We tried to keep you away from anything critical within the Illoreaen Habitat."

Questa was dumbfounded. She could not respond. Anger built up again. Her head felt as if it would burst. She felt numb, blood rose to her head.

JaYan did not notice the effect of his words. He was upset too and glanced around the table, "You have the ability to even Sense the presence of Giants from afar, Giants whose thoughts, emotions and very being are so drastically different from ours. How do we know you are not reading our minds this very moment? How can we trust you are not?

"Even our children know the history of the previous evil existence of Clan-members called Sensitives. They spread a condition called 'extra-sensory perception.' We understand it to have been a scourge that damaged the brain and turned Clansmen insane during the Inter-Clan Devastation. Many died horrible deaths from pain projected into their brains."

JaYan became intense and emotional as he spoke and sat down. He put his head between his hands with elbows leaning on the table.

The others now looked at Questa. She turned white, trembling with anger. For a while, she could not speak, and then she exploded, pounded the table and stood. "What nonsense! How can you be so stupid? How *dare* you!"

Her entire body burned with anger. With a shaking hand, she reached for the goblet, spilling some of its contents before she was able to swallow. The moisture helped, but on the second sip she choked and coughed until tears ran down her cheeks. She struggled for breath, but no one got up to help her, they just stared.

She was furious. *JaYan has known me long enough not to come up with such nonsense. He should have investigated the truth before speaking.*

She stared, her eyes sweeping across the group, at first in anger, then in a challenge. The assembly looked back in silence. At last she managed to recover a semblance of equilibrium and spoke with a trembling voice. "We cannot manipulate! We certainly cannot take control of a mind! Again! Nonsense! We can only share emotions and images! Of course, the Dynasty told you such a horror is impossible!"

She took a few deep breaths before she continued more calmly, "We also know the history, but your version is a gross distortion. The group of wise Clan-members you mentioned, those who warned the Clans, were Sensitives, called Sages at the time. I traced my family line to several of them and can recite the details. They warned against the wild exploitation of the environment and the explosion of the Clan population on the plains before the Inter-Clan Devastation.

"We use the same term for that terrible time. Their Sensing abilities were still basic and undeveloped but they were the ones who suffered the devastating pain when Sensing the hurt of others. They were the ones driven out of their minds when they could not isolate themselves from the emanated pain projected into their minds when the Clans tortured and killed one another!

"I know first-hand! I also suffer when anybody is in pain, despite my training. My Clan protected me. Even before birth, my mother blocked pain from affecting me. Later, as a baby, I was kept deep in our cave for protection. There the moisture in the ground and cave walls shielded me from thunderstorms or Sensing any Clan-member in pain.

"During my birth, highly experienced Sensitives blocked my emerging Sensing ability. Later I learned to control and block off Sensing, when required, which is often. Slaughtering of animals for food requires me to block out the emanation coming from the animal. It is another reason why we require the killing of animals for food to be painless and without stress.

"We Sensitives know of pain! Your interpretation of history has misled you. I'm certain the Dynasty assumed you knew all about Sensitives. The Healers you met must have been highly trained Sensitives, who completely blocked off their Sensing, as good manners prescribe. There would be no reason to mention the ability, which is known to all Clan-members. You would not suspect their ability if you had never been told. You also did not realize that I am a Sensitive even though I did not try to hide my ability! You only became aware of the fact when I Sensed the presence of the Giants and warned you. I cannot believe any Sensitive can be as dishonest as you suspect! There must be a different explanation!"

Questa paused, still angry but now in better control. "Let me tell you what I was taught about our history before you start your questioning. I can Sense truth without invading privacy and those who explained our history, believed their version to be true. My grandmother, Chiara, taught me the history as she heard it from her ancestors, and so have all the Sensitives from generation to generation. Good memory is part of our ability and training.

"The true history is as follows: during the Inter-Clan Devastation, it was the Sensitives who escaped from the killing and torture, hiding in the future Dynasty Valley. There, the Orrox, and all tutors are Sensitives. They teach us better control, allowing us to survive in a painful world.

She inhaled deeply, closing her eyes, then slowly exhaled. "I'm very tired now and wish to sleep. Please, I must leave now. You can ask me anything tomorrow and I will answer truthfully."

She got up and followed JaYan out of the Chamber as he led her silently to her habitual sleeping area.

With only a nod, he left her to return to the Committee, who discussed her words and the probability of Dynasty secrets, until very late.

#

Questa did not sleep well. She revisited the meeting in her mind, going over the heated discussion repeatedly. In her dreams, Giants replaced the Coordinators, yelling and grimacing, arms outstretched in hideous threats. She got up tired, with an aching head and slowly made her way to the eating area. She quickly gulped down some food without tasting anything and then returned to her sleeping area, where she sat, staring into the distance, eyes unfocused.

When JaYan came for her late in the day, he noticed dark rings under her tired eyes.

He explained, "The Coordinating Committee discussed the meeting through the night and we accept we may have been misinformed. Until we can investigate further, we accept that you believe your version is the truth. We informed all Illoreaens of the error. You are not dangerous, you are an ally. You must understand, we often use the image of Sensitives in our children's tales as a scary presence. For us, the concept of a benevolent Sensitive is a difficult transition. It will take time. Please follow me."

Anger nearly overwhelmed Questa again, but she meekly followed, suppressing her feelings. She was a guest with no options. In the meeting chamber, the Coordinators all looked tired. They had not slept either but they did not look as aggressive as before. A large number of mature Illoreaens, looking interested, sat on chairs arranged against the walls.

At least JaYan believes part of what I told them. I'm sure it was he who convinced the Committee to consider my story as truth, Questa thought.

JaYan started the discussion again. "According to our records, at the time of the Inter-Clan Devastation a group of talented survivors was identified and asked to study the causes of the drought, the availability of food and the levels and sustainability of resources. They were the original core of what later became the Illoreaens. To allow the group to work unhindered, the Chiefs decided the other Clans would provision them. Later the Dynasty and the Council accepted the obligation and they have been supplying us ever since. Our ancestors relocated to this infertile area, far from the Clan valleys, to enable us to work unrestricted. The location was a fortunate choice since we found many minerals and substances, as well as useful gasses escaping from fissures, which helped us develop many items. We always had little contact with the Clans until all communication routed through the Council and the Dynasty. We consulted our records and found no reference of the first Illoreaens interacting with the Elders you call Sages. Their only contact was when serving together on the Council. Even if those Council members knew of Sensing, it is not mentioned. We stopped attending Council meetings once our knowledge search began.

"Please tell us your version of what happened when the Chiefs and Sages gathered after the Inter-Clan Devastation, when the rain returned." JaYan sat down and sighed. "You are tired. We all are. Take your time, but we really need to know more before we can decide what to do."

Questa sat in thought, squeezed her forehead with her fingers to suppress a headache, and took a deep breath before she began. "The first Sensitive to gather the young with Sensing ability and train them to handle the pain they Sensed, was named Ollionox. He rescued many of the first Sensitives by insisting mothers isolate and protect those of their young, who showed certain symptoms as babies. We still use similar indications to identify and protect babies with emerging Sensitive abilities. We can detect the potential early in the womb. An awareness of life is inherent to our ability and we Sense life as soon as a fetus forms. Mothers are always very proud if we detect the Sensing ability in a fetus. The whole Clan helps to protect the baby. Before Ollionox's time, any fetus, baby or child with such abilities, suffered extreme mental pain and often died or suffered irreversible brain damage.

"After the Inter-Clan Devastation, the Clans formed a supervising Council and they recognized the importance of the Sages with Sensitive ability. They knew of the valley where some with the ability previously gathered. The Council decided the Sensitives needed a facility for their protection. Within the valley of the Dynasty, a group assembled. They were dedicated to the identification, protection, and training of Sensitives."

She took a deep breath, "The inherent empathy of a Sensitive makes us ideal Healers. Our training includes knowledge of herbs and enhances our ability to read trends. We do this by analyzing many small clues. Indications the non-trained might subconsciously notice, but are usually not even aware of, and instead call instinct. Our training makes us notice these and their individual importance. The training greatly increases our ability. Each Clan needs a Healer. Preferably, this should be a Sensitive trained in healing, who can also help to advise the Chief by observing trends. They are the Oracle-Healers. Our abilities have grown far beyond anything originally anticipated until we can now Sense the health of a newly fertilized embryo and arrange the gender during fertilization."

She paused before adding, "We do not read minds. We do Sense pain, but learn to block it because it can be overwhelming. We can vaguely read emotions when specifically asked and allowed to do so."

Questa looked at the different Coordinators with a sweeping view. She did not like the expressions on their faces or their body language.

MaGan spoke first, "We never imagined the Sensing ability could be so powerful. Sensing fetuses, indeed! Sensing Giants from afar! You must understand how the thought disturbs us."

Before anyone else could comment, JaYan turned to the other Coordinators, "We have great respect for the Clans, even though we keep much hidden from them. We believe the well-being of the Clans requires them to remain self-sufficient for their necessities. Our existence is a secret, kept from the Clans and, now we understand, therefore also from many Sensitives and Oracle-Healers. Before the Dynasty reveals our existence to those who need to know about us, they must have reached a high level of expertise and competency. When the next courier-messengers from the Dynasty arrives, we will have much to discuss and they will have much to explain. Before you make any comments, allow me time. I wish to think."

There was unrest in the gathering, but the Coordinators managed to keep everyone quiet. Those who persisted were gestured to leave.

JaYan was quiet for a time. Then he turned to the gathering, "I think, until proven otherwise, we'll have to accept that Sensitives, and Questa specifically, are not dangerous and use their power to benefit the Clans and by extension, us. This seems quite similar to how we use our developed knowledge to benefit the Clans while at the same time keeping it secret from them, and also in many instances from the Dynasty. The reason for our secrecy is to avoid disruption and unrealistic expectations.

"It is not clear why we were not informed of the power of Sensitives, but the conclusion must be: our developed knowledge and your Sensing abilities were both kept secret, by each group from the other. Only the Dynasty knew both secrets. I believe we must trust Questa and summon the Orrox himself. He has much to explain!

"Let us end the meeting and continue later. We have a great deal to think about and many questions to ask. I trust we'll all sleep well." With a nod to Questa, he stood up and left, leaving her to find her own way back to where she slept.

She could not sleep. *What will become of me? How can I live in a community where everyone distrusts me? When will I ever return to my Clan?*

Chapter 23 – Primitives Attack

The Primitives charged towards the fire where Jupex, Orrox, and their companions formed a defensive circle. Orrox turned to his acolytes, speaking softly, "Quick, concentrate! We must project something to scare off the Primitives! Follow my guidance, project the same emotion and images as I do. Concentrate hard. Synchronize with me. Now!"

The Clansmen did not understand what Orrox and the acolytes were doing until black fear overwhelmed them. The feelings started faintly and then grew in intensity. Dark, horrible images formed in their minds, enhancing the emotion. They had never experienced anything as terrifying before.

Orrox shouted, directing his voice at the Clansmen, "Do not close your eyes. Look at the fire. Think of your Clan! It will help!"

The Clansmen complied. They stared at the fire. As they changed focus, the images in their brains weakened in clarity. The intensity of their own fear diminished.

They noticed how the Primitives hesitated, clearly confused as the projected images formed. They pulled faces and cringed with wide eyes under the onslaught of the emotion and terrifying images. Nevertheless, they continued advancing.

The leader of the Primitives carried a spear made from a sapling with a sharpened point, hardened in fire. He threw it, aiming straight at Orrox's heart. Then, raising his club, he stormed forward, ready to smash Orrox's skull.

Orrox ducked, lunging to the right, stumbling against Camla. The spear just missed him and clattered against the rock behind, and fell to the ground.

The images in the Clansmen minds, dimmed, while the Primitives seemed to revive. They followed their leader's example and also threw their spears. Armed only with their clubs, they followed him and attacked.

Orrox, recovering his stance, whispered urgently, for his acolytes to hear, "You have it wrong; they are emotionally unlike the Clans. Their brains are different! Synchronize with my emanation. Read my Sensing of the leader's mind. Sense the inner self of the leader and adapt. Concentrate on the leader. Then project."

The Primitives were approaching fast, ready to smash skulls. The effect of the renewed projection of fear and ghastly images had a visible effect on them. They recoiled and dropped their clubs. The leader's reaction was even stronger. He clamped his hands over his ears and screamed.

Orrox threw some powder onto the fire. It caused a sudden flash of light and a loud boom. The Primitives froze, their eyes widening further.

The leader spun around and ran away, yelling. His reaction increased the terror of the other Primitives. They followed him as fast as they could.

The Clansmen could hear them falling over obstacles, as they ran away in the dark.

"That is enough!" Orrox cried and the phenomenon and images in the Clansmen's minds disappeared.

#

Orrox collapsed, exhausted, while the acolytes also sat down in a circle, breathing rhythmically, heads bent. They were obviously tired, wiping their brows and massaging their temples. Orrox sat with closed eyes.

Jupex and the Clansmen stood near Orrox and the acolytes. Their spears and clubs still clutched in their hands. They had never used them. Unsure of what to do next, they shifted their weight from leg to leg, flexing their shoulder muscles.

None of the Clansmen, not even Jupex, had realized how powerful the abilities of the Sensitives were. They watched them in silence. Giving them time to recover from the ordeal, which had visibly tapped their energy.

After a while, the acolytes started whispering amongst themselves. Ammox said, "That was incredible! What an experience! The fear and horrible images we projected were so much more intense than I ever thought possible! Orrox's imaginings pulling and coordinating ours! I was barely able to make my projection synchronize."

Bronnox answered, "That flash and boom! Orrox made that happen at exactly the right moment. Just when the flaming monsters they imagined, engulfed, swallowed them. No wonder they ran!"

The acolytes gave Orrox a sip of water.

Orrox looked up at Jupex and the Clansmen, "I'm sorry. I did not intend for you to experience the emanation. There is always the risk our projections can leak into those who are near to whom they are directed. We focused on the Primitives but some of the energy spilled over to you, partly because we are not in tune with their psyche."

Then, turning to the acolytes he said, "You have done very well, I could not have achieved this alone, but do not ever try such an emanation on your own. I trust you will never have to project such ugliness again. You will probably develop a headache and need soothing."

He took a sip from a small gourd he produced from the folds of his kaross. It visibly revitalized him. He allowed each of the acolytes a small sip too.

After a short delay, Orrox and the acolytes got up.

"We have to go," Orrox said.

"What an incredible experience!" Jupex said as they doused the fire. "You have shown how much we have always underestimated you; how powerful and dangerous Sensitives can be. It scares me. However, you have saved us from a lethal fight we might have lost. We must thank you," he paused while Orrox remained silent. Then he continued, "Why did they attack us?"

"Although they are aggressive, we of the Dynasty can normally control them and keep them from entering the valleys." Orrox's voice was still weak. "Our patrols spy on them continuously and can anticipate raids into specific valleys and ambush them when they approach."

He paused taking a deep breath, "Even so, they often attack Clan-members when we traverse the plains, trespassing in what they regard as their territory, even though they are late arrivals. We discourage attacks by trying to create scary myths concerning us, and limiting contact by infrequent travel through the plains.

We react quickly if a Primitive enters any of the Clan valleys. Our main defense is to play on their superstition and fears.

He paused again, "This strategy has now turned against us. From their abusive language, I understood they are blaming us for the Catastrophe, including the disappearance of the prey. They are already suffering from hunger—you might have noticed the leather straps tightly wound and knotted around their stomachs—they do that to reduce hunger pains. Extreme famine cannot be far off. I fear they might attack again. Let's go!"

#

They hurried along, as fast as was possible in the bad light. Orrox was always proud of the fitness of the acolytes, but projecting tired them and they struggled to keep up with the Clansmen. Orrox and Jupex conferred.

"You can move faster than we can," Orrox said. "Hurry along and warn your Clan to prepare for a possible attack."

Jupex and his Clansmen disappeared in the gloom while Orrox and his acolytes followed as fast as they could. With the Clansmen already far ahead, Orrox said, "Despite the danger from Primitives, who might be following our tracks, we'll have to rest often to preserve our strength. Now I must rest for a short while. I need it more than you do. I had to force your efforts to synchronize your emanations with mine and to focus correctly. It was very demanding."

He found a protected alcove, formed by a number of huge boulders. They all sat close together. The acolytes watched the approaches with wide eyes. They listened intently. Every movement attracted their attention. The slightest sound made them jump.

Orrox wanted to distract them, "While I rest, remember and analyze the strangeness of the Primitive psyche. We concentrated our projection on their leader and with my help you all managed to read the unfamiliar, to synchronize, and adapt your emanations. A very important ability, but I would have preferred imparting the technique in a safer way!

"Although we focused on the leader, the emotion and images pulsed through the brains of the other Primitives as well. Remember, all Primitives are similar."

Orrox closed his eyes and the acolytes could Sense him clearing his mind of thoughts. They tried to rest too, but they did not succeed as well.

After a while, Orrox opened his eyes. "I wish to sit still for a bit longer. Tell me, what do each of you remember? How is the Primitive psyche different from ours? Ammox, you have a talent to see the extraordinary. Tell us how you experienced the encounter."

Ammox thought for a few moments before answering, "It was horrible even though I always knew you were the source of the projection. Something specific to you was always there. Kind of like when a Bard tells a tale, I can recognize the voice and know who is speaking without affecting the content of the tale or its presentation. Then, when we synchronized our projections with yours, your adaptation to fit the Primitive leader's psyche became clear and I could adapt and focused better. It gave some understanding of the difference between us and them."

Camla looked at Ammox intensely, "Yes, you have explained it exactly. When they fled, I could Sense their fear and the differences between them and us."

The acolytes each explained their different experiences, then emanated their perception of how they Sensed the Primitives' mind.

"Remember, the inner self of the various Clan-similar types is different, even though there are parallels," Orrox said. "You need to be able to recognize this and distinguish the unique type of brain of each of us, Clan-similar types. We should be able to Sense their presence and emotions if we concentrate hard enough.

"As an exercise and for our safety, you must try to Sense the presence of any Primitive approaching. Practice to focus on their strangeness as we continue on our way. I fear they will attack again. Now we must hurry."

They rested twice more. Despite the breaks, the acolytes noticed Orrox's continued exhaustion. Their own tense nerves denied them effective rest.

#

By the time Orrox and his companions arrived in the Second Valley, it was already getting dark. Jupex was organizing his Clan's defenses, strengthening the palisade. His companions were telling the others of the Primitives' attack and how they experienced Orrox's emanation. The tale grew with each re-telling.

They could not put the feelings, images, sounds and smells into understandable words. One of them said, "Even my mouth went dry and was filled with a horrible taste. I wanted to retch. Looking into the fire helped, especially while I tried to remember my loved ones. When I closed my eyes for a moment, the images in my brain sharpened and seemed more real. Then everything was even scarier."

Another added, "At the ceremonies where the Oracle-Healers projected pleasant images, the feelings and imaginings are only faintly discernible. What we experienced was overwhelming."

Whenever Orrox or one of the acolytes walked by, Clan-members stopped their preparations and stared.

#

They all spent an anxious night with no visibility. Orrox was sure the night was too dark for the Primitives to assemble and approach the valley.

Orrox allowed himself and the acolytes the sleep they desperately needed. At the first glimmerings of light, they spaced themselves in a semi-circle at some distance, from the protective palisade of the Clan. To detect Primitives approaching, they had to limit the cross-interference caused by the minds of the nearby Clan-members. Distance was required. They had hardly taken up their positions and focused their minds, when they Sensed the overwhelming presence of the Primitives, an angry volatile emanation, growing fast and indicating many Primitives approaching in war frenzy.

Orrox yelled, "No! I was wrong! Get to the palisade!" They rushed towards the rough barricade, warning the Clan-members of the Primitives approach.

"Open the barricade! Let Orrox and his companions in," Jupex cried but there was no time.

They all heard the high-pitched cries of the Primitives. Orrox and the acolytes could not join the Clan-members inside the palisade before the first wave of Primitives reached them. Instead, they were forced to rush up the valley, where they found a secondary protective position between large boulders. But it was not good enough.

#

Jupex saw Orrox and the acolytes disappearing up the valley as the first Primitives reached them. *I don't know what Orrox can do to help us now. Any emanation to scare the Primitives, will affect us too,* he thought before concentrating on the attack.

When the Primitives reached the barricade, they threw stones and jabbed at the defenders with their spears. They pulled and hammered at the barricade using their hands and knobbed clubs.

Jupex and the Clan launched their spears accurately and used their clubs effectively, killing several Primitives.

But reinforcements stepped onto their dying fellows and continued attacking.

Primitives appearing on the cliff above initiated a secondary attack, pelting the Clan with rocks.

Avoiding the thrown rocks reduced the effectiveness of the defense.

A mass onslaught at one point of the palisade resulted in a desperate battle. Clan-members streamed to support, weakening the defenses elsewhere. There were just too many simultaneous attacks. The Clan was greatly outnumbered. They couldn't keep up on all fronts.

A part of the palisade leaned inward. A few Clan-members let go of their weapons to push it upright again. They were clubbed by the Primitives until they had to let go and the palisade fell flat.

Primitives streamed in.

Then further sections collapsed.

Many Clan-members were injured.

The Primitives' numbers where overwhelming. The onslaught was unstoppable.

"We cannot hold out!" Jupex yelled. "We have to flee up the valley. To the Cave! There they can only enter a few at a time. There we will stop them. It is our only hope. MaXiox, we must protect the injured!"

#

Orrox and the acolytes were at a great disadvantage. The horror and agony of the Clan-members being hurt, tortured and killed, emanated strongly. Despite their efforts to block these feelings, the horror broke through, entering the Sensitives' minds in overwhelming waves. Orrox managed to suppress his own reaction—the instinctive need to cringe and hide. He yelled at his acolytes, loud enough for his words to overpower their natural reaction. Mixed in with the painful emanations created by the hurt of their own, they also Sensed, although at a much lesser intensity, the Primitives suffering from injuries.

The Primitives on the cliff added their simple sapling spears to the stones they were throwing. A sharp stab in Orrox's side, a pain as excruciating as those he experienced in his mind, made him realize a spear had seriously injured him. He had to flee up the valley with his acolytes. The remaining Clan-members soon followed.

As the distance between the Sensitives and the wounded increased, the effect on their minds lessened but the physical suffering caused by the spear-wound in Orrox's side, remained. He shielded the pain from emanating, but the acolytes saw how he struggled to keep up.

"Bronnox, you are the strongest! Help me support Orrox!" Ammox yelled. His eyes large.

Camla and Lonna with ashen faces stayed close behind the two who kept their arms around Orrox. They were partly running and partly dragging Orrox over the debris littering the valley floor and up the steep incline.

#

Jupex and his Clan-members burst through a collapsed section of the palisade and rushed up the valley. The Clan youths and men formed a protective shield behind the fleeing Clan-members, as they escaped towards the Clan cave.

The Primitives first attacked the injured, making easier targets.

Jupex, MaXiox and a few men—relatives of the injured—fought them off.

Most of the wounded had difficulty clambering over the boulders and debris blocking the valley and could not keep up.

For a time, the men managed to protect the wounded Clan-members, killing Primitives with mighty swings of their larger clubs, all the while moving up the valley.

The Clan dragged along those who were unable to walk. It soon proved impossible to support the injured while swinging their heavy clubs. One by one they had to leave the injured behind.

"We will not be able to save them!" MaXiox yelled. "Jupex, you have to reach the main body of the Clan and save them. I will stay with these injured ones. We will buy you time. Save the Clan!"

Unable to save all, tears of frustration nearly blinded Jupex. He hesitated for a moment, then conceding the logic behind his friend's demand, he nodded and squeezed MaXiox's shoulder in a farewell gesture.

MaXiox returned the gesture with a nod.

The Primitives rushed forward to tear each of the ill-fated, abandoned victims apart. They gathered around the victims' bodies, danced and stabbed and clubbed until the remains were mangled, unrecognizable mounds of flesh.

Jupex rushed up the valley to overtake his Clan. They were nearly at the site of the cave.

Meanwhile, the oldest and slowest Clan-members in the main group could not keep up. A few of the younger Clan-members stayed with them for protection.

When Jupex reached the rest of the group, he called out, "We must barricade ourselves inside the cave. There the overwhelming number of the Primitives would make less of a difference. Only a few Primitives will be able to attack at the same time."

Some Primitives who had attacked from the top of the cliffs, managed to reach the cave before the Clan could.

Jupex and his companions launched a furious attack, swinging their heavy clubs and smashing Primitive skulls.

Before the Clan could enter the cave, more Primitives arrived, forming an additional barrier, keeping the Clan from entering. They were doomed.

In desperation, the Clan left the cave site and continued their flight up the valley.

"We must stay together! Do not separate!" Jupex yelled.

The Primitives followed.

Jupex and the remaining men formed a rear guard but were not able to protect everyone.

The Primitives managed to isolate and catch the slowest Clan-members, including a few children and women with small babies who tried to fight them off. The Primitives had no pity and savagely impaled babies and finally killed those left alive with their knobbed clubs.

The Primitives danced around these dead bodies as well.

The Clan-members could do nothing. Parents who turned around to protect their offspring were quickly killed.

The bloodfest of the Primitives gave the few remaining survivors time in their desperate flight. They scrambled on, believing they had escaped.

Having satisfied their bloodlust, the Primitives stormed up the valley, ready to attack once more.

Despite the speed and endurance of the Clan-members, they were no match for the Primitives, who were hardier, lighter, and faster, tempered by their harsher lifestyle on the plains and in the marshlands.

Hearing the yells of Primitives advancing on them proved that the pursuit had resumed.

Death was upon them.

#

Orrox and the acolytes were already farther up the valley and did not see the atrocities. They only felt the pain of the injured and the shock of death in their minds. Agony intense enough to make them cringe and hold their heads in their hands. With difficulty they overcame the instinctive reaction.

Orrox led the acolytes, flying up the valley. He struggled to continue and finally fell down. Pointing in the sunset direction, he urged the others on with signs and sounds. The acolytes stopped to help him, while the rest of the Clan-members streamed past, continuing their headlong flight.

Orrox was bleeding freely despite a hasty bandage applied by the acolyte girls. He continued in desperation to urge his companions to escape, but they refused.

The shouts and yells were getting closer.

Instead of fleeing, the acolytes dragged Orrox towards a clump of boulders and bushes nearby. They quickly obscured the marks where they dragged Orrox with branches, kicking up dust.

They focused on the source of the aggressive sounds.

A large group of Primitives appeared. The dust still hung in the air, hiding the remaining marks leading to the boulders and bushes behind which Orrox and the acolytes were crouching.

The Primitives stormed past with threatening yells and disappeared in the direction in which the Clan had fled.

Orrox and the acolytes collapsed with hands spread and clasped over their ears, their elbows nearly touching in front. They were unable to overcome the terrible pain in their minds, caused by the emanation of injuries, and the death of so many Clan-members.

#

At the head of the valley, the Primitives finally caught up with the Clan and surrounded them. The final battle did not last long. There were too many Primitives.

Jupex fought on. He swung his club with devastating effect, killing many of the Primitives surrounding him.

They stabbed at him repeatedly. One spear penetrated his right arm then another pierced his shoulder.

With a mighty heave of his huge club, he crushed two more skulls. His right hand was sticky with blood. He swung again.

A Primitive's club crashed onto his knuckles.

Desperately Jupex grabbed his mighty club with his left hand and swung it a last time. It splintered bone and then fell out of his grip.

The last thing Jupex saw was a flash of light as a Primitive club smashed his skull.

He had killed many Primitives. Now they took revenge. They speared and clubbed his lifeless body with barbaric vengeance.

Chapter 24 – Explanations

The next morning, at the Illoreaen Habitat, JaYan joined Questa, who sat alone.

She looked up at his approach, "Yes I am a Sensitive, through no fault of mine. I do not threaten any Illoreaen. I would remind you again: we Sensitives have been part of the Clans and the Dynasty for many generations, since before the Inter-Clan Devastation. The Clans have always appreciated and honored us for who we are and what we do. I do not know why you should treat me so poorly."

"You are quite right to be angry," JaYan responded, "but the dread of the mythical Sensitives is deeply rooted in all Illoreaens, and has been since our youth, it is hard to discard. For us, the memory of the dreadful Inter-Clan Devastation includes a connection between Sensitivity and the pain and instability experienced. In the myths, as we know them, the Sensitives were intimately involved with the madness.

"Of course, I believe you and know it is wrong to regard you as a menace, as some Illoreaens still do. The Coordinating Committee is trying to keep an open mind. I'm inclined to think the distortion of the truth developed within the Illoreaen community itself and was then expanded into negative myths about Sensitives."

Questa was not satisfied. *He talks too much!*

She just looked at JaYan, who forged ahead, "You told us the Clan-members fighting and killing each other, caused the Sensitives to 'Sense' their pain. That it was the Sensitives who suffered. That the myth distorted the truth and confused the offenders and the injured. I believe such a misunderstanding could follow naturally. We Illoreaens never noticed Sensing ability within our members and therefore, do not understand the possibility."

"I hear and will consider what you said. You Illoreaens are unreasonable and have treated me dreadfully," Questa repeated, standing up to get away from JaYan. She wished to be alone to consider her options.

I will have to educate the Illoreaens, she thought. *They know nothing about Sensitives. Our abilities are essential for the well-being of the Clans and would be very useful for the Illoreaens as well. The current distrust must be removed, must disappear. I'll have to consider how. It will be difficult to achieve but I am the only one who can do it.*

#

The Coordinating Committee had never before felt the need to meet every day. Although they scanned their records, recalled conversations and interrogated those who had joined the Illoreaens from the Clans, they found no deliberate lies or falsehoods.

A prominent Illoreaen called SkepTan, the agriculturalist, was the most negative, "There were never any Sensitives within the Illoreaens. We did not even think they still existed in the Clans. They were just mythical entities. I heard the Sensitives kill surplus babies when a Clan-member ignores the strict taboo of the one child per person policy. The Clans don't have the self-discipline to use our preventatives and medicines effectively!"

"You know that is nonsense, SkepTan," MaGan answered. "You're quoting stories created to frighten children. Do you believe them? Come on! Surely you do not think Questa is a murderer!"

SkepTan kept on grumbling under his breath, giving MaGan a dirty look and then looked down with a frown on his face.

JaYan sighed, "You're not satisfied, SkepTan. Do you have a suggestion of how we should handle Questa? We cannot abandon her."

MaGan smirked, "I think SkepTan wants to isolate Questa in a hothouse, permanently, like an exquisite plant, to look at but not touch."

He took his eyes off SkepTan and addressed the others, "I was furious when she entered our chamber of life. I feared she might have affected the strict cleanliness we maintain there. Her claim to Sense life was so ridiculous. Now I'm not so sure."

He paused, "We must accept Sensing is an integral part of Clan life and their contributions are valuable. The Healers are the ones who distribute the potions and powders, many of which my group develop. I evaluated Questa's recommendations when she helped to mix and pack powders and other medicaments. She is very knowledgeable and told us how the Healers diagnose and monitor the healing processes. Now we know, she meant by

Sensing. Her wording hinted at her ability, but I ignored it because it was not logical. The concept was outside my experience.

"She explained how the Healers, like her, evaluate the effectiveness of the medicaments they collect at the Dynasty and share the information. She never knew the origin. And we never knew the information the Dynasty sent back to us, the feedback on the working of our medicines, originated with Sensitive Healers."

"We don't know enough about Sensing," JaYan said. "MaGan is right. I propose we ask her to tell us more about her abilities and to demonstrate them."

SkepTan looked up with flashing eyes and straightened his back, his head held high, "You tinkerers with materials are always experimenting, searching for the limits of some device you have made. Now you want to experiment with Sensitives. I think Sensitives are dangerous. Go ahead, but remember I was against it and warned you."

#

As the gloom outside darkened, indicating the end of the day, JaYan asked Questa to accompany him again.

Many Illoreaens filled the Chamber. As they entered, a few of the Coordinating Committee nodded with a neutral look, while others frowned or looked down.

JaYan stepped forward, "Questa, you have seen the members of the Coordinating Committee before. Now many Illoreaen Elders have joined us. The Committee has discussed your case. You are a guest, but your situation must be resolved. We know so little of Sensitivity. Please help us understand what the ability consists of. Please tell us as much as you can."

JaYan sat down.

"I must think how I can explain," Questa said and then realized, *This is the opportunity to rebuild trust. I will have to demonstrate something they could not even imagine, something mental, something to demonstrate our abilities without scaring them, something to convince them they can benefit from our abilities... from us.*

Questa thought for a while before she started. "I was told you thought Sensitives are dangerous... that we are monsters. To me, your belief and reaction were—are—a great shock. Nobody has ever regarded me as dangerous. No! The Clans always ask for our help and they appreciate us as Sensitives. I would prefer to leave and return to the Clans who know and like me. Had the Dynasty messengers arrived in time they would have shown me proper respect and I would not have been here anymore.

"However, you would have remained ignorant of the Sensitive ability. I feel obliged to help you understand our abilities and how they have benefitted the Clans and how much your ignorance has harmed you."

SkepTan jumped up, "We must isolate her until the Dynasty messengers can take her away! Who does she think she is? We cannot listen to this!"

Some Coordinators agreed with SkepTan and they all looked offended.

With difficulty, JaYan restored order, "We decided to let her explain the Sensitive ability. We cannot make a decision until we know more."

Turning towards Questa he said, "You must explain why you claim that not having access to the Sensitive's abilities has been and is harmful to us."

"I apologize. I am upset and I used too strong words. However, our ability distinctly improves Clan life. It isn't as strange as you seem to imagine. You are all able to detect or discern the intention or emotions of another by observing what is called body language, which includes tone of voice, facial expression, involuntary body twitches, and many other small hints. Surely, you realize that it is very difficult to suppress all of one's emotions. Anyone can read body language. There are those who are better at this than others, depending on their natural predisposition."

Questa paused, allowing the idea to sink in, "With us, our inherited ability is well developed and enhanced through training. However, all Sensitives inherit additional abilities. We are able to Sense pain directly, as if our minds form a sympathetic connection with others when their brains give out strong impulses, created by intense emotions and feelings, like pain. We call it to 'Emanate'. I believe our brains are able to automatically synchronize with pulses emanating from other brains. This is chaotic for an untrained Sensitive mind. During training, from birth, other Sensitives train our brains to block these impulses and discriminate. It allows us to synchronize our emotions and feelings with those of the others and we can then focus and emanate sympathetically. We call this ability to 'Project'. We can change our synchronized emanations to soothe emotions, reducing pain by sharing it. It is as if we absorb some of it. A diseased or inflamed body emanates similar, but much weaker impulses. By Sensing these weak emanations, we can visualize body functions and discover the location of the pain or disease."

MaGan leaned back, steeping his hands. His eyes were bright, and he stared at Questa with intense interest. "That must be a powerful way to find the correct remedy."

Questa continued with a thankful glance at MaGan, "Intense emotions, for example, anger directed at us or extreme pain will penetrate our awareness, even if we block our Sensing. I have told you how frail we are until we have learned to control and suppress Sensing. When Heropto's hate penetrated my awareness, I isolated myself to try to Sense the Giants' strange brain impulses and therefore presence. My ability to Sense his intense anger from afar allowed me to quickly warn you of their approach before the Look-Outs discovered them.

"As Sensitives, we learn to switch off Sensing. It is essential, otherwise we can succumb to too many or overly strong inputs. It also respects another's privacy. We call it 'Blocking', which is our normal condition.

MaGan interrupted. "You said you can detect life? Sorry, please go on."

"Yes, we all can, since all life emanates impulses, however weak. It warns us if predators approach and is useful in the hunt. Trained Sensitives can remain Life-aware, except when specifically blocking the emanation of pain or the influence of stronger electrical pulses, for instance, those created by lightning—"

"Nonsense!" SkepTan interrupted. "I am the expert on life. My group selects the best of all kinds of plants and animals and knows their properties. There is no such thing as 'Sensing' life. I would know!" He got up from his chair and glared at Questa, "I have experienced the Dynasty's superiority and contempt of our knowledge as Illoreaens. They think they know everything because they grow a few trees and grass types in their valley. Things we have improved or created and they only increase in quantity in their fertile valley. They know nothing!"

SkepTan sat down. His face flushed.

Questa looked down and took a deep breath, then surveyed the Committee members. Ignoring SkepTan, she continued, "Not only are we Life-aware, but, more importantly, Sensitive Healers can detect Sensitive ability during the early development of a fetus. We can synchronize with other minds, allowing a greater depth of understanding."

A few slight nods encouraged Questa to continue, "As I said, all life emanates impulses, however weak. Nature itself emanates impulses too. The greatest example is during thunderstorms. Everyone can observe and even feel when the potential for lightning builds up, when the hair on one's head stands up or even small sparks crackle. Earth movements, shakings, storm winds and even changes of moisture all generated impulses, however weak. The farther away the source is, the weaker the impulse. At the Dynasty our mentors teach us how to increase our ability to focus on and Sense even these weak indications. We learn to enter an Abstract state where we can Sense the wider, expanded reality, which non-Sensitives cannot perceive."

Questa thought for a moment before she resumed, "The Super-Sensitive experts at the Dynasty have recently, just before I was abducted from there, demonstrated how powerful this ability can be when they synchronized their minds together. They warned of the imminent Catastrophe long before it occurred. They knew that the source was far away in the sunrise direction."

The Illoreaens looked at her with wide eyes. No one moved. There was a deep silence. Everyone held their breath.

Then SkepTan jumped up, "I told you! I told you! The shakings and the storm winds came from there. They knew. They caused it. They are devils!"

Murmurs of agreement rose from the assembly.

JaYan spoke up, "Sit down SkepTan. Questa is not hiding anything. We have to know more." He turned towards Questa, "You must understand how alarming your revelations are. You must reassure us. What does the ability entail? Can you explain it in such a way that we can understand?"

"It is a difficult concept. To Sense the faint emanations created by the interrelationships of life and nature, we must visualize and experience a reality beyond what our normal senses can detect.

"To advise the Chiefs and leaders of the Clans, we view and analyze reality from a different and often mental point of view. That is part of our function—to read trends—an Oracle function if you wish. To do that a fully trained Sensitive can enter an Abstract state, as we call it. I can try to show you, demonstrate how we discern, the additional reality.

"It might also convince you of our ability to serve the Clans. A talented and fully trained Sensitive is an expert in all these aspects. However, we do not all succeed in attaining efficiency in all these features, few do. Continuous training from youth helps. I believe the exercise will convince you that an extended reality exists. The demonstration will not affect your privacy, nor is it threatening."

JaYan looked around, "If your demonstration will help us understand the power of Sensing, it is essential to proceed."

All except SkepTan and a few Illoreaens sitting near him nodded approval.

"SkepTan, you and your knowledge group can leave if you feel threatened and do not want to see the demonstration," JaYan said.

SkepTan looked at his companions. "We'll stay. But I'm sure she will try to trick us. We will reveal the falsehood."

"Please continue," JaYan said looking at Questa. MaGan nodded his agreement.

"I plan to demonstrate our abilties by projecting the additional reality we are not normally aware of. I have to start with basic concepts. Because you are not used to experience projections by a Sensitive, I can start off with easier projections. Please be patient. It gets better as we proceed.

"Our earliest training, before we are half-doucia of age, is not only how to block and control our Sensing ability but much more. To bring our ability to full potential, we must be able to imagine strange concepts and visualize reality from an unusual perspective. We are trained to do this while still very young. After that age, our brains start to specialize. A brain develops and adjusts to processes it most often uses, while its ability to process anything never experienced, fades after the age of half-doucia years."

Another Coordinator interrupted, "That is why it is so difficult for an adult to learn the languages of the Giants, Primitives or other Clan-similars."

"Yes, I learned both when still very young and so did those of you who must communicate with them," JaYan said.

"Yes, exactly!" Questa continued. "To develop the immature brains of Sensitives when still very young, we are exposed to a strange and difficult concept that deals with 'Sensing directions.' It sharpens our mind and makes it easier to Sense how health, life, and materials are interconnected.

"We all know objects have length, width, and height. Similarly, we can move in three familiar directions: forward and backward, left and right, as well as up and down. As an example, we can direct someone to go to a certain point by saying, 'To find the bird's nest, walk gracia paces beyond a specific tree, doucia paces left of the boulder you find there, and then climb halfway up the cliff.' In this way we have used the three primary directions we experience daily to determine a fixed position. That is our reality, which we all understand. Without training we cannot visualize or imagine any other directions can exist."

SkepTan said, "That is so obvious! Why teach a small child such nonsense?" His followers nodded.

"SkepTan, please allow Questa to explain in her own way!" JaYan said, "Please continue, Questa."

"I told you I must start with the basics," Questa said. "To continue with the obvious, we call perception beyond our normal senses—sight, hearing, touch, taste, and smell, —abnormal or supernatural..."

"That makes the working of our light cubes supernatural," JaYan interrupted. "Sorry, continue..."

"Yes, but seriously, we Sensitives can visualize and Sense the abnormal and the mental, which cannot be detected by the five primary senses. There is nothing frightening in that. By sharing emotions and pain or by projecting a mental image, we help the Clans understand complex problems and help them cope with difficult situations. That, and the Sensing of life, is what you Illoreaens lack. That is why I said the Illoreaens are at a disadvantage without the services of Sensitives."

SkepTan grumbled under his breath.

"We have developed knowledge and methods to compensate," MaGan said.

Questa looked at MaGan, "That might well be and might be why I Sensed life when I entered your work chamber by mistake."

MaGan looked surprised and then nodded his acknowledgement. "You have guessed its purpose?"

"Yes, I think so." A faint smile touched the corners of her mouth. Returning her attention to the Coordinating Committee she continued, "While I explain the exercise, I will form an image in my mind of reality beyond the normal. I will emanate an image and then intensify it so that you can also experience it. This is to 'project.'"

She waited until she saw a few of the Coordinators nodding before continuing, "I believe you will find it strange. Should any of you feel nervous or threatened, raise your hand and I will stop immediately. I will only project images and not Sense at all. It will obviously not harm you."

Questa looked around at the group's faces, many looked unsure, but no one objected.

JaYan noticed her hesitation and said, "Please continue."

She took a deep breath, "I must build up to the final demonstration starting with the basics. Imagine an ant living its whole life on a string. It can only move either forward or backward. Those are opposites and together we regard that as one primary direction. Let's call it length. For this ant, no other direction is conceivable.

"You must get used to my projections before I handle more complex ideas. Here is the image. Please close your eyes and concentrate."

Questa paused. Her audience experienced the effect for the first time. In their minds a picture of a string with an ant crawling along it formed. They couldn't be sure whether they imagined the picture or received a projection.

"What a strange experience," JaYan said. "It's as if imagining something."

Looking at the others he asked, "Have you all perceived the image? Are we all still at ease?"

The committee members looked at Questa with large eyes. A few gave slight nods.

"I will take that as approval," JaYan said. "You can proceed, Questa."

"We have a toy for Sensitive babies to play with before they have even learned to crawl. At first, it is just a wooden bug in the form of an ant. It is attached to a string. The purpose is to teach a baby to understand the left and right, directions. As they grow older the toys become more sophisticated to teach them the concepts of different primary directions.

"Please be patient while I discuss the basic, yes, maybe obvious, concept further. The ant can only move within its world, which lies along the length of the string, left or right. If the string is a loop and the ant continues long enough, it will return to where it started. For the ant, its world is of infinite size. To visualize the loop, an observer must be able to visualize a second 'primary direction.' Let's call it width.

"If an outside force, like my fingers, pushes the two sides of the loop together, two points previously far apart can be brought near to each other or can even touch! The two points are then only near to one another in the width direction, not in the length direction, which is the only reality of the ant. The toy string and ant can be manipulated to do all of that."

Questa projected an image of a looped string marked with red dots at opposite extremes. An ant crawled onto one of the marked dots. Two hands with extended fingers appeared in the image, pushing the points together until they touched. The ant jumped to the other part of the string, onto the other dot.

"Now surely my projection is not threatening!" Questa said.

"It is weird," MaGan said, "But not threatening."

More than half of the audience nodded agreement.

SkepTan objected, "This is stupid! Of course, we know of the different directions. I'm just surprised that anyone in the Clans understands this."

Questa's face flushed red.

JaYan looked at SkepTan with a frown, "That is uncalled for! Again, anyone who finds this boring can leave."

No one left. Turning to Questa with a friendly expression on his face, JaYan said, "Go on!"

"Now imagine another ant living on a bladder, which can increase in size, starting extremely small, of no size, just a dot. Let us expand the bladder until it becomes a huge sphere with two specific points, unreachably far apart.

"The ant can now move forward or backward, length wise, and left or right, width wise, and in some direction between these two. Continuous movement in any direction within the two primary directions of length and width, will return the ant to where it started. While the ant is only able to move within the constraint of the two primary directions, two points on the sphere can be unreachably far apart.

"However, we know another primary direction exists, height and its inverse, depth. An outside force can push the two sides of the bladder towards one another until they are near or even touch. The ant can take the shortcut by moving through a third primary direction which we now call depth, which is outside its experience and its world definition." she paused, glancing at SkepTan who looked away.

"Let me project the image."

Her audience experienced an image of a sphere with an ant crawling on the surface. Two points on the sphere collapsed inwards until they touched, forming two connected funnel shapes. The ant slid down the slope, crossed and crawled up the other side.

The Illoreaens experienced the image. A few laughed aloud. They were now all interested.

Questa said, "I have to stop between explanations. Projecting images is tiring,"

SkepTan spoke up. "What has this got to do with predicting Catastrophes? I assume what you call your projections, are more like thoughts in my mind, not really pictures. Can you control my thoughts? If so, you are a monster!"

Everyone started talking simultaneously. Some agreed, but most waved their arms angrily at SkepTan.

Eventually JaYan was able to restore order. "I do not for a moment agree with SkepTan! But before you continue with your fascinating demonstration, please explain, can your projections control thoughts?"

Questa's face flushed red again, "I'm trying to show the alternative reality. But you must first get used to my projections. I can only project images, not control thoughts, but surely, if we were able to control thoughts, the Clans would never have accepted us. And I certainly would have prevented you from insulting me, as you have!"

JaYan took control again. "I'm sure you would never have considered such an action, even if Sensitives had that ability! But in any case, I would like Questa to continue her fascinating demonstration. We will ask her to teach us how to block Sensing later. Please go on, Questa."

"Now we come to the strange part, outside our frame of reference. You realize of course, we live in a world where we experience only the three primary directions of length, width and height. Our experience and world definition only allow us to imagine things in these three primary directions—except if specially trained!"

The gathering looked at her with large eyes. Many guessed where this was leading to and they were unsure.

MaGan looked at JaYan and whispered, "You have wondered about distances and limits. She might have answers."

JaYan nodded, "This is very interesting. Have you noticed how the bladder world consisting of two primary directions stretched to accommodate the movement in the third direction?"

MaGan's eyes stretched in wonder, but before he could respond, Questa continued, "I will try to project an image showing a further primary direction beyond length, width and height. It is intended to expand and sharpen the young Sensitive's mind. It is quite difficult and I can give you only a glimpse. If you close your eyes the projection would be clearer. I will only be able to project it for a short moment since I must create an image which is very alien to your minds and your minds are not practiced and attuned to receive projections."

The audience closed their eyes. The image formed and stayed for a while. A picture of two red spheres in a landscape, formed in their minds.

"The points, which are far from each other when perceived in the three primary directions, can move until they touch in the additional primary direction."

The spheres remained static as the picture of the landscape transformed to a strange bigger convolution, much more than the simple landscape. Unnoticed features and details got amplified, then the strange image in the Illoreaens' minds twisted and turned in an inconceivable way. The spheres moved together, certain features blended, then the image was gone.

Questa sat down, visibly tired.

JaYan whispered, "Did you see? The landscape stretched!"

MaGan nodded and then spoke up, "That is so strange. It is as if you helped me to focus."

"Yes. Improved focus is only one of many benefits. What we did was mental. Even for me, it remains strange and tiring to create the complex image so far removed from our experience of reality. I had to project strongly to create the image in your minds, which are so unaccustomed to synchronizing with a Sensitive. Projecting sapped my energy."

"Can I bring you a potion to restore you?" JaYan asked.

"Yes, thank you. But the demonstration is not finished. I have to show you how we use our ability to Sense the additional primary direction to enter what we call Abstract mode. In Abstract mode we Sense how everything, nature and life, is interconnected through this additional and other primary directions. For instance, we can detect where water can be found."

"How many directions are there? Is the one you showed us special?"

Even SkepTan looked interested.

"At the Dynasty our Mentors tell us that doucia minus one or two is the actual number of directions. The one I, and most Sensitives can Sense, affect nature more than the others, but not as strongly as the three primary directions. The others are miniscule and few at the Dynasty can Sense their working. None can Sense all. I was told they influence strange phenomena within cells and other things extremely small. A better answer only Mentors at the Dynasty will be able to give. Allow me to finish what I am able to show.

"I will have to enter the Abstract mode, as if living and observing in the fourth direction I showed you. I will Project at the same time. Sensitives will not normally enter this Abstract state without another Sensitive monitoring the process. We can get lost in the visions and might need help to exit. It can be addictive to remain in that state. However, to help you understand, I will Project how I can visualize the area around your Habitat in Abstract mode, highlighting water sources. Distances of our normal world loses importance when I visualize the world in this mode. Please close your eyes again."

A picture of the hall in which they sat appeared in their mind, as seen by Questa. The image twisted and turned in an inconceivable way, and then transformed as if from an observer looking down at them from the roof, but with all of them and the walls in shades of grey and different colors, heads glowing in soft rose.

The representation transformed to a strange bigger convolution, then twisted again and the hall shrank and disappeared, as if in the distance, images flashed by in their minds until a strangely twisted overview of the area around the Habitat was outlined in shades of grey and many colors. Fountains and water courses stood out in glimmering blue. Different parts and areas stretched and seemed to connect. Suddenly the picture exploded in a rainbow of colors, collapsed and was no more.

Questa remained sitting with a dreamy expression on her face. Her eyes turned up until only the whites showed. Her head fell back.

MaGan stormed towards her and slapped her face hard.

Questa's head jerked upright. Her body trembled and her mouth fell open. Her eyes stretched wide open and then returned to normal.

The Illoreaens jumped up and all started speaking simultaneously.

Questa sat with her head in her hands. After a while she looked up to say, "Thank you MaGan, you brought me back. As I said, we are not supposed to enter this mode except if supported by other Sensitives. It is dangerous and can harm our minds if the environment is unstable. I was sure I had enough control to exit on my own. I was wrong."

She supported her head on her arms and sat still with eyes closed. After a while, she added, "I felt I must show you why Sensing additional primary directions are essential. Without that, we cannot Sense the greater reality of how material and life forms are interconnected. We can interpret the colors and movement to show danger and relationships. It is a powerful tool to warn the Clans if something strange is threatening. That is how the experts at the Dynasty knew of the imminent Catastrophe. I should have realized; I was already too tired to try to enter the Abstract state safely. I can do no more. May I leave to rest?"

"Thank you for the demonstration, Questa," JaYan said, handing her a tumbler of an invigorating draught. "It was most illuminating. I am sorry you had to put yourself at risk to show us and that MaGan took such a drastic action. I trust you will sleep and rest well. Of course you are free to leave."

Turning to the others he said, "The Coordinating Committee has much to discuss, but later. We will leave as well."

Questa hoped her demonstration would ease the tension and mistrust but only said, "It was necessary," before leaving.

As they left, MaGan addressed JaYan, "Strange that there are no Illoreaens with Sensitive abilities, don't you think? Have the Dynasty's Healers removed those showing the ability by asking them to visit the Dynasty Valley? You know how often some young ones have left for the Dynasty and only return occasionally to visit their family. Have the Orrox's kept the ability from us, fearing we would become too strong? Something to wonder about!"

Chapter 25 – Discovery

Anja saw a large group of Clan-members storming up the slope, raising a cloud of dust, making it impossible to recognize who they were. She thought a few looked familiar, members of her father's Clan, the Clan of this valley. However, she could not be sure.

They were scared, looking back, falling and pushing each other. Many were wounded, bleeding, and emanated pain and fear. Their emanations slammed into her.

She forcefully blocked her Sensing.

The fleeing Clan-members were consumed by fear for whatever chased them. In their headlong flight, they destroyed all previous tracks and did not notice her recent passing.

They are scared. What are they so afraid of? It must be something terrible!

Fear washed over Anja. She wanted to help them. However, her limbs refused to obey, she couldn't move.

Close behind them four figures, supporting a tall stranger, came struggling up the valley. The stranger bled freely from a wound on his side. Then he fell down. She saw how he urged his companions to flee, using words and signs, pointing in the sunset direction.

They ignored his urging but looked back in the direction from where they came. Instead of fleeing, they dragged him towards the clump of boulders and bushes in which Anja lay concealed.

Trembling she watched them through the covering leaves. She did not move. As they came nearer, she noticed the nicely worked pelt with many pouches, which the stranger wore.

He is important!

The four concealed their injured companion behind a bush. They were far enough from where Anja was hiding, not to see her. They proceeded to sweep away the marks of dragging and pulling. Then, with their attention still focused on whatever followed them, they crouched out of sight.

Sounds of shouts and yelling came from lower down, getting closer. A large group of Primitives appeared, wielding spears and knobbed, hardwood clubs covered in blood and muck. The dust had not yet settled and hung in the air, obscuring all marks leading to the bushes.

Anja's fear increased. *If the Primitives discover me, they will kill me.*

Carefully, silently, she slid deeper into cover. The Primitives stormed past with threatening yells, following the fleeing Clan. She heard the sounds and shouts of fighting until that also faded into the distance.

Something horrible is befalling the Clan!

#

In her hideout Anja shivered, rocking back and forth where she sat.

It might be my father's Clan. It cannot be! I cannot lose them as well! Not my remaining loved ones!

She took a few deep breaths and forcefully unclenched her jaw.

I must help them, even if I get killed.

She was ready to rush out, when she remembered the strangers again. They sat hunched together, still not moving. It diverted her attention long enough for the opportunity to have passed. She saw them talking softly, looking around. They soon discovered Anja, they looked scared, then glared at her. The four moved forward, hiding the injured figure behind them and took up a threatening stance. Anja was sure they could see she was not a Primitive, but from the Clans. However, they were obviously not going to take any chances.

Anja's inclination to ignore all consequences and follow the doomed Clan, subsided as feelings ran high. Anja allowed herself to Sense and make sure there was no threat. *They are Sensitives, all of them!*

She projected friendliness and Sensed their surprise: *She is also a Sensitive.*

She spoke first: "I am Anja." It was a simple statement, which explained nothing, but her voice was shaky. She did not even mention her ancestry.

The injured figure looked up at her, a puzzled expression on his face. His eyes softened, hiding pain, before he answered, "I am Orrox, son of Orrox and Orrianne." He grimaced before continuing, "These are Ammox, Bronnox, Lonna and Camla," indicating the four young adults. "We are Healers and Oracles."

Anja managed to focus her attention on the strangers, to think rationally, to control her anguish.

A stranger called Orrox!

Memories flashed through her brain. Visiting bards often recited myths and stories about the Dynasty and the Orrox scions. Her grandmother indicated with a wink when the stories deviated from the truth. They told how the Orrox descendants sometimes became roving Oracle-Healers to enhance their knowledge and experience, to prepare themselves for future roles within the Dynasty.

The others must be acolytes following the Orrox as their mentor. Why do I feel so hostile towards him, even though he is injured?

Then she remembered, *Grandmother did not like the Orroxes. It showed whenever anyone mentioned them. I'm sure something horrible happened!*

Anja noticed Orrox looking at her sharply.

Orrox Sensed my dislike despite my control!

"Are you Jupex's daughter? How can you possibly be here?"

Eyes flashing defiantly, Anja answered, "Yes, I am the daughter of Jupex and Chiara-the-younger. My grandmother is Chiara-the-elder, the best healer and Sensitive of our time."

Orrox nodded, a hint of a smile again overrode the pain reflected in his face and just touching the corners of his mouth. "Yes, I guessed as much."

Anja got up and move out from her shelter, intent on following the Clan.

"Your words confirm what I suspected, this is the Second Valley, the valley of my father's Clan," she said. "I must go after them to help. They are in trouble."

Orrox grimaced and moved his hand to the wound on his side, which was bleeding even though still bandaged with strips of worked medicinal bark and flax.

With his other hand he indicated the acolytes must stop her. "The Primitives are too many. If we want to help the Clan, we must survive. The Primitives might come back. They will kill us if they do. We must find a place to hide."

Anja was not convinced and shook her head.

Orrox took a few deep breaths. With his hand clutched to his side, he continued in a low voice, "If you are injured, you would be a burden to the Clan. If you are killed, you would be of no use to them at all."

The acolytes supported Orrox's argument. "It is far better to hide and help them when it's safer."

Anja found it hard to comply, even though her training forced her to admit the logic. She collapsed into a fetal position. Her hands clutching her head. She rocked back and forth.

While the acolytes checked Orrox's bandages, he drank something from a gourd. It visibly improved his condition.

Memories of what her grandmother had told her intruded into the darkness overwhelming her mind, *Think of Grandmother's lessons! It might push the current reality to the background, might help me regain control and clarity.*

Grandmother had explained long ago, "The Clan Council consists of Chiefs, Sensitives and at least one Orrox descendant who annually meets in the Dynasty Valley. When I was training at the Dynasty Valley, an Orrox controlling the Council misused his powers." Grandmother looked sad, as if she avoided the memory.

She heard elsewhere how her grandmother trained with an Orrox as an acolyte, how she left after an intense argument turned into ugly accusations. Out of sympathy with her grandmother, she developed an ingrained aversion to all mention of Orrox descendants.

Anja remained silent while the others discussed their safety, "We must hide our tracks. Where shall we go?"

Their words slowly broke through into her consciousness. Reluctant to share her hideout with an Orrox, she nevertheless admitted in a trembling voice, "I have found a protected valley with water and food nearby that has a narrow entrance. We could hide there."

The acolytes turned to her in surprise, "Won't the Primitives catch us there?"

Anja forced herself to concentrate. After a moment she replied in a steadier voice, "Not easily! Pursuers would have to come down a very exposed access crack, one at a time. If necessary, I believe we can stop them there, while we can remain hidden."

The acolytes turned towards Orrox for guidance, despite his injuries. None made any alternative suggestions.

"Bronnox, see whether there are any Primitives in sight, but don't expose yourself," Orrox said in a weak voice.

Bronnox silently disappeared into the bushes. They did not hear him return.

"I see no sign of any Primitive. I think it is safe to move," he said.

"Allow the dust to hide our tracks. I will be as quick as I can," Orrox said. "But you will have to help me."

They hastened in the direction Anja indicated. Then crossed the Clan valley, furtively glancing in the direction the Clan and Primitives had disappeared. The young acolytes supported Orrox as he shuffled along. They swept the powdery layer of dust to obscure and hide their own tracks.

They climbed up the slopes of the Clan valley, onto the smooth rock slabs and continued towards the fissure, giving access to Anja's Hidden Valley. She pointed out the cairn, the small pyramid of stacked stones she had built to mark the top of the crack. Dismantling it, they left no indication of their passing.

"I Sense Primitives!" Anja whispered, causing them all to duck behind a weathered rock pillar near the top of the crevice.

In his hurry, Orrox moved too fast, causing his wounds to start oozing blood again. His soft groans alerted them to his pain.

Some blood smeared Primitives came running down the Clan valley in the far distance. They were laughing and yelling, swinging their bloody spears and clubs in the air without paying attention to their surroundings. Their passing raised a dust cloud again, erasing all marks or tracks Anja, Orrox and the acolytes might have left.

#

Despite the feeling of darkness, a depression she had been fighting since the Catastrophe and which has now returned with a vengeance, Anja climbed down the crack first. Bronnox followed closely, supporting Orrox. He couldn't suppress groans escaping through his suppressed lips, proving how suffered. On the way down he slipped twice, making the wounds bleed even more. When they reached the bottom of the crack, the acolytes supported Orrox through the gully until they reached the valley floor. From there they slowly followed Anja to her hiding place, at the large tree.

Bronnox stayed behind, secure in a nook where Primitives who dared, would have to descend the crack one at a time, exposed and clinging to protrusions. There he could easily stop of an intruder who persisted.

Suddenly the screech of a hawk reverberated through the Hidden Valley, bouncing off the cliffs. Anja had grown used to the loud noise, when the bird dove down to announce its hunting prowess when successful capturing a prey in its large claws. The hollow cliffs near the waterfall amplified the sound until the echoes seemed to surround them. The acolytes froze and dropped to their knees, their eyes large.

Orrox waved his hand weakly, "It's a hawk. The sound reverberates off the cliffs, making it louder. Anja, I can see you know. Tell them."

Despite her confirmation, the acolytes were visible shaken.

When they arrived at her the big tree, Anja managed to suppress al thoughts of what she had seen in the Clan valley, the realization of the slaughter of her father's Clan. She managed to distribute some of the edibles hidden in the hollow beneath the roots. As the most experienced Healer, it was her task to attend to Orrox's wounds. To her chagrin, she found she was reluctant to help the Orrox scion. The distrust, nearly dislike of anything to do with the Orrox dynasty, which she had inherited from her grandmother was ingrained.

Anja forced herself not to emanate the skepticism or emotion she felt. Despite her effort, Orrox seemed to know her feeling but submitted to her administrations. Duty forced her to perform the healing task efficiently. Using some of the herbs in her stash as well as medicaments the acolytes supplied, Anja dressed Orrox's wound, never looking him in the face. When she was done, he said, "Thank you!" and no more.

They made Orrox comfortable in the hole under the tree, Anja's previous sleeping nook. His condition had worsened and he was barely conscious. The acolytes stood around, seemingly at a loss of what to do. When the night approached, Lona and Camla looked at Ammox, who said, "We must think what Orrox would have expected us to do. I don't think it is necessary to have a guard at the crevice during the night, but I do think we must take turns to look out for danger and keep the fire burning, while the others sleep. Lonna, please call Bronnox. I will take the first turn to guard here."

Too overwhelmed by the recent escape and the horror of what they experienced, no one talked. Very tired, they soon found comfortable niches in which to sleep.

Anja suffered a long night. Fears about the fate of her father, her sister and the Clan, memories of her own Clan and their loss, haunted her dreams. She was glad to take her turn as a sentry when Bronnox approached her. She could see he was unsure whether she was going to share in the guard duties and reassured him with a nod.

When her shift was up, she woke Lonna to take her turn and lay down again, but she could not sleep. She remained awake until dim light announced dawn. In the light of the fire, she noticed the same restlessness in Orrox but whether it was memories, worries or the pain of his wound, she did not know.

During the morning, Orrox became feverish and the acolyte girls took turns to cool his brow, keeping it damp.

To Anja's irritation, Orrox tried to organize his acolytes even though he could barely speak. They quickly reassured him, "We can handle security. You must sleep. Fight the fever. Look, Camla has made you a healing broth."

They forced him to sip the warm potion, which made Orrox fall into a feverish sleep. He tossed and turned, mumbling his concern for the Clans and the Dynasty.

"You seem to have things well under control," Anja said as she watched the acolytes organizing what she previously regarded as her private sanctuary. There were dark rings under her eyes, which glistened feverishly. Her voice trembled as she got up onto weak legs.

"I have to find out what happened to my father's Clan now that you are all safe. My father, sister, and stepmother must have been part of the group fleeing the Primitives. I Sensed a horror connected with my father. He would not have run away; he would have fought. I must find them!"

"Please don't go!" Bronnox said. "You cannot go alone. Yes, we must help them, but we have already encountered the Primitives earlier on the Plains. They are angry, in a killing frenzy. In this place you discovered, we're relatively safe."

Ammox, Lonna, and Camla barely followed the conversation, their attention mostly on Orrox. One by one Bronnox's words seemed to register and they agreed with him. However, Anja insisted. With the acolytes in control, she felt redundant, "I have to discover what has happened to my father and his Clan."

"Anja, you are tired and traumatized. Please let one of us accompany you," Ammox said. "Two can keep a better lookout and are safer than one. You can be back before dark. Bronnox, will you go with her? We can keep guard and look after Orrox."

"Bronnox..." she looked at the powerfully built acolyte, thought for a moment, "Yes, it could work."

"With pleasure," Bronnox answered. "We'll be careful!"

"I know how dangerous it is. Thank you, Bronnox."

Ammox followed them as they climbed out of the crack. He stayed hidden until they were out of sight. Then he climbed down the crack and concealed himself in the same nook Bronnox had previously used, to guard and confront any intruder with his spear and club.

#

Although a sleepless night filled with nightmares had left Anja weak, she took the lead. She carefully negotiated the flat slabs of smooth rock extending from above the crack half way towards where the gloom obscured the mountains.

"We must not leave any tracks," she said over her shoulder.

Bronnox followed her. At the head of the valley, they saw a dark bundle. As they drew nearer the form became distinct. It was the horribly mutilated body of a small girl.

"Oh no!" Anja's groan warned Bronnox. He managed to stop her from wildly rushing forward, "She is dead and long beyond help. We cannot go near; we'll leave tracks and signs for Primitives to find should they return. Let's first look for any sign of danger. Follow me."

Bronnox carefully climbed onto a stack of high boulders, making sure he did not form a silhouette against the gloomy sky.

Anja hesitated for a moment then followed reluctantly. There was no sign of any Primitives, but farther down they could make out more bodies.

"Let me go to look at them alone, one of us will leave fewer tracks," Bronnox said. "It is better if I go first, they were mostly strangers to me. Please, let me go alone."

"How can I? What should I do while you are down there?"

"Just stay here and keep a look out. Later we can look for survivors together, find any who have escaped."

The bodies of many Clan-members lay together, surrounded by bodies of Primitives with smashed skulls. There were no tracks of any Clan-members beyond the grisly scene. Bronnox did not think any of the Clan had escaped. They were all dead, the whole Clan.

As an experienced hunter, he could read the signs on the ground. The Primitives had ignored their own dead and wounded, letting the latter die unattended. Instead, they danced around the bodies of the Clan-members they had killed, mutilating most. From the tracks of the Primitives, it was clear that they then split up. Some headed back down the Clan valley and others continued over the saddle towards the next valley.

Bronnox dragged and positioned all the bodies in a neat row. At the least sound or movement, he froze, looked behind him and then up to where Anja hid. Then he would lick his lips, take a sip of water from his gourd and continue.

The bodies of Jupex and their recent companions were barely recognizable. He forced himself not to emanate, to block his emotions, but couldn't help the tears from streaming down his cheeks. Jupex's body was pierced by multiple spear wounds and his head twisted to the side in a strange angle. He was surrounded by dead Primitives, all with crushed skulls. A broken club, too large for a Primitive to have wielded, lay nearby, Jupex's club.

He laid the body of Alena next to Jupex, tried to wash away the marks of the horror with water from his gourd. He covered the mutilations with leafy branches and protected the rest of the bodies with more broken branches, safe against predators.

Anja kept guard, wiping away tears as they welled up, blinking to keep her vision clear. She detected no movement, nothing stirred.

Bronnox was the first to Sense something… It was similar to the strange emanations he had Sensed when he was with Orrox and the other down on the plains between the marshes. Not anger this time, something more controlling and harsher.

He made a warning hand signal, grabbed two spears and shields of the dead Clansmen. Then he quickly made his way up to Anja, leaving as little sign of his passing as he could.

"Primitives are coming. I sensed them. We must hide somewhere where they cannot hurt us."

"Back there. The cliff! There's a fissure. We must worm ourselves inside."

They scrambled up a steep slope and some smaller ridges until they reached the rock face. Anja was right, the gap was narrow and deep enough to accommodate them both, one behind the other. Bronnox pushed Anja in first. She was smaller and could force herself deeper in.

He handed her a spear, then backed in also, pulling up his knees and covering them with a shield.

"Here, takes hold of this other shield. Protect the rest of me. Point your spear past the shields. We'll have to peep around them the to observe."

A group of Primitives following a mean looking leader appeared, sauntering up the valley. They were looking around and picking up things, then throwing them away again in disgust. Suddenly they saw the neatly arranged bodies of the Clansmen. The leader gestured. They all spread out searching the ground and found Bronnox's tracks. They stormed up the slope together. The leader looked sharply at the boulders where Anja had kept guard, then indicated with two fingers his conclusion: They are only two. Then they continued towards the cliff.

They soon found the crevice containing Bronnox and Anja. When the stabbing of their spears hit shields with no effect, the leader tried to grab Bronnox's shield, but received a deep gash from Anja's spear. He tried to grab the spear but Bronnox used the other spear to inflict a second wound.

The primitives' spears, sharpened saplings, could not penetrate the shields and after a while the Primitives resorted to the throwing of stones, which was even less effective.

After a while the only the leader continued the ineffectual attack. The rest of the troupe retired down the slope, searched the bodies, kicking some for sport. When the leader joined them they all crossed the saddle separating them from the next vale. The leader looked back frequently.

"He's not happy. He'll return," Anja said. "I Sensed that something is driving him, as if he is deranged."

"Yes, he is angry. He lost face but hunger is driving them. He might return with reinforcements."

At last Anja could ask the question which was haunting her, "Are they all dead?"

"I am sorry. I see no signs of survivors."

Tears flowed down Anja's cheeks. She collapsed between the boulders, crouching with her head down and hugging herself with her arms folded across her body.

Bronnox remained, standing nearby. After a while, when she had recovered a little, he added,

"I could see the men of the Clan fought bravely using their heavy clubs," Bronnox told her. "Most of the dead Primitives have cracked skulls. There were too many of them. In the end, the Clan was overwhelmed."

"Did you recognize anyone? The bodies of my father, Jupex, my sister, Questa, and my stepmother, Alena?"

"Yes, I knew Jupex and Alena. We helped the Clan after the Catastrophe. I found their bodies. They are both dead. I placed their bodies together and protected them with branches. Your sister was not with the Clan. Orrox can tell you more."

Anja looked at him inquiringly. When he did not respond she went down to the massacre site to look at her family, kneeled down and cried again, "Thank you for treating them so well."

Bronnox emanated sympathy to soothe her before he left her to her farewells. He stayed on guard duty until the darkening gloom indicated nightfall.

They returned towards the entrance to the Hidden Valley via a roundabout route, first into the mountain where the fear the Primitives have of mountains, would keep them from following their tracks. Then onto the huge slab, already clear of the dust layer and allowing them to leave no tracks.

Chapter 26 – Healing

At the crevice, the entrance to the Hidden Valley, Bronnox and Anja called down, confirming all was still safe. They heard Ammox's answer, "Orrox would probably regard my boredom as good acolyte training in patience. What did you see? What happened up there?"

"Don't joke," Bronnox warned. "It was horrible! Let's wait until we're back at the hollow tree. We have much to tell."

He later told Ammox, "You can't believe how fast and nimbly Anja moves. She left no trace of our passing. I must admit, she occasionally waited for me as I carefully avoided leaving tracks as well. You would never guess that a girl as beautiful as she is, can be so nimble. Have you noticed her poise? When running and jumping from rock to rock, she is even more graceful."

"Mm! Don't get infatuated with her. Lonna would kill you."

"What do you mean? Of course I won't! You know we acolytes may not form attachments."

"You're so right!" Ammox said and walked away.

#

At the big tree, Camla told them. "Orrox is more feverish than he was this morning. We've been treating him with potions and herb infusions. Tonight will be critical, if his fever does not break." She and Lonna were visibly exhausted from dampening Orrox's brow all day, trying to keep him cool.

Bronnox looked closely at Orrox, who lay comfortably between the roots in the hollow below the big tree.

When sure they could do nothing more for Orrox, he told the tale, "We found the whole Clan killed and mutilated. Including Jupex and the companions who visited the Dynasty Valley with us. I tried to arrange and protect the bodies. Then a group of primitives arrived and attacked us where we hid in a crevice in the rock face. When they couldn't reach us, they left. I do not think they will be able to follow our tracks to the entrance of this Hidden Valley, because we first went into the mountain. They would not dare following those tracks. But we will have to remain on our guard."

Orrox was in no condition to react or process the news but the others were stunned. They wanted to know more.

"Did no one survive?" Camla asked.

We saw no tracks leaving the area and no survivors appeared," Bronnox answered.

During the few days of traveling together, they had learned to appreciate the Clan-members. With Anja still a stranger, they were at a loss how to show their sympathy.

A groan from Orrox focused their concern on him.

Anja sat alone crying. Orrox was nothing to her. Her mind was occupied with the loss of her father and his Clan. *I am now alone in the world. Everyone I ever knew or loved is dead, both in my father's Clans and at my own. Now I must rely on these strangers, whom I only met a day ago.*

This realization was so devastating, she crept away to suffer on her own, taking only her bear pelt with her. Her suffering was impossible to share. She found a protected nook under a tree, against a few boulders. She sat there till nightfall, brooding and reminiscing. This latest loss finally overwhelmed her. She stayed where she was and did not sleep well. Illusions, alternating between pleasant memories of past experiences and horrible reconstructions of how her loved ones died, haunted her.

The acolytes' attention was focused on Orrox. They sat together in front of the tree, continually glancing at the unconscious Orrox while discussing remedies and planning how they were going to keep watch during the night.

In the morning Camla found Anja, "We missed you. Please drink this, it might help. We do understand how great your loss is. Tell us if there is anything we can do."

"Thank you. I needed to be alone."

She accepted the potion thankfully, drank and felt better, able to ask, "Thank you. How is Orrox?"

"He is still feverish. We have watched over him throughout the night."

Anja understood the acolytes' preoccupation with Orrox's health and wellbeing. How they feared his death. Without him, they would be leaderless, probably at a loss of how to proceed and handle the effects of the Catastrophe.

Anja accompanied Camla to where Orrox lay at the big tree.

"Is there anything I can do?"

"Not really. We are doing all we can."

"I still want to be alone," Anja said. She left the others to climb up the crack. She concealing herself at the top, between the weathered rock pillars. She wanted to visit the site of the massacre again, but dared not leave new tracks and could not face the horror. She held a lone vigil throughout the night.

#

During the night Orrox's condition deteriorated. The acolytes took turns to guard and care for him. While Lonna was sitting next to him, damping his brow, Orrox muscles contracted in a cramp.

"Help me," she cried.

Within moments the other acolytes crowded around the big tree. Lona managed to massage Orrox's muscles despite the limited space between the roots of the tree. She started with his calves and worked up to his arms. After a while, Ammox took over.

As soon as Orrox's muscles relaxed he forced himself into a sitting position and babbled incomprehensively, "Clans... Grandfather... Wrong... Colors, like rainbow... Cannot withstand..."

It took Bronnox and Ammox's combined strength to force Orrox down into a prone position again. The girls took turn damping his brow while he continued to mutter, then he broke into sobs, tears streaming from his eyes.

Camla brought a medicinal draught and together they forced him to drink. At last, he calmed down, looked at them with feverish eyes and then collapsed, his breath fast and shallow.

#

Bronnox saw Anja when she returned and filled her gourd at the little stream, "Where were you? We needed you and have been worried. We called but you did not answer. We struggled through the night to contain Orrox's fever. We are at our wit's end. Can you, as an experienced Healer, think of something else we can do?"

Anja felt guilty. She had shirked her Healer duties and ignored Orrox's condition in her pain and loneliness.

Anja accompanied Camla to where Orrox lay at the big tree. The Acolytes were all gathered near Orrox and Anja could barely reach him.

Orrox's wrist was in Camla's hand, "His pulse is weak and it's getting weaker. Oh, no! His pulse has stopped!"

Startled into action, Anja commanded, "Bring him out! I cannot work in the restricted space. We will have to massage his heart. I can Sense the heart muscle and I will emanate. Sense with me.

"Notice how I massage his heart. You can Sense when it is effective. There! His heart is beating again. You can also stimulate the blood flow when you massage here."

Anja projected her actions and observations, Sensing the contractions of the heart muscle, until the acolytes managed by themselves.

"My grandmother developed a powerful drug. I am sure it will break the fever and stimulate his heart," Anja said. "She would have left some of the drug in the Clan's Secret Cave. I will have to search for the cave. There will be hidden pointers. Bronnox, will you come with me?"

Lonna looked up with a frown, while Bronnox answered immediately, "Of course! We already know where the Secret Cave is. We gathered medicines during the Catastrophe to help the Clan. Come, I will show you."

Anja delayed for only a moment to make sure the acolytes continued massaging. Then she hurriedly followed Bronnox.

This time Bronnox ascended the crack first.

"This way, we must not leave tracks," he said as soon as Anja appeared next to him.

"The secret markers were probably destroyed by the Catastrophe. How will we find the cave?" There was a frown on Anja's face.

"As we told you, I know where it is. Across the valley where those loose boulders are stacked against the broken cliff. You can just see it. We fetched drugs and medicaments from the cave after the Catastrophe. Those we have with us, came from there."

Looking around for Primitives, they made their way, careful not to leave clear tracks in the dust. They saw no movement of life.

At the cave Anja inspected each container. The drug was in a stoppered gourd at the back of the cave, marked with a well-known rune.

"This is it. Here, take these as well. We might need them," Anja said, handing Bronnox a few containers containing liquids and herbs. "Now, let's hurry back."

As careful as before not to leave tracks, they traversed the head of the valley, descended the crack and soon reached the big tree.

Anja applied the drug while they kept on massaging taking turns. Anja kept an expert eye On Orrox, checking his heart regularly and applied the drug twice more.

With her attention on the patient, she managed to contain and overcome her sorrow.

They kept Orrox's head cool until the fever broke, deep into the night.

In the morning, Orrox was better. The Acolytes took turns sleeping, having been awake for two days.

Anja kept guard.

#

By the next evening, Orrox was able to sit comfortably near a fire, with his wounds healing.

"Thank you, Anja. You saved my life." There was a smile on his face and no grimace or other sign of pain. "The last I remember was when you and Bronnox went to search for survivors. What did you see? What happened up there?"

They all sat down. Bronnox sighed, "There are no survivors. We looked for Clan tracks everywhere. There are none."

"I, no... we sympathize with your incredible loss," Orrox said, looking at Anja. "I hope you will find us reliable companions and good friends. I trust our friendship will be some compensation for your loss."

"I'm sorry!" Camla said, touching Anja's arm. "We should have been more supportive but our concern for Orrox overwhelmed us."

Bronnox moved closer to Anja as a sign of sympathy. Lonna looked away, frowning.

Orrox watched the interplay of feelings between his acolytes. Lonna was jealous. Relationships between acolytes are strictly forbidden during their training, but still, feelings will develop. There is often something. He'll have to watch them. He saw Camla glancing at the two and realized, she also noticed Lonna's jealousy.

Orrox's attention shifted to Anja. She was looking at Camla while a small smile hovered at the corners of her mouth.

Lonna looked up, straight at Anja, saw Anja watching Camla and Camla watching her. She obviously understood the thoughts passing through each of their minds. Anja looked back and indicated with a small shaking of her head that Lonna had nothing to fear. Lonna blushed, jumped up, and moved away.

Anja noticed Orrox watching her and the others. She glanced around, then looked at Orrox again. He was smiling. She frowned.

Orrox could see she knew that he had followed her whole thought process.

She's very intelligent, Orrox thought. *I'm sure she followed the thought processes of each of us. She can handle intentionality to seven orders: Orrox; Camla; Lonna; Bronnox; Lonna; Anja and back to Bronnox. Seven orders, as I can.*

Bronnox noticed nothing.

Relationships between acolytes are strictly forbidden during their training, but still, feelings will develop. There is often something. I'll have to watch them.

#

The next day Orrox convinced them he could look after himself but will rest and sleep at the big tree. Ammox climbed out of the Hidden Valley. He concealed himself in a safe position from where he could also see the top of the Hidden Valley's entrance crevice.

As soon as he was sure all was safe, he signaled down for Anja and the other acolytes to join him.

Together they gathered branches and firewood for the pyre. Returning as the gloom darkened, they assured Orrox all was still safe. They ate a good meal and then sat around a fire.

"We must plan further," Orrox said. "I benefitted from the day's rest. It is my duty to organize the Clans and I must find survivors of the Dynasty. Until I am strong enough, we must continue to do our duty towards Jupex and his Clan."

The next morning, Orrox felt he was strong enough to join them. As the gloom lessened, Bronnox climbed out of the Hidden Valley first to reconnoiter. Ready to drop down the crack if he notices any danger. The troupe who had attacked him and Anja had not returned, there were no tracks.

Then they all climbed out of the Hidden Valley together. They insisted Orrox must rest, keeping a look-out, while they all were ready to scamper back to the crack at the first warning.

Now the difficult task of building and placing the bodies on the pyre began. The bodies of Anja's father and stepmother lay side by side on a patch of grass. Orrox came down from where he sat as a Look-Out and made them look as presentable as he could. Anja thankfully noticed the effort. She sat crying with her father's head in her lap and touched her stepmother, while the others readied the pyre.

With the pyre built and all the broken bodies carefully placed, Orrox performed the traditional rituals. They lit the fire and immediately moved away to a safe place from where they watched the fire consume the bodies. The smoke rose straight up to the gloomy heavens. No Primitives appeared.

Chapter 27 – Illoreaen Acceptance

At the next meeting of the Coordinating Committee, SkepTan jumped up to raise his objections, "The Sensitive is a conjurer! Lapsing into an Abstract state! What a hoax. Reading nature's trends! Indeed?" He inhaled deeply, "How did they manage to enforce the taboo of one child per Clan-member? Can she force an early abortion if a female exceeds the quota?" He wiped his forehead. "Yes, the ability she demonstrated is impressive. It shows how clever they are. How thorough their training. She said she projected the images, I say she deceives us."

He sat down staring at the table with a frown.

"Her name is Questa!" MaGan answered. Then, pursing his lips in thought, he said, "I believe her. However, to make sure, my group has a potion, a truth drug we have tested and found very effective. She can't know about it or protect herself against its workings. Will you be satisfied if she subjects herself to a test, where we can all ask her questions?"

He looked around. Most Coordinators nodded their agreement.

"Please prepare your questions. We'll agree tomorrow on which ones to ask. We must respect her privacy. Your questions should be limited to the Sensitives' abilities and to the possible underlying threat. We must assemble afterwards to hear her answers."

After long discussions, even SkepTan was satisfied.

MaGan and JaYan approached Questa late on the following day. "I'm sorry I slapped you. I felt I had to act," MaGan said. Looking her in the eye.

"Thank you. It was more drastic than a supporting Sensitive would have done, but it worked," she said with a smile.

JaYan looked down at his feet while MaGan spoke, avoiding eye contact. When he looked up he said, "I'm sorry, we have never been in contact with Sensitives before. Many Illoreaens are still skeptical. All the members of the Committee must be convinced of your good intentions. We must assure them your abilities are not a threat. The others will follow." Then he looked down again.

Questa waited silently to hear how they proposed to achieve this.

Have I put myself in danger without achieving anything? Do they still doubt me? she wondered.

"MaGan and his group have developed a potion forcing one to answer questions truthfully." JaYan continued. "Are you prepared to be questioned while under the influence of this drug?"

"What! After all I explained, you still don't believe me?" Questa's eyes flashed in anger, "I also have questions to ask. You have kept secrets from the Clans. I think it is your turn to answer my questions. Take me to the committee."

A small smile just touched the corners of MaGan's mouth but JaYan looked uncomfortable, "I can understand your anger. Please calm down. I'll take you to them."

On entering the Committee hall, JaYan immediately faced the Coordinators, "She has not agreed to the truth drug, but wants answers to questions of her own. It is only fair. Let us answer whatever we can."

He took his seat and gestured for Questa to sit down as well.

"Please ask your questions."

Questa looked at JaYan, ignoring the others, "How do you justify all the secrecy? Why can't we all share in the comforts you have?"

"The secrets we keep are all about the devices available here. They make certain aspects of our life relatively easy. I believe our use of them comprises what you refer to as comforts. However, we believe no one in the Clans ever goes to sleep hungry or cold except, maybe, during survival training. You all live a comfortable, self-sufficient life full of meaning, with daily challenges. In the Clans you stimulate your brains in many ways, not only becoming knowledgeable about nature and the mountains, but also devising complex games and competing with other Clans. With you, competition between individuals and Clans is never about the quality of life but only to test and refine individual abilities. Clan-members only change Clans to live with a life-companion from another Clan."

"How is this relevant?"

"It is relevant because what I have just described is the stable, comfortable life of the Clans. The Dynasty and your Council continuously device ways to keep your life interesting without due hardships, often tasking us to improve grains, fruit or other produce, which can be introduced as 'wild' in different valleys where they will flourish. We must also invent devices of high utility but seeming of low complexity to improve Clan life. It must not hint of higher expertise, which might disrupt Clan tranquility, exist elsewhere. Your oil lamps are a typical example. Directing natural gas using only localized materials is another.

"To accomplish what we believe as our task, we need many scarce resources, some available in small quantities right here in this infertile valley. The rest are often collected by the youths, both yours and ours, during their service period. Yours as requested by the Dynasty and passed on to us."

Questa frowned.

JaYan looked at Questa, but continued before she could interrupt, "There are not sufficient raw materials for us to create enough of our proven devices to supply all the Clans, and not enough knowledgeable persons to keep them working. The Dynasty Council believe that if distributed, the Clans will compete for access to the scarce resources and few devices, leading to skirmishes and even war between Clans. We Illoreaens agree with this view. To avoid this probability, we keep our developed knowledge and devices secret, except when all Clans can benefit equally.

"Our task is to make the Clan's life comfortable but challenging, without depleting the resources available. The proof of our success is the survival of the Clans, without serious hardships, during the many generations since the Inter-Clan Devastation.

"We do draw the best talent from the Clans to increase our abilities while some Illoreaens who are not interested in our knowledge building, join the Clans, all arranged in secret by the Dynasty."

He paused and looked Questa in the eye, "Any more questions?"

"Why are you Illoreaens allowed to be many more than the Clan limit of gracia members?"

"Yes, that limit avoids factions to form within Clans. We are also broken up into knowledge search groups, never allowed to exceed gracia in number. In fact, none of the groups ever grow to nearly that size, but some form associations for practical support and other reasons. The associations are bigger but not up to gracia in number. Anything else?"

"I'll have to consider your answer, but no."

"Well then, we were shocked when you told us the Dynasty is controlled by Sensitives. Even the existence of Sensitives was unknown to us. You have explained a great deal and we thank you.

"However, none of us Illoreaens must have any doubt of the true facts. The quickest way to achieve this would be if you should consent to take the truth drug and answer our questions. I will ensure all questions will be fair and not invade your privacy."

Questa hesitated the creese which had appeared between Questa's brow deepened and then she decided, *This might be the only way for me to overcome the distrust. I have to agree.*

Then she answered, "I will take the drug now, if you really find it necessary."

Questa drank the bitter-tasting drink and felt her eyes losing focus. She hated the feeling of losing control, losing the ability to block her Sensing ability. She feared for her sanity.

As the drug took effect, she was just able to say, "I can feel my ability to block out your emotions fading. Please do not hurt me! My Sensing ability is also disappearing."

When MaGan was sure the drug had taken full effect, he started with the first question, "How do you block Sensing and why do we not Sense? How do we differ?"

"I have been trained to visualize the full body in all its intricacies," her voice had an unfamiliar, mechanical sound. "It enables me to picture the position of pain, abnormalities, and ills. The area above our brows heats up when we Sense. We can cut off blood flow and nerves to that area. It blocks Sensing." Her speech quavered, "My tutors told me... all Clan-members have this organ. It is usually under-developed. You must have it too. It does not exist in other Clan-similars."

I have a different question, SkepTan said, "Can you still Sense me?"

She paused, "Not really."

There was silence and then soft murmurs.

"What does 'not really' mean?"

"I can only feel you are here. And you dislike me. That is all."

MaGan took control before the meeting got out of hand, "Tell us of the involvement of Sensitives in conception, pregnancy, and birth?"

"We are trained to Sense the presence of new life. After conception. Strongest when we touch the girl."

"And?"

"It allows the Chief to give her a potion. Prevent embryo developing. Chiefs get it from Dynasty... Must do it within six days."

SkepTan looked sharply at MaGan, "Did your group develop it?"

MaGan nodded while keeping his eyes on Questa. She did not hear the interruption. "We identify the man. If they broke the taboo, Clan will shun them... That is enough punishment. Prevent breaking taboos."

Many Committee Members nodded their agreement. One murmured, "It works here too."

Questa continued, "We can Sense gender. Also the health and abnormality of a fetus. The girls are used to us. Emotions and bodies respond to Sensing. If the fetus has harmful defects... pregnancy terminates. Spontaneous and natural. Healthy ones grow better."

MaGan asked, "What if it does not work? Do you use your Sensing ability to force a termination?"

Questa seemed to recover for a moment, "No! Of course not. If nature fails, we discuss the matter with... other Healers and with... the Chief... If all are convinced the fetus is flawed... Cannot develop naturally. The Chief gives a potion. We do nothing...."

She paused and her head fell forward.

MaGan took the opportunity to explain: "I'm sure they use a potion we developed. As you know, we have studied each phase of conception and fetus growth for many generations. We know enough to make sure we do no harm."

He looked around for reaction before continuing, "For a few days, potential new life is just a single cell the female body can reject. It happens every moon. Thereafter the egg starts to divide, but the whole is still just a drifting bundle. From the seventh day, we can start tests on the new life to ensure the bundle turns into a healthy fetus attached to the mother. As you know, we often do this in the chamber into which Questa inadvertently intruded. If our tests show the developing life is unhealthy or abnormal, with no chance of developing naturally, we apply the potion to terminate the new life. Their way must be much more efficient and accurate. As I understand her, they only apply our drug in extreme cases."

Turning back to Questa, he asked her to continue.

The members of the Coordinating Committee had to listen carefully as her voice faded.

"During birth we can absorb... some pain... Sense position and growth of baby."

Many more questions followed until she remained silent; her chin on her chest. She could not remember all she said afterwards.

MaGan looked at the Coordinating Committee members, "She is suffering. Should we go on?"

Some looked skeptical but a group under SkepTan's leadership was unsympathetic: "Yes!"

One of the group continued, "What other abilities do you use within a Clan, when any Clan-member is sick or wounded, during a hunt or during famine?"

Questa tried to recover from her swoon to continue. Her voice was faint, "Our Sensing is... like feeling the same emotions... like seeing pictures other minds emanate... if not blocked... we Sense hurt... pain... share it... absorb it... life... Nothing more..."

She slumped on the bench, sliding to the floor.

MaGan hurried forward, opened her eyelids and felt her pulse. "She has lost consciousness. She can do no more."

"From her explanation, we can deduce all her abilities," JaYan said. "It must be true. She cannot defeat the drug. She has had enough. We must take her to her sleeping cubicle and allow her to rest. MaGan, you must have a potion to help her regain her strength?"

"Yes, but sleep is now the best remedy. Let's take her to her cubicle."

A draught helped Questa sleep.

The next day MaGan and JaYan came to her.

"The truth potion does not normally have such a strong effect," MaGan said. "I trust you have fully recovered?"

Questa just nodded. She was angry, "Was it really necessary?"

JaYan looked uncomfortable but did not answer directly. Instead he said, "The Coordinating Committee has sent us to thank you officially for submitting to the truth drug. They are still curious and have many more questions to ask later, but in a friendly manner."

He paused, "Meanwhile you are officially welcomed as a special guest within the Illoreaen community. Until now many Illoreaens thought of Sensitives as mythical, supernatural beings associated with pain and madness. The Coordinators are satisfied we know the truth and are explaining the mistake to everyone. We apologize for previous mistreatment and promise to treat you well until you leave with the courier-messengers from the Dynasty."

MaGan added, "We have sent out a search party to find out why they have been delayed."

#

A few friendly Illoreaens invited Questa to their work areas to explain their activities. Questa suppressed her remaining anger.

They are really trying their best to compensate, to make me feel welcome. If I know and understand what they do, I might be able to contribute. Then, enduring the affronts will prove to have been worthwhile. They must accept the Sensitive ability as useful and essential.

She accepted with pleasure, interested enough to ask intelligent questions and was amazed at what she saw. Each hall seemed to have a different specialty where Illoreaens experimented with some device or plant. Very bright lights, shining from small cubes with no visible flame, created as much light as bright daylight. JaYan often accompanied her to different halls, explaining the activities in simple terms.

In an area housing a number of cubicles, MaGan was busy looking through a small tube at a thin slice of an unknown substance.

JaYan, pointing at MaGan, said, "We are cousins and have always been friends. He cuts up carcasses to inspect them. We have little in common, since I prefer logic to blood. What's more, he loves adventure and makes fun of, what he calls, my delusions. How we can even manage to tolerate each other, is a mystery."

They both laughed.

"Yes, his head is in the clouds. I prefer things I can touch," MaGan said, smiling.

Then, looking directly at Questa he said, "My team created the potion you drank before the questioning. I apologize again for having made you suffer. Please forgive me."

"Yes, I was very angry. The drug affected me more than I expected. But perhaps, if it helped to remove the misunderstanding, it was necessary. I'll forget it."

His friendliness emanated without him realizing it.

They lingered while MaGan showed her drawings and samples of the insides of the body. She could see JaYan's deep interest in all of MaGan's achievements. Their bantering reflected the sincere friendship between the two cousins.

Questa was very curious. She wanted to know more of how MaGan searched for knowledge. She was able to Sense the working of the body and visualized it, based on what she saw when hunters cut up prey. MaGan now displayed fascinating detail.

My knowledge of herbs and medicinals has value here, she realized.

"How did you see the small details to make these drawings?" she asked MaGan.

"I use something similar to the vision tubes, based on special Transparents. JaYan, go show her how we make them."

JaYan led Questa to an area lit up by the intense glow of a melted substance in a trough.

"Here we have three generations: grandfather, father, mother, son and life-companion all working together. Each generation has learned the technique from their elders. It is often the case in most of our searches for knowledge. Here they work with, 'Transparent.' Specially formed discs are used to enlarge things we wish to look at, including the vision tubes you inquired about as well as to examine the very small items MaGan likes to examine. Transparent can be made in any color. It is mostly made of melted sand, similar to the obsidian we collect from near volcanos and chip into sharp cutting shards."

Questa picked up a beautiful figurine of an auroch made of dark Transparent with different colors highlighting the bull's features. "These are beautiful! No one in the Clans has ever seen anything like it. Why can't these be shared with the Clans?"

"We're back to that, are we? The secrecy of the Illoreaens would be compromised. How would we be able to explain an item of such highly developed knowledge without the Clans becoming suspicious? You know how clever they are. We have great respect for the Clans even though we keep much of our developed knowledge away from them."

The grandfather approached and offered Questa the auroch figurine as well as the matching one of an auroch cow, made of lighter Transparent, "Please have this. The Illoreaens are so accustomed to our art, they don't show appreciation the way you do!"

They all laughed. "We make these in between our main activity of creating utility items."

JaYan explained, "They will appreciate your acceptance of the gift."

The gift made Questa feel welcome and she cherished the beautiful auroch statuettes as her most valuable treasure.

#

As she wandered from one group to the next, the Illoreaens found pleasure in explaining each activity. They rarely have the opportunity to show their achievements to an interested outsider, who knew nothing of their art or skills. Questa was fascinated with the sophistication and depth of their knowledge.

In a large hall, under a multitude of light cubes, SkepTan was busy with a number of Illoreaens, tending plants and nursing small animals in cages. She remembered his animosity but decided to be as neutral as possible.

"Hello, would you mind showing me a few of your activities?" she said.

"You can see for yourself; we adapt plants to improve certain properties." SkepTan frowned, "I have sent samples to the Dynasty, but they ignored them. They claim the plants are not adapted to the different valleys. What nonsense! I understand they distribute their own selections to specific Clan valleys. Who do you lot from the Clans think you are?"

SkepTan gave her a hostile look. Then he looked down. When he looked up again, he continued, "We also breed small animals, selecting individual characteristics."

Questa did not like his attitude, and blocked all Sensing, but she decided to remain friendly.

"Very interesting. Do you have much success?"

"I cannot think of any success eluding me. I'm the top expert in all aspects of breeding."

She was sure she misunderstood the implication, with a nod of the head she quickly left, not looking back. Certain she would not like the expression on his face, she was glad she did not Sense whatever he emanated. He effectively destroyed her growing feeling of acceptance.

#

The implication contained in SkepTan's comment brought back Questa's feelings of insecurity and loneliness, *Am I a specimen required for breeding, to preserve an interesting phenomenon? Am I regarded as a freak?*

She kept to herself and chose to eat at times when few Illoreaens were in the dining area. She reluctantly followed JaYan when he asked her to join him at his work area, "Would you mind helping me with my search for knowledge? When I'm not busy with my tasks as spokes-person for the Coordinating Committee, I like to indulge in an interest of mine. I have inherited the project from my parents but I'm continuing alone."

JaYan explained, "Long ago my ancestors discovered strange effects when using materials other groups found and purified. You saw the groups fashioning long, thin strings of copper, gold as well as from other materials. They use it to attach the different areas and materials to one another."

Nearby a girl was working with a companion. Questa recognized her as the friendly girl with whom she often enjoyed many easy exchanges.

"This is my sister Merpa and her life-companion, MalaGat," JaYan said. "They are busy making and playing with luminous quartz."

Merpa explained, "Our group have observed strange properties when handling the quartz. They exhibit the most beautiful effects. We'll show you later. Come, MalaGat, we have nearly solved the contamination problem. Sorry Questa, next time we can spend more time together."

JaYan laughed, "You can see why they abandoned me to continue on my own on the basics of quartz. Many generations ago, my forebears discovered a strange effect. If we dip two rods made of different materials into a jar filled with fermented fruit juice, we experience a tingling feeling when touching both rods, most pronounced when touching it with the tongue. This discovery caused excitement and interest.

"Different groups formed to experiment with different fluids and materials to enhance the effect. By using rotating mechanisms, they managed to intensify the effect and we now use this phenomenon widely.

"My ancestors continued working on this phenomenon. Through the generations, we made many more strange discoveries. They concentrated on the interaction of the effect on certain pieces of quartz. We have progressed far in finding useful applications. For instance, the light emitting cubes are made of pure quartz."

Questa was intrigued, especially when he showed her how the quartz glowed and even more so when she realized the bright shining cubes, which she saw in many of the halls, came from these experiments. JaYan showed her how they melted pieces of quartz at very high temperature, dipping an existing pure piece of quartz into the material and gradually, over many days, rotating and extracting it allowing more pure quartz material to crystalize.

She accompanied JaYan to his workplace where he was trying different configurations to examine the many abilities of the pure quartz. He carried on, describing more details of his findings.

Questa was surprised and pleased, *This might be an opportunity where Sensing will be useful.*

In his enthusiasm, he did not wait to see whether Questa understood. Questa concentrated hard. As JaYan went into more detail, she found she could vaguely grasp aspects of the difficult concepts.

"I can picture it! It is a bit like Sensing. From your explanations, I have created an image of what I understood. The image is a creation within my own mind. May I project it back to you? Then you can correct where I have it wrong. The projection cannot harm you."

"Yes, please do. If you can Sense a bit of what I'm trying to explain, it would help even more." JaYan watched her response.

Questa was very careful to limit her Sensing to just the essentials of what JaYan explained.

JaYan was amazed, she could Sense some of his thoughts if he tried hard to visualize the problem. On a few issues, she could re-project what she understood. This allowed him to correct her and in doing so, he gained better insight.

"I wonder," JaYan said. "Can you concentrate on this light emitting quartz I am using for my tests? You might detect something I'm not aware of."

Questa looked at the glowing crystal, closed her eyes and concentrated hard. Projecting and Sensing in turns.

"There is a feeling of flow. A bit like water but faint. And it pulses with energy. It is tiring to focus so intently."

"The light changed in brightness and color," JaYan said. His eyes bright. "I think you influence, and possibly detect, its inner workings."

JaYan concentrated so hard to understand or while stating his ideas, Questa sometimes thought he forgot her presence. Then he would suddenly turn to her, concern in his voice, "I have neglected you! Are you happy with us? Tell me about your Clan and valley."

She told him of the valley where she grew up and where her father Jupex was the Chief as well as of her grandmother's valley, where her sister lives. She also spoke about the little she remembered of her mother. He showed real interest.

Other personal matters she could not share with him and she longed for female companionship and started searching for a female friend. She liked Merpa very much but they tended to talk about quartz, instead of having the female discussions she craved.

#

Questa noticed a few friendly glances as she moved through the halls of the Illoreaen Habitat. A group of Illoreaens she had not met before approached her. "Is it true that you Sensed and Projected images to help JaYan solve complex problems?" one of them asked, "Splendid!"

But others were still cautious.

Questa was with JaYan when MaGan approached. He glanced at JaYan who gave a slight nod, "Hello Questa! JaYan and I have discussed the amazing results of your collaboration. It is as if your two minds worked on the complexity together, approaching it from different perspectives and clarifying the problem."

"I don't grasp all the complexities," Questa said. "After all, JaYan has many years of studying his subject. It is as if a picture of the thoughts he is trying to convey forms in my mind."

MaGan nodded, "We have always known, many in the Clans think in words, especially the bards! However, most of us Illoreaens think in pictures." He thought for a moment. "I'm curious, how do you experience bards reciting myths?"

"I can associate myself with the tale and visualize the story, forming images in my mind."

#

Questa climbed up to the highest observation window in the cliff every day, partly to get away from the competing attentions of JaYan and MaGan. Looking out into the gloom, she could make out the plain in the distance. The woods and shrubs surrounding the Habitat were more discernible and the palisade was in the near field of her view. She knew the layout in front of the cliff well.

She sat thinking in comfort for a while before she opened her mind to Sense for any threats against the Illoreaens. She felt an emotion of hate and aggression, faint but definitely there. She concentrated hard and Sensed the strangeness, the minds of many Giants! She focused on the minds she knew and Sensed Heropto, filled with hatred and revenge.

He is approaching. Heropto's horde is again sneaking in under the Illoreaen guard, intent to kill!

Chapter 28 – Moving on

In the Hidden Valley, they all sat by the fire at the hollow tree.

"We have done what we can for Jupex and his Clan," Orrox said. "Anja, we grieve with you." He paused and closed his eyes. "Yet now we must plan to leave. Our tracks are evident despite all our efforts. We had a respite, allowing me to heal. Let's restore the Clan cave, perform the rituals to abandon the Clan cave and then leave.

In the evening the acolytes used the opportunity to tell Anja more about their visit to the Dynasty valley. She began to understand the extent of the disaster and how the destruction of the Dynasty affected all the Clans. She realized Orrox had also lost his family and his future, everything. Although his losses were comparable or even greater than her own, she *could not suppress her lingering irritation.

At least he has the acolytes for company. And they admire him.

They have not spoken privately as yet. Orrox was still a stranger to her, a stranger whose forebears her grandmother despised.

With her strength returned, Anja was determined to search further near the second valley, "If I can find any survivors of my father's Clan, they can join us and help us stop any intruder attempting to descend the fissure. I have always understood the Primitives to prefer open spaces. They dislike the mountains and even dense forests. I cannot believe they will try to climb down the narrow crack."

Orrox replied using a soothing tone, "You may be right, but we cannot stay here much longer. You cannot search alone. It is not safe. Furthermore, we have used up much of the edibles available down here. If we find survivors, there would not be enough for all of us to live on. We would deplete the rest of the provisions in the Cave of Secrets. The danger of the Primitives discovering us increases every day. We have only the single exit. If they discover it, they may stop from leaving. We would starve."

Anja bent her head, "Where shall we go? Where can we ever be safe and secure?"

"I need to go up the crack to investigate and plan the best route to a Clan valley where we can be safe. We do not know how the Catastrophe affected the other Clans. I must find the best Clan where we will be safe where I can arrange the safety of all the Clans."

The acolytes immediately protested. "You cannot go! What if something happens to you? You have only just recovered from a serious wound and accompanying fever."

"I am strong enough now and will be careful."

"You convinced me I should not go alone," Anja said. "Now you want to do exactly that. Why shouldn't one of us go? I can go."

"No. It is my responsibility. To explore one needs more knowledge than your excellent ability in hiding tracks. I know the valleys and the routes through the mountains and over the Plains. I also know the habits of the Primitives and their language. I *must* go alone and, but for my serious injury, would have done so before."

"You are still weak from your injuries. Surely, one of us can accompany you!" To her surprise, she wanted to join him.

The acolytes readily accepted his opinion, therefore Orrox concentrated on convincing Anja, "Alone I can hide and conceal tracks better and also escape easier. But, before I leave, you and I can go out and search for survivors for a full day. We can then bring them here to the Hidden Valley."

Anja did not respond. He glanced at her, and then added more seriously, "But I do insist on going alone. I promise to rest often and not to let myself get as tired again."

She and Orrox left early the next morning. They searched all day, careful to leave no tracks or other evidence of their existence, even though searching through all the wooded areas in and around the Clan valley. They Sensed no Primitives, but found no survivors either. There were no sign of the leader and his troupe who had attacked Anja and Bronnox many days before.

Strange, Orrox thought. *During my search to discover the fate of the other Clans, I must also determine why that troupe did not return to search for our hiding place. Something does not make sense.*

Orrox has kept his promise and treated me well, Anja admitted to herself.

"We have done what we can for Jupex and his Clan," Orrox said. He paused and closed his eyes. "We cannot stay here much longer. Yet, now we must prepare to leave. Our tracks are evident despite all our efforts. We had a respite, allowing me to heal. Let's restore the Clan cave, perform the rituals and then leave.

The next day Orrox left alone.

#

Orrox carefully climbed out of the crack exiting the Hidden Valley. There was no indication of Primitives, even though he concentrated hard, trying to Sense their presence. *No Primitives. We are still safe!*

Never relaxing his vigilance, he carefully moved down the valley, past the abandoned Habitat cave and down to where Jupex's temporary Habitat had been. Stinking bodies were scattered all along the route.

I dare not look, I hope it is all Primitives' carcasses. I must continue down.

Orrox kept his head turned away, his mouth and nose covered with a soft cloth.

When he had passed the last bodies and the air was clear, he sat down. Sitting with his head in his hands, he managed to force the dreadful scene to the back of his mind. Only then did he walk on.

Where the valley and the stream merged into the marshes of the plain, he found a safe spot to spend the night. The experienced horrors haunted his fitful sleep. He woke up tired but pressed on.

On the plains most plants and many trees were dying or dead. Moisture mixed with the yellow-brown powdery dust in the air had formed a hard crust covering the vegetation. The polluted water in the streams stank and had an unsavory, ugly color. It was undrinkable.

As he stealthily moved from one hiding place to the next, he saw a few emaciated antelopes, rabbits, and rodents moving slowly in search of food. All suffered from thirst. Trying to save the provisions he carried with him, he looked for herbs and edible plants, but the Primitives had already gathered the little left. There was nothing left to eat on the plains and no drinkable water. The meat of an emaciated, recently dead rabbit, tasted foul, disgusting. Many rotting animal carcasses lay stinking near depressions, poisoned by the scarce water.

The Primitives had ignited the dry material in the valleys, Orrox realized. *The effects of the Catastrophe, after the cold season, had desiccated everything.*

He sensed no Clan life and climbed higher up to replenish his water from clear fountains, fed by seeps flowing from underneath rock slabs, and to get provisions from the Secret Cave.

He approached carefully, *Good! The Primitives did not find the cave!*

Then he moved on to the next valley. The bodies of the Clan-members lay together at the Habitat. From a hideaway, he observed several groups of Primitives raiding the remnants of the dead Clan's food stores.

By inspecting the signs in different valleys, he began to understand, *The first frenzied attack, which we experienced in Jupex's valley, is not the normal pattern. The killing is much more methodical. The small bands of Plain Primitives have either combined into large dangerous groups or were exterminated. They burned and chased each Clan from their Habitat, surrounded them and then killed them quickly. They gathered the available food and moved on. It also explains why the troupe who had attacked Bronnox and Anja never returned.*

At each valley, Orrox did the required rituals for all of them together, but was not able to build a funeral pyre and burn the bodies. There were too many. He just covered them with branches for protection against scavengers.

We can return later, when things are safer.

Sometimes, while inspecting a valley, he faintly Sensed a Projection. As if some intelligence or Sensitive was probing the valleys in search of information. When he concentrated to determine the source or confirm the feeling, it was gone.

He did not dare investigate many more valleys, but the pattern was clear, the valleys have all suffered.

#

A number of days passed and Orrox did not return. Anja and the acolytes knew he was still weak.

It probably causes him to move slowly and rest often, they repeated, over and over. They doubled their vigilance and collected more supplies from the Secret Cave, taking note of the concerns Orrox expressed. Still, the lapsed time became more and more worrying.

Anja and the acolytes were all at the bottom of the crack when they finally heard Orrox whistle a few identifying notes. The relief was visible on each of their faces.

As soon as he joined them, the acolytes fired questions at him "Did the Primitives threaten you? Did you see signs of survivors? Did you go to my Clan valley?"

Orrox held up his hands, "Please wait! I will tell you all and answer questions as soon as we arrive back at the tree."

He was exhausted, drank a potion and ate before telling what he had found. Although Anja was sure he had exerted himself too much, she said nothing.

"I have only bad news. I did not find a safe Clan valley for us to go to." Orrox held up his hand to stop any questions. When he could see their shocked expressions, he told them what he had seen.

Orrox decided not to mention the mutilations and how the Primitives' instinctive cannibalism was evident in the harvesting of the edible parts of the bodies. This memory was too ghastly to recall. He paused before he mentioned the specific valleys in a neutral tone. None had detailed knowledge of those Clans, but they were deeply affected.

"We must assume the worst. We cannot plan on finding any of the Clans to be a safe refuge... I have thought about the Catastrophe," Orrox continued. "Very little snow falls and the existing snow cover on the mountains does not melt and is not white. We have not seen the sun nor the moon since the Catastrophe. The gloom and darkness remain. We have to think of a new way to survive. The old ways cannot continue and will not return."

He waited for them to absorb what he had said, *They must understand, everything has changed.*

They were accustomed to seasonal changes where cycles always repeated, famine alternating with plenty, deaths alternating with births were normal but always in a repetitive pattern. Permanent change was a new concept. Nobody spoke, reluctant to accept the Catastrophe could have such dire and permanent consequences.

After a long silence, Orrox continued, "Please follow my logic. The evidence is, the Catastrophe's origin lies in the sunrise direction, from where the wind and shock waves arrived. The time between the shock waves proves it occurred very far away. Their strength and that of the storm wind indicate the extent of the Catastrophe. The wind, arriving so much later, and still so strong after covering an incredible distance, confirms the magnitude."

He looked at each of them in turn. "I predict we shall not see the sun for a long time and it will become colder. The darkness and cold will remain. Our valleys will not bring forth the plants and edibles we need. The comfortable way of life we in the Clans have been enjoying since the great Devastation, has come to an end. The Catastrophe has caused a new era to commence. We will need your individual abilities and talents to survive."

Orrox's words confirmed their worst fears. Nobody could add anything.

After a long pause, Camla asked the question, "What of our Clans? We must go to their aid. Warn them. Help them. We know more of the danger than they do!"

Murmurs from the acolytes confirmed their concern.

"I gave the matter a lot of thought, we won't be able to help any of the Clans yet. Their situations must be difficult but, as I said before, the Healers and Oracle-Healers know of the hidden provisions in the Secret Caves and they have the ice caves as well. High up the valleys they will be able to clear water seeps and fountains to get water.

"Most Clans, including yours," he looked at the acolytes, "lie in the sunrise direction. Erupting volcanoes and collapsed ledges have blocked the way. The only feasible route, to reach those Clans, would be to travel over the plains and marshes, where there is no food or water. If we nevertheless try to cross the plains, the surviving Primitives, who formed large gangs, will see our footprints and will attack us. Even if we do find survivors in a Clan valley, our presence will be an additional burden on them. No! We will have to find somewhere where we can survive and come to the aid of the Clans when we know more and are able to bring provisions.

"In the sunset direction, there is only one more Clan valley and then the desert and dry open slopes the Primitives seldom visit. Farther along the mountain range, there are many more small valleys. They are not as fertile as the Clan valleys and the food sources will be scarce. However, there will be enough to sustain us as well as any survivors we find. There we should be able to find a safe refuge."

They listened to Orrox attentively. It was time to make difficult decisions.

"We must take a lot of water, find extra gourds, and take as much food as we can gather here and from the Secret Cave, all we can carry." They nodded in agreement. "We have to follow the mountain range in the sunset direction. There are few edibles to gather on the way, but the route avoids the areas where we might encounter Primitives. We'll find the valleys and there is a possible refuge, mentioned in myths, where it is warmer. If it really exists, it will be very difficult and dangerous to reach. But we should try."

#

They started preparing for the journey the next day. Orrox and Ammox climbed out of the valley to find more gourds and if possible, meat and skins. They returned triumphantly with a dead antelope they had found higher up the mountain, below a cliff, half-buried in mud and ice. When it died it was not yet lean from hunger and the ice preserved the meat. They tanned the skin using tanning bark. Tears came into Anja's eyes as she remembered the tanning tree in her valley. There the tree was a source of comfort.

They smoked the meat over a fire, made pouches and carrying bags from the skin and cut the rest into leather straps of different sizes and lengths. When a darkening of the gloom indicated the late afternoon of their last day, Anja thought, *This valley has treated me well, it helped me heal from injuries, process the trauma and to find peace while I remembered my loss.*

She looked at Lonna and Camla, "As a last farewell to our lovely Hidden Valley, I am going to bath in the pool higher up. Are you coming? You others stay away!"

The three girls splashed, plunged and washed, using some of Anja's herbs. They returned refreshed, allowing the males their turn to use the bath.

Sitting around their fire, Orrox looked around, "Are we all prepared? We'll first go to the Clan cave, clean it out and remove all signs of Clan habitation. Anja, will you perform the ritual? The four of you must help her."

At first gloomy light, Orrox added dry wood to the fire for the last time. They all ate a good meal, then strapped their belts, heavy with gourds and pouches, around their waists and slung skin bags onto their backs. They each carried three spears, spare spear points, a spear thrower, and a knobbed club, ready to face danger. With a last look back at the hollow tree, they extinguished the fire, and climbed the crack out of the Hidden Valley.

"Anja, you go to the Clan Cave first. Call when you are ready for us."

The flame in the cave was still burning, removing the toxicity.

"A sign of continuity," Orrox said.

Ammox kept guard, aware of the danger Primitives still posed. The others removed all signs of Clan habitation from the cave. Anja then performed the rituals. When finished Orrox said, "The cave will remain safe for as long as the flame burns. May we one day return, to see it still burning! We are in constant danger up here, we have left too many tracks and evidence of our existence. Now we must hurry to the Cave of Secrets to collect the final provisions for our long journey. We must reach the safety of the mountain's ledges before dark.

Ammox, was there any sign of Primitives?"

"No, none."

Together they ran up the valley to the cave, packed their bags and then continued towards where the narrow ledges on the high mountain cliffs gave some protection, where attackers would have to attack in single file, eliminating the advantages of overwhelming numbers.

When the gloom darkened, they were already at a broken part of the cliff, from where a few ledges diverged. Orrox decided to spend the night on a level area behind some bushes. There were enough dry branches and splinters to allow them to make a fire.

"We should be safe here," Orrox said. "The Primitives don't know the mountains and the heights scare them."

Chapter 29 – Mountains and Desert

After spending a quiet night safely, Orrox selected a specific ledge leading in the sunset direction. He led the way, moving carefully and, whenever possible, selected a route where they remained invisible from below. Even though he could not see the sun or even use the mountain peaks as a reference in the continuing gloom, he had a knack of always finding the correct route. Everything was silent and cold, with no sign of life.

After a long slog, following different ledges, Orrox stopped on a narrow shelf, high above a marsh. "Wait here! I'm sure this leads down to the Clan of the First Valley," Orrox said. "The furthest Clan valley in this, the sunset direction. The last valley before the desolation. You will be safe here where you can see as far as the gloom will allow. Bronnox, come with me. Leave your belt and bag, but bring an empty one and your spears. We must see whether the Clan of this valley was spared the Primitive onslaught. If we find the Clan, we'll join them. Otherwise, we must get provisions from the Secret Cave of this valley and continue."

Orrox and Bronnox scrambled down a broken rock face to reach the marshy ground where the stream, running down the valley, originated. Following the stream down into the valley, Orrox scanned the ground, then looked up to where a break in the cliff gave access to the high mountain slopes, "Strange, all footprints are old and I see few tracks of small animals and none of predators. The Clan-members must pass here on their way up. I see no sign of any Clan-member having visited the ice caves since the Catastrophe."

"I smell rancid smoke. Has this valley also been burned?" Bronnox asked.

Orrox looked worried, "I was sure the devastated Clans lay in the sunrise direction, not here. The Primitives seldom venture towards the desert, which starts just beyond this valley."

They dodged between the black skeletons of burned trees, forcing a way through the ashes of destroyed undergrowth, until they reached a scene of a great massacre. The carcasses of dead Primitives lay outside and partly on the remnants of the palisade, which previously protected the Clan's Habitat cave. The cave's roof was blackened by smoke and the coals and ashes of a great fire were heaped at the entrance. Deeper in the bodies of the Clan-members lay, horribly mutilated, with their heads smashed to pulp by the Primitives' rudimentary clubs.

Orrox and Bronnox started cleaning and arranging the bodies for the last rites when Orrox whispered urgently, "I Sense Primitives! We must hide!"

There was nowhere to go.

Anja sat on the ledge with the other acolytes. It was cold and not very comfortable. In the gloom, they could not see enough of the valley or the surroundings to distract their attention from negative thoughts and imaginings.

The view must be magnificent in sunshine, she thought and then said so in an effort to start a conversation. The acolytes responded, made a few comments and fell silent again. There was not much to say.

Trained to be patient while watching an injured Clan-member, during a long night or when out on a hunt, Anja sat in a dreamlike state, when a feeling of Primitives intruded. She focused her Sensing. The frenzied anger was faint but came from somewhere lower down in the valley.

"Do you Sense that?"

The acolytes frowned and wrinkled their eyes in concentration.

"Sense what?" Ammox asked. "I Sense nothing."

"Primitives! I'm sure it's no illusion. Sense with me. I'll emanate to allow you to synchronize. And I believe I weakly Sensed Orrox's presence too. Just for a moment. They are in danger."

"Yes! I now Sense it too. What can we do to help? Can we project anything helpful over this distance?"

"No, I do not think so. It's too far. Even if we could, whatever we Project might affect Orrox and Bronnox too.

"We might Sense their presence if we try together. Synchronize."

"Nothing!" Lonna said.

Hands clenching and unclenching, shifting uncomfortably, they sat together.

"There must be something we can do. I cannot stand the uncertainty. Surely, we will Sense if something happens to them, if they get hurt," Lonna said, when the stress became too much.

"Maybe I should enter the Abstract state," Anja said. "In that expanded reality I should Sense the whole area and all life."

"You cannot," Ammox warned. "Orrox has warned us not to try except when accompanied by an experienced Oracle-Healer Sensitive. He did not even do that when he Sensed the imminent Catastrophe. He said it can be very addictive and it is difficult to return from that state."

"Yes. My grandmother warned me too. I only once experienced the beginning of it with her. It was as if she held my hand all the time."

What will we do if they do not return? Anja thought. *We will just have to be patient and, if necessary, wait till morning. Then we have to decide what to do.*

She guessed the same thoughts mulled through the acolytes' minds.

Orrox and Bronnox's only option was to scramble deeper into the cave. There was no nook or other hiding place. The Primitives had destroyed all partitioning and dividers in their ferocious attack.

"We will have to hide underneath the dead bodies," Orrox said. "We have no choice. Throw off your skins and coverings and drag them through the soot. Throw them deep into the cave. Then we must roll in the dirt too. It is our only chance."

Naked they crawled under and pulled over themselves the already putrid bodies over themselves. They nearly gagged.

A number of Primitives walked up to the cave. When they saw Orrox and Bronnox's footprints, and the arranged bodies, they stormed into the cave swinging their clubs. They looked around in the shimmering darkness, did not approach or touch the bodies and then left.

Nervously stamping their feet and stalking to and fro in front of the entrance, they yelled at each other before storming down the valley.

When Orrox and Bronnox could Sense the Primitives no more, they collected their garments and splashed into the polluted stream, washing themselves as well as they could. Before they were clean, they Sensed the return of Primitives.

A quick escape up the valley to join their compatriots on the narrow ledge, was their only possible refuge. They followed the watercourse upwards as fast as they could when three Primitives, dirty with clotted blood, confronted them.

From under his garments, Orrox pulled out two long, gleaming shafts, each as long as his forearm. He folded his hand around a handle at one end. From there the shaft flattened out to form cutting edges on both sides, ending in a sharp point.

"You are not trained in its use, but swipe and trust as much as you can. I know how to use it and can defend myself. See how I handle it. Then cover my back." Orrox said as he handed Bronnox the one weapon.

Bronnox grabbed it by its handle and pointed the shaft at the Primitives while Orrox advanced. The Primitives stood their ground and the foremost raised his club, aiming at Orrox's head. Orrox dodged the blow and swiped at the Primitives arm, drawing blood. Bronnox sidestepped a blow from the second Primitive, watching Orrox from the corner of his eye. The third Primitive sidled around to attack the two Clansmen from the back. Bronnox edged sideways until he stood back-to-back with Orrox.

Meanwhile, Orrox had dispatched the first Primitive with a deadly thrust and ducked underneath a blow from the second one, thrusting forward. The shaft slipped between the Primitives ribs and killed him instantly. Bronnox did not handle the weapon as well and continued dodging blows. Orrox turned around to attack. The movement confused the Primitive allowing Bronnox to effectively slice open the attacker's arm. Orrox's swipe decapitated the primitive. All three Primitives were dead.

The fight was fierce but short.

"We call these weapons 'Thruster-Slashers'. We must clean them," Orrox said, wiping off blood on some grass. Bronnox did the same.

"Their existence is a great secret, Orrox continued as he replaced them in sheaths attached and hidden inside his kaross.

Only the Orrox and his son carry them as emblems of their status. Please don't tell anyone what you saw."

Anja Sensed the Primitives moving away as their angry emanations diminished. She still could not Sense the presence of either Orrox or Bronnox.

After another long wait, she said, "I Sense them!"

Then, "There are Primitives too, they are fighting!"

The acolytes sat straight, staring down towards the valley. There was nothing to see. They synchronized their Sensing with Anja until they Sensed the death of the Primitives and the relaxed tension of Orrox and Bronnox. The relief was written on all their faces.

Orrox and Bronnox returned when dusk was already falling. Streaks of black soot showed in their hair, on their arms and feet as well as on the skins they wore. A pungent odor surrounded them.

The two summarized their experience in only a few words.

No Primitives followed them and they Sensed none during the night when they took turns to guard.

Orrox and Bronnox were very tired but they smelled so bad, they were not allowed to remain near the others. They slept farther away and downwind on the ledge, making themselves as comfortable as possible. The next day the two managed to find a water source and clean themselves properly.

#

The ledges petered out further on and the area became drier as they continued, hugging the mountain slope. At a prominent stream, they paused.

"I believe the great river, the one crossing the desert, has its head-waters here. It is the only water in this dry desolation. We call it the River of Doom. Very few Primitives ever come this far in the sunset direction. If they do they remain near the river. We should be safe if we stay on the slopes," Orrox said.

Ammox tasted some of the water carefully, just using the tip of his tongue.

"It is bitter," he said, spitting.

Bronnox and Ammox walked upstream until they found a little water oozing into the stream from a marshy patch to the side. There they dug a catchment trough, allowing them all to drink and fill their gourds.

"This river features in a myth telling of the entry to the underworld, also called the Chasm, but we must continue along the mountain chain towards sunset. There are a few valleys beyond the mountain we call 'Erejefischt.' They should contain enough edibles to sustain the six of us."

After a final wash in the bitter water, they entered forests where it was a little warmer than in the open. There they found a few roots and herbs in sheltered nooks.

They remained as high up in the foothills as possible. Lower down, deep dry gullies were entangled with spiky brush, making them nearly impossible to cross. They tried to hug the mountains at the edge of the tree line, keeping their level, moving into the slopes to pass the head of a valley and moving out around a spur thereafter.

"This is crazy!" Ammox cried at last. "We have walked in from that spur and out again onto this one. We have not progressed at all. You can repeat the in and out to the next spur. Not me, I'm going straight down and up again!"

Ammox joined the others long after they arrived on the next spur. He was scratched and exhausted. The brush hid many ridges and crests with thorny growth below each of them.

"I guess we just have to continue in and out. I will not try a shortcut again," he admitted resignedly, accepting the teasing in good grace.

One morning, Orrox pointed out scratches made by a bear, "The Cave-bears have been chased from the Clan valleys long ago, but they are still abundant here in the sunset direction. I don't believe any of us have ever encountered one before. Although their diet is mostly restricted to plants, remember, they are huge and extremely dangerous, especially when cornered. Keep your eyes peeled."

He paused and thought for a while. "Should we encounter a bear, we will have to escape up a cliff or along a narrow ledge. The bears are too big to follow us there, but they are able to climb any tree. Do not think of trees as safe refuges."

Their progress slowed. They kept near the small cliffs, which allow the steep slope to rise in stages towards the high rock face of the main range. Traversing the slope, the left foot always lower than the right, was difficult. Orrox noticed how quickly they all tired but insisted, "From here we can escape quickly."

Anja still did not feel part of the group and walked on her own.

The next day Orrox was the first to see a cave-bear approaching.

"Throw down your bags and climb the cliff! High enough to be out of the bear's reach."

The acolytes reacted immediately and quickly scrambled up the nearby cliff. Although vertical, it provided many hand- and footholds.

Anja was some distance behind and did not react immediately, then scrambled up the nearest cliff, still carrying her bag.

"Anja! You too. No, not there where the cliff is broken and forms steps. Throw away your bag and come here, where it is more vertical."

Before she could respond, the bear reared up on its back legs and lumbered forward, blocking the way.

It lunged towards the broken cliff and scrambled up, following Anja. The air vibrated with its roar.

Anja climbed higher, trying to stay out of its reach. A front paw reached up and clawed Anja's leg. Blood spurted out of a deep gash. Her foot slithered off a sloping protrusion. She slipped to within reach of the bear's powerful claws.

Meanwhile, Orrox had jumped off his safe stance, grabbed his spear and stormed. Bronnox followed. Ammox managed to fit his spear in his spear thrower and launched with all his might. The spear hit the bear's broad back.

The bear reached back towards the spear, lost its balance and fell to the ground. It got up immediately, reared up again and waggled towards his assailants.

Lonna and Camla had meanwhile picked up Orrox and Bronnox's spear throwers, where it lay next to their bags, and flung it forwards. Then they armed themselves with their own spears and throwers.

Retreating fast, both Orrox and Bronnox threw their spears accurately, hitting the bear in its eye and throat. The bear roared and grabbed at its eye, allowing the five to each stab it repeatedly with their spears. The bear clawed at them in desperate defense. The loss of blood weakened it, until, at last, it succumbed and died.

Anja managed to join the others at last, bleeding. "Thank you. You saved my life," She said as she collapsed to the ground.

The acolytes sat down, breathing hard, while Orrox attended Anja's wound.

"Somehow we managed to kill a cave bear. It normally takes many hunters to perform such a feat," he said. "Now we have ample meat. Pity we cannot carry it all."

When he had cleaned and bandaged Anja's wound he said, "We'll have to stay here for the night. Anja should not walk until the wound has stopped bleeding. Ammox will you start a fire while Bronnox and I start skinning the bear? Camla and Lonna, we can use a nice hot energizing drink."

They started late the next morning.

"We must stay closer together in future. Anja, please allow Lonna and Camla to support you over difficult terrain. We must avoid your wound bleeding, Orrox said. "I am still surprised we managed to kill the bear. I think it was on its way to a cave to hibernate although still thin, without enough fat to survive long," Orrox said.

Further along, they saw a cave in a band of rock above a steep slope.

"That is a typical bear cave," Orrox said. "The bear might have been heading there. It has turned cold and gloomy. I wonder. Let's inspect the cave."

Narrow ledges to the side made a safe approach possible. Helping Anja to climb, they peered in from high up. A few bears were lying on the cave floor and a heap of bleached bones and bear-skulls filled part of the cave.

"I thought this might have happened," Orrox said. "They have gone into hibernation again due to the cold and dark. As you know, many die in their caves during hibernation, either from old age or from having accumulated too little fat during the season of plenty.

They are lean. I have little hope for them. I don't think we will encounter any more roving bears, they will be hibernating."

They all gazed at the bears.

"Imagine how much meat they represent," Bronnox said. "We could each have a pelt as good as the one we are carrying."

"While they head for caves high up the mountains or are hibernating, we are safe," Orrox said. "One less danger to face. Let us continue on our way. At least we can go back to traverse along an easier route lower down."

#

They traveled farther. Anja's wound was sore, especially in the morning before she got into a walking rhythm. She was careful not to overextend herself and only limped slightly. Orrox's salves and ointments had prevented infection and sped up the healing. He applied them and replaced bandages twice every day, using soft skins and bark, which he carried with him. They drank as little as possible from their gourds, sharing when necessary. With depleted gourds, they occasionally found moisture at the head of a gully, near the mountain. With the aid of hollow reeds, they sucked up any water which accumulated in small basins, just enough to wet their lips and mouths or swallow small amounts of the scarce water.

As they crossed a prominent spur, Orrox stopped suddenly, staring ahead and up, to the right.

"Erejefischt must be up there. Look, it has erupted! I always believed Erejefischt was dormant. Look at the lava flows. The lava filled this depression and continues all the way down the slopes and beyond. The lava is still red hot, we cannot pass. We will have to follow this spur down to the river."

Orrox turned, leaving the mountain slopes facing the sun at their back. "We will have to stay between the dry gullies descending from the mountain. They are steep and filled with thorny growth. Carved out by flash floods, they are nearly impossible to penetrate. We will have to follow the line of the river into the desert, up to where the gullies peter out to become shallow depressions in the desert sand. Beyond the lava flows, we can make our way back to the mountain."

Continuing towards the river, they saw emaciated antelope and deer, ribs protruding, barely able to run away. Then any signs of life disappeared with very few animal tracks. Orrox decided to follow a dry stream. A moist patch occasionally indicated where water had previously accumulated. The gaunt bodies of large and small mammals lay nearby. The animals had dug out the covering goo, attempting to drink the foul water and died in agony.

The slopes and gullies flattened out and merged with the desert. Endless stretches of rocky slabs, alternating with areas covered in wilting shrubs, held no promise of cover or edibles. They crossed a sandy patch, where they saw several tracks with prominent claw marks.

"Wolves!" Bronnox said. "See, the track of the hind foot is placed within or directly in front of the forefoot. That identifies them. Wolves, not wild dogs. A pack of at least half-doucia."

When they were near enough to see the river, they followed it down, keeping far to the right, where large slabs hid their tracks.

Orrox looked down at the river, to his right, "It is only a large stream, a collection of the waters draining this part of the great mountain range. Despite its small size, some of the water must percolate through the sands, filtering out the worst contamination. We should find some edible roots near the banks, not affected by the impurities. But we dare not go there. We will leave tracks and the signs of digging, which any group of Primitives following the river in search of food, will see. It would be our death. Approaching the river must be our last option. We must hold out."

When the deeper gloom indicated the end of the day, they sought refuge.

"We need a site where we can defend ourselves," Orrox said, looking around. But they found none. They stopped for the night in the open and doubled their guard.

"We dare not keep the fire burning," Orrox said, covering the embers with ash. "This will keep them glowing. I will keep flammable powders ready. We must collect enough dry wood to create an emergency fire quickly."

Even the night sounds were silent, except for the far-off howls of wolves. To their relief, they passed an uneventful night. Anja was the only one not sleeping well, her wound tended to hurt during the nights.

They suffered from thirst and hunger. Expending energy to find routes around or down ridges made it worse. During the descent, the temperature gradually increased. The sparse plants and grass were dead. The little food in their pouches was running low. They rationed themselves to very small portions twice a day, eventually to only a small portion daily. The lack of nourishment and fluids rendered them weak and listless.

Orrox was proud of them all. They all made sure not to emanate how they suffered, effectively blocking the pain of thirst and hunger.

"Sucking something round and smooth, even a small stone, helps against the thirst," Orrox said.

Anja was not sure whether Orrox's advice was effective. Even so, she joined the others, sucking on fruit pips. To forget the thirst and the dryness of her mouth, she tried to think of good times past, but it did not help.

The cries of Primitives interrupted her thoughts and she Sensed terror. It was the same as before. She tried to suppress her fear. *It must be an illusion this time,* she thought, *brought on by my wound.* But the Sense and sounds increased. Then she called out, "Primitives!"

Chapter 30 – Giants attack

Questa rushed down from the observation portal high up the cliff of the Illoreaen Habitat. She found JaYan and MaGan in conversation.

"The Giants are coming again! There are many more this time."

JaYan said, "Are you sure?"

When she nodded her head the two immediately reacted to her news, rushing away, leaving Questa standing where she was. A number of Illoreaens passed by in a hurry, heading towards the exit.

At least they believe me now, and they are reacting, she thought.

Not knowing what she could do to help and not wishing to be in the way, she went to her sleeping cubicle and sat down.

Soon JaYan came to her with a few members of the Coordinating Committee, "Thank you for warning us. MaGan has gone to gather all the Illoreaens outside the Habitat. Even though there were only a few Giants last time, we nearly got the young ones trapped outside in their ambush positions. We'll now all remain safely within the Habitat."

The Illoreaens don't take the threat seriously enough, she realized.

"What can I do to convince you how serious the threat is? The Giants are intelligent and Heropto very much so."

"We appreciate your abilities. What exactly have you Sensed and what do you know?"

"There are many more Giants than last time. I also Sensed Heropto's emotions. His anger has reached a fever pitch. He seeks revenge and will not spare anyone. That is all I know."

#

When they arrived, the Giants did not storm the palisade, which they could have easily breached with their great strength. Heropto kept back his cohorts, pointing out the narrow entrance to the Habitat itself. There, only two Giants would fit side by side. Their bodies, if killed, would soon block the entrance. He also pointed to Illoreaens watching from the Look-Out positions, high up the cliff, overlooking the entrance and palisade, ready to fend off a frontal attack.

Questa understood Heropto's ability to evaluate the situation and his resultant reluctance to launch a frontal attack. The Giants were encamped in front of the Habitat beyond the palisade and she worried, *How will the visitors from the Dynasty manage to reach us safely? And when I leave with them, won't Heropto follow us and try to catch me again? He would love that. I'm sure he will try.*

The Illoreaens were still able to move freely within the palisade. Their reluctance to regard the threat as serious, increased Questa's concern. However, when the Illoreaens tried to move outside the palisade, the Giants' vicious intentions became clear. They yelled, threatened and threw stones from their protected positions but never exposed themselves to projectiles.

Two Illoreaen youths decided to show off their courage and challenged the Giants with gestures and abuse. When the Giants did not react, they ventured past the palisade misjudging the strength of the Giants and the distance they could cast stones. The Giants bombarded them with stones and suddenly stormed out from their encampment. A few of the projectiles hit. The youths just managed to scramble to the safety of the Habitat before the Giants reached them. They were not seriously injured but still needed treatment inside the cave system.

The Illoreaens were not sympathetic. "They should not have taken chances by exposing themselves," Questa heard one say.

She also overheard a discussion between two older Illoreaens, "The Giants' presence is really inconvenient."

"Yes, and the additional guard duty wastes time. My son was planning to work outside the Habitat. Now he sits at a Look-Out point."

"At least there are enough stored materials from the excavations. Most of us can continue with our knowledge searches and play-work."

"They will disappear soon. They'll get bored and run out of food. Then we can continue as usual."

They listened politely but ignored Questa's repeated warnings, "Heropto is clever. He will not give up."

Questa overheard quiet comments and snippets of conversation mentioning the many devices the Illoreaens could use to protect themselves and prevent possible attacks. They did not share the details with her and she remained concerned.

The young men found the guard duties, watching the Giants, an exciting diversion and they commented on the Giants' shapes and habits.

On one of the very dark nights, a few Giants managed to creep up to the palisade and they stayed there during the gloomy day. The palisade protected them from any projectiles the Look-Outs could launch from their positions high on the cliff. They taunted the Illoreaens from beyond the palisade, creeping in and out in the dark of night.

From an empty Look-Out post, Questa's unimpeded view of the Giants and their encampment, allowed her to study them well, to watch their habits and actions. She Sensed carefully while blocking out the Illoreaen presence.

She could still Sense Heropto's simmering hatred whenever she focused on him. But he clearly managed to control his impatience. *It makes him even more dangerous. I believe his plan is to exterminate all of us.*

JaYan saw Questa observing the Giants and noticed her concern. "We don't regard the Giants as a direct threat. Our Habitat is safe; we can keep the Giants at bay with our spears and flyers. They are quite slow and prefer to wait in ambush with their short stabbing spears and knobbed clubs. Their traditions match the environment in which they live and to which their bodies are adapted. When hunting large animals or even predators, they will physically tackle their prey using only their short stabbing spears and clubs. Do you Sense anything else?"

"I believe Heropto ignores traditions and I believe he's very intelligent," Questa answered. "His brain is very active, different from the others. They are all intelligent but I Sense he far surpasses them all, always scheming. There is a darkness surrounding him. He emanates an intense feverish hatred, focused on us. The other Giants have a very weak connection with him," she paused. "How will the Giants sustain themselves? There are so many. How long will they stay?"

"I don't really know. I think the Giants will soon run out of provisions or just get bored and go away."

"I don't understand how the group from the Dynasty can reach us safely and how I can travel with them and return securely to the Clan valleys."

"Yes, my main concern is for the messengers from the Dynasty. They should have arrived long ago. We have left warning messages about the Giants who surround us. We have not received any acknowledgement or answers. I believe the Dynasty will send a strong contingent to help us. With their help, we'll chase the Giants away. We are too few to do so alone."

Meanwhile, the Illoreaens stayed within the Habitat and continued with their tasks, sometimes joining the guards at the portals high up the cliff to watch the Giants. The Giants erected shelters and rolled boulders in positions, giving them effective cover and screening them from Illoreaen projectiles.

#

The situation changed. Questa overheard worried remarks, "The Giants are patrolling the slopes above the Habitat as well. We cannot use the alternative exits. We'll have to do something about them soon."

JaYan found Questa. He had a worried expression on his face.

She allowed her concern to show, "What is the matter?"

"The Giants have managed to block our ability to leave the Habitat. The foodstuffs we have stored inside the Habitat, are enough to last for an extended period, but our water position is critical. Our water comes from fountains in the mountains. The Giants patrolling the slopes have discovered how we feed water into our Habitat and have blocked the flow. There are only a few water drips within the cave system. We now collect all we can in vessels, but it is barely enough for all of us to survive on. We implemented rationing."

"What will you do and what about the group from the Dynasty?"

"Yes, it is worrying, but we have options. There is a secret escape tunnel leading out higher up the mountain, far to the side of the main entrance. Only a few of our fighters, equipped with special footwear allowing their tracks to meld with the large footprints of the Giants, can use it, and only when essential. They will intercept the group from the Dynasty and coordinate our efforts. The Giants are patrolling the area above the cliffs and Heropto has positioned them well. I think I need to talk to the Giants. I would like you to come with me. You might notice or Sense something useful."

"Certainly."

From a portal high up the cliff, JaYan called out in the strange guttural tongue of the Giants, "I am JaYan. I speak for the Illoreaens! Why are you threatening us? We have no fight with you!"

Heropto sat with a few of the Giants at one of the many barricades they had built surrounding the palisade. He stood up and stepped nearer, "Me Heropto, lead Giants in hunt. Me kill prey much bigger, bare hands! You small creatures take my Prize! You not interest me. You give Prize back, me go. Me see Prize behind you. She mine! Give her, me go!"

"You have no right to her!" JaYan said. "You abducted her from the Dynasty. They will wreak terrible revenge on you! Go away!"

Heropto gave a deep laugh, "The Dynasty! They finished! You not know!" All the Giants broke into the laughs so horrible to Clan ears. "You think they help you! They gone!"

JaYan quickly translated the exchange, leaving out the demand for Questa's surrender. The few words Questa had learned did not help, she could only judge the exchange by sound and body language. However, she Sensed Heropto's confidence, "He is so sure of himself. I shudder just looking at him! What does he mean when he said the Dynasty is 'gone'?"

JaYan could not answer. More exchanges on the following days did not clarify the mystery but made Heropto more aggressive and insulting.

A few of the Illoreaens told Questa tales of the fights amongst Giants, "They customarily exterminate opposing troupes with horrible cruelty. They have no feelings. They are terrible and kill one another on the slightest provocation!"

The Illoreaens' attitude towards her had changed, which pleased Questa. They now shared information as if she was one of them. They were not prepared to hand her over to the Giants.

"In the Clans, we know very little about the Giants, only that they are huge," she said, "For us, the main threat comes from the Primitives who, I believe, are even worse. The tales about them claim they cannibalize their vanquished and prefer nice fat victims with soft meat like the young and babies. We in the Clans are always very careful not to fall into their hands and to ensure they never enter our valleys!"

The next day Heropto renewed his demands. He said, "We got ice caves, plenty meat. We stay long! You die slowly! Better you leave hole you hide in. Come out now, you die quick."

The Illoreaens began to understand the real threat. The Giants intended to kill them all, even if they surrendered or handed over Questa.

#

The three Illoreaens, previously sent to search for the courier-messengers from the Dynasty, returned many days later than expected, "What happened? Giants surround the Habitat! We saw your message and noticed their tracks so we approached very carefully. We saw Giants patrolling and knew they were up to no good. We managed to slip in through the secret entrance, unseen in the dark. We were careful to leave no tracks. Why are they here?"

JaYan quickly explained the situation.

The Illoreaens all assembled to hear the bad news, "The route is now very difficult and destroyed in many places. The mountain passes collapsed or shifted and well-known landmarks have changed and are unrecognizable. When we did not meet the expected courier-messengers from the Dynasty, we continued on. Our adequate supplies and knowledge of the mountain, between here and the Dynasty Valley, allowed us to try many alternative ways. At last, we managed to find and force a route.

"Even worse. We found the Dynasty's home volcano erupting. It was horrible! We always believed the volcano was inactive, but it poured out lava, melting the snowfields above the valley. The whole side of the volcano, the side above the Dynasty Valley, exploded and is now just a smoking cavity. Mud lies thick in the valley. We believe it flooded. Lava and snow engulfed the Habitat. The Dynasty is no more."

The Illoreaens listened in shocked silence.

"We looked for tracks and searched for survivors, but we found none. We managed to penetrate the mountain slopes up to the next Clan valley. A layer of choking yellowish-brown dust, which tends to rise up when disturbed, covers the slopes. We found the remains of the members of the Clan. The Primitives herded them into a corner of the valley where they killed and mutilated all the Clan-members horribly. It was a massacre. We fear for the fate of all the Clans. I cannot describe what the Primitives did to their victims!

"We managed to gather enough food in and around the devastated valley, before we returned over the mountain. It was difficult. We saw the track of a single Giant near the Dynasty Valley and were very careful as we approached the Habitat. We noticed Giants sitting on rocky outcrops, etched against the yellow-brown sky, keeping guard. We waited until the gloom darkened before creeping to the secret entrance. The Giants are slouching around, disturbing dust and plants, making it easy to hide our tracks. The Giants disappeared as soon as the gloom darkened. They joined their companions at their fires lower down, in front of the palisade."

Questa's instinct overcame her shock. All her training urged her to soothe them and to absorb some of the pain, to share pain and suppress her own. It was her function in the Clans; that was what she did. The Clans did not regard soothing as an invasion of privacy. However, she dared not display her abilities. JaYan noticed her involuntary gesture but did not understand.

Shocked and worried about her own Clan she wanted to know more, but the three Illoreaens knew only about the one Clan near the Dynasty Valley and knew nothing further. She retired to her sleeping cubicle to worry through the night, *What will now become of me? How will I ever get back to my Clan? Are they safe?*

#

JaYan spoke with MaGan, "This is devastating. We will have to change our way of life. We were too dependent on the Dynasty.

We must now handle the Giants, without the Dynasty's help. What do you think?"

They discussed and made plans, sitting together for most of the day.

MaGan brought up another aspect of the disaster, "We did not know of the existence of Sensitives and their important role. We must not allow the ability to disappear, to die out. Questa might be the only surviving Sensitive. With her ability, she is very valuable." He paused and then added in an aside to JaYan, "She must have many offspring! The ability must be preserved!"

"What a cold way to look at it," JaYan answered, but he did not contradict MaGan.

It was a crisis. JaYan now understood Heropto's mocking bravado. The Illoreaens had been certain of aid from the Dynasty, who, with their many trained fighters, could have created a diversion, time enough for the Sharp-shooters to reach strategic positions and drive off the Giants. Now they were on their own.

The return of the search party brought valuable information. Individual Illoreaens were now able to exit from the secret entrance when the gloom darkened, after the Giants patrolling above the cliffs left. They brought in amounts of additional water, but the ration allowed for each member remained critical and washing was severely limited. The rain seldom fell and was acidic and poisonous, irritating the skin, affecting trees, plants and all growth. In the gloom and darkness, the plant cover of the plains and forested valleys was dead and the animals had vanished. Food stocks were slowly diminishing while the Giants seemed to have settled down for the long-term, feasting on the adequate supplies in the Illoreaen ice caves, which a few Giants guarded permanently.

A deadlock developed; the Illoreaens were safe in their Habitat and the Giants safely patrolled the surrounds without attacking, waiting for the Illoreaen provisions to run out.

When not at the Look-Out post, Questa watched the Illoreaens working at their work-play and knowledge searches, most often helping JaYan or Merpa, with whom she formed a close and friendly relationship. SkepTan met her in a corridor as she emerged from a discussion with Merpa one day.

"MaGan and JaYan are both pursuing you. No wonder! The Coordinating Committee was very clear, you must have as many offspring as possible to ensure the continuity of Sensitive abilities. There is no single child taboo for you and they are foremost in the queue. They plan to also get many offspring. Are you going to give the rest of us a chance too? Remember, I'm the expert on breeding. When is my turn?"

Questa froze in horror. *This was terrible. Was JaYan's friendliness only a way to have many offspring? To avoid the limitations of the single-child rule? And MaGan too!*

As soon as she could move, she ran down the corridor to her own sleeping cubicle, tears streaming down her face. How could she remain with the Illoreaens, if she was only seen as a breeding opportunity?"

#

The Illoreaens were trapped within their Habitat. The older boys and young men were becoming restless. The gloom hiding the sun was bad enough, but to be confined inside the Habitat made everything worse.

"This is our Habitat and our mountain slopes, where our ancestors have lived forever. The Giants have no right to be here, no right to bother us and to restrict our movement. Something must be done!" the young men expressed their sentiments virulently.

JaYan and MaGan tried to appease them but with little effect. Anger increased in intensity until a small group decided to confront the Giants, in secret and without approval.

Early one morning, before any light glimmered, a group of young men crept out through the main entrance tunnel. Only the Illoreaens on guard, who were friends of the group, knew of the exploit. They crept up to the palisade surrounding the Habitat, from where they could see the glow of the fire's embers. The Giants, bored with non-activity and never good at discipline, did not bother to maintain proper guard or even to keep their fires burning.

The group stormed the sleeping Giants and wounded the guards and a few others, not managing or intending to kill. Heropto and a few of his closest companions were more vigilant and moved quickly towards the palisade, When the young men saw Heropto and his supporters preparing to intercept, they rushed back to the Habitat and the safety of the palisade.

Heropto was the first to arrive at the palisade entrance. He seized the leader of the group who fought desperately, swinging his club. Heropto grabbed the club and threw it to the side with disdain. The young man discarded his spear thrower and tried to jab Heropto with his long throwing spear. The spear was long and difficult to swing. It did not work.

Heropto seized the spear with a yell, throwing the youth off balance. He grabbed the youth by the neck, squeezed, bones snapped, and threw the lifeless body against the palisade wall.

"You small. You insects!" he roared, spitting at the body. Turning to his companions he continued, "You kill all. *All!*"

The other Giants joined the massacre and attacked with their knobbed clubs, short stabbing spears, and axes with heavy stone blades.

The Illoreaen group fought for their lives, desperately. Their throwing spears were useless against the brute strength of the Giants.

Many of Heropto's followers did not even bother to use their weapons but followed Heropto's example of throttling and flinging their victims against the palisade, using their bare hands.

Two of the youths died immediately. Others were seriously injured and lay helpless, awaiting their fate.

The noise brought the Illoreaens to the observation windows in the cliff. There was not enough space to use spear-throwers. In desperation, a few grabbed their bows and flyers. It was difficult for the defenders at the observation windows to find a target. The Giants overpowered and held the youths as shields. Only a few flyers were shot, hurting but not killing the Giants.

The Illoreaens who were supposed to guard the entrance, rushed out to help, yielding their clubs with little effect other than confusing the Giants by suddenly offering several more targets, thereby delaying the Giants' killing spree.

The guards did not manage to retrieve the bodies of the dead Illoreaens, but had to scramble back to safety. They left one of their own behind, dead.

None of the wounded managed to reach the Habitat entrance.

Three of the guards, who reached safety, suffered such serious injuries, it was unclear whether they would survive. Despite all the care the Illoreaens were able to give, two of them died.

The result of the impetuous action was a disaster.

Heropto was furious, both with his guards and with the Illoreaens for surprising them. In sight of the Habitat but outside the range of the Illoreaen missiles, he personally mutilated the bodies of the dead Illoreaens, tearing them apart with his bare hands.

While his fellows killed the remaining wounded, Heropto grabbed one by the neck, using one hand. With the still living youth screaming and dangling from Heropto's outstretched arm, he slowly tore off the limbs from the wriggling Illoreaen, one by one.

Mercifully, the boy quickly lost consciousness and died.

Heropto threw the mutilated bodies and body parts over the palisade towards the Habitat and bellowed abuse, "It is the fate awaiting all of you!"

JaYan declined to translate.

Heropto treated his own guards with equal rage. He roared his frustration, grabbed the nearest by the neck, picked him and shook him, as if he was a tiger mauling a small animal.

The strongly built Giant was not so easy to dismember. All the effort only dislodged the guard's arms. Heropto's anger increased visibly.

With a face distorted in frustration, he flung his victim to the ground. Swinging his heavy club, he reduced the Giant's head to mush. The slaughter took considerably more time than he intended.

The other Giants enjoyed the spectacle. Before the remaining guards came to their senses and tried to escape, Heropto smashed into them. Their legs succumbed to his club first. Then their arms. Their yelling drowned the snapping and cracking sounds of splintered bones. At last, all the guards were dead.

The whole of the Illoreaen Habitat was devastated and the parents of the victims went into inconsolable mourning. The Illoreaen guards, who had helped the adventurers exit the Habitat, appeared before the Coordinating Committee. They tried to explain, "None of us realized how dangerous the Giants are. We did not believe in the Giant's strength. Our friends only intend to encourage the Giants to leave and did not even take bows and flyers, making sure they would not lose any."

Tears streamed down the guard leader's cheeks, "We never realized how absolutely barbaric and bloodthirsty the Giants, and especially Heropto, are!"

The Coordinating Committee could do nothing and said nothing about the lost flyers. Knowledge of the secret of bows and flyers, could make the Giants even more dangerous. The Committee did not need to punish the guards, or the young men. They would never forget the consequences of their actions, it would haunt them forever.

Every day was colder than the previous one, but this did not bother the Giants, because they thrived in the cold. The Habitat's temperature was slowly but steadily cooling down. Using their vision tubes, the Illoreaens could see the vegetation on the plains dying. There were no signs of the usual herds of browsers. Occasionally, they saw an emaciated predator slinking across the plain, far away. The wooded and forested valleys were stark in the gloom. Even the pine trees looked wilted and deciduous trees had lost all their new leaves.

Even without the Giants' presence and at the best of times, the plains and valleys near the Illoreaen Habitat were meager and yielded little sustenance. There was no hope of being self-sufficient. Without the supplies that the Dynasty regularly sent, there was no possibility of replenishing their stock of edibles.

It was becoming impossible for all the Illoreaens to continue occupying the Habitat,. The stink of decaying bodies of their kin, outside the Habitat, which the Illoreaens couldn't do anything about, added to the stress they experienced.

Something had to be done urgently.

Chapter 31 – The River

Orrox realized Anja's ability to Sense Primitives outdid them all. He took her claim of Sensing Primitives seriously—He stopped, listened, and focused his own considerable Sensing ability. Nothing. Then he picked up the faint emanations of fear and a killing frenzy. The emanations were not Clan like—the emanations of Primitives!

"Hurry! Hide!"

Anja and the acolytes followed Orrox to a clump of bushes near a natural rock bastion, still careful not to make easily discernible tracks. "We must prepare for an attack. Our few spears will be of little use against many. All we can do is frighten them with projections, explosions and smoke. We must hide until the Primitives have discovered us. Then we must take up a defensive position on top of these boulders. I will prepare some explosive powders.

"Bronnox, creep up to the top of the rocks and watch them. The rest of you, hide nearby. Anja, how is your wound? You Sense the Primitives best, we need your ability now. Please let the others synchronize with your Sensing to enhance their focus on the Primitive emanations."

"No problem. The wound has nearly healed and doesn't bother me much. I can concentrate. I only need to occasionally massage the surrounding muscles."

They followed Orrox's instructions and quickly clambered up the rock pillar, keeping a low profile, with only Bronnox peeking through a crack between two boulders. They kept silent while Orrox prepared his mixture.

"I still don't see anything. What do you Sense?" Bronnox asked.

"We are still focusing our Sensing," Lonna said. "Anja is projecting something I think emanates from different Primitives. The one lot is chasing another very frightened troupe. Oh! Anja, what was that?"

"The chasers are killing the others! It is horrible! Block your Sensing!"

"You are right! I can see them now," Bronnox said. "How awful!"

Bronnox needed to look away, just glancing through the crack occasionally to make sure the attacking Primitives did not approach them.

"What is happening? I'm allowing just a little of their emotions to vibrate in my Sensing, just to make sure I will notice if they approach," Anja said.

"I can identify the two groups. I think the chasers assembled as a mob to prey on weaker Primitives," Bronnox said.

The chasing group of Primitives surrounded their weaker victims and attacked them with their clubs. A short struggle ended with all the victims killed and slaughtered. In a wasteful display of their indifference to the value of life, the victors cut choice pieces of meat off their prey and ignored the rest.

Bronnox was still watching, "Oh no! They are butchering the others! They are cutting them up. They have started a fire. They are cannibals!"

Orrox joined his companions and took up a position near the top of the rock pile, "Block your Sensing! Follow my lead. I will show you how to completely block what is happening." There was silence while they all accepted Orrox's projection and strengthened their individual control, blocking the horror.

"I followed Anja's projection. Thank you Bronnox, you can move away. You have seen enough of their ghastly feast. I will keep watch now."

The companions sat in silence trying to deal with the horror of the Primitives, while Orrox forced his thoughts away from the awful display down below. This was the first time he witnessed Primitive barbarism on this scale. It was even worse than what he witnessed during the attack on Jupex's Clan or when he searched for surviving Clans. He came to understand better why the Dynasty always took such extreme precautions to keep the Primitives away from the valleys.

I am the remaining Orrox, successor to the responsibilities assumed by the Dynasty. Reassembling and redefining the Clans as well as their protection falls on me alone, until I have found others of the Dynasty. I must find a safe refuge for my acolytes and then discover what has happened to the Clans and those who survived the Catastrophe in the Dynasty Valley.

Glancing down at the Primitives, Orrox said, "You can all look now. The worst is over. They have finished and are lying around their fire. Do not show yourselves."

The companions cringed in fear. While the savage Primitives slept, they nearly forgot their continuing thirst. Orrox occasionally glanced briefly to ensure they were still safe. When darkness fell, they could see nothing and took turns to focus their Sensing on the Primitives to detect movement or danger, but nothing happened until the gloom paled to indicate morning.

"Wait!" Orrox whispered, "One of them is moving in our direction. I have the explosive surprises ready, be prepared to follow my projection," he paused. "What is he doing?"

They all looked, careful not to show themselves.

"He's digging something. Oh, how stupid of me! I know what he's doing," Anja said.

The Primitive dug out a tuber and then searched farther in a sandy area. He collected a few of the bulbs and carried it back to his troupe, where they grated them into pulp. Each of the troupe grabbed a fistful, squeezed the pulp and extended a thumb to allow the juice to flow down their thumbs into their mouths.

"I wondered how they manage to survive without drinkable water," Orrox said. "The water from the river and streams is foul and poisonous. And for food, they cannibalize the other Primitives. Unthinkable!"

Anja and the acolytes kept their ability to Sense fully blocked while the Primitives feasted again on the hideous meat, found more of the bulbs and drank the liquid. Only Orrox allowed a little of their emanations to penetrate his awareness. Then he Sensed a Projection, *Strange!*

Before he could focus it was gone.

The Primitives all got up, as if called, and moved upriver, away from Orrox, Anja and the acolytes. Their combined Sensing soon confirmed the greater distance as the Primitives moved farther and farther away.

Orrox concentrated but he never Sensed the strange projection again.

Was it my imagination? He wondered and said nothing.

The companions remained hidden, while Anja concentrated on the Primitives. By the end of the day, the Primitives were so far away, they no longer posed a threat.

"We must not leave any tracks for any Primitives to find, should they return down the river," Orrox said. "However, I don't think it very likely. They are probably on their way to their plains and marshes to find new victims."

#

From their rocky fortress, the companions continued downriver, keeping it far on their left. They were still scared and careful not to leave any footprints.

Anja headed for a sandy patch nearer the river where she soon found what she looked for. A small blade forming a single elongated leaf rose out of the sand. She carefully removed the sand around it to expose a large bulb, bigger than two fists held together.

"My grandmother taught me all about survival options. Here is one of those tubers the Primitives found. The juice has a tangy, bitter taste. They are the only source of life-giving liquid in the open desert. I have never seen these desert plants before but she accurately described the blade and the leaf."

Anja grated the bulb into a pulp. By copying the technique the Primitives used, squeezing the pulp in their raised fists, the six of them allowed the sap to run down their extended thumbs into their mouths. The tangy tasty effectively slaked their thirst.

#

"We must follow the river far enough to get beyond the lava flows and devastation of the Erejefischt eruption," Orrox reminded them. "Then we can return to the mountains and the smaller valleys where we should find enough edible roots and fresh water to sustain us. Once we have gathered adequate provisions, we can plan further."

Orrox did not show his frustration at moving farther away from the Clan valleys, where he felt his main responsibilities and obligations lay. He had no alternative. The threat of the Primitives was too great to return to the Clan valleys. They all wanted to search for survivors but they had to ensure their own survival first.

The river continued downwards, flinging its reduced volume of polluted water over waterfalls and rapids where high ridges crossed its path. The mountains disappeared in the gloom as they followed the river further into the desert. After three days, Orrox was desperately looking for a ravine leading up to the mountains. It must show signs of trapped moisture, where they could find oozing water by digging in the right spots.

The edge of another ridge with a drop beyond stopped their progress; the gloom and dust obscured any view beyond. Orrox, who was in the lead, took a pebble and threw it over the edge to estimate the height, as he had done each time they encountered such a barrier. The sound of an impact usually followed, allowing them to estimate the height of the ridge, even when the bottom was not visible. They all listened for the sound. One bounce, then silence. He then hurled a large stone as far as he could. After a very long time they heard the faint sounds of the stone hitting rock, and then faintly the sound of a second bounce.

Orrox was at a loss. What now? Their farther progress along the river was blocked while he was still searching for a suitable route back to the mountains.

They were standing on slabs of rock which ended in a sharp edge. It looked just like another ridge, which had blocked their progress before.

"Let me think," Orrox said, looking for a boulder to sit on. The acolytes looked worried, Orrox was normally more decisive.

"Memories of tales from when I was very young are stirring in my mind. It is late. Let's find a safe place for the night. With Anja's Sensing, we will have a fair warning if a troupe of Primitives approaches."

Orrox took the lead. The slab allowed them all to walk side-by-side, keeping the edge to their right. Eventually, they could see the river ahead, blocking their way. Looking over the edge they could see it thundering over the edge and disappearing into the misty gloom below.

To find a place to cross, they searched upstream, climbing a small ridge, and found an easy crossing. Here the stream widened as it passed over flat slabs. They waded through water seldom reaching up to their knees, and then only in the deeper rivulets gouged into the rock over the eons. A series of rapids descended the rocky ridge.

Orrox tasted the water carefully, wetting the tip of his tongue with a finger before he spat it out.

"The water is bitter and not fit to drink but we can cross here, he said."

On the far side they climbed down to discover the rapids ended in a waterfall, which tumbled into a large pool surrounded by big trees with spreading branches.

"Let's look more closely," Orrox said.

An overhang was hidden behind some wilting trees with few leaves remaining.

The approach to the overhang was protected on three sides. By the ridge from above, by the edge farther down river and, to the right, by the river and the pool.

"This must have been a very beautiful spot before the Catastrophe," Camla said. They all agreed, saddened by the change.

We can stay safely under the overhang through the night. I believe it is even safe to make a fire. We'll take turns to guard and keep the fire going."

Orrox woke each member to take his or her turn. When it was Questa's turn, preceding Orrox's, he moved quietly towards her, but she was already awake.

"My turn?" she asked and he nodded in confirmation. As she got up Orrox threw a few more logs on the fire. It flared up, illuminating the surroundings.

"If you notice anything strange, light this branch, swing it towards any threat and wake the others."

She expected Orrox to lie down again, but he sat down beside her. They were some distance away from where the others slept, making their conversation private. "Are you not going to sleep till it's your turn?"

"No, I have slept enough. I want to talk to you. More than a full moon has passed since the Catastrophe and at least half a moon since we met. We have only shared essential details but we still know very little about each other. Once we have settled, each of the acolytes will tell you their stories but now I would like to share a tale, a story of my grandfather and of your grandmother and mother. You will be surprised how much I know."

Anja was silent, suppressing resentment but strangely excited too.

Orrox sat silently for a while. "In the Orrox Dynasty, as elsewhere, an Orrox's offspring usually consists of only one boy and one girl. We keep close contact with our cousins, our aunt's boy and girl. The best qualified man can become the Orrox. Should a girl or boy, born in a specific generation, die before having their own progeny, we have rules and methods for replacing them, thereby ensuring the continuation of the Orrox line within the Dynasty. This is also the origin of the myths of Orrox immortality and rebirth.

"You surely have heard, the Orrox male of the main succession often chooses a cousin, often his aunt's daughter, as his life-companion. These intermarriages have greatly increased certain inbred abilities over the generations and increased the inflated opinion we Orrox have of our own worth. The Orrox's sister and male cousin bring new blood into the Dynasty line, typically by choosing outstanding Clan-members from distant Clans as life-companions. They usually join their companion's Clan and regularly become Clan Chiefs or a Chief's life-companions. Those are often allowed additional offspring. Our blood-line is widely spread within the Clans. You will be surprised to know how many Orrox ancestors you also have.

"As I have said, we are proud. We think we bestow a great honor on a woman of one of the Clans should the Orrox ask her to be his life-companion, especially if she isn't at least a distant cousin."

Seeing Anja's indignation, he paused and looked apologetically at her. "I must be truthful and can make no apologies.

"However, the story I wish to tell concerns your grandmother and my grandfather. She was a very accomplished and beautiful girl, whom my grandfather met they were both still young, in early adulthood as we say. My grandfather had a wild streak and, as the Orrox of the main succession, he was convinced he was destined to one day lead the Council and therefore, in his opinion, the Clans.

"The Orrox scions tended not to rate women from outside the Dynasty, especially if not closely related to the Dynasty, as highly as they should. We have much to learn from the Clans, who, I have learned, always treat all members with respect and as equals, despite the different roles they perform. The acolytes, you will notice, treat all as equals and with respect, and, I hope, so do I.

"My great-grandfather was overbearing, confident of his power and he sometimes bullied his life-companion, who was not a related Orrox cousin. Instead of protecting his mother, my grandfather adopted a similar attitude towards women.

"As you know, your grandmother came from a long line of Oracle-Healers, highly regarded in all the Clans. We, of the Dynasty, like to believe the Orrox blood flows strongly in your female line.

"Both your grandmother and my grandfather were selected for advanced training, as were a few very talented youths from different Clans. The selection was a great honor, even for an Orrox. The Dynasty expected the young attendees to become influential within the Clans. The talents of your grandmother, my grandfather and one other, stood out amongst the others and they often performed tasks and solved problems together. The three were strong Sensitives and super intelligent. Everyone expected them to become outstanding Oracle-Healers. The third was a girl, from a distant Clan.

"Their mentors made a great fuss, praising their individual abilities. Experienced Sensitives from all the Clans helped to organize special and intense training sessions for all three. The three were often together and it was probably inevitable a love triangle developed. I understand my grandfather enjoyed his position of working with two adoring women. Despite your grandmother keeping back her feelings, the two fell in love. Many have confirmed this.

"I am very loyal to both my grandmother and grandfather but I have to share the truth with you. The other girl was my grandmother and she was jealous, using every possible device to break up the couple. She enticed my grandfather to sleep with her and managed to conceive, breaking many Clan rules and taboos. My father was the result.

"My grandfather did not regard this as very serious. He thought his father, my great-grandfather's example, proved an

Orrox could bend or break the rules governing others within the Clans. Since both men and women may each choose the partner with whom to conceive their allocated child, he reasoned he was still free to choose your grandmother as his life-companion. He regarded the baby, my father, as my grandmother's sanctioned offspring.

"He just ignored the girl with child and arranged for her to be sent back to her Clan. He was sure he and your grandmother could still become life-companions and have their own two children. He did not understand your grandmother's principles. She believed in fidelity, therefore my grandfather had an obligation to his first-born and to the girl. She insisted on the first-born son being the true Orrox successor.

"My grandfather was furious and told your grandmother he would do whatever pleased him, because an Orrox was superior to any stupid, ordinary, and inferior Clan-girl. She would simply have to accept the situation. Your grandmother refused and returned to your Clan. When she discovered he had committed other infidelities, while they were together, she avoided contact with him."

This tale was new to Anja. She only knew her grandmother did not like, possibly despised, the Orrox scions, but nevertheless respected the Council and the knowledge dispensed from the Dynasty Valley.

"I did not know this," she said softly. She did not doubt the truth of the account.

"I'm afraid there is worse to come! To grandfather's surprise, my great-grandfather also insisted my father, the first-born, was the true Orrox heir. Great-grandfather also accepted the girl, my grandmother, into the Dynasty as the mother of the next Orrox and forced Grandfather to accept her as his life-companion. He punished my grandfather, restricting the power he craved so badly. The episode affected the Orrox predominance at the council. I have to admit, politics, not morals, probably motivated great-grandfather's actions. Too many experienced Sensitives and Chiefs from the Clans knew all the details. The reputation and hereditary succession of the Orrox was at stake.

"My grandmother was pleasant and pretty, and grandfather accepted the situation over time. My grandmother turned out to be fine, competent and influential in a positive way. I believe grandfather learned to love her. Her main flaw was to have fallen so deeply in love with him.

"After my grandmother died during a hunting expedition, Grandfather went to seek out your Clan. He again asked your grandmother to become his life-companion. It seems the break-up and heartache increased your grandmother's Sensing abilities and she asked grandfather to allow her to Sense his emotions and intentions.

"I think he knew she would not like him as he still was then, but believed, in his arrogance, he could hide his true self and project something she would like. He underestimated how phenomenal a Sensitive your grandmother was. She immediately knew and rejected his projection and read selfishness and a streak of cruelty in him. She read much more than he ever thought possible, more than he even knew about himself.

"Your grandmother then knew of his intention to increase his authority and power in the Council. He had no real remorse for having broken the strict Clan codes. He also allowed other girls to entice him, trying to conceive children. He kept out of trouble only because he knew how to prevent conception. According to my grandfather, your grandmother was the only one he ever loved.

"Your grandmother rejected my grandfather. He could not understand how his ambitions for the Dynasty, the Orrox, and for himself, or the admitted affairs with those he claimed not to love, harmed his case. She tried to explain the standards she expected of a life-companion and of an Orrox.

"Without fully understanding, my grandfather was adamant he would change. Without much hope, she told him to come back after five seasons. Should he have changed, she would accept him. This infuriated him. In his fury, he decided to use the power and influence of the Orrox name to force your grandmother to comply and started putting pressure on members of your Clan, nearly breaking up the Clan as factions formed."

"So, your grandfather was to blame! There were always two rival factions within our Clan with friction between them. No one would ever tell us of the younger generation what it was all about, but there were rumors of the involvement of my grandmother and the Dynasty," Anja said, her eyes widening.

"So, it continued until now! Even though factions do not usually form in a grouping as small as your Clan. I'm sorry." Orrox was demurely silent for a while before he continued, holding his chin as if in thought.

"After five seasons my grandfather returned to your Clan, confronted your grandmother and insisted on his right to make her his life-companion. By then he was an influential member of the Council where he used his superior Sensing abilities to manipulate opponents and advisors. His cruel streak was more prominent. Your grandmother Sensed it all and rejected him permanently. He was very angry when he left and later chose the daughter of a powerful Chief on the Council as life-companion. She was my step-grandmother and kind, but she never bore him a child and he never had another elsewhere.

"Despite my great-grandfather's opposition, my father was taken to my grandmother's Clan where he lived and learned throughout his youth. With my great-grandfather's help, they instilled the best instincts in my father. The Dynasty later called on him to train as an Oracle and herbalist. He proved able and talented and was chosen as my grandfather's successor.

"My father, probably influenced by grandfather's folly, overlooked Orrox cousins and second cousins but took a pleasant girl from another Clan as life-companion. She also had outstanding Sensitive abilities and is my mother. My father preferred to continue living with my grandmother's Clan, but he visited the Dynasty Valley often to fulfill his obligations as Council leader and for Council meetings. My sister and I, like him, grew up there, but were trained at the Dynasty Valley.

"My great-grandfather, who turned out to be a sensible man once he could discard his pride, blamed himself for his son's misconduct. He changed the training of Orrox scions to suppress any greed and unbridled ambition, which had emerged. My mentors and family often tell the story as a warning against pride and uncontrolled power lust and to remind us of a wild Orrox streak we must guard against."

"Do you know more about my grandmother?" Anja asked. "She never discussed her history and I never listened to gossip."

"I did hear the gossip!" Orrox continued. "Your grandmother took a childhood friend from your Clan as life-companion, one who was also a strong Sensitive. When your mother was born, she was expertly trained. She was the only child. Your grandmother did not want a son, afraid the Dynasty might target him.

"When it was opportune and with your grandmother's help, your mother looked for a strong companion with good instincts, whom she could love and respect. She found him, or as my mentors put it, they encouraged an outstanding young man to find her. He was Jupex who became your and your sister's father. We at the Dynasty never doubted your grandmother knew about the strong Sensitivity strain in his ancestors. Clearly strong in you and, I am told, in your sister. Your grandmother persuaded your mother not to have a son, only two daughters.

"I know all of this because your mother and grandmother visited our Clan, my mother's Clan, during a tour of many Clans, we believe in their search for a suitable life-companion. The story of their quest became part of my Clan's folklore. Our Clan mentored me from the beginning to be the Orrox successor. My father was probably in the Dynasty cave during the Catastrophe. I believe he is dead and I am the Orrox and the Council leader now.

"My grandfather never accepted your grandmother's rejection of him. She was incensed about his campaign within your Clan, which I understood caused her untold problems. She avoided all contact with the Dynasty and the Orrox and they never met again, thereby creating the myth of a deadly feud. I want to apologize for my grandfather's conduct."

The tale intrigued Anja. She did not doubt the truth even though neither her grandmother nor any of the Clan ever told her the whole story. Mention of her grandmother's youth was always taboo, but she recalled her grandmother's warnings against selfish power-hungry men. She fondly remembered her grandfather, PreTox, a kindly old man with a beautiful deep voice. He often took her on his lap to tell some children's story or sing a funny ditty.

"Thank you for telling me. It is mostly new to me and I did not know any of the details." She paused, deep in thought. Looking up suddenly, she exclaimed, "But then your losses are far more than just the destruction of the Dynasty! You must be very concerned about the fate of the Clan of your grandmother and father. Your Clan!"

"Yes, it would be easier if I knew their situation and I mourn the possibility of disaster."

While telling the story Orrox often looked around, never relaxing his vigil. Anja, so engrossed with the tale, forgot about her guard duty.

She was silent for a while, wanting to think but it was her turn to keep watch. Thinking would have to wait for later. "I'm sorry. I did not even notice how time has passed. I will be more observant now. Please go to sleep until it is your turn. You must not over-exert yourself – remember your recent injuries."

"No, I have already rested well and my wounds have healed. I'm wide-awake and have many thoughts to occupy me. You get some sleep until the dark lifts. I know you are tired and need more rest. I will start my turn now."

She lingered a little longer and then went to lie down again at her place near the fire, but she could not sleep. The story of her grandmother kept on coming back to haunt her, until increasing light announced dawn and the others started moving.

Chapter 32 – Flight

The Coordinating Committee asked all the Illoreaens to assemble. JaYan spoke first, "We have always depended on the Dynasty for supplies, partly because our valley and direct environment is infertile and therefore a poor source of food. The Catastrophe destroyed the little there was and the lack of sunshine prevents re-generation."

MaGan continued, "As you all know, our superiority over the Giants is based on the use of our unique weapons, most effective over a distance. If necessary, the Dynasty further support us with their specialist fighters. With the Giants remaining in the woods and hiding behind barricades, we cannot chase them away without the help of the Dynasty. But, the Dynasty was destroyed during the Catastrophe. Any survivors are in no position to help us. The Giants have now cut off our access to our provisions in the ice caves and have blocked our sources of water."

JaYan scanned the assembled Illoreaens. They all looked worried, "Yes, you are right, we are concerned," he said. "Under the circumstances we cannot stay here. We have to plan for the long-term and find a fertile enough area where we can survive until things return to normal. Our best experts have devoted much time considering what has happened and to estimate how long the effects would last. Our records show times when a very large volcanic eruption caused darkened skies, obscured by dust. The land-shakings and other similarities with what we are experiencing now point to something much, much bigger. The dust layers do not decline and still obscure the sun. Those knowledgeable in these matters, believe the sunshine will remain feeble for many seasons and little rain will fall."

MaGan continued, "We need to get rid of the Giants. We have been much too tolerant. After the disastrous adventure of the young men, most of us want revenge. We Illoreaens abhor unnecessary killing and find it especially hard to kill other Clan-similars. But this is different. We must remove monsters like Heropto and his horde from our area. We must eliminate them as a future threat. That is my task."

MaGan turned to JaYan, "Even if the Giants were not here, there would not have been enough provisions for all of us to remain here over the long term. The Giants make it much worse. Only a small group can remain in our Habitat, and only for a limited time. Most of us will have to find a fertile place with adequate food, where the effects of the Catastrophe are less. The obvious choice lies within the Clan valleys. A large group will have to cross the mountain and contact the Clans for aid, without the Dynasty's help. We will start planning immediately."

After the meeting, Questa confronted JaYan and MaGan, "You have developed so many things and your knowledge is so advanced. Surely, you can make better weapons than bows and flyers. Why don't you make something lethal enough to force the Giants to leave?"

MaGan answered, "Yes, we can make deadly weapons but, even if there were enough time, we will not. I'm the one who trains our young ones and enhances their fighting abilities during their service years. We restrict ourselves to use only the devices you have seen. Better weapons are always a solution for a short-term threat. But once made, they remain and become more deadly with time. To withdraw them from use is impossible. The Illoreaen policy to avoid developing newer and deadlier weapons, is ancient and absolute, decided on during the Inter-Clan Devastation. We prefer to suffer in the short-term. It is one of the reasons why you do not see the Clans use bows and flyers. Nevertheless, we will prevail."

JaYan agreed. "However, we appreciate your concern. To show you our trust, I will show you something we call a 'Thruster-Slasher'. A few reliable fighters are trained to use them as weapons. When wielding one of them, they can confront a Giant. In the Clans, the Orrox himself, as well as his designated successor carry them. They always carry two Thruster-Slashers, symbolically one for each hand. It implies no other activity may divert his attention from this primary task of protecting the Clans and their wellbeing... Please follow me. I will show you how they're made."

Questa accompanied him along a narrow passage. The air got hotter and stuffier as they approached a remote chamber. Gas roared out of a narrow fissure through a hole drilled in the rock, shaped to aim a flame onto a stone platform.

A broad-shouldered Illoreaen with massive forearms was hammering a white-hot, elongated piece of metal laying on the platform in front of him.

JaYan picked up a shiny object lying on the side and handed it to Questa, "This is it. Careful. It is very sharp. They were originally developed to clear undergrowth and bushes and only later became useful as weapons."

Questa looked and touched the sharp edges. "It is as sharp as an obsidian shard. How do you manage that and what is it made of?" she said. She understood the deadly possibilities. It could pierce a body or cut off limbs.

"We call the material 'Star-Splinters'. Light flashing across the sky is caused by white-hot objects sometimes made of this very hard iron-similars. It is pliable under great heat and force. We occasionally find one where it had crashed. We use the material to make these thruster-slashers and occasionally points for spears and flyers. The metal is very scarce."

They went back to where MaGan was waiting.

"I do not think you should make these thruster-slashers available to everyone," Questa said. "They are much too lethal, but I can understand your fighters' need to use them against the Giants."

JaYan agreed, but MaGan just frowned.

"However, your help and knowledge are invaluable," MaGan said. "Please tell us more about the Clan valleys. We know they are fertile. Is there enough food for the Clans to share, and do you know of other fertile areas?"

"I only know my Clan's situation. We will not be able to accommodate even gracia Illoreaens. Maybe we can handle a doucia or two for a few seasons. Other Clans might be able to accept greater numbers. Only the Dynasty knew the conditions within each Clan." Questa frowned, then thought long before adding, "The available information is just not enough. Maybe we can learn more. Please let the Illoreaens, previously sent to search for the courier-messengers from the Dynasty, describe what they saw and found. I will have to Sense what they observed and felt. They will have to give me permission to Sense them individually and agree to co-operate. I will only Sense their observations."

The Council considered the request, and then asked each of the search party's consent, before agreeing.

"Please close your eyes and you tell me what you observed," Questa said. "Think hard, remembering what you saw and thought near the Dynasty Valley and beyond. Create a picture in your mind if you can."

Each member told his story, thinking and telling of what he saw and experienced. There was broad agreed on most of what they remembered, but there were still discrepancies. Nevertheless, she could determine the level of destruction caused by the Catastrophe and eruption and separate that from the damage by the Primitive attack on the valley closest to the Dynasty.

They knew nothing of the valleys farther away, neither the Valley of the Sparkling Waters nor the Second Valley, where her loved ones lived. There was no news of her grandmother and sister nor of her father.

Questa thought for a while, explained her findings to the Coordinating Committee, and then left.

Questa already felt lonely and could barely face the possibility of her loved ones being in danger. Not knowing, was worst of all. She retired to her sleeping cubicle and lay down. She could not think. All seemed bleak and dismal.

#

The next day the Coordinating Committee again called all the Illoreaens to a meeting.

"The search party visited only two valleys across the mountains from here," JaYan began. "That of the Dynasty and one more. They found many of the plants and trees dead from the poisonous rain, cold and drought. The Primitives burned the rest. Questa analyzed what they saw and experienced. Even though the Clan valleys, on the slopes facing the sun, are much wetter, warmer and fertile than on this side of the mountain range. She believes many Clans suffered a Primitive onslaught and now live on hoarded supplies. It is not clear whether they will be able to accommodate us. Probably not.

"Farther away, in the sunset direction, it is warmer still with protected valleys, but they are less fertile. We believe we will be able to use our knowledge and abilities to produce enough food there, despite the difficulties.

"We'll have to find a safe refuge and our best chance lies there. It is a long distance from where the Giants live and also away from the plains and marshes, where the Primitives roam. We regard the Primitives as less of a threat than the Giants. We should be able to restrain them with our bows and flyers.

"According to Questa, the Oracle-Healers in each Clan valley keep stashes of supplies in Secret Caves high up the valleys as well as ice-caves above the snow line. The Dynasty, with the local Clans' help, always hoards a large reserve of supplies to use in case of famine or any other disaster.

"The Oracle-Healers collect the potions, medicines and herbs they need from the Secret Caves. Special marks and indications allow Healers to find the caves. The provisions are normally enough to feed and keep a Clan in health for an extended period, typically a year or more, until a new season can provide relief. Old supplies are always recycled and replaced with fresh ones. I am sure the Clans will be prepared to share some of this bounty."

The Illoreaens looked at JaYan with large eyes. He waited until their awkward shifting subsided, "We'll have to split up. The elderly and those parents with a small child will stay here, supported by those who are not so fit. Although a few of those who will remain will be old and slow, they are able to use bows and flyers as well as other deterrents effectively and will be safe. There are enough provisions for them and the drips yield enough water for those who will stay. Please, if you are unsure of your fitness, you must stay and protect your companions here. It is an important task and you can continue with searching and extending knowledge.

"The rest of us will consist of those who can move fast over rough terrain for extended periods while carrying heavy loads. We are going to cross the mountain range passing through thick snow. We cannot accommodate any laggards. Those who join our expedition will be subject to a harsh fitness test. I believe we will be able to travel much faster than any pursuing Giants will. We'll keep in open areas wherever possible, where our distance weapons are most effective."

A murmur ran through the Illoreaens. They were reluctant to leave the Habitat that served them well for many generations. They looked at one another and gestured to indicate in which group each wanted to be.

After allowing time for discussion, JaYan spoke out loudly. "We can decide later who will be part of which group. The final decision lies with members of the Coordinating Committee."

MaGan took up the explanation. "The mobile group must obtain a good head-start and will commence as soon as the Giants patrolling the top of the cliff move off to join their companions at their fires, in front of the palisade. I will organize protection and a rear guard. We must recover or destroy the provisions on which the Giants are still subsisting – our provisions! Our best Sharp-shooters must delay any pursuit. The Giants will have to leave when they don't have access to our provisions. Each of us will have a task and we must plan in detail."

JaYan spoke again, "The mobile group will contact those still in the Habitat when we have found a safe refuge. As soon as the meeting breaks up you must start thinking of how to preserve the results of the searches of knowledge you have been working on. We must later retrieve that."

The whole assembly looked at one another in silence. Slow movements and muted discussions caused small groups to form. The Illoreaens swamped MaGan and JaYan with a barrage of questions, but there was no dissent.

Even Questa was overwhelmed with questions, "What is it like on the other side of the mountain? Is it warm? Does the fruit often brought by the Dynasty's courier-messengers grow in profusion?"

She answered as well as she could.

#

During the preparations, Questa saw the Illoreaens mixing great quantities of black and yellow powder. JaYan saw her curiosity, "They know what they are doing; you still don't know many of our abilities. The Giants will never be able to enter the Habitat. We have too many ways to surprise and stop them. About your inquiry as to why we don't make better weapons, this mixture is the nearest thing we have, but it is not normally used as a weapon."

Everyone wanted to join the mobile group, but the Coordinating Committee allowed only the strongest and most fit to join. The final group consisted of the majority of the Illoreaens, including those older children, who could keep up and carry some weight. Parents of the smaller ones would remain. Questa, as did all the Illoreaens, tried to keep track of who would go along and who would stay. The Clan tradition of one child per person, a tradition the Illoreaens also followed, meant there were few young children to cater for while the tradition of three years of service and fighter training, ensured the fitness of many of the Illoreaens. The old traditions and taboos were proving their worth again.

The mobile group ate well and slept throughout the day preceding the flight. A Look-Out, hidden unseen just outside the secret entrance, watched the patrolling Giants. As expected, by the time it was dark, the patrolling Giants lumbered down to their overnight fires. The operation could begin. With the secret entrance out of sight above the cliff, the Illoreaens could move out quickly. The main group left the Habitat holding hands, taking a route through the mountain, which the search party recommended as still passable. They used shaded oil-burning lamps Questa had never seen before. They could adjust the lamp to give out only a dim glimmer, another secret! She assumed the oil to be made of animal fat, as in the torches the Clans used.

They are burning so much animal fat! Such a valuable commodity, more wisely used as food than for burning, she thought.

However, the oil had a very different, slightly unpleasant but distinctive odor—nothing like animal fat. This was no time to inquire, she controlled her curiosity, but she resolved to question JaYan as soon as they were safe and relaxed.

#

The flight worked very much as planned. MaGan led the fighting group, young men, friends and relations of the group the Giants had massacred. The youths, who had often fetched provisions and knew the terrain well, hurried up to the ice caves, invisible and silent in the dark. At the first cave, the Giants were relaxed and bored, lounging around a fire, roasting a fat hump of meat. The scene upset the angry and bitter youths. They had not tasted meat for a long time and to see the Giants feasting on their meat was the ultimate provocation. The youths crept up to the guarding Giants as soon as they fell asleep, one per Giant, with their clubs and spears ready. Using their obsidian blades, they slit the Giants' throats before they could make a sound. They repeated the operation successfully at the other caves.

Out of sight of the Giants at their encampment below, they removed the edibles. The mobile group took some of the meat and then helped those who were going to stay behind to carry the rest back to the Habitat. There they stored it in the newly iced-up cave chambers within. As soon as the mobile group left, those who stayed behind blocked the entrance from inside.

The mobile group only managed to travel half the night before forced to stop. The oil lamps were nearly empty. Stumbling over rocks and other obstacles took longer than expected.

JaYan called a halt, "Let's stop and rest! Get as much rest as possible. Eat and drink something from your pouches. We'll have to start again at first light, moving as fast as possible. The Giants will probably start a pursuit at the same time. We have a bit of a lead and I hope we can travel faster and for greater distances than the Giants can, but we are carrying heavy loads."

At first light, the group set out again, now moving much faster.

The fighting group consisted of many accurate Sharp-shooters who took up ambush positions at the places where the Giants usually ascended to the top of the cliff. The patrolling Giants were late in arriving. The fighters could imagine their irritation, not being accustomed to discipline and not alert. They clearly did not like the dull and useless task of patrolling the cliff tops above the Habitat. They obviously wanted to return to their leisurely life in their own forests, away from Heropto's bullying.

The Sharp-shooters remembered how JaYan's flyer had glanced off Heropto's brow and they made sure the flyers pierced hearts or throats. The Giants died without making a sound. By nightfall the next day, the fighting group caught up with the main group and could report, all was well and all the flyers retrieved.

Well-concealed spies stayed behind and arrived two days later. They reported on how Heropto failed to notice the absence of the patrolling Giants from the fires confronting the Habitat's palisade, before it was too dark for him to act. He clearly assumed the patrols joined the guards at the ice caves, to eat some of the meat stored there. He was furious and did not send Giants to look for them. He was going to make an example of them.

When they again failed to turn up the next night, he personally went for them late the next day. He only found their bodies as well as the bodies of those at the ice caves. By then it was too late to start the pursuit and the Illoreaen Sharp-shooters had already left.

The Illoreaens were allowed an unexpected additional day's lead.

#

The Illoreaens all carried heavy loads, including sleeping covers, spare drapes, cooking utensils, and food, making it difficult to keep up a fast pace. The young men kept their weapons ready and carried all they needed to erect a makeshift but defensible camp. Far ahead Questa occasionally spied the vanguard looking for the safest route, selecting open ground whenever possible. JaYan led the group but often fell back to arrange help for stragglers, and then joined the front again.

Questa had avoided walking with JaYan or MaGan or with any other male, remembering SkepTan's insinuation. She was afraid he might have started an ugly rumor. In defiance, she had only once purposefully gone to sit beside JaYan but now she tried to avoid doing anything to feed a rumor. JaYan fell back again and walked with her for a time. She was glad to see him but remained silent until, just before he left her side, she asked, "Are we safe? Will we get away from the Giants?"

JaYan had to be truthful, "I don't know, but this is our best chance. We can run faster and continue longer when not carrying heavy burdens, but the strength of the Giants can aid them in the rough mountainous terrain and in deep snow. For now, a fast walking pace will be enough and we should have sufficient warning of any pursuit. We have a few strong young men spying on the Giants, forming a rear guard under MaGan's supervision. I hope the loss of meat will deprive the Giants of their rations. Their alternative source of food is the meager plants and roots on the plain, which is far away.

"Here, high up on the mountains, there is very little food to gather and what there is, we collect ourselves. The plants are dying and have wilted, making even the roots less nourishing. The Giants will have to forage. I trust they will soon give up their useless chase. I do not know when we'll be able to return to the Illoreaen Habitat or what we'll find when we get to the Clan valleys. Meanwhile, the group left in our Habitat should be safe. The water drips yield enough for their reduced numbers. Similarly, the captured meat and other provisions will now last for a long time. They have enough flyers and other measures to protect themselves indefinitely."

They searched for a route through the mountains, aware of the danger of Primitives, a second set of enemies. The snow was deep. The Illoreaen mobile group walked in a single file up the passes forcing a route through the snow. They passed over a saddle near the highest crest carrying their heavy packs. From there they began the descent onto the glaciers and slopes facing the sun, the side of the mountain range containing the Clan valleys. The strongest were in front, avoiding crevasses. A strong rear guard followed. The open terrain made the group defensible.

The Illoreaens were not used to carrying heavy loads, not like the Clan-members who were always hauling wood or water or the spoils of their hunting expeditions. However, they were fit and determined and they did not complain.

I really respect them, Questa thought.

As they approached the first of the Clan valleys after crossing the mountain, the danger of meeting troupes of Primitives increased. MaGan enlarged the number of sentinels, slowing down the group. Questa Sensed terror, but did not know its origin. She was scared.

Chapter 33 – The Abyss

Orrox brewed a draught and brought Anja some, "I lay thinking while you slept. The river plunging over a sharp edge and vanishing in the depth, has reminded me of an old myth. It tells of the River-of-Doom leading to the underworld, the place where the spirits of the dead go. I remember a bard who visited my Clan and recited the verses. Afterwards, I asked my mentors whether the myth told of a real place. They told me the underworld of the myth is, in fact, a very deep but real place called the Chasm. An eternal haze obscures the invisible bottom of the Chasm. The hypothetical River-of-Doom is a large torrent in the desert, which falls over an abyss, into the Chasm."

He paused, "This is the only sizable stream or river flowing through the desert; it must be the one of the myth. Another mentor told me about a few adventurous Healers, searching for special herbs, ventured into the desert, followed the river and descended the Abyss. It is humid, hot and fertile at the bottom with canyons and many unknown features. They found the most potent herbs there. Neither they nor later herb collectors ever ventured deeper into the Chasm but stayed in the area near the cliffs. They said the Chasm was huge beyond imagination. I wonder, could this be the Abyss, the edge of the Chasm?"

Anja nodded, "My grandmother once told me she visited a place called the Chasm. They collected the herbs and other medicinals growing abundantly down there. She laughed when she told me how the myths called it the underworld."

He paused, "If it is, we may have found another refuge like your "Hidden Valley," but larger and with more resources. Let's hope!"

"Grandmother always said myths were created to hide important truths. She often narrated them."

"She was not wrong. The myth of the Chasm must contain important information. But I cannot remember more details. We have to decide. We should either try to find a route back to the mountains and the barely fertile valleys, or search for a route down into the Chasm, which, according to both our sources, may hide a profusion of resources."

Orrox and Anja looked at one another. Orrox could see she had the same idea.

"Now is a good time to use our ability to enter into an Abstract state and view the reality and possibilities of this area," he said. "However, there is something more I should tell you. My grandfather, the one who was in love with your grandmother, became addicted to the visions he experienced when in the Abstract state. The Dynasty kept him normal with difficulty. He suffered for the rest of his life.

"We Orrox scions, of the main succession, have inherited a tendency to fall into that dreamlike state and become addicted. We struggle to exit the state and often prefer not even to try to return to normalcy. I have only once entered that state. Four strong Sensitives synchronized with my mind and kept me aware of their presence all the time. They ensured my safe exit. I find it compelling to experience the visions again but do not dare. It is too attractive."

"I too have experienced the state, but only once and not fully, synchronized with my grandmother," Anja said. "I was supposed to repeat the experience with her until I managed full control while in the Abstract state, avoiding the danger of addiction. I know she intended to do the same with my sister, Questa. She expected us to reach the level of mature control only after reaching double doucia age. I will not try to view that reality except if no other option exists and then only if synchronized with other Sensitives. Possibly the Acolytes."

"No, they are still not experienced enough. We will have to search for the solution without entering the Abstract state."

#

The others joined them and looked at Orrox expectantly.

"Anja and I have discussed possibilities. We have to find a route down. But first, we need nourishment."

Their situation was desperate. The sound of the water increased their thirst and their longing for a drink. They had exhausted the supply of nearby tubers, of the kind that gave them the occasional mouthful of fluids. Their food supplies were exhausted and hunger pains racked their stomachs.

"We must stay together. We must accompany Anja in a search for more of the tubers and not use all we find." He paused, "While following the course of the river down, I made sure we kept well away in fear of leaving signs of our proximity, should Primitives also follow the river. I believe we are now forced to search and dig near the river for roots and tubers requiring more moisture. This putrid water, when filtered through enough sand, should have kept alive nearby plants." He paused again, "Anja, did your grandmother ever mention where to find edibles in the desert?"

"I'm trying very hard to remember," Anja had her hand against her forehead. "There must be something else. Let's search for some of the tubers. Maybe I will see something to trigger a memory."

They found only a few tubers, allowing each barely enough to swallow a mouthful of the juice. Orrox again inspected the nearby plant growth. With Anja's help, they recovered a few roots and walked around, searching for more.

"I remember now!" Anja said. "We must roast these roots to make them edible. The best way is to bury them in hot ashes and embers for a time."

Orrox suddenly jumped to the side. "Snake!" he cried. He used his spear and triumphantly held up the dead snake. "Meat," he said.

The companions could barely wait for the time it took for the roots and snake meat to bake.

"It's nice. The snake tastes a bit like fowl," Ammox said, his mouth still stuffed with meat.

"I'd never thought I'd enjoy snake meat. I'll eat it again any day," Camla confirmed. "It was a good meal and the roasted roots and tubers lessened my thirst a bit."

#

"If only we can find a way down. I'm convinced we will find water, edibles, and safety down there. Let's all look for a way down while we have the energy. Spread out. Search for any possible breaks in the cliff or marks indicating a possible route," Orrox said. "We must consider what the myths recounted. It would be best if Anja and I combine whatever we remember."

He led Anja away from the others.

"I remember a myth about the route to the Underworld," Anja said. "It descends the Abyss starting at a specific large tree, a Cecader with mystical properties,"

Orrox did not recognize the type of tree.

"I will recognize the tree and show it to you if we find one," she continued. "It isn't common in the desert; it normally grows higher up in the mountains in rock crevices. This particular tree grows with its roots in a deep crevice, near the edge of the Abyss."

"A crevice! Let me think." Orrox frowned and looked down with a hand against his forehead. When he looked up, he said, "Yes! My mentors told about a crack or fissure, down which one descends, is completely exposed with a void below as one wriggles down. My mentors said the river falls into the Chasm in a great waterfall. The greatest difficulty in the route down the Abyss is crossing behind this waterfall while following a tunnel in yellow rock. Together we might just figure out the descent."

"Why call the Chasm the underworld? My grandmother only told me of the special plants she found there."

"If half of what they told me is true, the Chasm could be a wonderful refuge. However, they warned of a danger. The myth tells of fire-breathing reptiles in lakes of blood. The Oracle-Healers were discouraged from exploring the areas away from the Abyss. The folklore tells of darkness and monsters, a frightening place."

"Yes, it makes the Chasm sound like some mystical place, made up as a children's tale."

"Did your grandmother present the Chasm as scary? I think not!"

Anja laughed, "No, she did not. According to her tale, she was safe while she remained near the Abyss. She also told me how deep the Chasm is. It is hot throughout the year and seasons barely change. Many different kinds of fruit and nuts, adapted to the heat, grow down there and ripen through all seasons. Let's hope it exists and is as attractive as she painted it and the Catastrophe did not destroy its wonders."

"If the Chasm is large we should find a refuge somewhere. According to the myth, to go around one has to travel along the Abyss for many moons."

"Let's not go around!" Anja said with a smile, "However, I'd like to follow the edge of the Abyss for just a little distance and look for a point of descent."

"I agree," Orrox said, and then thought, *We might have found a refuge. If so, I could safely leave you all there while I search for survivors. I must hurry. Duty calls!*

He added, "We must go back."

The sudden bluntness caught Anja by surprise. The sharing of memories gave her a feeling of intimacy, now he was cold and distant again. She managed to suppress a reaction. There was always awkwardness when they were in each other's presence, admittedly originating from her mistrust of the Orrox Dynasty. However, when he told her the tale of their forebears and now, discussing the myth, their relationship was friendly, almost normal.

"Let's climb to the top of the ridge," Orrox said, turning to the acolytes. "If this is the right river, we'll follow the ridge while searching for Anja's tree. I'm certain there is no other large stream crossing the desert!"

"My grandmother described the route from the tree to the crack," Anja said. "The tree is big and the only one of its type. We call it a Cecader. Skins stored between slats made of its wood, are protected against moths and insects and it gives off a lovely smell."

None of the acolytes knew the name. Orrox organized the search. "From Anja's description, the route follows a ledge keeping the rock face on the right. It should cross behind the waterfall, where the river plunges into the Chasm. Therefore, the tree should be farther on. Anja and I will search above this ridge. You acolytes must search below, up to the edge. We'll meet after the sun has moved two hands—you will have to estimate! If we fail to find one another, we must all return here. Be careful!"

Anja and Orrox continued above the ridge, occasionally looking down. Halfway towards the edge they started calling the Abyss, they saw a huge tree with wide spreading branches. They climbed down a rocky break, scrambling through bushes with limp leaves. It led them onto a smooth rock slab split by a deep fissure. The tree trunk was so thick, five Clan-members with outstretched arms would not be able to encircle it. Massive roots disappeared into the dark depths of the crevice.

"What a magnificent tree!" Orrox said. "No wonder the myth uses it as the main marker."

The other four arrived soon thereafter. They all sat down beneath the tree on sparse, withered grass.

"We're nearly there!" Orrox said. "The route down must be nearby. I'm afraid we left many tracks and clues of our presence. Anja, do you Sense any Primitives?"

"No, nothing. I think we are still safe."

#

The companions relaxed and Anja allowed her thoughts to wander, *Orrox has lost as much as I have and he has nobody to support him. We all rely on him, even I do. He has to remain strong and dares not give way to his sorrow, maybe even his despair! He took the lead when I Sensed the Primitives and I easily followed his instructions. This is so strange!*

She glanced at Orrox and saw him watching her with a faint smile just touching his lips.

He has guessed what I was thinking, without Sensing—just by looking at me. Angrily she turned her head away but could not stop herself from glancing at him again. His smile broadened.

She got up, "I will search for the descent. I have an image in my mind from when my grandmother told me about the place. She probably emanated and allowed me to form an image in my brain, without me realizing it. I remember how real her stories always were."

She returned after a while. "I think I have found it! There is a fissure farther on which widens near the Abyss, forming a large crack."

Orrox followed her to the crack from where the marker tree was still visible in the distance. Anja noticed Orrox's relief. On an impulse, ignoring conventions and taboos, she tried Sensing his emotions but he controlled himself and she Sensed nothing. She noticed Orrox watching her.

He has noticed something, she realized, blushing.

"It does look promising," Orrox said. "I will climb down a little way to see whether the crack leads anywhere. Wait for me. I will be back soon."

Anja was about to protest, to warn him of his recently healed injuries, but at a glance from him, she desisted.

He was back sooner than she expected.

"The crack has been climbed before. There are clear abrasion marks. I climbed down using protrusions to where an open tunnel or corridor starts. And, you won't believe it, in soft yellow rock. As in the myth. This must be the route! Let's get the others."

#

They all assembled above the crack.

"There are a lot of handholds and foot-supports but it is quite exposed," Orrox said. "Don't look down if you can help it. Ammox, you go first. Stand at the bottom of the crack and help the others down onto the floor at the bottom. There are a few boulders onto which you can step when you drop down from the crack. Leave most of what you carry up here. We'll have to climb up and down a few times to take everything down. After the first climb, we will know how much we can carry with us each time.

"Talk to the person coming down all the time. Should anyone get scared of the exposure, the sound of your voice will be reassuring. Each of you must sit down on the floor behind Ammox when you get down and wait for me. I will follow last."

Ammox disappeared down the crack. They soon heard his faint call, confirming he was down. Anja was the third in line to go down.

"How is your leg?" Orrox asked. "I noticed your limping until it warmed up from walking. I can climb with you."

With a defiant shake of her head Anja answered, "No thanks. I've climbed many times before and have no fear of heights."

Then, dropping her eyes she said in a softer tone while massage the scar area, "I'll just rub my leg for a moment."

There were prominent foot-supports and handholds on the rough, weathered rock. She moved down with her hands and back on the one side of the crack and her feet a bit lower down on the opposite wall.

The crack was quite wide at the top where they entered, but it narrowed and closed lower down, forcing her to move outwards until she was suspended over an overhang with nothing below her. The stiffness in her leg and the sudden change of perspective, changing focus from nearby to infinity far below, made her heart miss a beat. For a moment, the mist strands near the bottom swirled in her vision. She froze and then tightened her grip on a handhold and pushed out her feet to jam her more tightly into the crack.

"Strange effect the sudden exposure to the incredible height has," Ammox's soothing voice encouraged her. "We all experience it. Lonna and I are comfortable on a level shelf. It is easy to reach us."

She started moving again finding the crack widening, allowing her to move inward. A ledge appeared below her, hiding the depth. She moved farther in and down, over an edge. Below her, she could see Ammox and Lonna on a solid rock shelf. She scrambled down, stepping onto boulders stacked against a wall of soft yellow rock, and then she was safely down.

The others soon joined them. They were standing in a recess where a soft yellow chalk intrusion, between two layers of volcanic rock, had eroded over the ages. To the right, a ledge had formed, disappearing in the distance.

"This must be the route into the Chasm," Orrox said. "This yellow band probably extends for the full length of the cliffs. Rainwater flowing through the crack must have created this carved out ledge. Look, farther on the eroded intrusion forms a sort of open tunnel or corridor."

To the left, the ledge was less prominent and it soon disappeared around a corner.

"Where does it lead to?" Bronnox asked and followed it. He was back soon, "It peters out to a ledge too small to walk on, but the yellow intrusion continues."

"We should follow the ledge to the right, keeping the drop into the Chasm on our left," Orrox decided.

"What about the aggressive troupe of Primitives? They will follow us if they find any of the tracks we had made since crossing the river. I won't be able to Sense them through the layers of moist rock," Anja said.

"I believe we're safe for now," Orrox said. "They do not know mountains and hate heights. Nevertheless, we'll remain vigilant and will protect ourselves on this ledge if necessary. They would have to come one at a time and we are bigger than they are, and with good spears. Let's fetch all our belonging and go!"

They followed the ledge to the right. They could walk upright in the half-tunnel. Sometimes the roof was low and they had to crawl, while in other areas it rose high above, to become part of a broken cliff, showing scars of previous collapse. There they had to scramble over deposits of rubble. Areas of compressed soil indicated previous use of the route. They progressed in silence.

Not long after setting out, they heard a roar, first faintly, then louder and louder. The source was invisible, hidden in many turns and undulations. Ahead they could see wisps of moisture in the air drifting away from the cliff. The floor became wet and slippery until they came upon a precipice where spray drenched the ledge. The river fell down the Abyss in a huge waterfall. It had gouged a vertical gully out of the cliff and the swirling waters had eroded the yellow layer of soft rock deep into the mountain. There was just enough space to move cautiously deeper into the cliff. The deluge came down in waves, with wisps falling clear or splashing onto the edge causing a dense spray on its way down. The only way to continue was to pass behind the waterfall over a slippery, wet shelf, which sloped towards the waterfall and the vertical drop.

They stopped, damp and cold from the spray, huddling close together. Orrox started out to test the traverse but Bronnox quickly interfered, "You dare not take risks, we'll all be lost should something happen to you now."

Ammox could not stop himself and with a serious face he added, "We'll miss you later too!"

The suppressed panic of the companions caused them to break out in laughter, releasing the tension.

"I appreciate your concern. However, before any of us risk our lives, let us think. The same obstacle confronted all who were here before. There must be a solution, probably somewhere safe and dry. Wait here!"

Orrox retraced their steps along the ledge and soon returned, "I found a cord made of long leather straps, braided together in a rope. It was stored high and dry where a bit of a draught stopped rot and fungi. Bronnox, we must test it for strength."

They grabbed each end of the rope and pulled and plucked with all their weight. To make sure they inspected the full length of the rope, until they were satisfied with its strength.

Orrox tied one end around his waist, and asked Bronnox to belay him. Bronnox sat down with his feet pushed against a projecting rock for stability, the rope around his middle. Orrox carefully negotiated the shelf behind the waterfall while Bronnox slowly fed out the rope, keeping it just slack enough not to hinder Orrox.

The water had smoothed and polished the rock for eons. Orrox crawled on his hands and feet and sometimes nearly slipped but always recovered his stance.

The rope was long enough for him and Bronnox to tie each of the others to the middle and belay them from both ends. They each carefully moved across the slippery slope. Camla slipped, but the belay saved her. Orrox belayed Bronnox from one side only, when he followed last and managed to crawl across. They were all dripping wet but safe. Orrox coiled the rope around his waist to join the large number of practical items he carried with him.

"I'm taking this along to deny any follower its use. I can't imagine a Primitive trying to pass there," he said. "The crossing must be more slippery than experienced by previous visitors. An ash deposit has formed a slippery layer on the wet floor—and it is colder. If we move quickly, we'll soon get warm."

They followed the tunnel-like ledge for a long time, always with the Abyss on their left and always descending. At a stronger seep than most, Orrox stopped and tasted the water.

"Sweet! We're far below ground surface and all contamination is filtered out as it seeps through the earth. Let's fill our gourds."

The sweet water gave them courage and they continued, hoping to find food in the Chasm. Slowly green hills and plains became visible far below. The horizon remained hidden in the misty gloom. Sometimes they scrambled over loose rubble or across slippery areas, where moisture seeped or dripped out of cracks in the cliff.

They followed the ledge until they saw a spur rising up steeply from the bottom towards the cliff. At the spur, a scree-covered slope allowed them to clamber down. Before the light faded, they reached a sloping grass plain interspersed with slabs of dark rock and large trees. The tops of the cliffs behind them nearly disappeared in the gloom, even though visibility had improved. A layer of dust was also deposited down here, but new growth vegetation already penetrated and hid the contamination. High up a few wisps of white cloud were just visible below the edge of the Abyss, with the dusty sky far above, still a dark brownish, yellow-grey color.

Near a large cairn, a pyramid of packed stones, they sat down. A small stream bubbled out of a fissure between a few rocks nearby.

"This must be the beacon previous Oracle-Healers stacked to indicate the start of the route out of the Chasm. Visitors probably add a rock at each visit. The cairn must be a record of visits over many generations of herb gathering Oracle-Healers," Orrox said.

"Safe at last!" Anja said, looking at Orrox for confirmation.

"Yes, we have reached our first objective but we know nothing of the Chasm and what dangers it hides. Let's find some edible roots and plants. I would love a good meal. Anja, where do you think we should look for edibles?"

"The bank of the little stream, at its source up there, looks the most promising. The water should be sweet."

"Right, search there. You must all be back before dark. Keep a good look out for danger. I will start a fire."

Bronnox headed down the slope while the others started collecting near the fountain. They were all back at the fire in a surprisingly short time.

"I found some grasses with edible grains but the seeds are really tiny. Yet we collected enough for a meal," Anja said. "They are the same types as the ones in our valley, but our seeds are much larger!"

"Where is Bronnox? Did anyone see him?"

"I saw him disappear between those bushes down there!" Lonna said.

Bronnox soon appeared carrying a rabbit.

"Wonderful! We'll have meat as well!" Orrox said while Anja joined Lonna and Camla in congratulating him on his skill.

"Just remember, wherever there are animals to hunt, predators are also present. We'll have to be extra vigilant and take turns to stand guard and keep a fire going while the others sleep. I will take the very late shift. Tomorrow will bring its own dangers!" Orrox warned.

There seem to be plenty of edibles down here, Orrox thought. If I can get the acolytes and Anja safely settled down here, I can start out again to find the Dynasty survivors and re-organize the Clans. It will be safe as long as they stay here, near the Abyss. Then I must investigate and discover the lethal danger the Myths hint at!

Chapter 34 – Displaced

On the warmer, sunny side of the mountain range, the runoff of the everlasting snows had cut broad valleys into the mountainside, surrounding them with vertical cliffs. The ash of volcanoes had fertilized the valleys for eons, making them lush gardens. These were the Clan valleys.

Having reached these friendlier slopes, the Illoreaens continued as fast as they could, heading in the sunset direction. They stayed below the snow line but well above the tree line, allowing the forward and rear guards, with their bows and flyers, a clear view. The group bundled up, avoiding the long single file formation which they used while walking through the snow.

Questa was still furious at SkepTan's insinuation and walked with a few women, avoiding the men.

JaYan came to her as she sat with the women, during a rest break, "Why are you isolating yourself? MaGan tells me you have been avoiding him as well."

Questa did not answer but responded with a question, "I imagined danger. Weren't we vulnerable while struggling through the snow?"

"Yes, we were, but in the open snow the Giants are easy targets even though they are stronger and can handle the deep snow better."

"They must have a shortage of food. Are they leaving?"

"Our spies send regular reports on the Giants. They are still there. Two of our spies saw how Heropto killed some of his own troupe. He exposed their heads on stakes near the palisade and mutilated the bodies of those we killed during the escape. The Giants fear him and he is in control. They have found the secret entrance to the Habitat, but our companions blocked it from the inside. They are safe, keeping watch."

JaYan gestured towards two young Illoreaens with MaGan. He saw the gesture and joined them as well.

"These two were spying on the Giants and have recently come back from the Habitat," MaGan said. "Tell us again about the attack on the Habitat."

"We only noticed something was wrong when we heard the noise. We think they crept up to the palisade when the night was at its darkest, before the first glimmer of light in the morning. They stormed the main entrance with a simultaneous attack on the blocked secret entrance. We crept nearer and saw the guards in the Look-Outs posts on the cliff face, illuminating the area with torches, reflecting lamps and light emitting quartz. It gave the Sharp-shooters at the Habitat enough light and the Giants made excellent targets. The Illoreaens in the Habitat killed two Giants inside the entrance corridor and the rest retreated in disarray. We are sure the defending Illoreaens wounded or killed many more."

#

The Illoreaens put down their bundles when MaGan estimated it to be the middle of the day. They all filled their gourds, drank and washed in a stream of clear water flowing from underneath the ice. Guards encircled the group at a distance, ensuring all were safe.

JaYan and MaGan approached Questa together, "The mountain is unstable. We have sent out scouts to look for the best route," MaGan said. "They must also look for any threats we could encounter on our way. We now have scouts in front and behind as well as sentries above and below!"

"Shouldn't we have reached the Dynasty Valley by now?" Questa asked.

"Actually, we have already passed the Dynasty Valley," MaGan answered. "We know there is no help available there. To visit it would have required a difficult detour. Two scouts confirmed what we already know."

"You told us your training includes analyzing situations. We would like your advice." JaYan said. "But only if it does not require your entering the Abstract state again. I'm sure it's dangerous."

"No, analyzing is not the same," Questa answered. "The Clan Chiefs call it a Mentat ability. It is a state of enhanced awareness, approaching the Abstract state but not losing track of the immediate reality. No, it is not dangerous but I'll need quiet to concentrate."

"Can you see a flaw in our planning and deployment?"

"Please follow me as I walk around. I can then ask you questions."

A screen supported by poles was erected around the encampment, "What is its purpose and what is it made of?" she asked.

"The covering is made of a very light cloth, strong enough to withstand the cutting edge of an obsidian shard," MaGan answered. "It can resist the wooden spears of the Primitives and even the stabbing spears of the Giants. We brought our entire supply. The cloth is very difficult to make and a group, studying the strange properties of non-natural fibers, made the cloth. Young ones often make some as part of their initiation training. It teaches them the properties of materials and how to manipulate them to achieve specific objectives."

"What will you do at night, when we're at our most vulnerable?"

"Our scouts set noise traps after dark. We only remove them in the morning. We have a few light cubes to blind an attacker and light emitting paste, we smear on sticks and stones, to give our Sharp-shooters a visible target. Our power source for the cubes is limited and we will use them sparingly."

"Why did you send five scouts? Wouldn't three have done?"

"One must report back regularly and they must also be able to split up in pairs to investigate alternatives."

JaYan and MaGan answered many more questions.

"If you wish I can analyze what I have seen and heard, even though I'm only partly trained," Questa said. "I think of different scenarios. Images form in my mind and my subconscious works out risks and possible situations, which gives me an idea of probabilities and makes it possible to recommend actions. If you want me to analyze in a Mentat state, I will be in deep thought, unaware of my surroundings and will need protection. It is not like the Abstract state of enhanced consciousness within an expanded reality."

JaYan and MaGan looked at one another. JaYan nodded, "I think we need all the help we can get. We'll stay with you while you do this Mentat thing."

Questa completed a final inspection before she climbed onto a little hillock, viewed the surroundings and then sat down on a stone to enter the Mentat state. Now she missed the wisdom of Usux. Silently, she apologized to him in her thoughts. *He was an excellent mentor.*

She let her mind picture scenarios of possible attacks, regretting her incomplete training. She gave her mind free reign, recalling all she knew and was told about the Giants. She repeated the exercise imagining Primitives and then predators. Her eyes were closed and her breathing deep and even. Her Sensing registered nothing.

She slowly started noticing her surroundings. JaYan and MaGan were sitting on rocks near her, alternately watching her and the surroundings, on guard against any danger.

"I can't see anything wrong with your planning," she said. "It is excellent as far as it goes, but I know too little of your abilities and of the minds of the Primitives. I am not fully trained or experienced enough to give a very good opinion. However, there are a few things I would like to comment on, things you probably have already considered."

She listed a few improvements, which MaGan and JaYan either implemented or gave reasons why they were not practical.

"For the rest, I cannot find a flaw."

Questa felt a bit foolish. She had gone through the whole Mentat exercise and could not contribute much. JaYan noticed her discomfort, "Thank you. We feel easier to have our planning and precautions confirmed. We value your effort and marvel at your abilities. It's a pity we knew nothing about it before."

MaGan nodded his head and Questa felt better, pleased at being appreciated.

MaGan and JaYan kept Questa informed and she felt happy for the first time since SkepTan's allegations. Even though they were not safe, she now felt happier than she had felt since leaving her father's Clan, her valley, the Second Valley.

#

The next day, one of the scouts returned before they broke up camp. MaGan and JaYan gestured for Questa to join them, "We found a route to cross to the next Clan valley," the scout said. "It was very difficult. The slopes are unstable. We found the vegetation in the valley and ridges burned with only tracks and a few corpses high up."

"Was it Giants? Have they passed us?" MaGan asked.

"No, the Giants didn't kill them. The tracks were those of Primitives. We realized the danger and took care to remain hidden. We followed the tracks of the Primitives out of the valley. The tracks led us to the next valley over a high saddle. The valley and the whole mountainside are also burned. The fires must have burned for many days. The tracks went in and came back out. There were blood and charcoal marks where the Primitives rubbed against bushes or tall grass.

"I left the others to build a funeral pyre for the bodies we found while one kept guard. There are enough charred logs and half burned stumps for the purpose. They will do what they can and try to find out what the Primitives are doing. There are no tracks coming this way. You are safe until you reach the valley. Follow my route marks. I will go back as soon as I have eaten."

Questa saw him leave soon afterwards.

After crossing a high spur, with a strong rear-guard protecting their backs, they approached the Clan valley.

"MaGan and a few of the vanguard have entered the valley to investigate," JaYan told Questa.

#

The Illoreaens did not have any experience in foraging effectively. Under Questa's direction, they found enough roots and edibles surviving in protected gullies, where the fires did not reach. Soon their natural optimism caused laughter and even a few songs, exuberant enough to attract a warning from JaYan and the guards, "The sound of voices travels far. We don't want to attract unwanted attention."

They waited the whole day but MaGan and his companions only returned late.

The Illoreaens rushed forward with questions. "Did you find the Clan? How did the Catastrophe affect them? Can they accommodate us? Are we going to pass on?"

Then, seeing the expressions on their faces, they fell silent. JaYan moved towards MaGan, "What did you find?"

"Sad news. We found many bodies and a single Primitive scavenging the corpses. He ran away, scrambling down the valley as soon as he saw us. We chased him but even though he looked very thin and hungry, we could not catch him. He might warn other Primitives of our existence. Despite the danger, we all wanted to do something for the Clan. We built a pyre, stacked the bodies and then, ceremoniously, with rites, burned all, while keeping a lookout.

"We left a small guard. They can accurately launch a flyer every three counts and have many more. They can hold back a multitude of Primitives and will give us ample warning should any come up the valley."

The news destroyed the Illoreaens' happy mood.

MaGan called JaYan to one side, "The bodies have been mutilated. Body parts were missing. I think the Primitives are more horrible and dangerous than we thought!"

JaYan was shocked. "We'll have to keep moving. I thought the danger lessened as we moved farther away from the Giants."

He called Questa, "You told us of Secret Caves in the Clan valleys. Would there be one in this valley?"

"I'm sure there must be. I can look for signs. There should be provisions there."

"MaGan and a few strong Sharp-shooter fighters can accompany you and bring back as many edibles as possible. Are you prepared to go? It might be dangerous if any Primitives appear!"

"Certainly! When shall we go?"

JaYan and a few young ones accompanied her while MaGan arranged guards and a party to search for survivors.

The marks and signs Questa followed to the Secret Cave were obscure and difficult to follow. Nevertheless, she found the cave quickly and then managed to direct them to the ice caves too. They were back by midday.

JaYan was impressed. "I think she tracks even better than you," he told MaGan, but couldn't keep his expression serious.

"You might be right. Remember she grew up in the Clans where tracking was a daily necessity, while we only follow tracks when hunting as a sport."

JaYan slapped MaGan on the shoulder, "I'm just teasing you. I know how good you are! But she is impressive, is she not?"

MaGan agreed.

They took sufficient edibles to keep the whole group nourished for a few days. Although they found no survivors, they left enough provisions for any Clan member still alive.

#

The patrol, scouting ahead, returned the next day. Their leader reported, "At the far side of the next valley the cliffs get higher and the gullies deeper. The mountain slopes and ledges are unstable and filled with rubble. We realized the group will not be able to use a high route. We then descended and searched for a route across the plains, through the marshes.

"The bogs have dried up. The Primitives are starving and struggling to find drinkable water. They are fighting amongst themselves and killing rival troupes. I do not think the Primitives would be a serious threat on the plains since it is all open areas and we can keep them away with our bows and flyers. There we will be able to move faster."

The Illoreaen group descended, following the route the scouts recommended. The flat ground made it easier to find open areas to erect a portable palisade and form a protected camp.

Meanwhile, the scouts who entered the next Clan valley reported, "We were very scared and planned fast escape routes. We again found the vegetation burned and the Clan massacred. We found no survivors."

The patrol's audience was distraught, "Another Clan murdered! What next?"

MaGan and the young Illoreaens performed the necessary rites in the valley, burning bodies on a funeral pyre and returning the Clan cave to its natural state, ready for the cave bears. They then accompanied Questa in her search for the ice caves and the Cave of Secrets. They slogged up the valley, climbing over boulders and other remnants left by the Catastrophe and fires. As Questa expected, they found the Cave of Secrets near the top of the valley. Higher up the mountain, above the snow line, they found the ice cave containing the Clan's meat supply. They carried away enough provisions to feed all the members in the group for a few days.

They could not understand why the meat was still there until Questa explained, "The Primitives live on the open plains and marshes. They don't like the mountains. Even the valleys frighten them. They probably burned the trees and other vegetation to reduce their fear of narrow spaces when raiding the valleys. They will never venture onto the snow layers. I don't believe they know of the ice caves where the Clans save their meat and perishables."

They passed what was left of the pyre, with a faint smell of burned flesh still evident. Troubled, they turned their faces away. The horror, anger and disgust they felt, intruded on Questa's Sensing. She blocked her Sensing forcefully.

In both the valleys they visited, Primitives massacred all members of each Clan. The Illoreaens were upset and discouraged, wondering what fate awaited them all.

"I wish to have an overview of it all. I want to enter the Abstract state again. MaGan can bring me back if necessary."

"No! You must not. We know too little and you admitted yourself you are not adequately trained. You might harm your mind. Knowing what happened to the other Clans will not help. We will find out as we continue." JaYan looked at her intensely, putting a hand on her shoulders. "Please, don't!"

Questa looked back with large eyes. Then she dropped her head. "Yes, you are right. But I am so worried!"

MaGan tapped JaYan on the shoulder, "We must start again. We're taking much too long and must go faster. We're increasing the risk of the Giants overtaking us, should Heropto decide to come after us. In addition, we're on the Primitives' plains. Danger surrounds us!"

For those who could interpret the signs, the tracks and debris in the valleys told the story. MaGan showed JaYan all the signs and explained what he saw. When JaYan and MaGan returned from their inspection, the group assembled around them.

"In both valleys the storm wind destroyed the palisades at the entrances of the valleys and blew down trees while stacking rubble everywhere," MaGan said. "Boulders from the mountain lie scattered throughout the valleys. No rain has fallen since the Catastrophe. Dry material would have filled the valleys making them a fire hazard. The Primitives must have realized there were no patrols from the Dynasty to help the Clans. They used the opportunity to create fire-storms while attacking the Clan. They stormed up the valleys in great numbers. The Clans were fighting for their lives and could not fight the flames as well. The same thing happened at both Habitats. They burned the palisades, destroying the defenses and smoked both the Clans out of their cave Habitats, killing all. I think the success in one valley emboldened the Primitives and they repeated the same strategy in the next valley. They were in a frenzy of bloodlust and hatred and did not even bother to loot before rushing on. Smaller groups looted later. We have found no survivors in either valley."

Questa avoided the thought of the destruction extending to the Clans beyond. "My mother grew up in the Valley of the Sparkling Waters where my sister and grandmother still live. It is far towards sunset. Surely they will be safe?"

JaYan could not answer her.

"What about my own valley, the Second valley? My Clan, my father, and all my friends live there!"

JaYan could only try to console her. Many of the Illoreaens were weeping.

#

Questa and a few young helpers entered each valley. Although unrecognizable after the Catastrophe and fires, she always found the Secret Caves. The first two survivors appeared the third time they visited a valley, while she was searching for the secret signs leading to the Secret Cave.

The survivors were not sure of the Illoreaens but recognized Questa as a member of the Clans. They called weakly from their hiding place in thick shrubbery. The Illoreaen group treated them well at the camp, as if they were one of their own.

Each valley they passed showed the same pattern of destruction and massacre. MaGan spared the group the details but entered each valley with a strong group of Sharp-shooters with scouts running ahead. The Primitives never attacked. Often thin, emaciated Primitives scavenged amongst the now decomposing bodies, running off when the Illoreaens approached.

MaGan's young Illoreaens, who formed an important part of the fighting force, built funeral pyres and also accompanied Questa to each of the Secret Caves and ice caves. They carried back supplies and meat in great quantities. Signs of predators mutilating the bodies increased and the task of piling the bodies onto pyres became ever more gruesome. Questa admired their resilience and perseverance.

The fear for her loved ones grew as valley after valley revealed the same horror. She could not identify any valley from below. The gloom was too intense and she could not see the peaks for orientation. She always feared each valley would prove to be either her own or her grandmother's.

Occasionally a few more survivors appeared out of dense bush. In shock, they often did not know about the Secret Caves and lived on the meat in the ice caves only. Questa found solace in the presence of the survivors, who always recognized her as an Oracle-Healer. Many knew of her grandmother and they submitted to her healing and soothing with ease. Questa felt vindicated. She secretly hoped their reaction would show the Illoreaens how wrong they had been, *To have Clan-members around, who respect me, make it so much easier to handle my fears and the realization of constant danger.*

Their presence made her realize how much she missed the familiar routines and actions of Clan-members from the Clan valleys, even if they were not of her own Clan.

Questa always made sure they left enough edibles in the Secret and ice caves for possible survivors. Their many tracks made it easier for them to find.

<><><>

Chapter 35 – Settling Down

The first night in the Chasm was different. Anja, Orrox and the acolytes felt safe and made a fire in the open, bigger than any they had made since leaving Anja's Hidden Valley. No stars or moon were visible through the everlasting yellow-brown layer high in the sky, but dim light indicated a full moon somewhere even higher. Except for a few unfamiliar sounds, the night sounds were similar to those Anja knew and listened to every night of her life.

At least not the total silence of death we experienced up there, Anja thought. Life has a better chance to survive the effects of the Catastrophe down here.

Half asleep, she wondered about the deadly reptiles in the myth. Weird images flitted through her imagination before her mind emptied as she slipped into deep sleep.

When the light indicated a new day, the acolytes assembled around Orrox, who guarded the fire. Despite the gloom, the towering cliffs were a reminder of how deep the Chasm penetrated into the earth, how far they had descended. In the distance, the great waterfall was just visible. It seemed to fall out of the sky, the edge where it tumbled into the Abyss obscured by dust or fog and too remote to see.

From habit, Anja presented her hands to the fire. The day was quite mild and very different from the cold they experienced above the Abyss.

Orrox heated a couple of large stones, raked them out of the fire onto two carrying sticks and then transferred them to a gourd filled with water. He added a few herbs to the boiling water to make a refreshing hot drink. In another gourd, he used more hot stones to cook a broth made from the pulverized seeds they found the previous evening, spiced with more herbs to make a delicious broth.

"Come and have some food and drink," Orrox said.

"These herbs taste good. Where did you get them?" Anja asked.

"They are all around. I collected them as soon as it was light."

After the meal, Orrox said, "I believe we are quite safe from any Primitives down here, but we do have predators to fear. We'll all have to search for a place where we can stay safely. According to another myth, fire-breathing reptiles are only found near the middle of the Chasm. I believe we are safe here, even if they exist, but we will nevertheless have to keep a sharp lookout."

The acolytes laughed uncomfortably.

The air was clear, much clearer than they experienced above the Abyss. In the permanent twilight, Anja could discern the line of the yellow intrusion containing the ledge. It stood out against the darker cliff face. It ran in both directions, as far as the eye could see. A bit of green growth at the bottom and white frost descended half-way down the cliffs, made a beautiful multi-colored image.

"According to the myths, the Abyss is always shrouded in thick fog, making the Chasm very hot and humid," Orrox said, "The inability to see the bottom of the Abyss from its edge, must have lent credibility to the tale of the Abyss being the entrance to the underworld. The dry air and clear visibility down here must be unusual. No good rain has fallen since the Catastrophe, but here, so deep down, there will always be strong fountains. With the sun obscured, we can expect more cold. Keep it in mind."

"Ammox and Lonna, look for a safe place towards the river. Go around this spur and stay below the cliffs. Special herbs might not have been poisoned and still grow in the mists at the bottom of the great fall. You should be able to cross the river and explore on the far side as well.

"Bronnox and Camla, please explore to the other side while Anja and I will search the plains ahead of us, away from the cliffs. We must meet here again before dark—let's all collect edibles and herbs as we search, but be careful, dangers might surprise us."

Orrox and Anja watched the two pairs of acolytes, each moving away on their respective missions before walking together away from the cliffs down the sloping plain, "This is the direction towards sunset. Without the sun as an indicator, we have to use the orientation of plant and moss growth, to determine direction."

Irritation again grew in Anja: *Does he think I know nothing?* She quickly suppressed the irritation, careful not to emanate the feeling. Nevertheless, Orrox must have noticed something for he glanced at her sharply. Noticing, she said sweetly, "Yes, I regularly teach the young ones of our Clan to use moss growth to determine direction in cloudy weather.''

Orrox laughed, "I just thought aloud. You can teach me if you like!"

She was surprised at her continued irritation. Orrox's account of their history should have removed the ill will she feels. *Why am I like this? I am a positive person. I pride myself to always look for the best in any acquaintance. My antagonism must still linger from what I picked up from Grandmother.*

Then again, why must he always be the one to decide? He never asks me whether I would like to join him. He just assumes I will follow wherever he leads! Who does he think he is? Is he more like his grandfather than he likes to admit?

Trying to make sense of her feelings and not having a ready answer, she answered his laugh with a sweet smile. Then she cast off the negative thoughts and concentrated on their combined task.

A ridge crossing the plain blocked their progress. A little stream rushed over the rock slab to cast itself happily over the edge, forming a little pool at the bottom. Orrox tasted the water.

"Sweet!" he said. "These sources all drain from waters deep under the earth, not connected to the contamination on the surface." He paused, "I don't see anything promising here. I hope we can make our base in a good cave. Should we continue to follow the stream?"

"I don't think so," Anja said. "Let's look for overhangs or caves in the ridge. We can each follow the ridge in different directions and then up to the knolls, there and there," she pointed. "This will enable us to see the length of the ridge to both sides. We can then return here."

They each disappeared in a different direction, Anja to the left-hand side and Orrox to the right. As Anja walked along the foot of the ridge, she looked back. *The pool is out of sight from where we camped and perfect for a bath. I'd love a decent wash. It's been so long. Before dark, we three women must go for a bath and wash. I must find some herbs for washing properly!*

She followed the ridge until it petered out against the hillock. She climbed up to where the ground fell away sharply on the far side, becoming the edge of a deep canyon. She heard a faint, distant roar. The river plunged into the gorge, forming another great waterfall. The little stream found its way around the knoll, forming a gully and then also emptied into the ravine, releasing wisps of vapor.

Near where the river plunged into the depths, cliffs, banded in layers of different colored rock, formed a narrow canyon, which widened farther down. Several dark shadows were just visible low down on the opposite face of the cliffs.

Some of those could be usable caves, she thought.

Anja returned to the higher point and looked across to where she could see the other knoll far away. She could just make out the figure of Orrox. She waved vigorously trying to attract his attention, indicating a find. His answering gesture indicated she should wait.

Anja sat down leaning against a convenient boulder and waited. This was the first opportunity to relax in peace. Until now, she lived from moment to moment. Surviving one crisis after another.

Despite everything we suffered, fate was friendly in joining me, Orrox and the acolytes. How would I have survived without them? She wondered. *I like the acolytes. I must admit Orrox is strong and a great example for the acolytes.* Then realized, *I've never met anyone like him.*

When Orrox arrived, she did not notice him immediately. She was staring into the distance with a faraway look and a slight smile on her face, deep in thought. He looked at her for a moment and thought how pretty she was. The signs of stress and concern had lifted from her face while she relaxed.

She is the most beautiful girl I have ever met. She clearly inherited her grandmother's renowned beauty. No wonder grandpa fell in love with her grandmother, he thought.

He spoke softly, his voice nearly a caress but still very serious. "You must never let your guard slip. There might be predators around. You did not even notice me."

With a shock, Anja returned to reality. She was immediately on the defensive: "I have always been able to Sense danger. It seems you are not dangerous enough to activate my Sensing. I will sharpen it!"

She jumped up ashamed of her reaction, *What is wrong with me?*

Then, friendlier, "Come across! There is a huge canyon. Look! Down there. The dark patches. Those could be caves. Do you think we have enough time to explore? To descend down?"

She projected friendliness to soften the harsh words, but did not quite succeed. She noticed his slight frown, but he projected nothing and she could not Sense his feelings.

Ignoring the sarcastic reaction, Orrox followed her to the end of the hillock. "It looks very promising but we'll have to turn back to the others. I feel responsible and must set an example. We must be at our meeting place by the time they arrive and before darkness settles in."

Anja turned her face away to hide her guilty blush. Meekly she consented and followed him as they turned back to meet the others.

At dusk, they all gathered at the previous night's sleeping spot. The others told of lush vegetation and a few hollow overhangs in the cliff, but none were well protected or near fresh water. Orrox and Anja could give a more hopeful report of the canyon they saw. They agreed to explore the next day, before the girls hurried away for their bath in the pool farther down the creek. The males made do with a little depression in the nearby stream for a quick wash.

#

Descending into the canyon proved more difficult than anticipated. Orrox and Ammox tried several promising alternatives before they found a steep gully, the bottom polished smooth by floodwaters. They descended, sometimes climbing and sometimes slipping. At one point, Orrox slung the coiled rope of braided leather cords, which he still carried, around a convenient tree, letting the two ends drop all the way down a very smooth vertical section. Holding onto the doubled rope, they lowered themselves, hand-over-hand, until they reached the bottom. There Orrox pulled on the one end, allowing the rope to fall free. He then re-coiled the rope.

At Anja's glance, he explained: "We need the rope now. We will find somewhere else to climb up should this prove too difficult. We're all together with all our belongings in our bags and pouches. We can find a safe sleeping spot somewhere down here even if we don't find what we're looking for."

They scrambled farther down the smooth watercourse until they reached the river side, still carrying pollution from the surface. The river had carved a mighty canyon in the dolomite rock, topped by a massive and very hard granite layer. Lower down the canyon walls grew higher and higher until they disappeared in the distance and gloom. Dead fish caused a foul smell from the river and pools, while on the riverbank the trees and plants wilted.

The companions followed the river downwards, often crossing where stepping stones allowed an easy passage. They split into two groups, one at each side of the river, searching the cliff face while staying alert. Occasionally they disturbed a rabbit or small rodent but found no sign of predators. On their left, a strong stream flowed out of a cave near the bottom of the canyon forming small pools before joining the main stream.

"At least the ash will not have poisoned the underground water," Bronnox commented and walked forward for a taste. He rolled a mouthful around before swallowing. "Sweet," he pronounced.

"The stream gets a lot of fresh water from the tributaries with their sources down here. Plants away from the river have remained healthy and the river will clean itself," Orrox said. "There should be more caves. Maybe we can find one to suit us. Watch out for signs of cave bears. They would not have suffered as much down here as they did above. We don't want to surprise one inside his cave!"

Ammox called from the left-hand side of the river, "I think we have found a good cave!"

A grassy platform formed a convenient deck in front of the entrance.

"I don't see any signs of cave bears here," Ammox said.

"Did anyone see cave bear claw marks on any tree? Any sign?" Orrox asked.

Nobody did. Bronnox took the initiative, approached the cave mouth carefully and looked in. Dung from bats, small rodents and rock rabbits covered the cave floor. A few bone splinters proved small predators occasionally used the shelter. Fashioning a torch from bushes and tree gum, Ammox joined Bronnox. Together they entered the cave, their spears at the ready. Orrox soon joined them.

"The cave front is large and spacious," Orrox reported when they returned. "A few tunnels continue at the back but we can seal them off with branches and later possibly with a stone wall. We can explore those tunnels in the future and at our leisure. This cave is near enough to the cave with the fresh water stream. The plants are lush here and are not wilted like those above."

They took the rest of the day to make the cave habitable.

The next day they searched for a new route out of the canyon but found none. In the end, they climbed up the smooth vertical chute again. Bronnox went first, using tall saplings tied together with vines to work his way up, trailing Orrox's rope. The others used the combination of rope and saplings to follow him.

At the top, Orrox and Bronnox left the others to gather herbs and roots while they climbed all the way up the yellow ledge to the waterfall. Bronnox belayed Orrox as he passed behind the waterfall and climbed up to the crack. He raised his head above the edge carefully and looked around. He climbed up the ridge and still saw nothing.

When Orrox and Bronnox returned to where the others waited for them at the cairn below the scree slope, he shared his concern. "I saw no danger up there. It signifies nothing. We'll have to make it very difficult for any Primitive to descend into the canyon. A portion of the route down is visible from the cave. All we need to do is watch this section and then we can intercept anyone trying to come down the vertical chute. The chances of any Primitive following us are slim. I'm satisfied with this precaution."

#

The gloom persisted as they settled down. Orrox started preparing for a lone expedition to find survivors of the Clans. They all collected as much provisions as they could safely store, including enough for any refugees they hoped he would find.

The dust layers high above remained opaque. Rain seldom fell but dirty white frost covered the tops of the Abyss cliffs. The river, with the level down to a wide stream, cleaned up remarkably well. Only the water gushing from what they now called the 'water cave' remained constant. Normal life, as they knew it, did not return.

While they were all working near the cave, Anja overheard Orrox humming a tune she remembered from before the Catastrophe. A song her grandmother had often sung. He started mouthing the words softly under his breath, sometimes singing the song a little louder. She softly joined, her clear soprano voice in a perfect descant, supplementing his baritone perfectly. As they both sang louder, her voice rose in harmony with his, clear and pure. The joy of the pure sounds engulfed her. She forgot her original aversion towards Orrox, an irritation she forced herself to maintain. It was a feeling she could not explain or understand, but always present, prompting the need to be careful when he was around, one of not relaxing her guard in his presence.

She allowed herself to mellow in the full enjoyment of the pure sounds, the harmonies, the lilts and falls and the different tones beating in tune. The acolytes, who were doing chores in different areas in and around the cave, stopped and listened. When the perfect duet ended, tears ran down their cheeks and the girls sobbed softly. The experience was the trigger they needed to deal with the terrible stress they all still suffered from. Self-control had kept them going, but now the beautiful duet allowed them to indulge their sorrows and fears.

Orrox and Anja stared at one another, they were both deeply moved. Anja turned away and sat down sobbing. She released her pent-up emotions, emotions she had kept in check since the Catastrophe. Tears ran down her cheeks. The sobs washed away feelings of anger and desperation and removed the last vestiges of her aversion to Orrox and of his Dynasty. It left her feeling clean and refreshed.

The entire group sat where they were, in silence. Then Camla said softly "That was the most beautiful experience of my life! We need to hear it often."

Orrox walked out of the cave in silence, allowing Anja to cry and to regain her self-control. He returned after a long absence, and went to sit near Anja "How come you know the song?"

"My grandmother often hummed the tune and sometimes sang the words. There were often tears in her eyes and I always felt a sort of nostalgia, only partially suppressed, emanating from her.

I remember a sort of sad smile full of longing when she sang. Her voice was beautiful and she often made me practice singing."

"If her voice was as wonderful as yours, it must have been beautiful indeed."

Anja felt a strange elation as she continued her chores for the rest of the day. When she lay down to sleep she recalled everything.

Why do I feel so joyful? What a strange sensation. Then she realized, *I love him! He is handsome and strong and he impressed me even while he recovered from his injuries and fever. I longed for his return and was as worried as the acolytes when he was away. I was always in love with him.*

With the joyful thought, she was nearly asleep when she realized, *I cannot show anything. I fought against it as hard as I could and forced myself to feel irritated. The rules of the relationships between mentors and acolytes prohibit attachments. I'll keep my secret. But I'm sure he likes me too.*

#

They all kept very busy preparing for Orrox's expedition, working together on most chores. Bronnox and Ammox preferred to collect the special roots, herbs and plants growing below the Abyss cliffs. There they found agave plants with fat fleshy leaves ending in hard sharp thorns. Scraping the meat off the individual fibers, they twisted the strands together, rolling them over their upper legs with the palms of their hands, fashioning strings. Then they twisted the strings together in the same way, finally plaiting them to form strong ropes of any required length. Bronnox selected a thorn attached to a very long filament. He gave it to Lonna to use as a needle and thread.

On one such an outing, Bronnox climbed up a spur towards the cliff rising high above the plains. He was looking for a specific herb, which Lonna wanted. The air was exceptionally clear with only a few wisps of cloud below the edge of the Abyss. He looked up at the towering cliffs, rising up perpendicularly above him, engrossed in contemplating the massive scale of it all. As he stood with his neck stretched back, it felt as if the whole cliff tumbled forward, forcing him to step back to retain his balance. He blinked his eyes twice, convinced his eyes were cheating him. Then he was sure. He saw two small dots sticking over the sharp edge of the cliff. He blinked his eyes. More heads joining the two, and then he even saw arms gesturing, thin and spidery in the distance.

"Primitives! They must not see me!" he plunged to the ground trying to make himself small, trying to hide in the shrubbery.

He looked down to the plain far away, where Ammox collected agave leaves. He stood out, visibly etched against a light background. He waved his arms to attract Ammox's attention. When Ammox waved back, he pointed upwards. From Ammox's reaction, Bronnox could tell he also saw the figures above the cliff. Bronnox hastily joined Ammox, who quickly hid behind a clump of trees.

"We must warn the others! We must make sure they don't see where we go, but I'm afraid we have not hidden our tracks well, they will be able to find the access to the canyon."

They hurried back, tumbled down the chute and stormed into the cave. Orrox was talking to the women. They looked up in amazement, their eyes large. Orrox asked, "What's wrong?"

The two were out of breath and not coherent but soon Ammox explained, "We saw Primitives on top of the cliffs! They saw us!"

Gasping, Bronnox explained, "I was on top of a spur. When I looked up, I saw the Primitives. We rushed back here as fast as we could."

"Tell me exactly what you saw," Orrox said. "If they were on top of the cliffs, they were much too far away for you to make out details."

Bronnox thought for a while, "I saw a few small dark dots sticking out from the cliff, etched against the grey sky. They were heads. Then I saw more dots and arms waving."

Ammox nodded his agreement.

"We must assume the worst and prepare ourselves for a Primitive attack. Our best defense would be to stop them at the waterfall with a fallback position at the gully. There a few of us might be able to stop them or at least scare and discourage them from entering the canyon, and if possible, get them to turn around.

"If they descend into the Chasm, they will have to use the same route we used, the yellow ledge. They will be visible as they descend. Hurry, we'll have to block the gully in the narrowest and steepest places. Lonna, you have very sharp eyes. When you reach the top of the gully, you will see a knoll to the right from where large portions of the yellow ledge are visible. Conceal yourself there. You must warn us as soon as you see any of them descending the ledge."

Even though it was nearly dark, they hurried to the gully, to where their tracks would surely lead the Primitives. They blocked the bottom of the chute with thorny branches, just leaving space for Lonna to pass down and join them before the last light disappeared.

Orrox said, "They will not enter the Chasm in the dark."

All of the next day, they took turns to hide on the knoll, making sure they were not visible from the top of the cliffs, keeping watch. Only once did they see two figures on top of the cliffs, quite far from the crack, the only possible descent into the Chasm.

Anja knew Orrox was worried, even though he kept his feelings well under control, emanating nothing. By now, she knew him well enough to see the tension in his body. She wished she could soothe him, stroke his hair. The thought of his probable reaction, should she crumple his hair, amused her. Orrox was more attuned to her than she realized, he turned to her and gave her a bright smile, "I'm glad you are relaxed, we'll overcome this together, I promise!"

Turning to the acolytes he said, "Anja and I will ascend the yellow ledge up to the waterfall. There we can prevent them from crossing the slippery ledge with our spear throwers and long spears. There are so few of us, we dare not risk two men or two women of the group. You acolytes know one another well and must find a hiding place somewhere, should we not return."

The acolytes protested vehemently. "We cannot do without you," then added, "and we cannot lose Anja either. You are our mentors!"

Orrox was adamant, "I'm older and we are more experienced."

"Anja's Sensing, attuned to the Primitives, should help us," Camla said. "We might have to project something to scare them off!"

Orrox paused, then added, "In any case, you are younger and can recreate the Clans. We have to go."

There was a shocked expression on all the acolytes' faces. At last Bronnox said, looking down, "Do you really think we might be the last of the Clans, the last of our type of Clan-similars and the last with Sensitive ability?"

Orrox didn't answer.

Orrox and Anja climbed up the yellow ledge while the other four remained well hidden near the gully. They each carried a club, a long stout sapling, a spear thrower and a few spears with sharp obsidian points.

They moved up the ledge as fast as they could. Near the waterfall, a projectile swished past Orrox's ear. "Fall down!" he cried.

They both dived to the ground.

They pressed themselves into a corner where the ledge met the cliff and scrambled backward. Anja remained close behind Orrox, trembling with fear.

If we die here, at least I will be with him, she thought.

Chapter 36 – The Desert

A survivor helped MaGan identify the Valley of the Sparkling Waters, before Questa went in search of the Secret Cave. He asked JaYan to accompany him when he inspected the valley. They identified the position where the collapsed cave Habitat used to be. There was no sign of Clan life, only a set of very old tracks leading up into the mountain. The cave itself had collapsed and huge boulders and rubble had engulfed the site. It was impossible to look for the bodies of the dead Clan and there were no sign of any outside.

JaYan found Questa, "This is your grandmother's valley. The cave had collapsed and the Habitat is destroyed. All that is left, is a heap of impenetrable rubble. There are a few tracks, which tell us nothing useful. We found tracks of Primitives entering the valley, but they turned around before reaching the collapsed cave. We found no survivors, no bodies, nor any signs of an attack. I believe all members of the Clan met a quick and painless death inside the cave."

Questa was sad, "You saw no bodies and no life? Maybe they went to my father's valley. It must be farther on."

"I don't know. There is only a single pair of tracks from after the Catastrophe. They lead into the mountain. I think we should go on and not stay over. I don't think you should go up the valley to search for the Cave of Secrets. Please don't go."

While they were still talking, a messenger from the rear-guard arrived. He reported, "Heropto has started the chase with a strong contingent of Giants. They are some distance away and they are progress slowly over the difficult terrain."

"I'm sorry Questa. We must move on immediately," MaGan said.

Turning to the messenger he continued, "Tell SerGa his rear-guard must remain just ahead of the Giants in open terrain. Heropto will understand the threat of you launching spears or flyers whenever they pass over open ground. SerGa knows what to do. Remind him that you should fall back before total darkness. You can run faster than the Giants' gait allows them to move. Then, when light allows, harass them again. Now hurry back. I'll send reinforcements if SerGa needs them. Just keep me informed."

#

After passing more valleys, the Illoreaen group arrived at the Second Valley, Questa's home valley. MaGan and a small group of fighters entered the valley from below, fearing they would find the same scene they encountered elsewhere. They stayed away all day while JaYan found it increasingly difficult to prevent Questa from following.

She rushed towards MaGan as soon as he appeared. "What did you find?"

"The valley itself has not been destroyed but we found two burned out pyres. One at the top of the valley and a smaller one lower down. Funeral rites have been performed for the Clan. Many rotten carcasses of Primitives lie between the two sites, most near the top site. The cave Habitat has been ritually abandoned."

"I must go up. Will you allow a few Sharp-shooters to go with me? I want to go to the funeral pyres and look at the cave and the Habitat."

"I'll arrange that," MaGan answered.

Questa entered the valley slowly, avoiding the Primitive carcasses, looking around at the devastation. The vestiges of many Primitive footprints led up the valley to the site of the new Habitat. Parts of the palisade and shelters were scattered in the trees and boulders. There was nothing else. She approached the Clan cave carefully and entered. A small flame was burning at the back.

The smell has disappeared. Who did this? she wondered.

She noticed the signs left during the ritual abandonment of the cave.

Only a very few did this, not the whole Clan. A few Clan-members must have survived, she thought.

The Sharp-shooters accompanying her attracted her attention, "There is a smaller pyre just here but the large one is farther on."

At the top of the valley, they showed her the remains of the larger funeral pyre. She sat down near the burned-out pyre, while the others kept watch. She cried softly, thinking of her loved ones, trying to remember incidents involving each one and wondering who survived.

My father would not have survived. He would have fought to the last to protect our Clan. The survivors must be some other Clan-members.

The Illoreaens waited patiently.

JaYan came up the valley and joined the guards. He watched her sympathetically. He wished he could help to reduce her pain, but he could not think of anything he could do.

Questa held her head in her hands. At last, she looked up and saw JaYan. "Let's get some provisions from the Secret Cave," she said drying her eyes.

Questa knew the cave and led the others there. "There was a Healer here!" she exclaimed. "Someone found the cave. It must be a Healer but my Clan did not have one, only me. Who was here? Where are they?"

Questa looked around, "See what they collected? It was not much but they knew what medicaments to take. They must have helped members of the Clan to survive."

The idea of survivors comforted her, but, despite a thorough search, they found no-one.

"There must have been survivors." JaYan remarked, "Enough to build the pyre and to haul the bodies. As soon as we're safe, we'll come back to conduct another search."

"I'm sorry for your loss." MaGan, who also joined them, added, "But there is nothing we can do now. The tracks and signs of what happened here are old, impossible to read. We'll have to move on. The Giants are closer. Soon we will not dare to approach any forested or wooded area."

#

The rear guard kept the Giants in view.

"The Giants are using the Secret Caves and the ice caves to get provisions," the messengers reported. "They follow the many tracks we made to find the caves. Isolated Primitives raid the Secret Caves as well. The Giants kill them on sight."

"We must hurry! Their route above the valleys is more difficult than ours, but they spend less time at each valley than we do. They only collect the remaining provisions. They are catching up!" MaGan warned the group. "It is a pity we were forced to leave enough provisions for possible survivors! Now the Giants are using everything and leaving nothing."

Thereafter they did not visit or leave tracks to the Secret Caves, but only took provisions from the ice caves, leaving nothing for the Giants.

MaGan discussed the situation with JaYan, "We will soon leave the mountain slopes behind and approach the open desert sloping away towards sunset. There the Giants will also have to abandon the protection of wooded areas, if they still wish to follow us. We must avoid a situation where the Giants would be able to approach near enough to engage in close contact. We will have to be very vigilant, especially at night."

"The best would be to lead the Giants over open areas without wooded cover, farther from their natural Habitat on the other side of the mountains," JaYan answered. "They must then turn back."

The Illoreaens stocked up with provisions at the last Clan valley, cleaning out the ice caves. Then they moved away from the mountains. A rear-guard messenger reported: "The Giants have been collecting the Clans' throwing spears in the valleys and are practicing with them, throwing them farther than any of us can, nearly as far as we do with our spear throwers!"

The group was only a few days ahead of the Giants and managed to remain so. JaYan, MaGan, and a few of the most experienced Illoreaens consulted with the remnants of the Coordinating Committee to decide on their farther route.

"We can circle back to the Habitat using a roundabout way," one of them offered, but they rejected the idea as soon as it came up.

JaYan consulted Questa: "We have a problem. We cannot continue running forever. Your Clan lived in the second valley. What lies beyond the Clan valleys? There are tales, myths of mountains and a great plain with great waters beyond, in the direction of the midday sun. Have you ever heard of it?"

"Our Clan confirmed the tale of the great water, beyond a plain which grows drier as one progresses. There are also myths about the entrance to the Underworld. This lies towards sunset with a river of death to cross. I don't know what we will find there."

"Here is an idea," MaGan said. "We must travel down this sloping plain onto the open desert. There can wait for the Giants. When we have led them far enough away from any forests or woods, we can attack them. Our Sharp-shooters can move faster than they can. We should be able to cut them off and deny them access to water. Without cover, they cannot escape. If we destroy them we can return to the valleys for any provisions left in the Secret Caves."

It was a dangerous and daring plan, forcing thirst, hunger and hardship on them all, but there was no alternative. It depended on who could last longest in the desert.

#

The group followed the slowly descending plain in the sunset direction, following the course of a great river, which was reduced to a stream, flowing in the middle of its course, away from its usual banks. The shriveled plants gave way to dried grass, which became sparser as the Illoreaens continued down. Water seeps became more difficult to find but this suited them. The Giants would be forced into the open.

The messengers reported, "The Giants waited in the woods but they have now moved onto the plain."

"We must continue to draw them farther onto the desert, away from the mountains," MaGan said. "They must be at least three days away from any woods or forests before we attack."

Water became scarce and they rationed food. But still, the Giants followed. They remained too far away for MaGan's plan of cutting them off, to succeed. They did not attack but moved from one defensive position in outcrops or stacks of boulders, to the next. MaGan was worried. They could only safely return to the valleys after defeating the Giants. Meanwhile, they were depleting their provisions.

The attack came from an unexpected direction. A mob of aggressive Primitives came storming up the river, covered in blood.

Yelling and screeching with wooden spears and knobbed clubs, they attacked the vanguard.

MaGan's young fighters, protecting the main group, heard them coming. They formed a protective circle while the Illoreaens moved into an alcove where a dry gulch, the river, and the riverbank protected them on three sides.

A number of Primitives tried to approach from above the riverbank, but well-aimed throwing spears discouraged them. The whole mob then rushed past, running up-river.

The rear-guard, farther up-river, watching the Giants, heard and saw the Primitives coming and concealed themselves, their bows and flyers ready. From their hiding place, they witnessed the massacre.

The Giants saw the Primitives coming and waited for them in a loose bundle.

The Primitives relied solely on their knobbed clubs and spears of sharpened saplings. They approached the Giants carefully, casting their sharpened saplings.

A number of Giants stormed forward, but the Primitives were fleeter of foot and the Giants could not catch any of them.

Irritated, the Giants returned to the loose bundle watching the Primitives and ignoring any scratches the saplings caused.

When the Primitives saw the Giants with only stabbing spears, they attacked in their bloodlust and frenzy.

The Giants waited for them and instead of bundling up, as the Primitives expected, they spread out in a long line and curved around quickly, surrounding the Primitives. They grabbed the sharpened saplings, yanked each attacker forward, often killing them with a single blow. The clubs did little harm, merely increasing the Giants' wrath. They spread out and killed all the attackers.

The messengers from the rear guard reported, "We did not see any Primitive escape. Heropto yelled at us after the skirmish. We believe he threatened that we would suffer the same fate. He still thinks he will catch and kill us."

\#

The Illoreaens waited in the protected corner of the riverbank for a day, hoping the Giants would attack after their victory over the Primitives, but instead Heropto re-organized his followers and waited near a rock formation, safe from the Illoreaens' projectiles.

The Illoreaens were forced to continue their trek following the river. The terrain slowly sloped downwards in the sunset direction with ridges often slowing the group's progress. The Giants followed at a safe distance. The scouts could not prevent them from using the same water seeps where the Illoreaens dug deep wells and found clear water for their own use. There were too many places where the Giants could protect themselves from the Illoreaen projectiles.

MaGan mouthed his frustration, "What can we do? We're already on strict rations. We have to attack them!"

JaYan agreed. "Yes, there is not much else we can do. We cannot return to the mountain range and Clan valleys to look for any provisions still left in the Secret Caves. We would have to pass through woods and forests. Even worse, the Giants might occupy the caves where the Sharp-shooters' projectiles would be useless. Yes, MaGan, we will have to attack.

The Coordinating Committee agreed.

MaGan assembled all his fighters and they joined the rear guard before dawn. As soon as there was enough light to see, they rushed to within striking distance of where the Guards were sleeping near a few fires. Heropto had placed his guards well and they feared him enough to remain vigilant. They saw the Illoreaen approach in time for the whole group to retreat into nearby rock formations, safe from projectiles.

The Illoreaens, on their side, remained out of physical reach of the Giants. Heropto did not even try to use the throwing spears they had practiced with. To throw them they would have to expose themselves to Illoreaen projectiles. The attack achieved nothing.

Disappointed, MaGan retreated. The Illoreaens continued down-river on hunger rations.

A day later, the forward scouts reported the river's end. It fell over a cliff into obscurity. The Illoreaens could go no farther.

JaYan forged ahead to find a safe place before the main group arrived. Above a ridge he crossed the river, looking for an area where all the Illoreaens could camp, protected from an attack.

Below the ridge he saw footprints and the remains of a fire used for cooking.

"Someone was here and stayed for at least a night! No, there were more than one. It was after the Catastrophe. See, the tracks are on top of the layer of dust."

MaGan agreed and added, "This is a good place to wait. The space between the ridge and the cliff's edge is open. Ideal for a defense with bows and flyers."

Farther on JaYan saw a giant tree with its roots in a deep crack. Its limbs extended so far, all the Illoreaens could assemble underneath, and would have been in its shade if the sun still shone.

"Let's make our encampment there, away from the river, around the tree," JaYan decided.

"I agree. It's also easily defensible. The ridge is too high and steep for any Giant to climb down and the other side is protected by the cliff. A few of our Sharp-shooters above the ridge can dominate the whole area. We'll wait for the Giants to come nearer. They will have to attack from the sides and come within shooting range," MaGan confirmed.

The rear-guard came up to MaGan to report, with many of the Illoreaens listening, "A few Primitives, who survived the massacre, killed a couple of the Giants scouting alone. You will not believe it, the Primitives cut up the corpses and ate them."

A cry of horror escaped the assembled Illoreaens.

"The Giants have turned around and are killing Primitives, but from Heropto's gestures, we think he is even angrier than before. We believe he will lead his troupe to kill all the Primitives they can find and then he will return to wreak his frustration on us."

The Illoreaens built their camp beneath the magnificent tree with its spreading branches and prepared for a long wait and a proper defense. Sharp-shooters kept vigilant guard at the group's periphery looking outwards.

JaYan approached MaGan, "We don't have enough to eat or enough drinkable water. We cannot remain in this defensive position for long. What shall we do?"

"We will have to send a few of our young Sharp-shooters, the ones doing their service years, back to fetch any provisions left in the Clan caves. There is a slight chance of success. We might be sending them to their death. I will lead them."

JaYan could not offer an alternative, "We will have to wait till the situation is even more desperate. We can still last a few days and we might find a few water seeps in the open under the ridges. We'll all be thirsty. Attacking the Giants might be a better proposition."

The Giants were catching up, but MaGan decided to wait while the Illoreaens were setting up camp, others ranged far in search of seeps of fresh water or to dig wells away from the river, where the oozing water was not polluted yet.

Questa found more tracks near a waterfall and a pool. She followed them but soon lost them on the smooth wind-blown rock slabs edging the Abyss.

She rushed up to where JaYan and MaGan were in deep conversation, both looking worried. "Come see! I found footprints. They were made by Clan-members, not Giants or Primitives. There were Clan-members here, not too long ago. See, the breeze has not deformed the tracks too much. I can make out different sets. There were at least four of them here, I think six."

"That is impossible!" JaYan said. "How can Clan-members find themselves this deep in the desert? Please, show us."

JaYan and MaGan inspected the tracks and had to agree. "Definitely Clan footprints," MaGan confirmed. "I have to check our defenses. You keep searching. We can tell the others when we know more."

JaYan and Questa found no further tracks before night fell. They were looking over the edge the next day. Fog obscured everything. It slowly boiled over the edge to evaporate, only to be replaced by a new upwelling. The fog slowly descended as the day progressed, until it evaporated, allowing a clear vision of the Chasm floor far below. Suddenly Questa called out, "Look down there! I can see a figure. No, look there are two. They look like Clan-members. Giants and Primitives are built and walk differently!"

They both waved.

After a while, the one figure stopped. They could not see whether he looked up. He ran towards the other figure. Both figures stood still for just a moment, then both disappeared.

"I'm sure they saw us!" Questa said.

JaYan answered, "Yes. I'm sure they are not Giants or Primitives. They must be from the Clans. We might have made a mistake in attracting their attention. They might not allow intruders. What if there are other secret Clans we have never heard of? We'll have to be careful."

JaYan was now convinced an entry route into the Chasm must be close by and arranged for a search along the edge of the Abyss. They searched all day but did not find a way down. The next day, on an impulse, JaYan explored a prominent crack in the smooth slab. Taking a chance, he tried to climb down. He found abrasion marks, signs of recent use of the crack. When he arrived at the yellow ledge, he was sure, *this is the route.*

Climbing back up, he reported, "I have found the route into the Chasm. It is very exposed which means we can easily stop any descending Giant. He would be an easy target for our projectiles and he would not be able to respond."

The approaching Giants required an urgent decision. JaYan and MaGan conferred with those of the Coordinating Committee who were in the group. Long discussions followed. They decided unanimously to explore the route down.

In the end, MaGan's suggestion was accepted, "It would be better if the entire group were safely beyond the reach of the Giants with only my fighters in exposed positions."

"Then we don't have to protect the group and can concentrate on the Giants." MaGan added.

JaYan was given the responsibility to lead the group down and accommodate them down there for a few days.

"I would prefer MaGan's fighters to come down to protect the group. We don't know what awaits us down there. A few Sharp-shooters can easily cover and protect the descent," JaYan said. MaGan agreed.

The whole group descended slowly, many belayed down with the help of ropes. They spread out along the ledge. Sharp-shooters knelt in front of the growing group assembling on the ledge while JaYan talked the Illoreaens down the crack. Young fighters sometimes climbed below those most scared of the height. The Illoreaens allowed Questa to emanate soothing emotions. When the last of the group was down, JaYan went to the front to lead the group along the ledge. Sharp-shooters stayed behind to cover the descent and to wait for MaGan and the rear-guard to catch up. They knew they left tracks, clear enough for the Giants to discover the route.

JaYan said, "Two Sharp-shooters must stay with me in the lead. Send MaGan forward as soon as he arrives. We don't know what awaits us. If we see anyone, shoot warning flyers, near enough to frighten, but not kill."

Chapter 37 – New Beginnings

"Stay down! Don't show yourself," Orrox shouted. "These things can kill!"

Another projectile arrived hitting the rock at exactly the same spot.

Even at this distance, absolute accuracy. It is a warning only.

Orrox dared to peer around the rocky outcrop, "I cannot see much. No, I see someone looking around the bend on the far side of the waterfall. He is carrying... I don't believe it! I think I know who they are!"

He yelled loudly, "Wait! I am Orrox of the Dynasty! We are not enemies!"

The noise of the waterfall drowned his words. Then to Anja, "I will somehow have to communicate with them. I will tell you who they are later."

Orrox rose slowly from behind the shelter, leaving his spear and club on the ground. He waved both hands, showing they were empty and he did not carry a weapon.

He said, "Stay where you are until I indicate it is safe."

Anja peered out. Slowly, from behind a corner, a figure appeared. He carried a strangely bent stick with a cord tied between the ends. She wondered what it was. The figure was neither a Primitive nor a Giant, but, despite the strange garb he wore under a soft skin covering, he looked like a member of the Clans.

The figure squinted suspiciously and then relaxed. He clearly did not regard Orrox as an immediate threat. Orrox made a gesture to signal a greeting of peace.

Orrox and the figure both moved to their respective edges of the waterfall. Both were clearly wary of crawling to the other end, where they were exposed while negotiating the slippery shelf. Orrox motioned for Anja to approach, indicating with gestures, there were only two of them.

They both moved back, keeping their hands visible with palms forward. Orrox beckoned, inviting the other to cross.

The other hesitated and gestured towards figures hidden beyond a previous turn. Three of his companions appeared, each carrying one of the curved sticks with a straight sapling fitted cross-wise and pointing straight towards the two. Their intentions were clear. They would protect their companion—kill if necessary—using similar projectiles to those that landed near Orrox and Anja before.

Anja understood the threat all too well, even though she could not imagine how the devices worked. She glanced at Orrox, he clearly knew these strange bent sticks and projectiles. "Orrox," she said, "Do you know who they are and what those are? They look dangerous. Can I Sense them?"

"They are Clans and you may not Sense them, it would be extremely rude. Yes, those are very dangerous and can easily kill us at this distance. They will if they suspect a threat or trick. I will explain later. You will find them very interesting. Bronnox will be fascinated. He'd love to see their devices!"

Another companion, watching Orrox and Anja suspiciously, produced a rope. The first figure tied the rope around his waist and carefully negotiated the slippery shelf. He crossed behind the waterfall on all fours without slipping. When he reached safety, he stood and waited.

The stranger's crawling was embarrassing. Orrox approached him with a half stoop and bent head, humiliating himself as well to compensate. He held his arms outstretched, palms forward. He halted a few paces away and stood straight, both now standing proudly on firm ground.

"I am Orrox, of the Orrox Dynasty. I assume you are Illoreaens. I know about you, and you know of us."

The other answered, loudly enough for Anja to hear. He spoke in the Clan tongue but with a heavy accent and a strange pronunciation.

"We know the Orrox. We, the Illoreaens, often have contact with the Dynasty and the Orrox. How do I know you are really of the Orrox? I don't know you."

"I am the Orrox who grew up in my grandmother's Clan. Surely, you have heard of me? The Orrox delegates, who regularly visit the Illoreaens, tell my tale. I know of the Illoreaen developed knowledge. I know about bows and flyers. I know your Sharp-shooters could have easily hit their target and killed us. You missed on purpose, despite the risk of not being able to retrieve your flyers. Only an Orrox can have this knowledge."

"I concede, you must be from the Dynasty, possibly an Orrox, possibly the Orrox! I am JaYan of the Illoreaens, son of LaGos and Merpa the Elder, leading a large group of the illustrious Illoreaens. I am pleased to meet you. It is an honor! We were forced to flee from Giants who attacked our Habitat and are pursuing us. My cousin MaGan leads a formidable group of fighters, Sharp-shooters, as a rear guard. Is it safe here? Can my companions cross and join us?"

"We know the Illoreaens are peaceful," Orrox said. "If your intentions are amiable, and if you will not harm us, we would be pleased to welcome you down in the Chasm. It is safe there and the food is plentiful... Why did Giants attack you? How could they resist your strength? We have much information to share!"

"We also have many questions and information you will find valuable, but we'll have to wait until my Illoreaens are safe and settled," JaYan said. "If you agree, I'll indicate that my companions can cross behind the waterfall. We are weak and have suffered much. We have travelled continuously for many days. We desperately need rest."

The two looked at each other, wanting to trust one another, but were careful after all their recent experiences. Orrox unwound the plaited leather cord, still tied around his body. "We can help. I have a rope, which will make it easier to bring all your companions over safely. If you hold on at this end, I will go across and assist in tying each of your companions to the rope and then we can bring them across safely."

He gestured, "This is Anja. She is the daughter of a renowned Chief and a famous Healer. Anja, will you stay here as support?"

Anja was pleased. Orrox had decided the two of them should face the danger of the unknown intruders together. It showed trust. The danger has now passed. She exerted self-control not to emanate the sudden relief and responded happily. "It would be my pleasure!"

The Illoreaen was emaciated and Anja could see how tired he was. He signaled to the three still watching them with bow and flyers ready and pointing. They beckoned others, still hidden behind them. Slowly more figures appeared.

JaYan turned towards Anja and looked at her strangely, "We have a young woman with us who looks like you, with the same blue eyes," he said drily, tilting his head. However, Anja was too focused on her task to attend to his words.

Orrox crawled across the slippery shelf behind the waterfall, one end of the rope attached to his waist. On the other side, Orrox tied each Illoreaen onto the middle of the rope, in turn. Between JaYan and Orrox, and with the help of other Illoreaens, they belayed each one across the shelf behind the waterfall.

Anja helped them to sit safely farther along the shelf, where it was dry. She was returning to the moist area near the waterfall, when she stopped in amazement and dropped to her knees. The figure in front of her uttered a cry of astonishment, "Anja!"

Anja started trembling, looked up and clasped her hands to the sides of her head. Her voice was hoarse when she whispered, "Questa!"

She got up slowly. Then they rushed towards each other and hugged and cried and laughed and could not stop.

Orrox could not see the two, the waterfall and spray hid them from his view. JaYan, who was at their side of the waterfall and saw the meeting said, "I told you she resembles you; you must be sisters! Only sisters can share a renowned Chief as father and a famous Healer as mother."

They did not even hear JaYan's comment.

The Illoreaens, seeing the euphoric reunion, smiled happily, sharing in Questa's joy. One of the Illoreaens took over Anja's duty, leading the last of the company to the dry area on the shelf. Soon Orrox returned, moving carefully across the shelf and joined them.

Now Anja could tell him, "This is Questa, my sister! She's alive!"

Orrox was amazed. Both he and the acolytes knew the Giants had abducted Questa. How could she be here? Down in the Hidden Valley so long ago, when they found out who Anja was, they decided not to tell her about the abduction. Convinced of Questa's death at the hands of the Giants, they decided to spare Anja the horrible detail. Surely, it was kinder to let her think her sister died quickly.

He turned to JaYan and said, "How did this happen?"

"It is a long story, related to many other occurrences. Let's get away from this exposed ledge to where we can all sit safely. Then we can share our experiences. My companions have suffered and need to rest. We also need some sweet water and nourishment. If you can help us, you will do us a great favor."

"There are only six of us, but we will be honored to give as much help as we can. There is a seep with sweet water just a little farther along and plenty down in the Chasm."

Questa and Anja sat together talking softly, happy tears flowing. Although Questa saw the funeral pyre in the Second valley and therefore assumed their father, stepmother and the whole Clan were dead, she still held a faint hope of their escape.

Anja told her, "I saw their bodies and we built a funeral pyre. I performed the death rites myself. We also ritually cleaned the cave. It was all we could do, but we did it properly."

With the confirmed knowledge her loved ones had not somehow survived, Questa cried on Anja's shoulder. The only physical comfort Anja could give was a caress, while stroking her hair and emanating soothing emotions.

#

The group slowly made their way down, following the ledge, and then clambered over the scree onto the spur to arrive safely on level ground. Anja and Questa fell behind, absorbed in common grief and joy, with much to tell.

Before they left the waterfall ledge, JaYan sent fresh water with a confirmation of their safety as well as a promise of nourishment to MaGan and his Sharp-shooter fighters. They were still above the abyss, protecting the entrance to the crack, down which the Illoreaens recently descended. With bows and flyers ready, they were waiting for the Giants.

Orrox rushed ahead to tell the anxious acolytes, "There is no danger. This is a large group of a special Clan called Illoreaens. I know about them. They are weak and tired. Anja's sister Questa is with them. You should have seen their meeting! They cannot stop talking and hugging each other. Please go down into the canyon to fetch foodstuffs. Also, bring salves and herbs."

#

Orrox and JaYan waited until all the Illoreaens were cared for. A few refreshed Sharp-shooter fighters ascended the Abyss to relieve the rear-guard. After making sure the relief was in position below the crack, with an unobstructed view of any Giant trying to descend, MaGan was the last to arrive.

The acolytes brought all they could carry. They made herb infusions to refresh the newcomers. While they helped to apply salves and dressing bruises, they discovered the many ointments, the Illoreaens had brought along. Many were unknown to them.

When all the Illoreaens were satiated with food, water and herb infusions, the whole assembly formed a circle around Orrox, JaYan, MaGan, the two sisters and the acolytes. Both groups wanted to ask many questions. The Illoreaens knew more about the Dynasty and the Orrox Clan than either Anja or Questa or any of the Clans knew.

Orrox could explain his presence in a few sentences: "I am Orrox and these are my acolytes, Bronnox, Ammox, Lonna, and Camla," pointing to each. "We don't know what happened to their Clans. This is Anja. She is Questa's younger sister. She lived with her grandmother in the Valley of the Sparkling Waters. Her Clan died when a rock-fall destroyed their Habitat and their Clan cave collapsed. You have observed the happy reunion with Questa."

Orrox's voice carried well enough for all the Illoreaens to follow every word. They always lived with the knowledge of their dependence on the Dynasty and, therefore, on the Orrox. To see a descendant in the flesh, fascinated them. They wanted to know all the details of his experience.

Orrox continued to relay the story of Jupex, the father of Questa and Anja, and his Clan, the visit to the Dynasty Valley, the Primitives' attacked, and of Jupex's heroism. He looked down sadly while saying, "We were the only survivors."

Orrox noticed a movement in the crowd. An Illoreaen spoke up, "So, you are all Sensitives too!"

"SkepTan, let him finish. Questions and discussions can follow later," JaYan said. "Please continue!"

Orrox looked surprised, "Yes, of course we are all Sensitives. My acolytes are in training. They have already proven their potential to become outstanding Oracle-Healers, like Anja."

JaYan started his story, "I am JaYan," he pointed to a small group standing near him. "These are the members of the Coordinating Committee of the Illoreaens and I am the Coordinating Speaker. "Questa will tell you how we found and rescued her thereby attracted the wrath of the Giants. We also found survivors of the Clans on our way here. Questa has told them who we are. They are those standing near you, Orrox."

Orrox nodded. He had already spoken to them.

"Orrox also knows who we are, but Anja and the acolytes have probably never heard of us and do not know of our existence." He explained more, ending with, "We are proud of our skills and knowledge. We have managed to invent and make many things. Orrox is aware of some of them. A simple example is the bow with which MaGan's Sharp-shooters shot at Orrox and Anja!"

Orrox laughed, "Luckily you missed on purpose, but you gave us a good fright. You can tell more. My acolytes and Anja are all trained Sensitives and they know how and when to keep secrets. Knowledge of how special the Illoreaens are can be shared with them."

JaYan thought for a moment, "It would be best if you tell them about us, Orrox. However, there is another matter. We did not know of the Sensitive abilities of your Oracle-Healers. It was a great shock when we realized Questa is a Sensitive. We treated her very badly. I hereby apologize again on behalf of all of us."

A murmur rose from the others. JaYan signaled for silence, "MaGan please continue."

MaGan summarized the siege, their decision to travel, their escape and the suffering, "We are not strong enough to take on the Giants, except in open spaces. They committed many atrocities and we were all in danger of starving. I have very bad news. We passed all the Clan valleys. The Primitives burned, attacked and killed the Clan-members in each valley."

He paused again.

"We performed the necessary rites in each valley, built a pyre and burned the bodies. We also performed the rituals to abandon the caves. Questa will bear witness that we did it properly. I am sad to say we found only these few survivors."

MaGan paused and looked first at JaYan then at Orrox, "I'm afraid the Giants will try to follow us. If they do, we're all in mortal danger. However, from what I observed, we can stop them at the crack where we descended. Or, if not there, at the waterfall."

MaGan stepped back to allow JaYan to have the final word, "Thank you, MaGan. I'm convinced you and your Sharp-shooters can protect us from the Giants."

Turning around he said, "Thank you Orrox, Anja, Bronnox, Ammox, Camla, and Lonna for the friendly way you received us, attended to our injuries and shared your food. Now is the time to rest. We'll set up our encampment here near the streamlet and start gathering foodstuffs."

With a slightly uncomfortable smile, he added, "We Illoreaens are not very good at gathering, but Questa and the survivors from the Clans are teaching us and we are learning."

The Illoreaens were embarrassed and did not understand the acolyte's spontaneous laughter. Orrox silenced them with a gesture, "Please show the newcomers where and how the best edibles can be collected."

Turning to the Coordinating Committee he said, "There is not enough uncontaminated water for all of you up here. In the canyon there is plenty, also good caves and fish to catch. You are welcome to join us there."

JaYan scanned the group who indicated their agreement by slight nods.

"Thank you. We accept," he said.

Facing JaYan Orrox continued, "The stream down there contains an abundance of different types of fish. They give strength. We also have the meat of small game. Your companions will soon regain their strength. We prefer to go down now. We have not brought coverings for the night. Even down here, the nights are cold."

JaYan started to thank them again when MaGan interrupted, "Our priority is to eliminate the threat of the Giants and I believe my Sharp-shooters should stay here where guards can easily be relieved. I'm going to see to the organization of patrols and guards. Till later." He left to confer with some of the young men.

The rest of the Illoreaens followed Orrox and his companions to the Canyon. The smooth chute delayed them but with the Illoreaens' additional ropes and a ladder Bronnox fashioned from saplings, they managed well. Ammox, Lonna, Camla, Anja and Questa went ahead to point out a level spot near the water cave for the Illoreaens to stay the night and where they could collect firewood. By the time the gloom darkened, the Illoreaens were safely settled in their encampment.

#

JaYan asked Questa to show him a specific herb, which grew near where the river entered the Chasm, falling down the abyss in the previously mighty waterfall, still spreading its mist far around. They climbed out of the Canyon together, using the ladder now permanently positioned in the chute.

They walked towards the pool at the bottom of the great waterfall in silence. The water quality was already much improved. On a knoll, near the waterfall, they stopped and sat down on the soft emerald green grass.

"You were very angry with us Illoreaens. I sincerely apologize for the way we initially treated you. SkepTan's remarks made it worse. Yes, I have learned about his horrible accusation. Anything I said would not have improved things. SkepTan's bitterness is a reaction to the trauma he suffered when his father, HenGan the Elder, whom he adored, disappeared when he was still young."

Questa was silent and looked away. She had suppressed the hurt and tried to forget the terrible insult. To forgive SkepTan would be difficult.

"Please forgive him. His father heard about exotic herbs from a visiting Dynasty delegation of courier-messengers. The Dynasty later informed us he had reached the Clan valleys, attended the annual Clan feast to learn more and left in the sunset direction. Even the Dynasty's searches never discovered what had happened to him. SkepTan blames the Dynasty and the Clan Healers, and therefore the Sensitives, for the loss of his father.

"Enough of that. Surely, with enough Sensitives around, SkepTan's accusation has lost its sting. Let's forget about him."

Questa looked at him, and smiled, "I agree."

JaYan began again. "I dared not speak before. I was in a difficult position as the Coordinating Speaker. I dared not give an impression of misusing my position. I avoided doing anything to make you suspect ulterior motives. However, I am sure you always knew how I feel. You must know how much you attracted me from the first moment I saw you, even though you were unconscious, dirty, and dressed in a stinking, insect-infested Giant's kaross."

Questa looked away but could not avoid laughing.

"That's better. I fell in love with you then. When I found out how brave and intelligent you were, my love grew. Long before you revealed your Sensitive abilities, I was already forced to hide my feelings, also because you were a guest and I dared not take advantage.

"It hurt me when you wanted to leave us to return to the Dynasty and your Clan. I decided I would follow you there to woo you unhindered. Then everything went wrong. I now want the same chance as any other. For a start, I'd like to make something special for us to eat tonight and then we can sit together around the fire. Come, what do you say?"

Questa looked up, eyes shining, "I would like it very much!"

#

The Illoreaens regarded the Clan survivors as unsophisticated, who, on their turn, thought of the Illoreaens as helpless, nearly parasitic, unable to browse and feed themselves. They also looked at the bows and flyers of the Illoreaens and learned about their comfortable lifestyle, jealous of the Illoreaen artefacts and figurines made from Transparent.

Orrox experienced hostile glances and overheard mumblings of survivors, "If we had access to bows and flyers, we would have killed the Primitives. Our families, friends and relations would not have been massacred. The Clan's blood is on Orrox's hands."

And, "The Dynasty failed us."

Tension increased. Orrox, JaYan and MaGan noticed the split developing and did their best to pacify the groups.

Orrox realized the trust relationships within the Clans was in danger and explained, "The Dynasty patrols did use bows and flyers to protect the Clan valleys. They are weapons, meant for fighting, not hunting. The patrols served us well for many generations, keeping us safe. The Catastrophe destroyed the Clan's palisades and other safety measures as well as the Dynasty Habitat, the whole valley, and thereby the Dynasty's protective abilities."

A survivor called UniSux spoke up, "I was on patrol with four others when the Catastrophe struck. We were on the plains below the Clan valleys. Two of our group returned to the Dynasty Valley for instructions. We never saw them again."

The Clansman standing next to him nodded his head in confirmation.

UniSux continued, "The swamps on the plain became soggy and unstable and we had difficulty in moving from one valley entrance to the other. Primitive bands started to assemble and they attacked us. From a strong defensive position, we used our bows and flyers and killed many. All but three of us were killed.

"The Primitives retreated when night fell, and we managed to retrieve many flyers. The three of us, the only remaining members of the patrol, slipped away onto the mountain slopes, but another died of his injuries. We two survived until the Illoreaens passed by and saved us. A few of our friends, who were on different patrols, were also saved. Their stories are similar. Look, there they are."

A few in the assembly put up their hands and nodded their confirmation.

"There was nothing we could do!" one of them said.

"You have heard their stories," Orrox said. "The patrollers are heroes and all did whatever was possible. I cannot imagine what more could have been done to save the Clans."

Orrox, Anja, the acolytes and Questa mingled with the survivors, talking and explaining. Slowly, over time, emotions relaxed.

\#

Not long after the Illoreaens descended into the Chasm and settled in the canyon, figures appeared on the rim of the Abyss. MaGan and his group moved carefully up the ledge, ready to confront any danger. At the waterfall, MaGan left a number of Sharp-shooter fighters hidden in a position to cover the slippery ledge, before continuing.

They arrived at the bottom of the crack in time to hear the loud guttural sounds of the Giants. It sounded like an intense argument and loud shouting.

"What are they up to?" SerGa, the leader of those on guard there, asked, looking at MaGan.

"I don't know. They must have seen our tracks and found the crack. Heropto will understand the danger of descending. We must be ready. Do you have enough flyers?"

"Only these we each brought with us. Surely they are enough?"

"I'm not so sure."

MaGan sent back one of those who had arrived with him to fetch more, "Tell those guarding the waterfall to be prepared. I think the Giants are coming."

After a while, the noise stopped.

"Have they left?" a guard asked, shifting his position, peering up the crack.

Before MaGan could answer, they heard the shuffling noises of a Giant working his way down the crack.

"They're coming! SerGa, arrange your fighters! The ledge is too narrow, we are getting in each other's way. I will fall back a little way to form a second line of defense," MaGan said, gesturing his small group back, from where they could still see into a part of the crack.

The Giant climbing down was so large, he was forced far out of the crack, to near the edge of the crevice. There he became visible to the defenders below him.

He was holding one of the huge throwing spears, Heropto copied from those he saw the Illoreaens use. SerGa shot a warning flyer up the crevice, just missing him. He continued to descend. SerGa followed the warning shot with a flyer in his leg but the Giant kept on coming.

"Each of you shoot one flyer into his legs. Take careful aim!" SerGa said. The flyers did not stop him. His body and head were mostly obscured by his thick thighs and legs.

With a mighty one-handed throw, the Giant launched his spear at SerGa's fighters, who were bunched up on the ledge below him. The spear hit a Sharp-shooter in the head and he fell sideways. A companion tried to catch him, but the already dead fighter's body dragged him along to the edge. For a moment the rescuer toppled in precarious balance, still holding on to his friend's body. Then they slipped off the shelf together. A last grab for support was not successful. Together they fell to the Chasm far below.

For a moment the defenders all froze in horror. Then SerGa yelled, "Now he is without a weapon! Go for his body or head, if you can see them."

MaGan had an oblique view and could see more of the Giant. He shot three flyers in quick succession. One hitting the Giant above the brow. It bounced off his cranium and disappeared down the abyss.

That also happened to JaYan when he shot at Heropto, MaGan realized.

The others also managed to land more flyers in the Giant's torso. Bleeding profusely with flyers in his legs and lower body, the Giant gave up and climbed back up the crack, struggling to support himself.

As he bumped against the sides of the crack, the flyer-shafts broke free. Only the flyer-heads remained stuck in him. A moment later an intense yelling indicated the Giant's return.

"It must be Heropto venting his anger," SerGa said, glancing back at MaGan.

"Yes. We must remain alert and ready. He will not give up," He looked down past the ledge into the depths. "We will have to suppress our sorrow till later."

Sometime later the shuffling noises started again. The previous Giant appeared, still bleeding from his wounds. But above and behind him Heropto climbed, holding him by the neck. He climbed with only one hand while his victim shouted and cried, scrambling with hands and feet to keep from falling.

"It is amazing how strong Heropto is!" SerGa whispered while bringing up his bow with a flyer in place.

MaGan could see the front Giant's face, which was swollen. His body was covered in bruises and bleeding.

I'm sure Heropto assaulted and subdued this one before attempting the climb himself, MaGan thought. *With Heropto hiding behind the other, we are in trouble.*

MaGan, fluent enough in the Giant's language, uttered a warning. Heropto just laughed.

"We must kill him!"

They aimed at Heropto whenever he was visible behind his victim. From MaGan's position Heropto was more visible, but they were so bunched up that only two or three of the Sharp-shooters with him, could aim and shoot. All of them often missed, putting more flyers into the Giant in front and below Heropto. The latter struggled less and less and then loosened his grip on the handholds.

Heropto, with his incredible strength, now held the large Giant by the neck with one hand only, still using him as a shield. The Giant dangled free, which gave more opportunities to aim at Heropto himself. At last, Heropto let go of his victim-shield. The Giant fell all the way to the bottom. They then concentrated their flyers on Heropto.

Shooting up from below, SerGa's troop could not launch a lethal shot. MaGan's group's effort was slightly better. They kept on until Heropto looked like a hedgehog with its densely arranged quills. Heropto was bleeding profusely from many flyer wounds. The blood streamed down the sides of the fissure like a waterfall.

He continued to climb down until he was quite near and started to move into the crack to position himself safely over the ledge.

"Careful! He might land on the ledge. Move back. Try for a killing shot as soon as he becomes fully visible!" MaGan shouted.

They were running out of flyers when Heropto's feet slipped on his own blood. Then he lost his grip on the bloody handholds, let go, and fell. He let out a loud and furious scream, just hitting the edge of the ledge. He grabbed for something to hold onto, and then fell all the way. They heard his screams until he hit the bottom far below.

His screams were followed by loud noises made by the other Giants up above.

"I cannot believe such a determined, foolhardy attempt!" MaGan said.

SerGa and the other guards nodded and then exclaimed, "He nearly landed on the ledge. We were really scared. He might have kept balance!"

MaGan hastened back to relieve the guards, leaving the few of his fighters behind. When he reached the waterfall, he sent most of the Sharp-shooters, still waiting there, to the crack as further reinforcements. From below he sent up more fighters with many flyers.

"Heropto is dead. I believe the main threat has passed," He informed those gathering around him. "But we lost two of our brave fighters."

The next day they found the two bodies of their fallen companions. Everyone in the Chasm honored their bravery. JaYan arranged a special death ceremony at their pyre, while tears ran down the faces of the families of the heroes. The whole community attended, except those still on guard.

Nearby they found the mangled bodies of both Giants at the bottom of the cliff. Heropto was two heads taller than the other Giant, who was huge himself. Two Illoreaens worked hard to pull the smaller Giant towards Heropto's body, where they covered both with a pyramid of stones, to remind them of a terrible assault.

A day later the guards at the crack reported, "We don't hear the Giants anymore."

Two more days passed before SerGa climbed up the crack. He was tied onto a strong rope, recently braided from leather straps. He was ready to jump out of the crack into the void, should any Giant attack him. He trusted on his companions and the rope to catch him.

They teased him, "You are as foolhardy as Heropto," but admired his bravery.

SerGa made no noise as he climbed. When he reached the top and heard nothing, he stuck his head out above the crack and looked around. He did not see any Giants.

Back at the encampment, MaGan assembled a strong group of young men, all trained Sharp-shooters, "Without Heropto as an instigator, the Giants will be less of a threat. Now is the time to finally get rid of them. Follow me!"

MaGan was determined and inspected the area above the crack himself before allowing his fighters to emerge. They stayed away for many days while the guards stationed below the crack remained ready to react with only one sentry above, at the entry to the crack.

When MaGan and his fighters returned, the whole group, including the Sensitives, assembled to hear his report.

"We followed the Giant's trail past two valleys where we were able to retrieve some provisions from the caves. We made sure the Giants did not double back. They are disorganized and are rushing back to their own, distant forests. They rushed across the plains. We saw only dead Primitives in their wake. I think the Giants must have killed them all!

"Just before we turned back we met these three messengers from our friends who stayed in the Habitat."

He pointed to three Illoreaens who had remained hidden behind the others of his unit. "Come and tell them your news."

They advanced and one, called GaRop, spoke up, "When Heropto left, the Giants became demoralized and many left. Their patrols were disorganized and then stopped. It was soon possible to move in and out of the Habitat using a new exit. A few days ago, a Giant arrived. Those few who understand their language heard him bringing the news of Heropto's death at your hands. All the Giants left while we celebrated inside the Habitat."

The Illoreaens applauded loudly, many crying. First one then many voices called out, "Now we can go back!"

JaYan spoke softly with MaGan and the three messengers and then held up his hand, "There is more!"

GaRop said, "I'm afraid the rest of my news is not good. Those with the knowledge back at the Habitat used the time and our facilities to analyze the situation without the support of the Dynasty and the Clans. The consensus conclusion is, there will not be enough food for the Illoreaens to survive in our Habitat. We cannot go back. We must all find somewhere fertile, warm, and with enough water to sustain us."

The bad news silenced the crowd.

Orrox spoke up, "I believe the solution must lie down here. There is an abundance of fresh water down here and the temperature, especially farther down into the Chasm, is much warmer than up there. Why don't you transfer the whole Illoreaen Habitat into the Chasm? The Chasm is very big. In the canyon there are many suitable caves, which can be enlarged. There we'll all be safe and secure."

He didn't mention the myth's reference to dangerous reptiles. That threat would be confronted, should it ever appear.

There was silence and then a growing murmur of discussion. The outcome was positive but the Illoreaens were reluctant to lose their old Habitat.

JaYan said, "Thank you, Orrox! We'd like to pursue that idea after due consideration. We don't have to abandon the Habitat. It can remain as a reference and special knowledge facility with only a few specialists staying there. We can supply them with all their needs. The rest of us can then re-start our searches for knowledge somewhere else, possibly here."

JaYan's solution satisfied all. The Illoreaens would not lose their old Habitat.

#

All the survivors of the Clans, whom the Illoreaens had rescued, selected to stay in caves near Orrox. The survivors of the Clans tended to say, "Those Illoreaens are so strange. They are not like us at all!"

Many Illoreaens moved farther down the Canyon, where they found a series of suitable caves. They worked hard at improving their living conditions and became self-sufficient. They ignored the phenomenon of Sensitivity whenever possible. The consensus was, "The Clans are so primitive. They know nothing!"

#

Three years had passed. As expected, new commitments resulted in new lives. Questa and Anja both had daughters named Chiara, Chiara-the-Illoreaen and Chiara-the-Dynastist. Their life-companions, JaYan and Orrox, became best of friends, while MaGan found a life-companion from amongst the survivors of the Clans, also a Sensitive and a talented Oracle-Healer.

JaYan moved to live near the cave where the Sensitives had originally settled, where the Illoreaens had dug a large new cave complex in the soft rock face. There they installed all the important devices from the old Illoreaen Habitat and continued their knowledge searches. They kept the old Habitat secure as a reminder of a previous age.

Search parties found and rescued more Clan survivors while facing new threats, which manifested in the Clan valleys and on the Primitive plains with the disappearance of Dynasty patrols.

MaGan walked up to the Sensitive cave complex where Orrox and JaYan were sitting. Concern was reflected on his face, "You are doing well but at our Illoreaen site, we still have problems," he said as he sat down. "I believe we must call a meeting of the Coordinating Committee."

"I thought SkepTan was too busy experimenting with the new types of plants down here, to be difficult," JaYan said.

"No, his isolationist tendencies sometimes rankle. Some are angry with him for creating the new cave complex where he and his followers test plants and small animals. That doesn't concern me too much.

"However, many of his followers, as well as some of our other Illoreaens, are curious, as they should be. A few have ventured down the canyon. Many waterfalls and other obstacles blocked their progress. They found strange life-forms as they descended. They tell how the air gets thicker and more humid. Even a breeze blows with more force than expected. Standing at the edge of a series of cliffs, which barred their way, they saw huge winged creatures far below. They turned around there. I don't like the unknown and am concerned. We've had enough surprises for our lifetime! What do you think?"

Orrox and JaYan looked at each other with puzzled expressions.

JaYan frowned, "You say the air is thicker lower down? Surely then, wings will be more effective and will carry bigger creatures? I wonder what else live down here."

"I think you are right," Orrox said. "We need to stay vigilant. We've got unexpected threats developing above the Chasm and mysterious, and possibly dangerous, creatures lower down."

The other two nodded their agreement.

"At least, for the moment, we are safe," MaGan said. "But I'll keep my fighters trained and ready.

Special request:

If you'd like to be notified when the next book in the Illoreaen Saga series comes out, be alerted of free book promotions, as well as entered into regular raffles for signed paperbacks. Please join my community by sending me an e-mail to:

henry@hv-loren.com

AND PLEASE...

I'm trying to base the further books in the series on probabilities and scientifically based assumptions. To make them available at a low price I need sales and reviews help sales.

So, I'd really appreciate a review on Amazon. The number of reviews a book accumulates on a daily basis has a direct impact on how it sells. So, if you leave a review, no matter how short, it helps me to encapsulate my speculations into further novels.

Here is a link to review my book:

https://www.amazon.com/review/create-review/ref=cm_cr_dp_d_wr_but_top?ie=UTF8&channel=glance-detail&asin=B01M3WW42C

Postscript

The lifestyles of the Clans and Illoreaens could never be re-established. New ways to create a stable future had to be found. The devastation was less in the depths of the Chasm and a return to the outside was impossible, despite the lethal dangers still lurking in the depths. The new group of Illoreaens and Clans faced the dangers and adapted. They remained even after the effects of the volcanic winter, which lasted for a thousand years, had disappeared, not aware that the world outside was now safer than what they faced within the Chasm. The new group did not know that only a 'few breeding pairs' of the many groups of hominids who had roamed the earth before the Toba Super Volcano Catastrophe survived and never encountered any of those for many millennia. Those of the group who survived remained until, many millennia later, the Chasm was inundated with the water from what we now call the Mediterranean.

<><><>

End Notes

Quotes used:

'Happiness[1] consists in seeing one's life in its entirety as meaningful and worthwhile'

'A meaningless life[2] is a terrible ordeal, no matter how comfortable it is.'

Terminology and Concepts:

Abstract state – An out-of-body experience, which allows trained Oracle-Healers to become aware of reality in four spatial dimensions.

In that state, Oracle-Healers are aware of reality beyond those perceived by our normal five senses, Sight, hearing, touch, taste, and smell.

"The reality we perceive is not a direct reflection of the external objective world.

"Instead it is the product of the brain's predictions about the causes of incoming sensory signals."[3]

Abyss – The vertical cliffs encircling the **Chasm**.

Birth Group – To facilitate the one child per Clan-member rule, conception was organized for births to occur in three years (quarter doucia) cycles. Within each Clan a bond formed between members of the same birth group.

Block – The act of:

- Hiding the electrical impulses radiating from one's brain in electrical noise, thereby making one's emotions and thoughts unreadable.
- Reducing the blood flow to the Sensing area in the brain, thereby reducing or eliminating the influence of external electrical pulses on the brain.

---

[1] Yuval Noah Harari – SAPIENS – Page 437

[2] Harari – SAPIENS - Page 437.

[3] "Our inner universes." byAnkil K. Seth. Scientific American – September 2019

Catastrophe –The local effects caused by the Toba Super Volcano eruption (74, 000 years ago). Similar effects were felt worldwide.

Chasm – The cavity that flooded approximately 7 500 years ago, to become the Black Sea. The Chasm was still only a few kilometers below sea level near the Abyss, but much deeper near the center.

Clan-life – The Clans' concept of Hunter-Gathering, also the name of a game played by the Illoreaens.

Clan-similar – The description used by the Clans and Illoreaens when speaking of other Hominid species.

Coordinating Committee –The central authority in the Illoreaen Habitat with decision-making and executive authority. It consisted of selected elders and younger leaders.

Developed Knowledge – Technology.

Doucia, Gracia, Agia, Epia. –They are the names of the major numbers in the duodecimal numbering system (base-12) used by the Clans and Illoreaens and remembered by later civilizations (e.g. the Babylonians). Mathematically it is a superior system since twelve can yield a whole number when divided by 2, 3, 4 and 6. The decimal system (base-10 with 2 and 5 the only such divisors), was developed later when others found it easier to count to ten, using their fingers.

Each number was represented by a simple image, which consisted of rectangles and triangles. Each image contained the number of sharp angles equal to the number represented:

Therefore:
< - was called 'Doucia' (12 in Decimal)
< - - was called 'Gracia' (144 in Decimal)
< - - - was called 'Agia' (1728 in Decimal)
< - - - - was called 'Epia' (20736 in Decimal)

For accurate calculations the Illoreaens used a sexagesimal (Base-60) system, revolving round prime numbers.

Emanating – The term used by the Sensitives to depict the electrical impulses radiating from all life forms and especially from an active brain, which Clan members were able to **block**.

Knowledge Searching – The names used by the Illoreaens for general research and experimentation as well as projects run by different Illoreaen individuals or groups.

Life aware – The ability to be aware of the **electrical impulses emanating** from all life forms.

Obsidian Shards – A sharp edge, chipped off glassy, volcanic extrusion, used by all ancient Hominid species for cutting, slaughtering prey and cleaning hides. Obsidian shards can have an edge so sharp that surgeons have successfully used them as scalpels in heart and eye surgery. The Clans had perfected the manufacture and application of obsidian.

Play-Work – Same as Knowledge Searching.

Primary Directions – A term used by Sensitives to depict Spatial Dimensions. In the absence of jargon, the Sensitives used plain words to express the concept, i.e. the known three spatial dimensions: Forward and Backward, Right and Left, Up and Down.

The Sensitives were aware of the reality of other spatial dimensions. The technical curiosity of the Illoreaens motivated them to investigate further. Together they slowly came to understand the world from the perspective of more spatial dimensions and how these dimensions interact with our observable physical world.

For instance, when the Illoreaens encountered the phenomenon of entanglement, many generations later, the Oracle -Healers could see that two or more entangled objects are, in fact, parts of a single object existing in another spatial dimension. The entangled objects we observe are the parts of the whole object that sticks out or crosses into the three spatial dimensions our senses and devices can perceive.

Projecting – The act of focusing so that the electrical impulses radiating from a Sensitive's brain, representing an emotion, thought or image, induces a replica in the subject's brain. It entails synchronizing with the subject's brain waves.

Runes – The marks in the writing system originally developed by the Illoreaens to mark potion and medicine containers. The system was adapted to record the results of experiments and research and later to record history, myths, stories, and training manuals. Used by the Dynasty and Oracle-Healers but not by the Clans.

Sensing – The ability of a Sensitive to pick up emanations of (the electrical impulses radiated by) a subject's active brain, to interpret the subject's emotions or to synchronize with an emotion, thought or image recalled by the subject. (Refer to ESP=Extra Sensory Perception).

Sensing Ability – The name given to all the features of trained Sensitive's abilities. Few Sensitives achieve proficiency in all these features and very few become experts. They include:

- Sensing;
- Projecting;
- Blocking;
- Sharpened observation;
- Analyzing reality. During what is called a Mentat state, an Oracle-Healer recognizes the many different aspects and indications of his or her environment. By prioritizing these and giving each a weighted influence, they can predict probabilities and tendencies. We call the subconscious effect *instinct.*
- Mind self-control. Control of thoughts, emptying the mind for enhanced rest.
- Entering the Abstract state, which includes the Mentat state and awareness of, and visualizing, additional dimensions.

Service years – Each birth group served and trained for three years (one-quarter-doucia), starting at age fifteen (one-and-a-quarter-doucia). Their duties included general maintenance of the Habitat, water supplies and surroundings as well as patrolling and carrying heavy loads. They exercised, were kept fit, learned all the Clan traditions and went on short excursions and long expeditions.

Spear thrower – A piece of equipment to extend the human arm. It enables the operator to launch a spear at a greater speed and force than possible with the unaided arm. The version used by the Australian Aborigines was called a *woomera* and the American version was called an *atlatl*. It consists of a shaft with a cup or a spur at the end that supports and propels the butt of the spear.

Thruster-Slasher – A sword-like instrument with two cutting edges and a sharp point and a handle made of wood. It was originally developed to clear undergrowth and bushes. The Illoreaens hammered pieces of metal obtained at meteorite landing sites into the desired shape. It was easier to form when heated to near melting point. It was carried secretly and only issued to those with high status or ability.

Transparent Illoreaen name for glass. They had developed techniques to heat coals until they could melt silicon and other ingredients to form many types of glass. They also managed to blow the melted glass to form figurines and containers.

Traditions, Transitions, and Ceremonies

Traditions:

Clans voluntarily limited their size to allow long term stability. The distance between Clans, each living in its own fertile valley, ensured plenty of resources to gather and forage, a life without epidemics but still with enough challenges to stimulate human intelligence. Specialists created an environment where life was long and healthy. They also improved the quality of resources, without causing competition for unnecessary luxuries.

Some unbreakable traditions maintained the stability of the Clans.

The most important <u>was the one child per person tradition:</u> Each Clan-member was allowed to have one child of a selected gender, with the partner of his or her choice, usually his or her life-companion. If a child died before being initiation, the parent was allowed another child. To break this tradition was taboo. The only exception was when the Dynasty Council allowed someone to have additional children as a reward for some achievement or service. This tradition kept the Clans small, gracia or less in number, which all in the Clans regarded as ideal. Experience had shown that larger groupings led to faction forming and strife.

All babies were born in three-year cycles creating peer groups within each Clan. Older Clan-members, past their childbearing age and often approaching gracia (144) years old, spent much time in training and minding the young ones, allowing the parents more free time. Grandparents had a special role in sharing their experiences and recounting the myths and explaining the traditions.

When the older ones felt that their bodies started to deteriorate, despite the care of the Healers, they let go of their will to live and died in peace and without pain.

Transitions:

The transitions between stages of an individual's life were each marked by a Rite of Passage ceremony.

The Illoreaens recognized five major Rites of Passage:
1. Birth and name-giving;
2. Induction into maturity;
3. Committing to a life-companion;
4. Birth of the individual's child;
5. The rites at death.

They also recognized three minor Rites of Passage:

1. Taking up a position of responsibility;
2. The breaking up of a life-companionship;
3. Committing to a new life-companion.

Ceremonies:

Ceremonies punctuated life within the Clans to highlight specific events. Some were individual-specific like the rites of passage ceremonies, others involved a whole Clan or all Clans.

Ceremonies within a Clan:

Most ceremonies within the Clans were excuses for a feast and included the feast after a successful hunt, the start of the growing season and the cleansing or abandoning of a temporary Habitat or cave.

Clan wide ceremonies:

All the Clans celebrated the Vigil of the Fires, annually held in a different Clan valley on the longest night of the year. During the feast, fires lit on high points surrounding the valley symbolically entreated the sun to strengthen and bring longer days for the growing season. Even though the number of attendees per Clan was strictly limited, each of the trainees attended the feast at least once during their three service years.

Most Clan-members met their future life-companions at a feast.

Orrox succession:

During a secret ceremony of high symbolic significance, the Orrox nominated a successor for Council approval. By symbolically handing the candidate two Thruster-Slashers, he invested the latter with the obligation to protect the Clans. One is intended for each hand, implying that no other activity may divert an Orrox from this primary task. The ceremony is attended by the council only. The Orrox and his successor always carry two sheathed Thruster-Slashers hidden on their persons.

They are emblems of the Orrox status. It is a sign of extreme favor for an Orrox to let a follower handle one, thereby symbolically investing him with some of the Orrox obligation and power.

Only a few trusted fighters are trained to use Thruster-Slashers as weapons. When wielding one of them, a fighter can even confront a Giant. Within the Clans, only the Orrox himself, as well as his designated successor, carry them.

Facts:

The eruption of the Toba Super Volcano 74 000 years ago, caused far greater devastation than any other event during the whole of hominin and human evolution. It had a magnitude far greater than any other super volcano eruption within the past 25 000 000 years.

At the time, many groups of hominids still roamed the earth and our own species, Homo sapiens, had already been around for more than 200,000 years. The explosion was big enough to kill all human and related species, except for the 'few breeding pairs'[4] who survived. It plunged the planet into a volcanic winter and caused the extinction of many species, leaving a caldera one hundred kilometers long, in what is now Sumatra, Indonesia.

The Yellowstone eruption, which created the caldera containing the well-known park, was of much smaller magnitude and occurred hundreds of thousands of years before our species came into existence.

\#

After the Toba Super Volcano eruption, the temperature grew colder for another 100 years. It took up to 1 000 years for the last effects of the volcanic winter to disappear, but the ice age continued.

\#

During the recent glacial period, within a longer ice age, which lasted from approximately 120 000 years ago until 12 000 years ago, the sea level was up to 120 meters lower than today.[5]

---

[4] Stewart Brand, SALT talks

Sam Kean, The Violinist's Thumb

Prof Eugene I Smith. UNLV · Department of Geoscience, has a different finding

[5] https://www.google.com/url?sa=t&rct=j&q=&esrc=s&source=web&cd=3&cad=rja&uact=8&ved=2ahUKEwjL1Kf5-dLmAhUDsXEKHUv5Dj0QFjACegQIDBAG&url=https%3A%2F%2Fwww.giss.nasa.gov%2Fresearch%2Fbriefs%2Fgornitz_09%2F&usg=AOvVaw2ZnE9eM3VfQHnd986jx0Ur

The trough now containing the Black sea was not connected to the Mediterranean and was fed by a number of large rivers that flowed through a dry to semi-desert landscape. As the sea level started rising, the Mediterranean broke through the current Bosporus straight and filled the Black sea trough with sea water, approximately 7 600 years ago.

#

Nature creates high voltage electricity-producing and sensitive sensing cells packed into a specialized electric organ, in certain fishes and mammals. These can generate and detect a large range of frequencies at very high voltages. Other cells insulate these cells from normal cells.

All brain activity generates electric waves that are measurable, detectable, and can be used to manipulate artificial limbs.

<><><>

Things to wonder about:

- Why are we the only homo species alive while many homo species still existed before the Toba eruption?
- Why do certain researches assume Homo sapiens only developed intelligence (and maybe speech) as recently as 40 000 years ago? Prof Robin Dunbar has studied the development of the size of homo (and other) brain sizes and came to the well-motivated conclusion that we had developed speech and fifth-order intentionality[6] (which I understand to be our level of intelligence amongst other properties) by 200 000 years ago.
- Why was much of our level of technology only developed over the last 150 years? Our forebears, although only a few in number, were as intelligent and had hundreds of thousand years to achieve the same results.
- How much water did the Black sea contain during the ice age?
- How much water did the rivers contribute during the very dry and cold conditions?
- How deep was the Black sea trough? Current depth is over 2000 meters. How deep was the silt layer?
- Why are the myths describing crystal balls the same as a description of a theoretical ultra-powerful computer?
-

<> <> <>

---

[6] Dunbar, Robin. The Human Story (p. 192). Faber & Faber. Kindle Edition. And other publications and presentations.

Assumptions:

Where possible the setting and assumptions in the novel are based on possible extensions of the published findings of many researchers.

Researching the assumed reality of the ancient world allowed me to create the setting of this novel. I imagined Clans living stable, meaningful lives for many generations until disrupted by the Catastrophe.

Clan details are based on facts and assumptions of the conditions when Toba erupted as well as my understanding of the time. The following are relevant:

First premise – Extent of the Catastrophe:

All the human species experienced a Catastrophe during and after the Toba explosion.

Supporting arguments to the first premise:

The shock waves, tsunamis and storm winds generated by the Toba explosion would have travelled around the earth, possibly converging and peaking in the Atlantic Ocean. They triggered earthquakes and eruptions everywhere. During the volcanic winter, with the sun barely visible, very little rain fell. Water sources and lakes dried up, extending the Catastrophic effects[7] for centuries.

Second premise – Many hominin species existed 75,000 years ago:

When the Toba Super Volcanic erupted, causing shock waves and windstorms worldwide, there were many hominin species

---

[7] Environmental impact of the 73ka Toba super eruption in South Asia. – Martin Williams et al.

(modern and extinct humans)[8] roaming the earth in small bands and groups.

Supporting arguments to the second premise:

Although we are the only (known) human species alive today, many hominid species[9] flourished until the Catastrophe wiped out most of them. Examples are Homo erectus, Homo denisovans, and Homo luzonensis,[10]. Others survived longer, Homo neanderthalensis[11] until about 30,000 years ago and Homo floresienses until a few thousand years ago.

Third premise – Ancient Intelligence:

Some of the human species were as intelligent as we are and were able to choose their lifestyle and could have developed sophisticated technology[12].

Supporting arguments to the third premise:

The literature, art and other evidence show that during the past, humans were at least as intelligent as we are today:

- Greeks, 3,000 years ago
- Egypt, Babel, Sumer and Accad 5,000 years and longer ago
- The Plimpton 322 tablet [13]proved that more than 5,000 years ago it was used to calculate trigonometric

---

[8] Harari –Page 8: 'Who knows how many lost relatives are waiting to be discovered...';

Page 9: 'The earth of hundred millennia ago was walked by at least six different species of man'.

[9] Rebeca Rodgers et all – Evolutionary Biology vol 43 "The Hybrid Origin of 'Modern' Humans."

[10] Katsnelson, Alla (24 March 2010), "New hominin found via mtDNA", The Scientist.

[11] Volcanoes Wiped out Neanderthals, New Study Suggests". ScienceDaily. Oct 7, 2010. The research is reported in the October2010 issue of Current Anthropology.

[12] https://www.ncbi.nlm.nih.gov/pubmed/17136087

[13] Abdulaziz, Abdulrahman Ali (2010), The Plimpton 322 Tablet and the Babylonian Method of Generating Pythagorean Triples, arXiv:1004.0025

equations more accurately than we could with the help of the tables used before electronic calculators took over.

- The Lebombo bone[14] (carved prime numbers) and other numerical devices, 35,000 to 55,000 years ago.

There is evidence that a hunter-gatherer lifestyle could have been superior to the sedentary agricultural lifestyle that developed in response to population pressure at the end of the Ice Age.

Prof Robin Dunbar's[15], studies of brain capacity and organization, shows the ability for higher levels of intentionality, which might be equivalent to intelligence, is unique to humans and points to language and intelligence developing 200kya.

If one assumes that brain size is an indication of intelligence, then Neanderthals, with a brain size larger than ours, would have been more intelligent than we are. Prof Dunbar points out the 'possibility that their brains were organized in a different way from that of modern humans' and 'much of this extra volume was in the visual areas at the back of the brain'.

Other human species (e.g. the Denisovans of which we only know through fractions of DNA) might well have been very intelligent.

Fourth premise – Ancient Technology:

Intelligent humans have developed sophisticated technology and mathematics in the many millennia before our time.

Supporting arguments to the fourth premise:

There is proof that the Greeks and the Chinese had developed sophisticated technology thousands of years ago. The Antikythera

---

https://www.sciencedirect.com/science/article/pii/S0315086017300691

[14] originalpeople.org/ishango-bone-worlds-oldest-math-tool/

[15] Anthropologist and evolutionary psychologist form Oxford in his book, 'The Human Story, pPage 191 and elsewhere..

mechanism[16] is a good example. The technology was often abandoned in favor of cheap or slave labor.[17]

Many thinkers and experimentalists developed our current technology[18] in only the last 200 years.

During the many millennia before and after the Toba eruption, a smaller group of humans could easily have developed as much. Especially if they shared and transferred their expertise from generation to generation. The Illoreaens lived longer productive lives and had adequate time and resources to concentrate on developing technology.

Fifth premise – The Ideal Clan Size:

The Illoreaen sagas are based on the idea of an advanced prehistoric society organized to remain viable for many millennia without needing growth to avoid degeneration or stagnation.

To achieve this, the numbers within the society were limited to a birth rate of just over two per woman and the size of a Clan limited to approximately 150 individuals. In the Illoreaen novels the number used is 144 – a round number in the duodecimal system.

---

[16] https://www.scientificamerican.com/article/antikythera-mechanism-eclipse-olympics

https://www.ncbi.nlm.nih.gov/pubmed/17136087

https://en.wikipedia.org/wiki/Antikythera_mechanism

[17] For a tyrant, king or noble, technology was a threat. It could allow his dependents to become independent. By being the only person who could afford an army or many slaves, the tyrant, king or noble could enforce his will.

[18] Electricity is an example: Humphry Davy (later Sir and Baronet) was from humble origins, attending grammar schools. While indentured with a surgeon he built electrical batteries based on a paper published by Volta in the same year, basically from scratch. It was the first useful form of electricity. He later used electricity to discover many elements by electrolysis of different salts and built the first electric lights.

He appointed Michael Faraday, who had no formal education, as his assistant. Faraday discovered electro-magnetism and the basics of the electric motor, electric generator and transformers (essential in the transmission of electric power). All this technology was developed in less than 25 years in the late 1700's and early 1800's, with little precedent to build it on.

Supporting arguments to the fifth premise:

The birth rate was controlled[19] by allowing each person the right to one child, the gender of his or her own choosing, with a partner also of his or her own choosing. Usually the partners were life-companions. To avoid shrinking numbers, Clans allowed certain individuals another child under exceptional circumstances, maintaining an average birthrate of just more than 2 children born per woman.

The complexity and potential for conflict were reduced by the size of the Clan where many in the Clan took care of Clan children. Women had the first claim on rearing the children she had born, even if she had joined her life-companion's Clan and later moved back to her birth Clan.

The target of 144 of members in a Clan was established over many generations and is supported as practical by modern studies. Prof Dunbar's research shows we humans can only maintain about 150 meaningful relationships[20] (acquaintances) at any time, 50 general friends, 15 close friends and 5 intimate friends.

The thresholds is imposed by brain size and chemistry as well as the time it takes to maintain meaningful relationships.

Sixth premise – Archaeological Evidence:

The lack of archaeological[21] evidence of the sophisticated technology the Illoreaens developed, is no argument against its existence.

---

[19] Sub-replacement fertility: Many references available on Google and other search engines. Too many to select or show here.

For example of a discussion see https://en.wikipedia.org/wiki/Sub-replacement_fertility

[20] Prof. R.I.M. Dunbar in *Royal Society Open Science* and others.
The Human story etc

[21]

https://www.theguardian.com/science/2000/sep/14/internationalnews.archaeology

Supporting arguments to the sixth premise:

The Illoreaens originally developed sophisticated technology on the northern slopes of the Caucasus Mountains. Their culture, shared with the Clans, required the clearing of abandoned cave Habitats, restoring it to a natural state. Thereby allowing nature to heal and cave bears re-occupy the areas. This action destroyed possible archaeological evidence of their existence and technology. After the Catastrophe technology was restricted to the cavity now filled by the Black Sea, where no detailed archaeological research is possible.

Seventh premise – Black Sea Cavity:

74,000 years ago, the Black Sea Cavity[22] is several kilometers deep and was mostly dry with a deep layer of silt deposited during the ice age as the kilometers high ice-fields scraped the continental surface as it advanced and retreated.

Supporting arguments to the seventh premise:

The recent glacial period, which ended approximately11,700 years ago, was part of a longer ice age that started 2,000,000 years ago. During most of the ice age the great rivers, the Danube, Dnieper, Dniester, and Rioni carried little water. The ice advanced and retreated repeatedly scraping huge amounts of stone, sand, and dust from the European and Asian continental surfaces. Flash floods washed it into the Black Sea cavity and exposed new rock surfaces to be ground into more sand and dust. The dust from the Toba super volcano as well as that from the two eruptions of the Campi Flegrei [23]super volcano in Italy, added to the silt washed and blown into the Black Sea cavity.

---

[22] Wilford, John Noble (17 December 1996). "Geologists Link Black Sea Deluge To Farming's Rise".

Özdoğan, M. (2011). "Submerged Sites and Drowned Topograhies along the Anatolian Coasts: An Overview". In Benjamin, J.; Bonsall, C.; Pickard, C.; Fischer, A. Submerged Prehistory. Oxford: Oxbow. pp. 219–29.

[23] Campi Flegrei". Global Volcanism Program. Smithsonian Institution.

Eighth premise – Mild Climate:

The effects of the volcanic winter[24], following the Toba eruption, were much less in the Black Sea cavity and a mild climate prevailed in its depths.

Supporting arguments to the eighth premise:

Despite the desert conditions outside of the Black Sea cavity, ground water was fresh and abundant deep down. Heat from the thinner earth mantle heated the ground surface so deep down. The thick air, many kilometers below sea level, had a hothouse effect despite the weakness of the sun, allowing abundant plant growth.

Ninth premise – Sensing:

Sensing and emanating abilities could have evolved in hominids by the increased sensitivity of a set of brain cells to electrical impulses and the strengthening of the electrical impulses generated by a different set of brain cells.

The premise is that Sensitives were always Life-aware except when specifically blocking the emanation of pain or the influence of stronger electrical pulses, for instance, those created by lightning.

Supporting arguments to the ninth premise:

Electric eels and other Gymnotiformes[25] with their electric organs and electro-sensory systems (ESSs)[26] have cells that generate very high voltages as well as electrical signals at specific or variable frequencies. They can transmit and sense these signals over long distances, even thru water.

----

[24] Robock, Alan, 2000: Volcanic eruptions and their impact on climate, Earth in Space, 12, No. 7, 9-10.

[25] Moller, P. (1995) Electric Fishes: History and Behavior. Chapman & Hall
  Electroreception and Communication in Fishes / Bernd Kramer - Stuttgart; Jena ;Lübeck ; Ulm : G. Fischer, 1996. Progress in Zoology; Vol. 42.

[26] Physiology of Tuberous Electrosensory Systems, by Masashi Kawasaki

The literature indicates Electroreception[27] exists in vertebrates and invertebrates.

Sensing brain waves using 'brain-computer-interfaces' (BCI's) is already known technology and amongst other uses, is used to manipulate artificial limbs.[28]

Since the first writing and publishing of this book, in 2016, advanced experimentation in the use of brainwaves to communicate has continued. The techniques are both non-invasive (e.g. using EEG's or fMRI's to read the brain waves) and invasive (using implanted electrodes)[29]. Articles in 'Nature' and searches for 'Brain-to-Brain Interfaces' yield much more details.

Tenth premise – Additional Spatial Dimensions:

For a Sensitive to be fully conscious of the universe, the Sensing ability included awareness of additional spatial dimensions as well as the very specific values of a number of universal constants.

Supporting arguments to the tenth premise:

The idea of a fifth dimension beyond the usual four of space and time, i.e. a fourth dimension in space, came from Theodor Kaluza, who sent his results to Einstein in 1919. In 1926, Oskar Klein gave Kaluza's classical five-dimensional theory a quantum interpretation. In the 1940s the classical theory was completed,

---

[27] Electroreception in Vertebrates and Invertebrates– Encyclopedia of Animal Behavior, 2010, Pages 611-620

[28] A Johns Hopkins team has already developed and tested small wireless device with 100 electrodes, each capable of measuring signals from individual neurons in the brain.

Jan Scheuermann, a Pittsburgh mother of two, volunteered to have surgery to implant the neural transmitter into her brain. Her brain's messages manoeuvre a robotic arm.

Many more examples can be found through relevant searches.

[29] Miguel Nicolelis' book 'Beyond Boundaries' and further continuing experimentation creating a 'BrainNet'.

and the full field equations including the scalar field were obtained[30].

String theory looks at particles and postulates the aspects of the particles we see in our three-dimensional universe are actually reflections of higher order spatial dimensions or rather, in this case, non-spatial dimensions for these particles. If we could see them in a higher number of dimensions, we could see they're strings, but all we're able to see are the tips of the strings in our three-dimensional universe[31].

The basic numbers of the universe each define a key aspect of our universe. If they had different values the universe would be a changed place, and life on earth would never have arisen.

26 dimensionless constants describe the Universe as simply and completely as possible.

1.)   The fine-structure constant, or the strength of the electromagnetic interaction.

2.)   The strong coupling constant, which defines the strength of the force that holds protons and neutrons together.

3–17.) We have fifteen particles in the Standard Model: the six quarks, six leptons, the W, Z, and the Higgs boson, that all have identical rest masses. It takes fifteen dimensionless constants to describe these masses, relative to the gravitational constant, G.

22–25.) The neutrino mixing parameters.

26.) The cosmological constant.

Other values define our universe:

27.) The mass-density of the universe.

Others constants are universe independent:

28.) The gravitational constant, G.

29.) The speed of light, C.

---

[30] Goenner, H. (2012). "Some remarks on the genesis of scalar-tensor theories". General Relativity and Gravitation. 44: 2077–2097.

[31] Publications by Brian Green, Leonard Susskind, Gabriele Veneziano, Edward Witte, Barton Zwiebach, and others.

Especially Brian Green's talk on additional spatial dimensions:
https://www.ted.com/talks/brian_greene_on_string_theory?language=en

30.) The value of Pi.

Eleventh premise – A stable society without constant growth must be possible, even today:

To expect companies to report growth every quarter is unrealistic in the long term. As is the statement that the only alternative to growth is stagnation.

In this novel, both the Clans and the Illoreaens were fully employed in interesting, fulfilling activities. If there was greed, it was for power, not possessions (supposed to increase investments in production). The taboos were designed to work against that obsession.

Supporting arguments to the eleventh premise:

Many of our most respected researches have expressed the fallacy of perpetual growth:

Despite Moore's law still running decades longer than expected, there is a limit.

"Only Idiots and Economists believe continued growth is possible[32]."

"Capitalism's belief in perpetual economic growth flies in the face of almost everything we know about the universe.[33]"

The capitalist creed: "The profits of production must be reinvested in increased production."[34]

The decline of powerful nations can be attributed to the lack of understanding the implications of this creed.

Historically the typical wealth cycle is:

- Entrepreneurship – the first generation creates wealth, or, in the case of a city-state or nation, the first development phase creates the strong city or nation;

---

[32] Jared Diamond in a 2019 BBC interview amongst many others.

[33] Harari– SAPIENS – Page 352

[34] Harari– SAPIENS – Page 349, interpreting passages within Adam Smith's 'The wealth of nations' first published in the 1776, on which capitalism is based.

- Usage- The second generation builds upon the wealth; or, in the case of a city-state or nation, the second phase creates dependencies or colonies, which has to create wealth for the mother city or nation;
- Waste – The third-generation waste the wealth, or, in the case of a city-state or nation, during the third phase the mother city or nation lives in leisure off the wealth and abilities of the previous phase, and becomes degenerate;

Examples abound from Greece to Rome to the Italian city states.

Recent examples are the Dutch and English empires:

In the 17th century the Dutch became the best producers of wooden beams and planks, the best ship-designers, and the best shipwrights. They created the concept of shares, and many other financial tools. By the 18th century they became financiers, investing worldwide and especially in the UK. The English became the better ship designers and shipwrights.

In the 19th century and early 20th century the English were innovators, sparking the industrial revolution. Much of their great industries have now disappeared and London became a financial hub.

In future books I intend to show a more complex Illoreaen society, which is stable over millennia.

Made in the USA
Monee, IL
06 June 2021